HUMANITY'S
FIRST TEST

IGNACIO RAMIREZ BAUTISTA

Paperback ISBN: 979-8-9901083-0-1
E-Book ISBN: 979-8-9901083-2-5

https://www.facebook.com/humanity.s.first.test.book
https://www.goodreads.com/book/show/208126236-humanity-s-first-test
https://twitter.com/iggy_rb

DEDICATION

To everyone that lost a loved one to the Covid Pandemic
To my mother.
To all hard sci-fi, near future, first contact fans out there.

CONTENTS

ACKNOWLEDGMENTS

PROLOGUE

In a laboratory inside a hollowed-out asteroid turned space station laid all three of them, like statues but very much conscious and aware of their surroundings. The fragility of the human body forced them to try and prolong their lifespan to be an antenna until the First Test concludes. The Observer had told them he would contact them again when the time was right.

They have been asleep, if you could call it that, for 20 years. Every time The Observer entered their minds, a flash of light gave off a soothing blue hue through their eyelids, while their loose straps tightened to control their shivers. Then he would convey a simple message: The time is approaching. The likelihood of the first of the last three tests starting has increased.

The irregularity of its outer surface danced

between shade and light and accentuated its rotation, reflecting billions of streams of faint light from all over the universe, like it had done so for billions of years before humans discovered it. A small supply ship would arrive occasionally and refill the necessary resources. They were alone and had been for two decades. This was their mission: wait for an unknown amount of time for the first test and see if the fruits of their collective labor ended sweet or sour.

All three of them spoke, "How close?"

The Observer, "Depends on the next couple of days..."

The Observer's physical presence had never been seen, heard, felt, smelled, nor tasted. But The Observer's presence was undeniable. Two men. One woman. The Observer always spoke in probability and likely outcomes. The Observer did not experience time as linearly as humans did. Every time an important event in human history occurred, or the likelihood of it occurring increased, The Observer would *reach out and communicate with humans as a guide in some way or another.*

If the event was seen as likely to happen in the immediate future, The Observer would say: Depending on the events happening the next couple of days we will see.

If the event had already taken place The Observer would answer: One of the least likely outcomes is now present. It has happened. It will happen. It will forever have happened. It is now locked in to your universe like Plank's Constant or the Fine Structure Constant.

BOOK 1: THE NEXT COUPLE OF DAYS

CHAPTER 1: THE STUDENT

The shadow of their building was long as the sun was barely above the horizon. The sun illuminated their neighborhood well and the horns of the boats in the distance were loud, long, and uninterrupted. The fresh and humid air rustled the leaves of the trees outside the building, sneaking in through the opened windows. The delivery drones were busier than usual today as well, and their buzz gave perfect examples of the Doppler Effect, casting fast moving shadows over the tightly packed row of parked ultra-smart cars. In the mornings, these cars leave one by one in perfect order, going to pick up their owners.

Elton waited for his alarm to ring, watching the seconds tick in anticipation. His nose confirmed the smell of bacon and coffee after hearing sizzling and the sound of a small coffee pump suffocating at the end of the brew cycle. His wall screen flashed the weather, some news articles about protests and important messages from friends and family wishing him luck along with his bank statement and schedule for the day. He put on his earpiece that was charging and walked by the automatically opening door and into the bathroom, where his shower turned on at the perfect time. His automated shower head valves threw water, soap, and shampoo over his body like a synchronized water fountain show. He dried himself with a towel, not trusting that the electricity would be on long enough for his body dryer. The lights flickered away and his earpiece indicated the network was down.

He rolled his eyes and got dressed. As he made his way to the kitchen he noticed Alexa, with an oversized apron, warming up breakfast for him on the propane gas stove. Her jacket hung on a cupboard knob, far enough to avoid splatter from her rushed hand over the food.

"Mornin', babe. Did you see your mom's message?"

"Power went out..."

"Network is back online." His earpiece said.

Alexa and his earpiece simultaneously read him the message, "Good luck today. We will see you at 8PM to celebrate."

He pointed to his ear and Alexa smiled. It is common for Alexa and the A.I. to inform him simultaneously. She's usually up before he is. The power goes out intermittently a couple of days a week. When that happens, Alexa beats Claire, the A.I., to the punch. All day outages were rare but with no power, none of their semi-modern conveniences worked properly. So, the disabled their automated meal prep machine and switched to an old gas stove. In fact, a lot of the modern conveniences like the meal prep, automated closet and self-cleaning bathroom and kitchen were rarely used. Hell, even the elevator wasn't used by many residents. Gas stove or not, they didn't have time to cook fresh food. It was mostly used to warm up pre-cooked vacuum sealed food.

He just finished his master's in applied physics and she was busy prosecuting protesters by the dozen. It was getting increasingly more difficult to find fresh meat and vegetables and with limited time, getting fresh food was more trouble than what it was worth. He had read somewhere that frozen food and fast food replaced fresh food many times in the previous century.

'Fresh food is overrated anyway,' he thought.

He helped her finish breakfast and prepared her coffee just how she liked it: 5 packets of creamer and 7 packets of sweetener. They sat down at their island, setting down their plates.

"You nervous?" she asked.

"No," he replied.

"Your blood pressure is slightly elevated and you are sweating, despite it being 72 degrees in here," he heard, coming from behind the screen, temporarily minimizing a news story about the recent protests turned violent. These protesters, which were a good mix of age and race didn't like that the government was sending more spaceships to terraform Mars for future generations, "We can't wait another 200 years for Mars to be ready. We want a better life for everyone, not just the top 1%. We need jobs, food, and adequate healthcare pods in urban areas. UBI isn't enough to live comfortably..." he heard a young woman say. Universal Basic Income hadn't been increased in 25 years. Or was it 35? He wondered.

"Looks like you're going to be busy the next couple of days," he took a sip from his coffee, slightly nodding at the screen and making eye contact with her light brown eyes.

"Yeah, what with these idiots protesting instead of looking for work and my boyfriend suffering from high blood pressure. What's his glucose levels?" She asked, looking at the screen. One of the A.I. cameras was there.

"Normal," Claire replied. "Heart rate is a little elevated, however. It could be from the caffeine. Your sugar was a little low this morning before breakfast."

Another news story from Tijuana started. The screen showed a line of tiny electric cars next to a restaurant for government subsidized food. These restaurants were no longer selling food. They would just give food to citizens and get money straight from the government. Sometimes it was more efficient to hand people food, instead of letting every single tiny home have fully stocked kitchens. At least, that's what the Mexican government said. This government program also existed in the USA but on a much smaller scale. Protesters objected to this, fearing that the government controlling the food supply so tightly could demand easier control over its populace. Alexa finished her croissant & licked her finger to pick up the last of its flakes off the plate while he took his last sip, feeling a couple of tiny grounds coarse his throat.

"I gotta go," she said

He nodded. She wore her work clothes. Her long light brown hair draped over her blue top and white collar. She grabbed her A.I. link, jacket and attached it to her left forearm. He was wearing his lucky suit with his own link on his forearm. She finished her coffee and he loaded the dishwasher, hoping to come back to clean dishes.

As he stepped outside, he noticed several cars in front of theirs move out of its way. Their owners worked a 9/80 shift & the cars were not needed this early. Their car showed up in front of the staircase like clockwork and the doors slid open. Sure, it was one of the oldest cars in the garage but it was completely self-driven. It charged itself when it could and by the looks of it, it had enough juice for 800 miles. Not bad.

Both screens inside the car showed some more protests with weather updates and the route on the map. As they left the garage the car jolted to a stop.

"Ugh," he said and rolled his eyes at the sight of the hooker stumbling in front of them. She waved good-bye to her John in the other car. He was waving with a bottle of beer in one hand and blowing her kisses with his other as his car was slowly accelerating away with a light hum.

"Hey, at least she's working. and at least it's legal now," Alexa said.

"It's not legal. Not yet."

"Might as well be. The DA instructed us not to prosecute. and cops don't even arrest them anymore."

"I guess…"

"It could be worse. She could be protesting."

The hooker, Candy, made eye contact with them as Alexa opened the window. He signaled her to close it.

"Hola papi. Hola mami. You wanna party?"

"No, thank you," he yelled out the window uncomfortably.

"How about later? To celebrate you being accepted to the program?" She yelled back, smiled, waved, and winked at them. His eyes fell wide open and shot Alexa a glare as she giggled, covered her mouth, and closed the window. They drove off.

"Did you tell her about me?"

"Of course. We were talking and your name came up."

"What?"

"Hey, the city wants to get ahead of this. Prostitution is going to be legalized by next week. The city council was instructed by the state, which was instructed by the federal government to play nice. Perform... outreach. They'll be law abiding citizens soon and as such they have every right and protection just like us... even protestors have..."

"Play nice?"

"Yeah. We want to know what is going on with them. We have to protect them. If they see crimes or protestors organizing, they need to feel comfortable enough with us to provide info..."

"So that's it, huh? You want spies?"

"Well... No. But they need to be able to talk with us. We chatted and your name came up...."

"How long have you two been friends?"

"We're not friends. She hangs out around here. Sometimes I go out for a smoke and you've been super busy with school and we just talked a couple of times," she replied. "Don't worry. It'll be fine. I'm not going to have her up for tea or anything."

"I know. It just threw me off a little," he replied.

"... At least ... Not yet," she laughed and patted his arm. He was especially tensed today. If he was rejected from the government PhD program, he'd have to teach high school kids how to make fake volcanoes and about the periodic table. He shuttered at the notion of his mind being used for such demeaning work.

"I just want to help everybody, not just the super wealthy... even her..." Elton whispered to her, noticing she look her up and down.

He let out a small grin as she kissed him. The rest of the drive was uneventful. After a couple of turns and a short time on the freeway, Alexa was dropped off at her office. She's a lawyer for the city of San Diego in California and spends most of her time going after protestors and murderers. He spends most of his time studying and at UC San Diego.

Downtown is closer to Mt. Hope Cemetery, which is south a couple of blocks from where they live on Morrison St. The cemetery hadn't been open for new customers for over 20 years. After light outbreaks of the latest new virus, it filled up quick. Most visitors were over 60 years old, having lost people 20 to 30 years back.

There are still a couple of single-family homes there but most were replaced by mid-rises 80 years back in the 2050s. Their building was one of the first to be built and is a little older and their apartment is a little bit bigger than average at 780 square feet. Newer apartments were 650 square feet or 700 square feet for two bedrooms. This was done at the turn of the century to ensure all 15 million residents of San Diego could stay in San Diego and to accommodate displaced citizens from the downtown area that habitually flooded.

The car sped up as he re-read his last paper. His professors said it showed great promise but not to get his hopes up. The private companies and government agencies were very selective about who they accepted into their program. Going to Mars on scientific trips was riddled with red tape. Space tourism was a buzzing industry but he couldn't put space vacation on his resume. Mars terraforming was going slow, painfully slow. The population was nearing 10 million on the red planet, which was a drop in a giant-ass bucket of 11.1 billion total human population. Building settlements was the easy part. They could physically house another 50 million right now but the problem was growing food, which stemmed from shittier than normal soil.

Early scientists over estimated their capacities and the

quality of soil and so human migration almost grinded to a halt 40 years back. Only 15% of the people were being relocated. The last 200 missions to mars were automated and their cargo was dirt. This happened in response to the protestors becoming increasingly violent 10 years back. Sabotaging manned flights were bad publicity. Sabotaging cargo missions didn't make the news as much. This backfired and sending dirt over feeding people on Earth led to more protests all over the world. It was a vicious cycle with no end in sight.

Then, rumors about shutting down the terraforming project after the rich and powerful were comfortable enough erupted more violent protests. The wealthy had double the stakes: their money and their life. If the planet went to shit their lives would also. No amount of money saved their ancestors from the sinking Titanic. And no amount of money would save their planet. It just so happened that they shared it with everyone else. They had no choice but to give their money to the cause. A nice side effect was looking like heroes to the rest of the peasants. Being admired by the peasants made them feel good like the good old days. His thoughts rambled on about what it may be like to be wealthy for a couple of more moments.

His car reached a building at UC San Diego. More kids were protesting and walked around with signs and projecting holograms to synthetic clouds. He stepped out of the car and made his way to the building as he programmed his car to take advantage of the uninterrupted nightly charge and offer rides to others until it was time for him to go home again.

It was only 4 floors high with huge windows all around. They reflected the synthetic clouds. Today they looked nice. But on most days, when the sun was out, it hurt his eyes. He looked up and made out the leaning giant air conditioning unit. He remembers being involved in a pool to see when it would fall when he was an undergrad. The pot was still open, last time he checked.

He walked by the lobby's large flat screen with a directory and planned events in various halls. A lot of those were taken up by students to discuss what the protests meant and why they were happening. After many arguments it was agreed that: Old people suck and they don't care. Fair enough, he remembered thinking & being disappointed at the superficial reasoning. That's when he attended his third and final symposium.

His meeting was moved from D Hall to M Hall. 'Fuck me,' he murmured. The farther down the alphabet the smaller the hall was, which was a bad sign. The smaller the room meant the smaller the crowd, which meant the worse the news. He groaned, again. The school didn't want a public audience for a rejection, fearing a falling in their prestige. Rejections always got the smaller rooms. He made his way down a long narrow hall which leads to classrooms, private study rooms and some small conference rooms. He took the stairs to the second floor and walked towards M Hall. He was early and decided to leave his coat on his chair and head to the bathroom. On his way back he saw two of his professors along with two strangers enter M hall. He followed them in.

"There he is," Dr. Patrick looked at his direction. He extended his hand and was greeted by Dr. Rodriguez. Dr. Patrick was his last professor, which taught him about how string theory could be potentially tested using quantum entanglement. Dr. Rodriguez was his professor from his first year. He had a crush on her and even asked her out once. She accepted but during dinner it quickly showed that she was there as more of a mentor instead of a love interest. He wore her down and soon after her first divorce they hooked up. Just once. She said it was a mistake and that she wanted to continue as professionals. He thought he loved her and said as much. He was embarrassed but she assured him they could remain in contact. They did. After he met Alexa, their communication dwindled.

He tried shaking her hand, but instead received a hug and

a quick peck on his cheek. "I'm so proud of you," she said into his ear, similar to what your aunt would say at the end of your graduation ceremony. His eyes moved sided to side, confused. M Hall is the size of a broom closet with one screen and one light bulb. Her reaction didn't jive with his surroundings, lowering his confidence. He could feel his brain overthinking everything.

He was introduced to the last two individuals. Simply known as Mr. Smith and Agent Lopez. You could tell both were from Hispanic descent and didn't talk much like secret service agents. Weird. Elton wasn't getting that warm fuzzy feeling from either of them. Agent Lopez was cute but way too old for him. She was probably already married with kids his own age, he thought. Mr. Smith didn't seem like the kind of guy who'd share a beer with you. In fact, he looked like the type of guy who only ate oatmeal and drank water. He didn't seem to be much for flare. And that simple title didn't help much neither.

"Please, Mr. John, have a seat," Dr. Patrick motioned to Elton to sit down on one side of the long table and they all grabbed their seats on the other side. Mr. Smith moved like a robot. Even his clothes didn't bend naturally. He sat down, taking a second to make eye contact with every one of them. Dr. Patrick' hand trembled slightly. Dr. Rodriguez let go of a subtle grin. Mr. Smith looked like he was constipated, and Agent Lopez looked unimpressed by any of this.

After almost an hour of small talk, mostly between him and Dr. Rodriguez, the conversation covered part of his past, which inspired him to study what he did. Him, Dr. Rodriguez and Dr. Patrick compared him to other students and praised his work in front of Agent Lopez and Mr. Smith. Then, after some more exchanges the mood changed a little.

"Mr. John, we have read your report and verified your conclusions on your last few experiments. Long story short, even though you didn't verify nor conclude anything tangible, your theory is sound. Solving the Wheeler-DeWitt equation for specific conditions, showed great promise and sparked the interest of the scientific community in the government." He glanced over at the two suits. Their interest didn't seem sparked at all. They were looking at him like his parents were looking at him at the principal's office back in 3rd grade after he pulled a prank. He re-programmed the teacher's tablet and A.I. to immediately show the answers to a test. He got caught after everybody got a perfect score.

Dr. Rodriguez interrupted Mr. Smith, "Yes. Our friends here mentioned to us that their scientists only recently solved this equation and they think it could be the key to providing faster than light travel within our lifetime. Isn't that exciting?" She smiled at him. He hated that smile. It showed she knew she could have him if desired. She had and then discarded him. She was older, showing signs of crow's feet and more white hair than he remembered. But she still looked great and had a hold on him. He would love to be with her again and she also knew that. It bugged him.

"Wait, so... does that mean I'm in? This room doesn't really scream let's celebrate." Elton looked at the two suits. They sat there like sitting statues. All they needed was pigeon droppings on them to complete that still and lifeless look.

"Yes," Agent Lopez said, with a colder tone than even old A.I.

"And No." Mr. Smith quickly added.

Dr. Rodriguez smiled uncomfortably and glanced at her colleague, "It's a bit more complicated than that. It depends... how badly do you want this? How well can you keep secrets? How far would you go to help humanity? Everyone, not just the super wealthy?" She said this with an intense, uncomfortable glare thrown at him. She was not joking.

CHAPTER 2: THE SCIENTIST

The silence increased the tension for several seconds which seemed like an eternity. Agent Smith tapped on his tablet and Elton's lit up. "The first form you will sign, and date confirms that you are accepting assignment from us. The second form confirms that you will not tell anybody anything about what we talk about and during your time with us or any of your work." It sounded very Men In Black and Gestapo-like. He continued, "all you can say is that you are engaging in research that will aid in the terraforming of Mars. The third explains what may happen if you talk too much. You will be tried as a biological terrorist and quickly executed and your past present and future will be erased permanently from Earth's database. You would never have existed. Remember 1984?"

Elton felt the seriousness go up a notch and let out an uncomfortable smile. That last part Robot Smith said was not in the form, but he didn't doubt his ability of keeping his word. Smith's summary was concise. He continued, "Your former professors have been involved with us for the past decade. They helped guide your research to align better with our work."

He wondered why Dr. Rodriguez pushed him away so long ago. Was she just using him for her own benefit and then regretted her brief involvement with him? Or did she manipulate him and use him as another asset as a spy? Or maybe she just wanted him to focus on his work and she didn't want to distract him. Other questions like this ran through his head. He questioned all his research and his choices. Were they even his choices? He had to say something.

"Wait a minute. My solutions to that equation showed that faster than light travel was possible on a miniscule scale. Inverting space and time quality variables merely indicated that this is possible. Why would you want me to help if you guys solved it before I did?" Elton asked, eyeing the two suits. This was fishy. Either they hadn't discovered squat and needed him, or they had already discovered it and didn't need him. Why not just use his research themselves? They couldn't test this theory without the power of 100 large cold fusion reactors. The world only had 8 fully functional at this time.

"We are not at liberty to state why we would like you to work for us. Not before you sign those documents. Then, it is on a need-to-know basis." Agent Smith said, emulating a robot again. "All we can say is we would like you to work for us and help develop a prototype for faster than light travel. I'm sure you've heard the rumors. FTL drives are within our reach, and we are recruiting as many scientists, and engineers to work with us and taking them to Phobos to work on our terraforming project." The last couple of words hinted at a sarcastic tone.

Agent Lopez stared and sighed, "Mr. John, we know this is a shock. Rest assured that those forms are standard procedure. Initially, you will work from a lab on earth, but may need visit Phobos for testing, if you ever get that far."

"Have you guys ever been to Phobos?" Elton asked his former professors. They both shook their heads in perfect sync.

"We haven't had the chance. Our research is not there yet. But with your help we may be able to build a prototype in 10 to 20 years." Dr. Rodriguez responded. It sounded rehearsed. She was hiding something. That Phobos line smelled like... like... yeah... bullshit.

Elton thought about rumors surrounding FTL drives. No evidence of one existed; not even prototype testing. Theories and math were fun and games and his mouth watered at the thought of his involvement. This is what scientists must have felt like in the early days of rocketry in the first half of the 20th century. Except, it seemed, those scientists didn't know what it would lead to and these two suits seem to know more than they led on. This whole secret police vibe bugged him. The alternative was less appealing. He signed the tablet three times with his complete name: Elton Cuauhtemoc John.

CHAPTER 3: THE FORMER LOVER AND A HISTORY LESSON

The rest of the meeting continued much differently. He was given his job requirements and responsibilities. His location was to be in a basement lab in one of the old buildings on campus. There, he would perform research and lab experiments confirming previous test results. This would serve two purposes: One, it would catch him up on what he would be doing and prove himself and, two, he would confirm the findings and ensure that the theoretical work done before him had no holes in it.

A small part of him was already regretting this. He didn't want to be a lab rat nor a paper pusher. At least it was a research job for the government. They had vast funding and he would get to stay near family; for the time being. He liked San Diego ever since he moved there for his Bachelor's. Despite half of its downtown area being permanently under a couple feet of water, the effects of global warming were mild. The inner part of downtown now has levees and walls.

Initially, he will report to Dr. Rodriguez as Dr. Patrick was retiring soon and wanted to move back to India. Alexa's possible objections crossed his mind and he easily brushed them aside.

He was sent encrypted emails about his assignment for the foreseeable future and was told to report to the Ramirez-

Huang building's basement on Monday, in three days. After the suits informed him of his duties, pay, title, obligations and reminded him of the documents he signed they were on their way. Mr. Smith looked up at the lights in the room as they flickered and walked out. Dr. Patrick excused himself after congratulating Elton and he was left with Dr. Rodriguez.

"Katelyn, thank you for recommending me and for your guidance in my career," he felt very uncomfortable and stuck his hands in his pockets. "But what is all this secrecy stuff?"

"You are most welcome.... it may seem overwhelming. Those suits are just doing their jobs. To be honest, I only talk to them once a quarter through video chat. They check in periodically. Do you job. Show progress. They'll be out of your hair. Those meetings are a mere formality from when NASA, NSA and the EPA were combined into one entity because they already know all of your work and when you do it. Don't let them scare you." She waved her hand, dismissively and cleared her throat. "Just work, once in a while you'll find a mistake or make an improvement here and there and you'll be on your way."

"Thanks. I hope I can live up to the challenge."

She nodded, "To show there are no hard feelings let's have lunch on Sunday. Are you available?"

He glanced at her and rubbed his chin as he pushed in the chair he was sitting on. "Thanks for the offer... but because of how we were..."

She rolled her eyes and let out a slight giggle, "No... not like that. I know you are still with Alexa, right?"

"How about Monday?" he suggested, trying to keep his professional and private lives separate.

"Sure. That works." She seemed unaffected by his request. She opened the door for him and said she'd walk him to his car. Once outside, he told Claire to bring the car back. Apparently, it had just dropped off some college kids at a local diner and was a mile away. Parking is expensive & instead of paying to park his car, he could rent it out as a private taxi while he was not using it. The car knew when & where to pick him up and charged on the slow charging lanes for a while before returning to its owners.

"Is your car on its way?" she asked

"Yeah. Yours?" he replied

"No." she said after looking at her A.I. on her arm and nodding at words in her earpiece. "It went home but the rolling brown outs only let it charge for 90 minutes last night. It was enough to pick her up and go back but she lived more than an hour away. Katelyn was one of the few who did not participate in car sharing. She didn't bother programming it to pick her up since she thought this would take a lot longer. She hadn't been to one of these meetings in a long time and was, like Elton, expecting a large hall with vibrant discussions about his research and newer research and the inevitable 'are you hiring?' from many undergrads.

"My car has 600 miles left of charge, I can take you home and you can fill me in on what my first 90 days will be like," he said.

"I can also test your Ramirez-Huang engine knowledge."

"Sure."

The car showed up and they got in and got comfortable. After getting settled he started the conversation.

"Thank you for coming. Two professors are recommended and while Dr. Patrick volunteered, I only sent you my invite as a formality. I never thought you'd accept."

"You didn't want me to show up?" she asked, teasing him.

"It's not that." He replied, not noticing her sly smile.

"Well, truthfully, I wasn't going to come. I haven't had anything scheduled on Friday in years and live so far away... But I read your paper. Very inspiring. Reversing the time and space variable attributes sparked my interest. To cut time you need more space. At first it seemed impossible but realized that the Ramirez-Huang engine could possibly be modified to make this work. Honestly, that's why I think they need you." Her words flowed naturally, now.

"It went through my mind as well. But the drive would need

gravitons, and anti-gravitons and strings and anti-strings. If anti-strings and anti-gravitons even existed. There is some evidence... but would need to go through 8 dimensions instead of 4. The energy required would be gigantic. I don't know if it's possible." He said, wondering what would be needed to make this work.

"Don't worry too much. You will be paid to discover if it's even possible." She shot him a subtle Mona Lisa smile.

They sped down the freeway at 110 mph, on their way to New Temecula. This city adopted its new name after a population explosion 45 years back or so. The lanes were tightly packed with cars. All of them were moving at the same exact speed only mere inches away from each other. The smart road navigation was always on. Its electrical and AI have multiple back up layers. This let traffic flow smoothly and quickly

It permitted people to use that time to their liking. Some slept or read. Others drank in a mobile bar & others worked out. Smooth and constant speed meant no stop and go like 100 years ago. Most transports carried over 100 people and its passengers were stored like those Japanese hotels that were famous in the previous century. Other cars had tinted windows, which meant people were having sex in them. Public nudity was still a crime and enforced by asshole cops who needed to meet their arrest quota and wanted to embarrass people.

Law enforcement was still a very much human activity. The revolts of the 2070s changed the constitution permanently: robots and machines were to take orders from humans. It was not the other way around. Although, lately A.I.s progressively controlled more of their humans' lives.

"What do you know about the RHE?" she asked.

"I suppose the same as others do. Ramirez and Huang were scientists working from Canada. One was American and the other Chinese. This was before the UN, under the influence from the superpowers, took a more proactive role in third world countries under the disguise of 'eliminating poverty and providing democracy.'" He scoffed.

He continued, "The year was 2039. The first humans were still 20 years from reaching the red planet when these two decided to experiment with an ion engine at the newly built particle collider facility meant to make the original LHC obsolete. They were in... Green Fork... or Yellow Fork... or spoon..."

"Yellowknife. Well, they were a couple of miles east of there," she corrected.

He nodded, "Scientists had recently discovered the new four particles. But these two found the anti-quarks to these particles. They had the smart idea of feeding them through a small modified ion engine with a special type of magnetic field and their little engine vanished. It wasn't until 6 months later when the Chinese Spy satellite discovered its rare radiation signature coming out of Great Slave Lake. Their next test was with a small engine with a black box, and discovered that it was subjected to 5 Gs of acceleration for approximately 50 seconds. And that was with those anti-particles that were relatively easy to find and it was a miniscule amount of mass."

"Remember, it was the fact that it was so cold that permitted these particles to interact with residue from previous tests with an atomic layer of ice and the enzymes from the newly discovered bacteria that enabled this huge acceleration." She hinted.

"Yeah. Apparently, the residue with an atomic layer of frozen water with bacteria gave it its extra acceleration. It worked for batteries and so it made sense that it would work with propulsion. At least it makes sense now. I remember it took them 4 years to perfect their first test engine. That was possible because both governments tried to outdo each other in a grant-giving war. The public didn't really understand the gravity of such a discovery. Going at 5Gs wasn't impressing anybody. Especially when they heard it only lasted 48 seconds. I remember classmates made fun of that and that they could last longer and harder. But it was a huge deal. What most people missed was that the propulsion mass was basically nothing compared to the size of the rocket. These handful of quarks propelled a 100 g engine with no effort. The trick was to find more of these particles. That's where most of the funding went. The engineering was already there."

"Impressive. The de-bending of spacetime undid the distortion of it due to earth's mass slightly."

"That's right. It wasn't until a couple of years after the first proper prototype was built and tested that it was discovered that this new engine was traveling above our third spatial dimension" he replied. "That's what enabled the rest of the world to fund the first manned space flight to Mars which only took 6 months roundtrip.

Their talk continued, mostly about the RHE and how his first task at the lab would be to reproduce it. This will easily take up to a year. Then, he would re-discover the advanced method used by one of Huang's students to calibrate and tune instruments in the particle accelerator in Canada to detect and capture those same particles. This would take him another couple of years. He had to write the program from scratch, without the help of A.I. He looked forward to this as he always wondered where the inspiration originated. Before, all the sensors were set to find the same exact particle in a very tiny space. However, she decided to use many sensors that only detected partial side effects independently over a large volume of space and used them together to find many of these particles in various locations over a wide volume. It used the disturbance in EM and gravitational waves. That, was inspired. This made her an international celebrity and a household name.

The car reached its destination and Dr. Rodriguez got out after a brief casual goodbye. On the drive back home, he fell asleep and when he awoke, he mentally revisited their conversation and was lost in his thoughts while looking out the window at the hundreds of other cars that passed by.

Beyond the rows of cars laid buildings upon buildings over the desert landscape that was now a stranger to sunlight. Shadows replaced sunlight near the freeway but beyond these buildings, patches of golden yellow tall grass and bushes swayed back and forth in an endless dance with the wind.

He thought about the essence of the RHE. The engine was modified but the particles and their interaction to our world was what really made a difference. That was the real key: the partial flattening of spacetime basically made interplanetary travel more like traveling on roads. Spaceships were no longer complete slaves to orbital mechanics and Newton's laws. In the early days of space travel, calculations were completely dependent on the body being orbited. But after the RHE, with its accidental mixture of regular fuel, ice, and some amino acids from unique bacteria, flying a spaceship was more like driving a car, or more appropriately, flying a helicopter. It wasn't until the second prototype that this engine was nearing perfection. The third and fourth versions of the engine were improved slightly and now, we were stuck on the fifth iteration. With plenty of exotic particles to go around, countries fought less among themselves until oil was drained from the earth. But by then cold fusion reactors and better batteries made wars over oil nearly obsolete. But global warming made water sources and workable land scarce. This created new conflicts.

Humans always found new reasons to fight and kill each other.

Soon after the second RHE was perfected, politicians pushed to use this new found technology as the main power source for the world's electrical grid. It made sense at first. Through trial and error, it was discovered that distorting spacetime so close to earth or inhabited space resulted in adverse side effects: anything within a couple of meters of these small test engines were ripped apart by shock waves. Government agencies soon decided that this would be exclusively used for space travel once in orbit and away from

29

space stations as larger engines had their affected volumes multiplied.

The RHE travels in the 3.5th-ish dimension. It wasn't quite hyperspace, if such a thing was ever something humans could visit. The best way to describe it, it was agreed upon, was to take the example of the Brazilian Pygmy Gecko. It doesn't swim nor does it fly but it can walk on water. Its special skin, which repels water is analogous to the engine's magnetic field interacting with these exotic particles rejecting space and kind of gliding over it but still touching space. It was above it but still very much interacting with it more than with higher dimensions

Later, it was discovered only small spacecraft can achieve this. Of course, every subsequent spaceship generation grew and put into question just how big was too big. The math revealed that the mass of a spaceship could not exceed %0.0000001 of the Earth's core. The largest spaceship ever built was nowhere near that mass and scientists predicted that by the time humanity needed a spaceship anywhere even close to that we would have better forms of traveling and such a problem would be considered moot.

The RHE vastly reduced the solar system's size. But it couldn't get you to your destination instantly. For every traveler one would need to take food, water, space radiation protection and air. 5Gs was not only impractical technologically speaking, but also impossible for normal humans to handle. Sure, a fighter pilot could handle it for a couple of seconds but normal people didn't want to feel like a horse was sitting on their chest. Recent declassification of government documents showed that some of the manned flights subjected to high Gs in the RHE disappeared forever. Some scientists predicted those ships with its inhabitants reached the fourth dimension and died. Others said they reached the 4th dimension and became energy-type beings, abandoning their bodies. Others speculated a bit more simply: these ships went so fast for so long that they had left our system entirely. This didn't sit well with the public once it was declassified because it meant that these brave pilots starved or suffocated to death.

Elton likes to think they passed out and died without suffering. He switched thoughts to explorers who did make it to their destinations and grinned. It was amazing. Humanity had entered the 20th century on trains traveling 50MPH and left it with jet engines that could take you halfway across the globe in less than a day. It left the 21st century going to mars in 6 months. In the first 10 years of the 22nd century those travel times were cut a little. Cold fusion reactors and fully automated spaceship building decreased ship building time drastically. That, along with better versions of the LHC produced fuel much, much faster at a drastically lower cost.

Now, in the year 2141 one could go to Mars and come back in 7 weeks. Sure, it was only for the super wealthy, but it was still possible. Most people made the one-way trip in 6 weeks. Sleeping pills were plentiful and highly encouraged.

CHAPTER 4: TWO MEALS AND THE FIRST BANG

Alexa released a loud condescending laugh and people near them interrupted their talking and drinking to look over.

"Babe, what's so funny? I genuinely thought you might be bothered by me working with Katelyn," Elton said, raising a brow at her.

Her laughter died down a bit as she made eye contact, "Oh. Wait. You're serious? Let me laugh louder." She did. It was a strong high-pitched laugh. Very feminine.

"Jesus Christ..." he started but rolled his eyes and laughed a little. At least he didn't have to worry about her worrying.

She finally calmed down and explained, "It's cute that you thought I'd be worried. It's also cute you can call her Katelyn again." She took a small sip. They were waiting at the bar for his parents. They were meeting her parents the next day for lunch. All four of them were genuinely happy them, and wanted to celebrate.

"It's just that she's a lot older and obviously not interested in you," she mentioned casually.

"Fine. Let's forget it." He said as she nodded. His parents came in to the restaurant and navigated through some tables and after a casual wave they sat down for dinner at their reserved table. They ordered steak. Real steak. None of that tofu crap. It was from a cow, too: not from a lab that grew meat.

This meat came from an actual cow. It moo-ed and ate and shit. Maybe it also had a soul. Either way, it was good.

After dinner and once at home getting ready for bed they overheard the news, again. More protests erupted. They seemed peaceful enough. No tear gas and no vandalism. Alexa seemed annoyed at the notion of her maybe being called in on a Saturday to work on paperwork for those who were going to be inevitably arrested. Luckily, the power went out and, while living on the top floor, made love under the stars once the ceiling was pulled back like a curtain.

The next day lunch was very pleasant. It was early June, and the sun was high above them. It if wasn't for the umbrellas, they would surely be getting sunburnt. They ate on the sidewalk patio. All of downtown San Diego, what was left of it anyway, was all pedestrian friendly. The cars would drop off patrons about half a mile from the new coastline and they could walk or get automated golf carts.

After the food was finished and the glasses empty, as Alexa's dad asked for the check a loud explosion was heard coming from Coronado Island. Everybody stood, with shock in their eyes, and loud thumping in their chests. They looked at each other and all their A.I. tablets lit up. Breaking news. Drones surveying the shorelines captured a video of a propane tank being purposely lit by a person wearing all black and quickly running away. It was near an apartment building, and one could see the side of a wall being broken and after a couple of seconds the dust settled and one could see what seemed like dust covered bloody legs.

"What the hell?" was all Alexa could say. Everybody else was watching the same thing and turned to everybody else dazed and confused. His A.I. started speaking to him: Terrorists have been seen planting explosives near the Naval Base Museum. Once this was heard that video disappeared and no one could find it again.

Firefighting drones could be seen taking off from boats and land and hurried over to the black smoke. First aid drones also made the trip across the channel. Police drones, each carrying a team of 3 cops were also lifted and placed at strategic locations. At the ferry port, bridges, and other important locations.

Claire spoke, "For your safety it is recommended that you stay indoors. Your home would be preferable. Avoid federal buildings and other important landmarks for the rest of the day. Elton's link automatically went into emergency mode and opened communications instantly to all of the important people in his life. This included the mayor, his family and boss and anybody else he had added. He quickly added Alexa's parents to his list, wanting to avoid an awkward conversation later.

Alexa nodded and simply said, "Sure. No problem. I'm really close. I could walk there now."

"Wait. What?" Her mom asked, worried.

"They want me to go to work and start filling out paperwork for search and arrests warrants," she replied simply. "We have a pretty good idea of who was behind these attacks. The evidence is being looked at now and we could have some arrests by tonight."

"OK... so what should *we* do then?" her mom asked.

"I guess we could just go home and wait it out. I was done with lunch anyway." Her dad said, casually. He seemed less concerned than them.

"We could all just go to our place. It's pretty close."

"No. We should really go home. It'll be alright. This reminds me of the riots back in 2111. Remember?" Alexa's dad looked at her mom. She blushed.

"Wait. The riots back in January of that year?"

"Yes. We were confined to our tiny apartment for a whole week." Her dad said. Mike is his name.

"Wait. Isn't your birthday in early October?" Elton looked at Alexa. She had a disgusted look on her face.

"Dad?!" she protested. Elton smiled. Mike hugged his wife, also named Alexa, and motioned to pay the check and they

were soon on their way. Alexa, Elton's girlfriend insisted this was just going to be lots of paperwork and that he should just go home. He reluctantly accepted, after realizing he couldn't do much. This wasn't the first time they were told by the all-powerful A.I. to go home. It hadn't happened in over a year. The best thing to do was to stay calm. It would blow over soon, they thought. The truth is: this is only the beginning.

It was decided that Alexa and her parents would walk to work where her mom had ordered the car to go and wait for them. It was the courthouse and so traffic was always moving down there. The car would decide to leave a nearby skyscraping garage at the perfect time based on their location and take them home back to La Jolla. They were near Elton's and Alexa's apartment and with very little to do he decided to walk home the 1.5 miles. The nearest pickup location was half a mile away and there was really no need to get the car to rush home. The car was on its way to the border anyway to drop off travelers or the overly-panicking Mexican citizens that would prefer to go home.

The walk to where car traffic was permitted was very pleasant. No loud noises were heard, and he even heard the beautiful song of the House Sparrow on multiple occasions. The sun was a little lower in the horizon, which made the long shadows from the tall buildings even longer and the wind cooled. It reminded him of the fresh air he had felt when visiting Alcatraz up in the San Francisco Bay when he was a kid.

His mom's voice was heard, "Elton, we just got home and heard. Are you alright?"

He confirmed he was fine. His parents always took out their earpieces and unplugged themselves from the network on the weekends. Sure, they still had their smart car, smart appliances and ultra-smart A.I. within reach, and their vitals were always being recorded and shared with family. So, he knew they were fine. But it was nice to hear her voice.

They briefly spoke about what they had learned. They lived

east in El Centro, much farther away from the small explosion. After a couple of minutes of conversation, they heard over their earpiece that more protests were planned for the day at UC San Diego, USD, Cal State San Diego, Cal State El Cajon, Cal State San Marcos and Cal State Poway. Apparently, all the students saw the initial video as well and were upset that the official report was a complete lie when compared to what they saw. This happened more frequently now. Something would happen, videos would be shared and then the official story would be different then the video. Many times the initial videos were staged and so these protests were just an annoyance. However, this time, the reporter emphasized that the protesters genuinely believed the video over the official report. This was common as well.

"I hope your school will be fine. You don't want to be out of a job before you start it," his dad jokingly said. Elton smiled as he looked down at his A.I. on his wrist. The camera drone hovered, also displaying a little screen with the image of his parents. They pleaded with him to be careful. Elton, dismissively agreed and said he was going to be home soon. Then the line went dead and all he saw was the same news articles that were being pushed through the emergency network.

When he got to within a couple of blocks from his place, he noticed his A.I. go dead. Then, it quickly came back to life and showed two warnings. First, was a plea to avoid the smart car network because it was temporarily down. Odd. That never happened. Sure, the power would go out for many places like offices, schools, homes and even government buildings, but never the smart car network.

Second, the mayor's voice was heard. She was nervous and asked all citizens to comply with the immediate, yet temporary lockdown. Any groups of more than 5 people would be stopped and searched and possibly arrested. He was beginning to worry. Maybe it was a prank. It had to be. But he didn't see cars on the road and the birds got louder. Then when he was a block away from his place the birds suddenly went quiet. All of them. The wind stood still. and then a small rumbling and thundering sound was heard in the distance. It seemed to be coming from the abandoned nano factory park a mile east. The thunder got louder and as he reached his building he saw Candy with her co-worker there, standing on the sidewalk, looking up at the sky, scared. Both were wearing miniskirts and low-cut blouses ready to work. The thundering grew louder.

Then, almost instantly he saw the source of the sound. People were walking towards him. But it wasn't just a couple of people. No. It wasn't even a large crowd of people. It was a mob comprised of smaller mobs. It was a mega-mob, if such phrase could be used. He heard indiscernible chanting but as they got closer, he could make it out. Candy slowly backed away, closer to his building. The chanting became unmistakable, "Stop the lies! Remember Fry!"

It confused him at first but then remembered. When human cops were being replaced by droids and robots a police chief named Felipe Fry from Boston exposed that the new robots were purposely editing videos to use in prosecutions and achieve convictions. It wasn't just a handful of bad apples. It was a huge scandal, which resulted in a mini civil war, forcing the president to resign, was arrested and subsequently exiled. That's when the constitution changed. That video really must have pissed them off. OK. Maybe the video was real, and the government had scrubbed the network.

The mob moved closer and grew louder. They were down the street now and Candy and company looked at him scared. She yelled something but was muted by the mob's chant. He signaled them to follow him and open the door to his building. The building's local A.I. was severed from the network but had a failsafe. As he entered the lobby, he saw some protestors point and run after him. Some ran into the building through the garage opening. He quickly activated the failsafe. He broke the glass cover with a small hammer hanging next to it. The red button was exposed. He punched it. The screen above the large mushroom button sprung to life with the message, "insert finger for sample to confirm total lockdown in 10... 9...8..." Beneath that was a physical sign: IF FAILSAFE FAILS TO BE ACTIVATED AFTER BUTTON IS PRESSED, YOU WILL BE SEDATED and ARRESTED. They weren't messing around. Activating the failsafe was a serious action. It was like calling in a terrorist attack, while yelling fire in a theatre and pulling the fire alarm and opening the emergency exit all while having sex in a car without tinted windows and flipping off the president of the United States and kicking a puppy with your spare foot. OK. Maybe that last part was not actually illegal, but it would be frowned upon.

He had never activated this before but knew the process just like everybody else. Now the only way in or out was for an actual live blood sample. This ensured that someone couldn't get in by simply providing a sample of a dead residents' blood. He stuck his finger in as the countdown showed a 3. The door to the outside showed several dozen people outside approaching it. He felt a little prick on his index finger and two seconds later, which seemed like an eternity, steel doors 6 inches thick started coming from the ground completely surrounding the bottom level. He heard the garage gate close almost instantly and then similar steel gates closed access to it as well. Then, the wall next to him lowered, exposing a manual crankshaft that required 30 manual rotations to release the lock and eliminate Total Lockdown Mode. He noticed some people get into the garage level. If they were lucky, they hadn't found the other entrances to the building open and the elevators deactivated. If they were unlucky a handful of people were now locked there and if there was a resident down there, they may be in trouble.

CHAPTER 5:
LOCKDOWN WITH
TWO HOOKERS

Emergency lights lit the stairs and hallways and every single door to every single apartment. The mob was still heard from the outside through the windows that were partially open. He guided his guests to his apartment. His neighbor came out and looked worried.

"Did you activate..." he asked. The retired cop never married and lived alone. Elton nodded at Jake. He was holding Candy's hand. She was holding her friend's hand.

"Is that why you have..." Jake looked confused. Elton rolled his eyes. "I couldn't leave them outside with the mob now, could I?"

"No. I guess not." Jake said. "Is your A.I...."

"No. The smart car grid is down as well. My direct line to Alexa is also down." Elton seemed worried. "But the building should be able to contact her shortly once the emergency systems are up and running." He touched the doorknob and after it read his biometrics it opened.

He offered his guests a place to sit and some water. His left hand was shaking. The building's A.I. went to work, connecting to his A.I. It read his vitals along with his guests' vitals. The sensors throughout the building showed the 6 people in the garage breaking car windows and puncturing tires. They were stuck down there for now. Now that he was connected to the building, securely from within is apartment his signal was rerouted to Alexa who was connected to the city's emergency network. Claire automatically contacted and reopened communications with her.

"Elton? Is that you?"

"Yeah. How are you?"

"I'm fine but the mob that went by is getting closer to my building. As soon as the emergency cameras and drones detected the mob the building went into total lockdown mode. I was already in but some of my co-workers weren't."

"I activated TLM at our building as well. How are your parents? I heard the SCN is down, too. Is that true?"

She nodded. He saw different camera angles in her office. People seemed worried but were otherwise safe. "I guided a drone that was out over the freeway closer to where I think my parents should be. But with just the basic A.I. functionality it's almost like looking for them manually."

"Yeah. I barely made it into our building..."

"Hey. Is that... Candy?"

He nodded and looked at his guests. The other woman waved, looking at the obvious spots where cameras would be found. Just like he had access to some cameras near Alexa, she had access to all of their apartment's sensors.

"I found them outside our building. The mob was literally barreling down towards us so I brought them inside." As he said this she pulled up video from one of the cameras closest to their apartment. She watched it in double speed and her eyes widen and then she showed relief when the video showed them safely inside.

He got as much information from Alexa as he possibly could. Over 100 small attacks similar to the propane tank exploding were executed at the same exact time by a group of people called Earth First. They demanded the Earth be taken care of first, or at least transport the most vulnerable people to better places. They felt that all those missions to Mars took up funding to better the lives of most people on Earth. They weren't wrong.

Earth First had seized control of many government buildings up and down the west coast. This included Canada and Mexico as well. Their demands were simple: dismantle or severely hinder the systems that target protestors and violent offenders. Then, they would liberate previous leaders that were wrongly imprisoned. The last demand: North American Coalition's Government shall use funds from future missions to Mars to help people on Earth.

San Diego was one of the first cities to be attacked. It is an important port city that connected it to a neighboring country and had a powerful hold in the NAC, along with Tijuana. Other sites were also targeted: Ciudad Juarez/ El Paso, Laredo/ Nuevo Laredo and Brownsville/ Matamoros, St. Stephen/ Clais, which was now the size of New York back in the year 2030 and the Mega-metropolitan area of Vancouver/ Bellizngham which was the main port connecting to the East. All were still in NAC control, for now. Mobs were marching down these cities as well, going to the main federal and NAC buildings. But so far, the mob in San Diego was one of the largest they had seen. The St. Stephen/Clais mob was slightly larger.

Shortly after their quick discussion the network came back online momentarily. A young lady was the only thing on the screen. It was a looped video of her making her demands. The rebels had secured control over the network and were locating those responsible for locking up their leaders, brothers, and sisters. Alexa's face became pale as she swallowed. Elton's eyes looked terrified as he noticed a lot of movement in the back of some of the live feeds coming from Alexa's building. Then, screens showed the lobbies and ground levels revealing sunlight and sidewalk. Shit. The TLM system had been overridden. All screens went blank. They flickered back on for a moment, only showing still images of the aftermath. Some of the federal employees that were closest to the stairs, elevators and doors were overrun by dozens of protestors with stun guns. They approached Alexa, as if knowing who she was and where she was. A bald white man with a handkerchief slightly covering his face hit her in the face with his stun gun. The feed went dead. A second later, it came back on showing the man carrying Alexa out of the field of view of the camera, while others stayed and tied up the rest of the victims. Other members of the mob started connecting to all of the computers and screens available with their own equipment. Then, the last thing he saw was another masked person look up at the screen and shoot it.

Elton tried to let out a scream, but his shock made his knees buckle as he grasped for breath. Candy and company approached him and his eyes went dark.

CHAPTER 6: THE PRISONER

Loud explosions rang in Elton's ear and dust from the ceiling made him sneeze. He heard the mob outside screaming and chanting incoherent phrases. He was on the floor, in between the kitchen island and a sofa chair and table. He stumbled to his knees and grabbed his pounding head. He must have hit his head when he passed out. His hair was getting stuck to his hands. It was like he had tiny amounts of honey on them. He looked at his hands. They had stains of dried blood. What the hell? He checked his other hand and it was also stained. He felt around for a cut on his head, and then his neck and then the rest of his body. Nothing. Whose blood was it?

He heard what he first thought was thunder. Then he realized they were large boots making their way down the hallway. They were getting louder.

"This is it." The muffled scream came directly from the other side of his door. The stepping sounds quickly dwindled to a silence. He got up, still with a headache. He saw Candy's friend on the sofa where she first sat with an empty bottle of water and her throat slit open and her body drenched in dried blood. A knife was seen on the cushion next to her. Her eyes were open and looking directly at him. They were lifeless. His mouth opened to scream something and he took a step in her general direction. He was confused. Where's Candy? Maybe in the restroom. What happened? Why was he alone with her friend? and why were his hands, arms and entire clothes stained with blood. There was very little blood on the floor.

Most was absorbed by the couch. He didn't see a continuous stain from her body to where he was laying. As soon as he tried to muster enough strength to take another step in any direction, he saw the door swing open.

"That's him. That's him." A couple of people yelled when they made eye contact. The half dozen group looked him up and down and then looked to their right, towards the corpse.

The mob paused for a bit and made way for who appeared to be their leader. "Yeap. That's him." Mr. Smith said. He looked him up and down and then at the dead hooker. Elton could tell one of his eyes was recording, scanning and he wanted to yell at his surprise of Mr. Smith approach him with the mob. Smith seemed genuinely disgusted, "You sick fuck..." was all he said as the butt of his shotgun hit Elton's face. He fell asleep once more.

CHAPTER 7: MR. SMITH; AKA BIG MIKE

Elton regained consciousness laying on crappy office carpet. You know the kind. That thin and scratchy gray carpet that when you get close to it you notice that individual sections are actually individual colors. He felt his face and it hurt. His upper lip was itchy from the dry blood. This time he was sure that was his. He noticed desks and chairs and computer terminals along with black screens in the wall on all four corners. He was definitely in a government office. But which one? The room he was in had no windows and the door, after checking, was locked.

He saw a single camera aimed at the center of the small room on top of a dusty bookshelf in the opposite corner of door. He recognized the bookshelf and the chairs after thinking about it. Lonely nails were on the wall where pictures or other frames hung. It seemed like a Judge's office. This wasn't the NAC Supreme Court justice, this was a low level, petty judge that was assigned to a crappy post because he couldn't be fired. It didn't seem like a state judge's office either. This office belonged to a county judge at the most. That meant this was a government building. Maybe it was even Alexa's building. His head started pounding and as some dust made him cough, he felt his lower left front chest hurt. It was sore. He lifted his shirt. A bruise.

The door swung open and he saw Mr. Smith, again. He put his hands up and looked down, giving up and backed away a couple of small steps.

"Why are you doing this to me? I didn't tell anybody anything. How could I? I haven't even started my job…"

Mr. Smith approached him, slowly. "Hello, Mr. John. Long time no see…" He got closer and snickered.

"Usually, I don't like violence but the citizens needed to see strong leadership and since you had just killed a working woman, I figured it was ok."

"What?" Elton tried to gather more thoughts. "Why…"

"It still is," Smith said as he hit Elton with a broken leg from an office chair. Luckily, the blow had hit his upper arm. He didn't think he could take another blow to the head.

Smith walked over and grabbed a seat while Elton backed up.

"I go by Big Mike these days," Smith said giving Elton a quick glance. "Smith is my corporate name. I'm just trying to make life better for the 99%."

Elton opened his mouth to speak but Big Mike's raised index finger stopped him.

"Like most of us, I tried to make a better life for myself and family but the deeper I got into the beast, the harder it became to ignore the signs. I spent many years searching for answers, using my post to my advantage. Eventually I found likeminded individuals and many of my fears were proven correct." Big Mike sighed and waved the chair leg pointing at their surroundings, indicating it was all a facade.

"Long story short – Earth First – my team, discovered that world governments are doing something very secret and are simply using terraforming Mars as a cover. We're not sure exactly what… but we suspect, based on history and recent laws passed, that the intention is to only save the wealthiest among us. How, exactly, we don't know. Dome cities are unlikely because they can get overrun by most of us. The most likely scenario is that, as soon as Mars can support the top 1%, Earth will be abandoned and the rest of us will continue to destroy ourselves while they are at a safe distance."

Elton squinted and felt sore as he moved. "So, your plan is to kill normal people that haven't even started working?"

Big Mike laughed a little and shook his head. "It is apparent that the beast needs people to do its bidding. The side effect is that the rest of us... most of us... fight for scraps. You are just a victim of circumstance.:

Elton exhaled loudly, unwilling to believe Big Mike could just minimize human life so quickly. Not just his, but everyone else.

"My associates and I are not stupid. We were able to hack systems and A.I.s with friends to the cause in high places sprinkled throughout. This is a suicide mission. We calculated we can only hold our positions for two weeks max. Right now, we control over 300 buildings and each building houses people like you and your bitch. Your public executions will show we are serious. If the people meant to solve problems don't solve problems immediate to the masses, then they are useless and we will all go down with the ship."

"What are you talking about?"

"Earth First has learned that the terraforming is severely underfunded. We don't have 10 million people there. We only have 2.4 million. However, we suspect that number is bullshit, too."

Elton refused to believe Big Mike. There was no way most people would be abandoned on earth to fend for themselves, would we?

Big Mike stood, and moved closer to the door, "we are performing trials on traitors and executing them on live feeds. We are short on time and Alexa's trial is being held in two hours." He looked at the camera and nodded, acknowledging a message. "I apologize. Her trial ended 10 minutes ago. It was ahead of schedule and she was just executed."

Elton couldn't believe his ears. All of the monitors turned on and before he could react or call Big Mike a big piece of shit he saw and heard the trial end. The judge ordered her execution by hanging. This was obvious since the noose was already around her neck and she was standing on a chair which was on a small unstable table. It looked like Alexa but her hair was different. Too different. A masked man kicked the table out of the way and the chair fell. She dangled there for a little bit after a large crunch and snap was heard. Then she hung there. Lifeless.

"I'll fucking kill you!" Elton screamed and rushed towards Big Mike. He was waiting for it and Elton was aggressively kissed by the shotgun once more.

CHAPTER 8: BEING LIBERATED, KIND OF

Every time Elton woke up in his makeshift bureaucratic prison cell he found a paste packet of nutrients, water and saw trials and executions repeatedly. On the fourth day, EF was on execution number 178 inside that lone building complex. The real number must be in the tens of thousands, he thought. One by one was taking a little longer than expected. But as Big Mike pointed out on his third and final visit: this was a suicide mission and they planned to continue until the bitter end. Elton's trial and execution was planned towards the end. What would be better than to fry a newly hired scientist who was dating one of the best prosecutors and was found with a dead hooker while his girlfriend worked? Only two other people were more morally corrupt than he was. Their activity with animals was not mentioned. You can use your imagination. Elton will be moved to the prison, and executed by electrocution.

On the seventh day, having freed most of the prisoners from the local jail in the basement of the federal courthouse, which was next to his area in the same building, Elton was moved to where the electric chair was. This was a remnant from the 2060s when executions were an everyday phenomenon and since most prisons were backlogged with death row inmates, the city council decided to make an execution chamber in its basement. It was seen as a badge of honor. Countless criminals used that chair as a gateway to the afterlife. That is where Elton would find his ticket to meet with Alexa once more.

Elton's knees failed him again and he had trouble breathing, picturing his family and Alexa's execution on repeat in his mind.

The executioner strapped him into the cold and rusted out chair and whispered, "Do not speak. If you want to live, then listen. These straps are tight on your arms and ankles but connected with Velcro to the chair. When the power goes out simply get up, quietly walk to the door we just came through. At eye level you will see a white stain on the wall to your right. Puncture it with your finger. An opening will appear in the wall. Go through it. Steps will lead you down where I will be waiting for you. You will have 48 seconds." The voice sounded familiar, but he couldn't make it out. It was a monotone voice that haunted him. Could he trust this woman? Was this a cruel joke to entertain the rioters?

She walked out and the door shut. In front of him was a large window and he saw a red light hovering at eye level. A camera. Behind the camera was a large red electrical handle on the wall being held by Big Mike. On the opposite side of the camera sat three bug-eyed giddy people wearing 17th century wigs to mimic the judges from the Salem Witch Trials. 'Adequate,' he thought.

Big Mike started speaking unrehearsed words. No doubt they were being fed to him through an ear piece or through the head band many people chose to wear to connect to the A.I.

"Elton Cuahu...Quauk... quak... cookie... cuahu... what the fuck," Big Mike couldn't pronounce his middle name.

"It's Cuauhtemoc, you big mierda," Elton yelled, correcting him. The judges giggled. Big Mike wasn't pleased and was about to pull the lever when the nearest judge stopped him and shook his head. He mumbled something to him.

"Elton Quack-A-Doo John," Big Mike continued, "You are hereby charged with the following crimes: Aiding the enemy of the people; Being morally corrupt by hiring a hooker; infidelity, obstruction of justice from Earth First by activating the TLM in your building, preventing easy arrest; murdering a working woman; murdering a minority; hate crime. What say you?" As soon as he finished saying this the three judges pointed their 6 thumbs down. How Elton wishes he could raise his hands to show them the middle fingers instead.

"I didn't hire her. I couldn't leave them outside with you maniacs coming for my building, could I?!" He screamed, not knowing how thick the glass was. Big Mike's words were muffled through the glass and he needed his words, his final words, to be heard.

"Them? There was more than one hooker? Fine. You are hereby now charged with hiring multiple hookers," Big Mike corrected.

As Big Mike pulled the lever, the power went out and it was completely dark. As Elton got up, he was knocked to the ground by an explosion that rattled the walls. Dust fell on his face as he landed on his knees and elbows. That was going to leave him more bruised. He quickly stumbled onto his feet and made his way to the door. To his amazement, it opened rather easily. He took a couple of steps in the dimly lit hallway. Very few emergency lights were on and he was having trouble searching for that stain. He tried to eyeball four feet from the door frame but couldn't find the stain. After a couple of seconds of desperation, he decided to just start poking the wall where he thought the stain should be. He didn't know how hard he should poke so he kept on hurting his fingers with every failed attempt.

Several seconds later the lights started turning on and he saw that white mark. It seemed to taunt him as he was sure he had poked that section of the wall many times. It didn't matter. He stuck his finger easily through it. It felt like a sponge which accommodated his finger and then the wall vanished. That was a neat trick. Old and high-quality smart materials, no doubt, made up that part of the wall. The outside lights showed the steps with a rail on the side that wasn't the wall. He only saw the first ten steps or so. The rest vanished into the darkness.

He made his way down the steps and once the entrance was clear, the wall filled itself up again. He had heard of those smart materials being widely used a couple of decades ago. They were a nice addition to a home and it was meant to make your home moldable to different times of the year and events. It never caught on as a popular choice as it was expensive and only practical in large houses. Who the hell wanted entire walls being shifted in their home on a regular basis? and so smart materials were mainly used for making small tables that seemed to form from thin air or maybe a frame around a screen to make it look like an ancient hardcopy of a photo. Cars implemented smart materials as it helped with maintenance.

At the bottom of the staircase, he met strangers. Then, he saw Katelyn. His eyes let out a gush of tears as she hugged him. It hurt his torso, but he hugged back. He saw her come in close for a hug and tasted a little bit of salt as he felt her lips against his.

Then, he saw Agent Lopez and conflicting emotions filled his heart and mind with rage. He didn't know if he should attempt to escape or attack her. He fidgeted back as Lopez reached for him. Her eyes begged him to not to leave. She looked considerably older without makeup. He noticed her wearing a janitorial jumpsuit but puffier. This made her frame look bigger than normal. She got closer and he let out a small smile. He fell to the floor again after feeling his knees failing him once more.

"Are you..." was all he could mustered with a catch in his throat. She shook her head.

"What about..." he gestured upwards.

"Smith is a traitor. Now we know he's been playing both sides for years. Let's never speak about him, again." Lopez said. He quickly understood.

"Take him to the back. Make him comfortable." Agent Lopez looked at Katelyn and a man who guided him. As they made their way behind shelves filled with books and boxes filled with paper, he noticed that this was a large basement. It looked like a library. But the shelves blocked the view from the stairs and the short ceiling didn't help. He continuously dodged low hanging light fixtures. The tables were all moved to one side of the large room. He passed smaller end tables and book shelves that were used to separate sleeping quarters where he saw even more people sitting. Some had a couple of bruises. Others had bandages. Some were sleeping. Others were reading. Others were huddled in small groups and interrupted their conversations as he was led by them. He made out over 200 people.

They made it to a study room turned into a bedroom with an actual bed. He was so in shock that he didn't even notice that the bed was already being used by someone else. It was a woman asleep. He got a glimpse of her swollen and bruised face.

"Why did you bring me here? With her? I'm not hurt too badly. I can sleep on the floor with everyone else," he whispered.

"That's Alexa," Katelyn said as she nodded at the woman in the bed. "She's sedated. No need to whisper."

Elton got a headache again. He felt dizzy and fell on the bed. He didn't fall asleep. His mind was racing to figure everything out. None of this made sense. He struggled to speak with a frail voice, "Wait... so how... why? But how?"

Katelyn fit a band around his head and fell asleep and instantly relaxed in dream land. He could tell it was a dream and was not scared. He was back at M Hall with only Agent Lopez and Katelyn readily visible. Dr. Patrick was missing and Agent Smith looked like a Jedi Ghost who quickly vanished. Elton clenched his fist as Smith disappeared.

"Ask your questions. To whomever you direct your question to will answer it." Agent Lopez calmly sated.

This dream interview lasted a lot longer than he wanted it to but it was necessary.

He was thrown into Alexa's mind recording of her watching the execution of her former co-worker. The judge declared that because Alexa's work on convicting protestors, he execution was revenge masked by redemption. The rest of the female inmates next to Alexa sobbed as they saw the end of the woman's life. She had asked Alexa to trade clothes after being gang-raped. She couldn't live with herself after that. Luckily the so-called judge didn't know what Alexa looked like. The soldier who escorted her didn't know either. As she was being judged, one of her companions hacked into the network and superimposed Alexa's face, showing those who watched a fake image. Those who knew what Alexa looked like were hiding away, avoiding conflict, and letting their pawns have their sick fun.

Dream Lopez reappeared, as M-Hall rematerialized and spoke, "To protect you and other victims we are letting the news report you all died. Don't worry. Your parents know the truth. In time, you will be permitted to speak with them."

"My parents... you mean... they're OK?" Elton feared the worse and was relieved to hear they were fine."

"Most family members were not targeted."

Elton nodded and swallowed hard, "How many total were killed?"

"Preliminary estimates have the count at 10,000 fake trials followed by executions. Thousands more died in the final battle."

Elton grabbed his head, trying to comfort his headache, "I'm still having a hard time understanding how this all went down. Weren't we prepared?"

"We got complacent and sloppy and Earth First was very coordinated and tech savvy. Their network virus penetrated our quantum supercomputers and A.I.s all over the USA and the NAC. That was just the beginning. It took down the Smart Car Network. We lost so many innocent lives. Mostly infants, the elderly and special needs folk. Starved mostly since they couldn't move."

Elton's stomach knotted up in disgust, "What about planes?"

"Fortunately, they fared much better. Autopilot landed & those who could, helped those who couldn't."

"How did it get so bad... all those executions..." Elton snarled.

"San Diego/ Tijuana was one of the last cities to be liberated. We stumbled."

"What other damage did they do?"

"We lost thousands of lives in a very public way. Some facts you would have learned in your first couple of years at work were leaked. For instance, the health pods used rare metals and thus we don't have enough. These health pods work great, but the waiting lists are extra long."

"Big Mike mentioned Mars... we're doing everything we can, right?"

Dream Lopez sighed, "That answer is a bit more complicated but we will tell you in time. In reality, only 1.31 million people reside on Mars. We can house 15 million and provide water and oxygen for 5.4 million. Food is the problem. Only enough for just over half a million. Earth and other specialized stations are picking up the slack."

"How is that even possible? Shouldn't growing food on a planet be easier?"

"No. Space stations are powered by RHEs, which distorts gravity to an affected volume beyond the station. In space that is not a problem. On a planet it can cause damage. You know that. We have to create energy by more conventional methods for everything from water creation to magnetic fields to lights and everything in between."

Elton nodded.

"We are trying to terraform Mars but it is painfully slow without RHEs on the surface. The sat energy network is not yet operational because those resources are being spent elsewhere. More on that, later. The dirt on Mars is crappier than we originally thought. Furthermore, the negative effects of the human psyche from living underground to prevent radiation damage can be detrimental to the human experience on Mars. Of course, living underground saves energy for magnetic fields and heating and so on..."

"So, life on Mars is hard? Is that where we are going?"

"For now, my answer is yes." Dream Lopez gave him a look of disapproval and he didn't push the subject.

"What about Candy?"

"She is dead. Sandy murdered her. Once they realized the gravity of the situation, Sandy suggested killing you in your sleep to avoid sharing food and water. They believed they could wait it out. They argued & fought. She is not on the priority list for arrest. Apologies."

"How long will I need to be here?" Elton motioned to his surroundings.

"The dream will be over during a normal sleep cycle. However, we will need to hide out, while the rest of the traitors are brought to justice and we get our infrastructure back up and running."

"What about my job..."

"Your future lab was destroyed. The Ramirez-Huang name is seen as a source of all of this. You, Alexa, and the rest will be transported off world for your collective safety. Your job will continue but not on Earth."

"Where?"

"I cannot say at this time."

"People are waiting just like you all over the NAC. They are in basements, bomb shelters and subway stations and even sewers. Believe me. This is only temporary housing."

"I see," Elton scratched his head.

"Suffice it to say that this event lit a fire under our asses. The Quantum Computer A.I. networks predicted an event similar in magnitude to this one to take place by 2181. It happened 40 years too soon. The bad news is that by 2198, we expect the current system of government and institutions to succumb to external and internal pressures and many lives will be lost. This, when coupled to the potential failure of the secret project made it clear: A New Dark Age would be imminent."

Elton's jaw dropped and he slouched on his chair. After a moment, his curiosity got the better of him, "What about

Katelyn's kiss?"

"She was overcome with joy and it was impossible to express in another tangible way."

"And now... now what?"

"The secret project will not be told at this time. Stop asking."

BOOK 2: THE SECRET PROJECT AND THE SECRET TRIP TO THE SECRET PLACE

PROLOGUE

The three of them, laying in their pods with their life-giving solution, spoke to The Observer: They made it. Right? The First Test is starting. The Observer: Almost. The likelihood of the First Test happening has increased ten-fold. Their station sent out an encrypted message: Guide them. Nourish them. You... we are close.

CHAPTER 9: THE LAUNCH

Chemical rockets were indeed still king in breaking ties with Mother Earth. The smoke trails from the Apollo, Shuttle, Atlas, Artemis, Omicron, Psi, Tau-Chi and Upsilon days that deafened spectators and awed children were a rarity on Earth as of late. Space manufacturing and industry had made everything originating on Earth a thing of the past. Space had overtaken Earth's need to supply everything. Now, limited supplies and materials from Earth, along with humans, were sent into space. The rest came from space stations or Moon stations. This propelled mass migration of humans and robots alike to Mars and beyond. Earth's strong gravity pull is no longer our weakness.

During the early days of space industry, many automated machines were launched to create habitable and industrial space stations placed in orbit around Earth and the moon. All of this happened slowly at first and quickly accelerated. Mohr's Law was also applicable on the time spent on manufacturing of our new asteroid-ships. These machines dwarfed those on the ground and human ingenuity permitted us to have a firm hold on the moon. Then, we went to Ceres and other asteroids. As more and more bases on the moon were erected, more metals for industry were discovered. This, coupled with the Moon's lower gravity let humans have a permanent presence elsewhere. We were no longer a single planet inhabiting species.

For years and then decades the moon was king in the

manufacturing of anything and everything humans needed for space exploration. Then, the RHE was no longer used to create energy for fabrication. Instead, asteroids relocation was perfected and those found to be filled with expensive metals and water were relocated just outside Earth's Sphere of Influence, the Moon's SOI and Mars's SOI. Smart materials and CPU making machines from Earth, coupled with these metals created machines, which created more machines. Once we had perfected these automatons, they went to work on creating ships and habitats for our frail bodies out of the hollow shell leftover from mining. Our bodies are frail and a couple of meters of hard rock and metals provided much needed protection from space radiation. These asteroid-ships, dwarfed those from ships from Earth. The ships that were made on Earth and on the Moon were now repurposed as Atmosphere Penetrating Vehicles and Landing Vehicles only.

The shortest travel time between Earth and Mars occurred every 26 months. However, in between these massively efficient 6-week one-way trips, other, longer missions would also be sent. These had luxury items like physical books, reputably branded alcohol, and clothing along with items with sentimental value. Soil to grow crops was sent to Mars. A lot of it. Humans were never on these trips, which would take up to 6 months to get to Mars in the worst of circumstances.

Elton thought about all this as his ship was taking off from Earth. He had flashbacks as a little boy watching holograms and even 2D videos about space exploration and other historical documentaries. Alexa was next to him. She was still bruised but was healing nicely. But only her physical wounds were healing. That one time he wished to speak about her ordeal she claimed amnesia. He didn't push the subject. She was still the most beautiful woman he had ever seen. Her brown hair draped over her bruised eyes. Her hand was clutching his as their elevation slowly, yet parabolically increased. Despite all the advancements in technology, it was common practice to send 30 to 40 people at a time. This ship only had 12 people onboard. Freak accidents still occurred.

Their trip started out as a common one. They left Earth in chemical rockets and rendezvoused with their RHE, which was already waiting for them in orbit. Once their CM was detached from the chemical rockets, they attached to their new RHE. This new RHE has two larger cylinders attached to it. Attached to that were four other cylinders. The 4 cylinders had cargo, food and supplies and dwarfed the other two cylinders, which housed their sleeping and living quarters. It came with everything they needed: basic sick bay, kitchen, bathrooms, and a small recreation area to unwind along with a small section to exercise in. These, in turn, dwarfed their CM, which dwarfed the ancient Apollo CM. Supplies, like food and water were already being manufactured and refined in orbit. Atmospheric gases were also extracted from the upper atmosphere and the moon. The small recreation area has a retractable portion of the wall where they could eat, work out, read, or even have sex looking straight at the stars.

These living quarter compartments were manufactured in completely automated stations. The RHE was manufactured in a manned station with a 24/7 military presence. A total of over 1350 large stations orbit Earth. Only a handful were dedicated to making RHEs. Other stations were for research and others were privately owned. Others still, created chemical propulsion for all of the other stations and ships. Other stations were farms that had scientists on board them and were quickly picking up the slack from Mars. Some were harvested and the fruits and vegetables were flash frozen and sent to Mars while others were grown on the way there to provide fresh groceries. Robots would automatically harvest and properly store the harvest. At Mars, the vegetation was sent to the surface automatically. It was an endless interstellar dance, being led by robots.

To feed a large population on Mars, it had to grow their own food. A couple of the newer stations were intended to make larger stations. They had new equipment from Earth and were approximately 10% done with the newest and largest station yet. Earth First released information on this a week ago. It's meant to house over 50000 people permanently. The purpose was not known.

A couple of minutes after running diagnostics on their systems Elton felt a light jolt which resembled an old elevator in a tall building. He briefly got a glimpse of the Earth getting smaller, quickly. But it wasn't an image which resembled any of those famous ones. No. Instead, he could see Earth and surrounding it were a dozen or so ghost Earths. But it got weirder as every ghost Earth seemed to show a different side of it. He had heard of this 'Higher Dimensional Projection Effect' but today was the first time he experienced it. Since he was now in the 3.5th dimension, he would see the 3 dimensions below him flatter. Since photons preferred 3 dimensions, which were all beneath him, he was able to see more information, but fainter. It was indeed a beautiful yet weird site. He ducked his head a bit and saw what was supposed to be empty space but instead saw more HDPEs of Earth. He felt like he was going through a tunnel with the walls showing the same image over and over again. The further away he saw the less opaque those images became as photons vanished from their new found dimension.

He swallowed hard and glanced over at Alexa. She had her eyes tightly closed and her grip on his hand got stronger. His heart raced as he clinched his jaw. But he could tell the notion of being in grave danger was stemming from within. He was indeed safe, above his home universe. The exotic particles in the engine created their own cocoon to protect itself from being ripped apart in higher dimensions; or at least up to 3.5 dimensions. This was a happy side effect, which still baffled scientists. These particles would raise their immediate vicinity to the 3.5th dimension and at the same time protect it and once the trip was done they would safely come back to our 3 dimensions. Another pleasant side effect is that while being in this new found universe, there was practically zero chance asteroids would damage their ship. Asteroids, how we know them did not exist in higher dimensions.

Once the dust settled Elton and the rest of them were transported to northern Florida, where the new Launch Site was built. Training and briefings took up most of his time.

He remembers sitting in a small conference room with a beautiful oval wooden table. Fourteen of them met daily for two weeks. Two pilots. Lopez as the security officer and eleven of them, including Elton and Alexa.

During the first meeting they debated what to call the ship. "Looks like we'll be transporting tons of cheese. Maybe we should call it the Cheddar." Michael Jacob Johnson giggled as he said this. He was an older man, nearing sixty with many years of experience in virology and astronomy.

A couple of them laughed around the table and Vera Ivanov replied, "Why not? They did say we could name the ship." She had a master's in History and originally from Chile. Everybody exchanged glances and Elton and others gave a slight nod and shrug in agreement.

No one at the table were even close to being Nobel laureates. This worried Elton. 'Maybe Lopez and the rest of them had to settle for us.' Elton's thought scared him.

CHAPTER 10: LOPEZ, THE TRUTH TELLER

The next day, while in their tiny sleeping quarters Alexa was ingesting her daily regimen of medicines and nutrients. They were accelerating but it was such a tiny acceleration that they barely felt it. They had to take meds to prevent 0G sickness. They were also all given a single dose of nano anti-bodies. These were tiny robots in the bloodstream that only let known cells live in the body: a super vaccine for all known and unknown pathogens. It was also a cure for future cancers, as this new generation of tiny robots also attempted to fix mutations in cells, they deemed unacceptable.

The down side was that if too many parts of the human body had cells developing cancer, these nano-bots would kill them and eventually the normal cells would die out. The jury was still out on whether this could be called 'the cure for cancer'. But as they were going near interplanetary space for a long time it was seen as necessary instead of wasting energy on protective shields from radiation which may leak up to the 3.5th. They could not use an asteroid-ship as their mission was a secret and an asteroid missing would be noticed by the independent astronomers. If these nano-bot trials proved successful they could be administered to all humans on Mars and would aid in the terraforming effort by redirecting much needed resources to something besides making huge magnetic fields.

Elton had come back from the shower and noticed she was next to the medicine panel, floating.

"Did you know I lost my grandmother to cancer when she was only 87?" she asked as she turned around.

"I didn't," Elton said, a little pleased at Alexa opening up a bit after almost a month. Today she seemed a little happier. Maybe because her bruises were almost fully healed, and it didn't hurt to smile anymore.

"Yeah. Stomach cancer. It fucking sucked. She refused to tell anyone about the bathroom analysis performed on her urine and she even damaged the computer and it couldn't connect to the doctor. When she finally showed symptoms, it was too late. She asked for euthanasia. She went peacefully with all of us surrounding her." She looked at her ring which contained some of her ashes.

"I'm sorry she had to suffer but I'm glad she went on her terms," was all he could think of to say.

"I still think about her. Sometimes I dream about her."

"Really?" He replied. "What do you two talk about?"

She shrugged her shoulders slightly. "The truth?"

He nodded, preventing himself from hitting his head on the habitat.

"Can't really remember…"

Elton lightly nodded at her and floated towards her and made at attempt at a hug. She came in close and buried her head in his chest.

"It's that time. Everybody, meet at the command module." Agent Lopez's voice echoed from the speaker system. They made their way to the doorway, being careful not to bump into the habitat. Only Lopez and the pilots had experience in space. As permanent earth dwellers, they were still being acclimated to space travel.

All were in the command module a minute later, waiting for some people to stop fumbling around. Agent Lopez floated so elegantly it seemed like she was standing still. Her ponytail gave her the 'I have my own gravity' look going on.

"Has everybody taken their anti-sickness meds for the day?" was all she asked. They all nodded and looked around to everyone else. Elton did that first thing in the morning. "Good. Because this may take a while and I don't want anybody puking breakfast all over my new ship." She petted a console briefly.

Some slightly laughed and others grinned. A pair of the younger scientists looked embarrassed. She took a deep breath and started her explanation.

"In the year 2089, while Huang was working on his latest project he discovered that those anti-particles that helped the RHE function were a side effect of other more exotic and heavier particles. He subsequently discovered that these new particles that were not discovered yet didn't seem to ever come near Earth. His calculations showed these 'parent' particles were forever stuck in the Oort cloud: specifically, at what one may consider the polar north and polar south locations relative to the Sun." A diagram on one of the screens popped up with the sun and the planets in the traditional horizontal middle line along with two red dots shown way above the Sun and way beneath it. Elton assumed correctly that the map was not to scale. He raised his brow as his lips lightly opened for a small gasp of breath.

"Hold your questions until the end," Agent Lopez reminded him. She continued, "The following year, Ramirez and his new team verified Huang's math. With this new confirmation, Huang and Ramirez teamed up again to design an easily assembled mega-LHC like particle accelerator. This one had to be bigger than 20 times the size of the one their famous experiment was held several decades ago in Canada. That's 370Km diameter, folks. Its purpose: to find and/or create these HPs.

"The Mega-LHC was designed and built in parts. It was never fully assembled and tested on Earth. A project on such a massive scale could not be kept secret. Building such a huge science lab would be seen as wasteful spending. This could have caused riots since the nation was still heavily in debt from the mini civil war, which had just ended a couple of years before.

"10 Launches were scheduled. One had the crew. Another had a new 3rd gen RHE and the other 8 had supplies for the crew and all of the parts and machinery needed to assemble the Mega LHC in the Oort Cloud way 'above' the sun. They had to grab most of the supplies from the moon or orbits around it. The ships were launched and kept on accelerating for quite a while. The RHEs were pushed to their limits and traveled the 15.261 light-days in 10 months. The size of this region where the parent particles could be detected varied from a radius of 0.58 light-days to 0.88 light-days. As soon as their sensors picked up 3rd degree evidence, and they were near their calculated destination, they went to work building that new particle accelerator.

"That Particle Accelerator is still there. That is our destination. Missions to this station regularly take supplies but for the most part it is very self-sufficient. Unfortunately, cheese uses too much energy and resources to make up there and so that is what we are taking with us. Also, this is a specific brand of cheese highly sought after up there. It will only take us 280 days to get there. This is why you may feel a little acceleration from time to time. It's minimal but can be nauseating. After 4 months we will stop the RHEs, cruise, run tests and then go retro and start our deceleration.

"We are not going to a simple science station. This is the most advanced space station humanity has ever built. It's also the largest. If you want to get an idea of how massive and sizes: it's basically a large city in space. Approximately 67.75 million citizens call it home. Most of our supply missions that were meant for Mars were redirected to this station. Most of the inhabitants have no family left on Earth. Do not make me regret taking you up there."

Agent Lopez smiled as she looked around the CM. Everybody had a surprised and 'ah yeah' look on their face. Elton's mind was racing and Alexa grabbed onto his hand and squeezed it hard. She leaned over to his ear. But before she could speak, Agent Lopez interrupted, "Question, Alexa?"

"... um... yes... so did you say 67.75 million people are onboard?" was all she could respond.

"That is an excellent question. Before answering, I will remind everybody that my answer is only known to me and my superiors and scientists at the station. The vast majority of those people don't know that everybody else doesn't know about them and honestly don't care. To them, Earth was where they lost their family, limbs, and love. Up there they have purpose and don't care if they ever leave that station. They have a great life minding their business. Most were brought here as teenagers and young adults after wars or pandemics took their loved ones away. Entire villages that were migrating were taken to a ship. To answer your question: yes. Almost 70 million people live up there. I think what everybody else is wondering right now is 'why?' Right?"

Everybody nodded, including Alexa. "So... why are so many people up there?" One of the younger crewmembers asked. John is an astrophysicist and was still finishing up his Master's program when he was taken prisoner.

Agent Lopez nodded and took a sip from her water. "These Huang Particles exist up there. These are the parent particles. The HPs are not from around here. It's hard to explain. Basically, that volume of space is like a hose that connect a water tank to your lawn. The water tank is the reservoir in the 8th dimension. It houses the HP, Anti-HP, Super-HP and Small-HP and that volume, coupled with our Mega-LHC bring them down to our universe, which is the dirty lawn. They also bring down gravitons, dark energy, and dark matter in unstable and smaller quantities."

As she paused Elton and the rest of them seemed utterly confused. Lopez had just admitted to Huang discovering and proving hyperspace particles, dark energy and gravitons existed. But proving them was the easy step for him. It seemed that he could harness their power. Yikes. He felt light headed and rubbed his eyes. It was all too much information about concepts he had never even imagined. Here he was trying to prove FTL in super short microscopic distances when he was being told, 'oh yeah, we have proof of higher dimensions. Oh, and by the way, all of you are too stupid to understand but you're all we have and therefore we need you to help us figure out what these particles do and if we can even use them.' He was dead wrong about her intention and Lopez was about to show him.

John said, "OK. So let me get this straight. Huang was a super genius who independently proved higher dimensions and was trying to figure out how to exploit these particles?"

Lopez nodded gently. "Yes to the first part and no to the second... and Huang is still alive."

She explained:

• Huang continued his work on these particles for several years. Ramirez branched off into genetics and biology.

• Then, one day Huang had a dream. These particles were being used incorrectly. Instead of trying to store them indefinitely, he needed to modify the RHE to be compatible. The MRHE was born. In his dream he told himself that the new MRHE would be enveloped in the older particles he and Ramirez had discovered so long ago. He basically put a blanket of these particles over his engine and then take all of the new particles and force them to interact with each other in precise quantities.

• The quantity of the largest particle was exponentially proportional to the next largest particle, which was exponentially proportional to the next and so on. He made these particles interact with each other in the engine bay. By doing this the test engine fired successfully at first and then stopped broadcasting and disappeared.

• From now on the original RHE will be known as the engine or E and the new engine will be called the M Engine or ME for short.

• Exactly 2.71828 seconds later they reacquired the signal. It was a bit fainter but it was the same engine. The engine was 814919842.7 meters away.

Elton shook his head and raised his hand. Agent Lopez stopped speaking and let him speak. She was used to being interrupted at this point in her speech. "So, you're saying that this ME which was now enveloped in 3.5th dimensional space interacted with 8th dimensional space particles and traveled instantly from one spot in our universe to another e light-seconds away? Am I hearing you right?"

John nodded nervously. He had his thumb and index finger to his mouth. He was perplexed and stood there like he had just seen a higher dimensional lizard alien ghost. Lopez was unaffected. "So now you want us to perfect this engine and fine tune it where possible and maybe within our lifetime we may have interstellar and even intergalactic travel?" Elton was getting a headache just thinking. "Or do you just want us to make MEs from Es and send them to Earth and migrate everybody to other star systems?" John said, without looking at anyone. He was lost in thought Elton couldn't believe that question was legitimately asked.

Lopez replied, "No... not really..." She gave them a sly smile. "It's simpler than that. Yes, we discovered the fuel to make interstellar and, yes, even intergalactic travel possible. Yes, we have ships with this capability right now as we speak. Us humans... us monkeys that barely learned how to use their thumb 200,000 years ago now have access to interstellar travel. But there is a catch. It's tricky to understand. Not even Huang does. He has theories..."

Lopez took another sip from her water. She moved the communications console a bit and confirmed that their comms array was down.

"There are several problems that won't permit us to go gun ho into super deep space," she continued. "Please bear with me. Once the ME was perfected and several unmanned tests proved successful in our solar system, we took the next logical step. We sent one woman to the Alpha Centauri system. After all, our telescopes showed the planets there had promise. Now we know that these telescopes from the early 21st century were flawed. We made two huge, stupidly simple mistakes. One: Huang assumed that the mass of the particles used in hyperspace travel was a fixed constant based on the e ratio. After all, fuel quantities in our 3-dimensional space lose all purpose and meaning when you include higher dimensions. Two: we also assumed that every single star system had roughly the same Oort clouds. Maybe these new HPs were further away from their host star or closer or in different locations but we assumed that we would find HPs everywhere. We were wrong. Dead wrong."

Lopez, for the second time, showed signs of being human and her voice crackled a bit. "On the first manned mission, my mother was the pilot. She was sent to the Alpha Centauri System. The mission was to go there for a couple of weeks. Gather data, program probes to orbit planets with regular Es, collect more data and come back. At first they were having trouble locating the new HPs. First they thought, their sensors were malfunctioning. Then they thought they were out of range and so they used their E for several weeks to travel well above each star and well below each star. The results were the same. No HPs were found."

Elton was confused as to why Lopez said 'they' but after the look on her face, decided not to interrupt. She cleared her throat and continued. "After a month of waiting for the ship and the second mission which was originally planned to go to the Sirius system was reassigned as a rescue mission. They took a state-of-the-art med-pod, a fully equipped sick bay and extra provisions. Since Huang assumed that when we ignited the ME all of the inside HPs were used, we filled up two MEs but only fired one. We figured we could store them and then bring them back using the unspent fuel in case their MEs were down. We ran dozens of tests for days to make sure that the HPs were there with mini bursts on the other ME. Everything checked out. The second ship jumped. A week passed. Then, two weeks passed. Then three weeks passed. In our desperation we launched the third and final rescue mission. This time they took 4 MEs and no pilot on board. The Quantum supercomputer would be in charge.

"Two weeks passed. Then two months passed. Then. A year passed. Nothing. After 2 years of running diagnostics and test that all ran perfectly well we felt confident to launch more missions. But the chief council overruled us. Then, exactly 4.243 years after my mom's mission was launched we got her messages. We heard everything as it happened just 4.243 years too late."

These particles that originate in the 8th dimension like it up there. They really like it up there. Once they are sent back through that dimension, which happens to be their lowest energy state, they stay there. The only reason why they could run tests flawlessly in our system is that these particles reach out to surround our sun in the entirety of our Oort cloud. Much later, Huang and his team would discover that HPs are present everywhere in the solar system. They just needed to calibrate their sensors correctly. The solar system 'poles' simply have a higher concentration of these 'hoses'. So when the ships jumped to where other of these hoses touched they would be mistaken by the original, since the engine was not shut off and recaptured new, yet mathematically identical HPs. The ME acts like a sort of magnet for these particles. If there are any nearby it will grab on to them without a problem.

And so, we discovered that not every Oort Cloud that engulfs its host star has these HPs in them. They just don't. In fact, our solar system is the only one that we have discovered that has these HPs. How do we know this? The torturous transmissions from the stranded showed them following the mission and protocol to the letter. All the data received checked out. They did everything right. Nothing malfunctioned. There just weren't any gas stations around. Each subsequent transmission from the crew proved that they were starving, and running low on oxygen. They tried to run their Es to come back to our system but it would have taken them decades, if not centuries to get back. Stranded. The last transmission was from her mom saying that she loved her daughter and husband and was sorry she couldn't come back but that was the job. That was duty. Sometimes you came back and it was great. Sometimes you didn't. She grabbed all of the now empty ships and instead of starving to death she decided to run all of the ships into Proxima Centauri. The probes were broadcasting messages with data from the few planets they were orbiting. None were habitable. They would have to look elsewhere.

CHAPTER 11:
LESSONS FROM
THE PAST

Lopez shed a tear after she played her mom's last recording. She dismissed everybody and said to reunite after a quick break to tell them what was being done and what was expected of them once they got to the Ramirez-Huang Super Star Orbital. The quick break turned into a whole day.

Elton didn't know what to make of all this. He knew that Phobos line form M Hall was bullshit. But he never imagined this story. What if they had contacted other beings? Was Lopez a Lizard person or shape shifter? Did the grays or lizard people or little green men and women all had embassies in the Orbital? What if we had embassies in those species' orbitals? What else were they not telling us? Is time travel possible? Is there proof of a God now? Did my hot high school English teacher want me just as bad as I wanted her? He needed answers and quick. Were we going to see aliens to be adopted as pets or be food in exchange for advanced tech? His mind raced incoherently.

He approached Alexa again. Their stare into each other's eyes said everything words could not express. They embraced, trying to comfort, console and even relieve this indescribable weight that had recently been placed on their shoulders. The burden was too much for some members and they could overhear them throwing up. Others were in shock, being suspended on invisible strings in the ship that Lopez seemed to have complete control over. He shook his head gently as he grabbed his forehead and top of his head, running his fingers through his floating hair. For an instant he thought about just going into the airlock and leaving the ship without a suit. Maybe Lopez had some magic technology that would pull him back in like superheroes. He didn't know what else to question.

He closed his eyes for a second and then was interrupted when he heard Lopez's voice again, asking them to come back into the CM. He motioned at Alexa and she confirmed it had been several hours. They all complied, like zombies; floating zombies; zombies that were smart enough to know they were zombies but not quite smart enough to stop being zombies.

"I hope I didn't frighten you too much yesterday. All I want to reiterate now is that all of your various reactions to this are valid. By the time we dock you will feel much, much better. As many of you have guessed – I have given this speech many times before. Before we continue, I would like to answer the most common questions we are asked. Please wait 'til the end to ask your question." She briefly looked around and continued.

"No, we do not have time travel capabilities. No, we are not developing a time travel machine. We have NOT, I repeat NOT, made contact with beings from another planet. We have not discovered bacteria, fungus, insects, humans, lizard people, gray aliens anywhere. Yet. All humans on earth are humans despite what their odors suggest." Some of them chuckled nervously.

"Big foot does not exist. The loch ness monster does exist. Or, did. Yes, we do have tacos on the orbital. Yes, we do have a Tuesday at the orbital and yes again we do have Taco Tuesday. Yes, we have margaritas and other alcoholic beverages but those are limited to Friday thru Sunday. No, we do not possess what you would consider superpowers. I cannot read your mind. We can share thoughts on our headbands through the A.I. but this is not essentially the same thing. We do not have proof of God and do not know what is in the afterlife. Yes, we do let you believe any religion you want if you don't hurt anyone or use some weird ass loophole to do something stupid, or what most countries would call illegal. The citizens on the Orbital are not slaves. They are not genetically engineered to be docile. If you fall in love with someone up there you can marry them no matter their gender." She paused for a bit and looked at everybody before she continued. No one was asking anything and so she gave a cocky smile and started, "Ramirez is still alive as well. His work on genetics and the nano-bots you were given will indeed extend your lifespan considerably. So far, we predict to have citizens live productive healthy lives up to 215 earth years. and we are not giving this to humans on Earth yet because this only prolongs their suffering down there. OK. Now that that is out of the way let me continue with our mission so far and how you will aid in providing desirable results."

'Too bad we can't take advantage of all that extra time to save humanity because we are on the clock against ourselves,' Elton thought.

The first couple of missions that were sent out to Proxima/Alpha Centauri were not a complete failure. Yes, brave lives were lost but much was learned. For instance, from now on no humans were going to be sent to their deaths outside of our Oort Cloud. Period. After these missions were confirmed to have ended, design changes were made to future spaceships to other systems. Besides not having humans on board, each spaceship would be sent out with two HP detector sensors and enough fuel to travel for up to 3 years using its E. This will remove all doubt that their system has or lacks HPs. Each spaceship scout would take 30 smaller probes the size of a large double decker bus. These were meant to scan one rocky or gas giant each. These would travel with their smaller, regular E and report back to its mothership. This mothership would then transmit the encrypted signals back to the orbital.

That is the plan and had been executed perfectly since 2095.

For 46 years, spaceships with its smaller probes that were fully automated were sent out as fast as they could be manufactured on a one-way trip. All space ships had gone to systems that were in our vicinity. This means they were all closer than 50 light-years away. All probes also had lots of seeds to plant crops. This was in the event they found a habitable earth-like world and wanted to start growing food even before humans showed up. They only carried corn and beans. Corn was very versatile and could be used as primitive fuel or to make plastic. Beans were widely eaten and are a good source of protein.

As far as Huang and his team knew, these missions were working flawlessly. They would get to their destination, travel around the system dropping off probes into orbits to many rocky worlds, collect data and then send it back as transmission signals at the speed of light back to the orbital. Then they would simply retransmit the data until they were destroyed, died or humans came back for them.

And this is where their problem laid. The oldest missions were 46 years old. All of the missions in the first 20 years of this massive project were indeed only 20 light-years away. Six years ago, they received the oldest of these transmissions via normal light speed communications. The problem is that some spaceships were launched less time ago than they traveled in distance. For example: a spaceship that was sent out 10 years ago to a system that is 11 light-years away had not had enough time for its signals to reach the orbital. Huang and his team were running out of options and time. Spaceships that were sent in the last 6 years were sent to systems that were over 50 light-years away. They would have to wait at least another 44 years to get data back. This was quickly becoming unacceptable. More and more probes were sent out each year to different, farther systems.

It was 2141 and if the Quantum Super Computers and A.I.s back on earth were to be believed in their social-economic analysis of humans, this Orbital had less than 57 years to fix their dire situation. Sure, they could send out hundreds and even thousands of spaceships into other systems but if they had to wait decades or centuries or even millennia to get a simple thumb's up or down then they might as well give up their noble quest now. We couldn't just send colonies of people and tell them, "Good luck in the nothingness of space. We don't know if you will hit the jackpot and find Earth. With limited supplies and obvious limited habitable planets and systems that don't have fuel to bring you back you will most likely die alone. Thanks for your sacrifice. Peace, dumbasses." Actually, this is plan D. Plan A is fix earth. This seemed impossible. Plan B is to terraform Mars. This was painfully slow. Some scientists argued that if we could terraform Mars then we should be able to fix our planet. The problem is: it is much, easier to warm up a planet than it is to cool it. Plan C is finding a habitable planet and colonize it ASAP.

This is where Elton's solution to the Wheeler-DeWitt equation came in. He and the rest of the new members of the secret team were expected to invent a new communications device. Just like telephones had replaced letters in the early days of transatlantic travel, they too would have to replace regular radio transmissions with something quicker or even instant. They needed to invent the Quantum Entangled Network except they had no idea what to make or even how to make it. They didn't even have the name picked out yet. It didn't matter. Working together they would find a solution because they needed to. There was no prize for coming in a close second. Humanity's fate depended on information and on the speed at which it was gathered as it always had.

CHAPTER 12: THE GIANT BUS STOP AND THE ONE-WAY TICKET

John, was looking around the ship at startled faces. He bit his lower lip and cleared his throat, "OK. OK. You need us to extract information from ships that can only travel one-way to any place in the galaxy. I'm still having trouble believing that our system is the only one with these HPs. Does it have something to do with our position in the galaxy, quasars, or neutron stars near us or black holes or anything else?" He shook his head, unwilling to accept what Lopez was about to tell him.

"Huang and Ramirez already eliminated those possibilities. We sent out 12 spaceships to 12 systems as much as 300 light-years away where we know the galaxial spatial environment was nearly identical to ours. We need to wait another 271 to 292 light-years for their data to return. But, remember, these ships are programmed to use their Es to orbit the star like a comet for several years to try and locate these HPs. If HPs are detected, they will return immediately. It is safe to say, and Huang would say 100% certain with a negative 10% chance of error, that if these ships have not returned in three to five years, then they could not find HPs and simply went into sleep mode. Even if these ships find a perfect planet in a system without HPs, we won't know until their signals reach us the old fashion way."

That was that. Agent Lopez wasn't dismissing them. They were all lost in thought, in deep space with new information that threw their minds into a frenzy of disbelief coupled with amazement and determination. Lopez looked around some more. She flashed a subtle Mona Lisa smile.

Elton's eyes got wider, "OH! Um... I know... why are there so many people living on the orbital?" Everybody stared at him, realizing they had been so distracted and in deep thought that they had forgotten about the question Alexa asked the day before.

"8.4 seconds, Agent Lopez," the A.I. was overheard. "Average time of realization is 8.9 seconds, with the fastest time being 8.2 seconds." It was then they realized everything they were doing, thinking, and experiencing was a test. Lopez emphasized that they always did this to everybody in school now to determine who had the most potential in helping with this project. Most were deemed unfit to help. Others showed some promise. John, and Elton were two of them. Alexa was too, but she went into law and prosecution. That tiny spark of inspiration helped people in any field they chose to go into.

"Ah yes..." Lopez started, "There are two simple reasons. Now that I explained what is done, and what we need you to do you can understand the answer. The main scientific work done on that orbital can be completed at roughly the same speed and efficiency with only 120,000 people. Reason 1 – If and when we find a perfect planet and can send people safely, we want to be able to send people that are prepared for it and will have an easier time adapting their minds to being uprooted and transported to an unknown location. We have over 200 spaceships docked that can hold over 150,000 settlers for a quick 3-day trip. They will be asleep for the duration of the trip, but once on the planet they will get to work with their machines and equipment and be the guinea pigs. If they fail and die, then the news will never reach Earth. If they succeed, then the ships will come back and be refilled and sent out again and again. Reason 2 – They are trained in basic combat to fight a hostile E.T. If the species we encounter is peaceful, then we would put our best foot forward and maybe impress them with our Orbital's capacities. Think of the Orbital as a giant bus stop. Everybody on board has a 'First available seat to anywhere' ticket."

CHAPTER 13: TRAVELING AND STUDYING

The day after Lopez's speech was to rest and let the story sink in. She discouraged conversation and analyzing it for one day. They all needed alone time to process it in their own way. Those who knew each other before the riots naturally gravitated towards each other. The next day conversations flourished. The Cheddar became a floating classroom with plenty of coffee and time to explore wild ideas.

These casual talks grew into organized meetings where people volunteered to work on what they liked. They tried to work out details, math, experiments concepts and simulations. At the end of every single unique idea, text would appear over their experiment in bold letters like a stamp indicating that this had been tried and failed or that the math didn't work out or this had already been disproven.

Elton noticed Lopez was letting them continue for a couple of weeks and one day when they were all in the CM, he asked Lopez for direction and everyone else was in silent agreement. She, once more, pulled those imaginary strings they all had attached. She explained that part of the program was to see how organized they could get and let their ideas flow freely. "Honestly," she started, "every single idea explored for the last two weeks and most likely will have for the foreseeable future have already been thought of decades ago. None work. We don't expect you to give us a solution any time soon. There are two reasons why Huang's work was fruitful: two accidental discoveries that would not have happened on any other system. The algae and the HPs. Habitable planets are extremely rare and HPs in our Oort Cloud seem to be just as rare or even rarer. We can't explain it. Huang and others have different theories. I hinted at this in my initial explanation." She paused for a moment and quickly looked around the CM, again. "Maybe HPs somehow prevented damage from foreign radiation and let life evolve naturally. Ramirez thinks these HPs interact with organic molecules which stimulated them into DNA and life grew out of folded proteins. Huang's student, Miriam Lee, who created the sensor calibration procedure, theorized that something or someone put these 8th dimensional HPs at systems that either will host intelligent life or were used by that something or someone to travel to those places similar to our system to start life in the first place."

Elton became both amazed and irritated. So what was the point of them even being there if all of their little brain ideas had already been thought of by Ramirez, Huang and Lee? Was humanity so desperate that these average scientists and engineers indeed needed to be called, taken to the edge of their known solar system to help these three minds that together had more computing power than every single other human brain that had ever existed? Yes, they all had various degrees and yes they were all seen as having above average intelligence but none of them had ever thought about testing FTL engines or extending human longevity into a third century or colonize a habitable planet.

His thoughts raced. Were they all going to be sent up there as errand boys and girls to get the marvelous minds coffee and tea that those other 70 million humans could never get right? The simple answer is no. They were being sent up there because time was running out for humanity. Our self-imposed demise was inevitable as had been proven throughout history. Billions on Earth resented above average intelligent people.

People froze to death in Texas and died of heat stroke in Seattle during the, now common, extreme weather patterns. Their fancy college degrees did not stop human suffering, let alone reverse it. Two birds. One stone. They tried to help humanity and got to work in peace.

As it had happened so many times in human history, some people stepped up to the challenge. Some ordinary people knew what was at stake while the rest of humanity either didn't care, didn't want to know, or even fought against them outright. Examples were sprinkled throughout history, from traitors in wars who saw the light and helped the good guys win, to pandemics that made some not care enough to comply with health safety tips. Other examples can be mentioned but the point is made: some people, even when others were against them for doing the right thing that benefited everyone, still did it anyway and were labeled as, and rightfully so, heroes by historians.

Lopez raised her hands in a pleading gesture, "we encourage free thinking, but we are also on a time crunch and need you all to become Nobel Laureates, in 10 years. That starts now. I have uploaded a plethora of courses to your individual stations. To start, all courses will be the same and as you progress you will be guided towards your strengths. By the time we get to the RHSSO, you would have completed the first load of courses and know where to report to develop your expertise. If by the end of the trip some of you do not like your assignment, then there is the airlock." She pointed at its general direction and some smiled nervously. Elton didn't doubt she would kill them if they didn't comply. She could have easily left him on Earth to be captured again in the next uprising and be killed. As far as he was concerned, she saved his life and he got to work on something bigger than himself. He looked forward to contributing. They all are. He just hoped he could do it before it all went to shit down there.

They were dismissed and all of them eagerly started on their lesson plan. At first, it seemed, all recordings were of history and records about the first E and then filler about their inventors' lives. Every so often, the video would pause and make them look at mathematical equations that seemed to have come from aliens who only spoke backwards Russian. It took Elton three days to merely follow the basic equations that Ramirez and Huang seemed to have solved over a cup of coffee. John took 4 days to solve the same set of equations. They were expected to be up to speed in 9 months.

Two months later, Elton was stuck on the experiment and calibration procedure Miriam Lee invented. He just did not understand this for 3 weeks. He let out a grunt of defeat and slapped his console, making Alexa turn from hers. She was busy studying to receive a degree in Bachelor's in Physics. For the most part, she was enjoying it. It was a little easy for her, as she had minored in mathematics back in college. She just never really enjoyed it but now she felt compelled to at least be better prepared than a useless lawyer.

***

Alexa and Lopez had agreed that after she earned a simple STEM degree she could, if she wanted to, start learning every single human language throughout history. She quickly agreed but asked Lopez why?

"Think about it. Everybody on this ship already knows science very well. We don't need another person to struggle with science if they don't want to. You would be part of a tiny group of people already aboard the RHSSO that will be trained, when/if the time comes, in a new alien language. Lee believed that if the ancient beings who put these HPs near our star were out there, maybe they created others like us. Of course, other species would evolve way differently. But, she firmly believed that if we had experts on languages, they could more easily decipher alien languages, and will permit us to communicate without the need for violence. Or, we could at least try to avoid conflict, initially."

Alexa was surprised at her full honesty and asked, "Are you asking me to be on the team that will be sent out to make first contact with intelligent beings from another star system?"

Lopez smiled, "Don't get ahead of yourself. We are very hopeful in not being alone in the universe. If they exist and communicate how we do, it could be possible. But it could take you years, decades, or centuries to ever use your new skill. But most likely, you will simply practice all your languages with humans. We may never make contact."

Alexa sighed, seemingly disappointed. "I'll still do it."

***

"Sorry," Elton said, annoyed. I'm going to get more food. You want anything?

"Apple juice and chocolate chip cookie paste."

He floated away from his console and out of their tiny room. The door closed behind him. He guided himself through the hallway, unwilling to use the Velcro on his shoes. That noise got old really fast, and everybody had an unspoken agreement to avoid it.

John, was sipping his coffee and speaking with Erica when he asked them to excuse him to gain access to the drinks' compartment. "Erica and I were talking about Lee's experiment. We've been stuck on it for over a week. Have you already passed it?"

He sighed. At least he wasn't the only one struggling. "The truth is; I've been stuck on it for three weeks myself."

John slightly choked on his coffee as Erica's eyes grew wide. "Are you saying you already passed everything up to this class over three weeks ago?!" Erica said, genuinely surprised.

"Yeah, the other stuff about how to perfect batteries was difficult and it slowed me down. I spent a whole day on that."

"This guy," John pointed at him looking at Erica.

Elton seemed a little confused and annoyed, "Why? You guys finished it in a couple of hours, right?"

"Hell no," John screamed. "Bruh, it took me 3 days to get

through that. Erica did it in two."

Elton looked surprised. Was he really the fastest learner there? Maybe they were just lying or maybe they only spent a couple of hours a day while he was spending at least 8. "Are you guys just like spending half an hour a day on this stuff or what?"

As he said this john, tapped his A.I. on his sleeve and the large screen in the kitchen lit up. It showed his progress. One day he spent 6 hours. The rest of the days averaged between 7 and 11. "Let's see your progress," Erica asked.

Now, Elton felt like a show off. He showed his chart. He had a couple of days of just 4 hours and the rest were averaging 6 to 9 hours. Erica went next. Her time was near his.

Days turned into weeks and the Cheddar's environment control adapted to the changing seasons back on Earth. Christmastime was quickly approaching which coincidentally marked the exact date at which their retrograde would start. During a weekly meeting with everyone they started talking about the progress each individual had. Erica had taken the lead and now was done %61 of the workload. John and Elton were tied behind her at %60 and the rest of the crew followed. The last one was the youngest member. Her name is Sonya and she had barely started college when she was taken captive in the riots. She was at %43 but Lopez assured her that despite her position she was doing quite well.

The first couple of months covered physics and mathematics exclusively, while the following two months were more heavily concentrated on chemistry and biology. They were all about to start or had already started the second to last lesson plan. This was more of what they were learning but more advanced with literature and in English, Chinese, Spanish and French sprinkled throughout. This, along with music was seen as a hobby and was highly encouraged to be participated in as a group after their arrival. In fact, the RHSSO had an orchestra and many Jazz and Rock bands. If they preferred to act, sing or paint, then they could develop those skills on RHSSO. But now, they had to focus on STEM courses.

The last lesson plan covered artificial gravity. Of course, this was only possible with a simplified ME engine and at lower levels with upgraded stationary Es. Having stuff spinning to create artificial gravity was tried on ships with Es in 3.5-dimensional space and it never ended well. Hyper-momentum would take over and eventually the ship would be torn apart into higher dimensions as the momentum vector was fully inside the 4th dimension. By the end of their trip, they all would have started the very last portion of their curriculum. This was meant as an introduction to the development and creation of anti-matter weapons.

As the Winter Solstice in the Northern hemisphere neared, the speakers on the ship were heard. Lopez announced that for the next week they would not be required to continue their curriculum and alcohol would be readily available during most of their time awake instead of just a couple of hours in the evenings on Friday and Saturday. Audible cheers echoed within the chambers.

"I am still going to continue my lesson plan." Alexa scoffed. She had already mastered Spanish, which was easy enough as it was a de facto requirement living in the borderland and having to interact, Mexican-American, Mexican and NAC politicians, criminals, and other citizens. She was finishing French as she spoke to Elton. Her plan was to start on Chinese before the end of the year. Hopefully, she would be done with Chinese and Russian by the time they docked. She wanted to push German off when, with one of her talks with Lopez it was revealed that there was a small group of people onboard the RHSSO that spoke and dealt mainly in Native American and Mesoamerican languages. She was excited to focus on that her first couple of years there.

CHAPTER 14: BUTTERFLIES

During the celebration, more alcohol was brought out by Agent Lopez and she handed out more pouches. She motioned everybody to gather and clinging glass was heard over the speakers in the CM, simulating toasts.

"I know this isn't how anybody planned on spending their Christmas. We are all alone right now, approximately halfway to our destination. If all goes well, we should be able to let Sonya Sarali celebrate her 19th birthday at RHSSO."

Everybody let out a small cheer and clapped. Lopez continued by thanking them and asking them to remember all those that were lost in the riots half a year back. They all understood that even though Earth First caused a lot of pain and suffering, that their end goal was the same as theirs: to better the lives of everyone back on Earth. and they had to be successful to prevent others like Earth First to commit violent crimes again. After all, the best way to prevent violence is to end the root cause: which was being in a situation that made life extremely difficult for most.

Everybody nodded and took a sip from their champagne pouches. Traditional and newer Christmas music started playing in that pod floating through space. It was getting into position to do a retrograde. The Stability and Control thrusters, which also ran on traditional chemicals and propulsions sounded. Sometimes backup S and C thrusters used waste with small amounts of water to make minor corrections. But on such a long trip the E had enough time to steer them in the right direction. These mini thrusters were only going to be used again while docking.

As the entire ship reoriented itself slowly some of them were moved slightly into one side of the ship. They had been expecting this but not with alcohol in their bellies. At least this made the ride more fun, Alexa told Elton. Lopez brought up the information panel for everyone to see. It showed the E, with its power source at full capacity. The reactor was working fine. They saw the traditional fuel tanks decrease by 1% in the entire re-orientation. The E used exotic particles to move the ship above our space but it still needed traditional fuel and regular electricity for its magnetic field. Also, once the ship dropped from 3.5 dimensions, the ship had to correct itself with a delta V that had to use traditional fuel. But since these anti-quarks and fuel mixture were so efficient, the fuel tanks only had enough fuel to take them from Earth to the Moon in an old rocket from the 20th century. These engines, when modified to use these exotic particles required much less fuel and could go so much faster. In the 21st century even the most efficient rockets before the E, would need to carry over %60 of its mass as fuel. Now, they typically only carried %5. This was enough to get them from Earth to the colonies around Neptune and back, 80 times.

The Cheddar, however, having to fly much, much farther away had %20 of its mass as fuel. They only needed a quarter of that but it was better to be safe than sorry. Furthermore, the RHSSO was not stationary, if that word could be used. Its distance to Sol varied greatly. The extra fuel was just in case. Of course, if they were running low on fuel, they could always send a message to the orbital and they could send help. This is why Alexa saw so much food being loaded in. All of it was for them and a good portion of it was set as emergency reserves in case they had to wait for RHSSO's AAA service.

As the party continued, the initial tension of the trip vanished as they all relaxed. The Cheddar requested Lopez's presence in her private quarters. As she left, she asked everyone to go to the recreational section and pull back the wall all the way. They complied.

Sonya took advantage of her small stature at 5'0" and moved all the way to the front. She sat by the giant bent window, which was approximately 100 square meters. This enabled them to see the Milky Way in all its glory. They were so high above Sol, if it could be put in such a way, that they couldn't make it out and their dear sun was swallowed by the sea of tiny lights all around them. It was a scary sight. They stared into deep space and could make out the constellation of Orion. It looked exactly the same as it did back on Earth.

"Hey, there is the southern Cross," Vera mentioned. "And look, Crater and Centaurus. My favorite, Eridanus!" As she said this she pointed to the constellations and outlined them with her index finger. The screen behind them sprung to life and diagrams of each constellation were shown in turn. Vera was born and raised in Chile. She lived in Parinacota, with her parents after her grandparents fled the Great Central Asian Wars of the 2040s. They barely knew how to walk. That's when Uzbekistan and Turkmenistan were swallowed by China and Iran, respectably. Her grandparents left as the Russian soldiers started their occupation of their hometown. She still spoke Russian and even Portuguese, along with Spanish and English. But her real desire was to be a painter and a performer on stage. She was captured, along with her girlfriend the same day everybody else was. After Big Mike's crew raped, tortured, and killed Alice, her girlfriend, she ran towards one of the members of Earth First and literally ripped his testicles and penis off his body with an improvised glove made of adhesive materials and topped off with surgery grade blades. As she was dragged outside to be executed the military took back the building. She was the first one to be saved. They gave her the choice of staying on Earth or leaving forever. Alice was pregnant via IVF and they were both supposed to be moms and get married in early 2142.

Agent Lopez entered the area and with a hidden smile,

announced that the last member of Earth First that was captured had been executed. The UN, along with all the other main 6 regional assemblies on Earth had voted to start sending twice as many of their citizens as before to space stations, the moon, and Mars.

After a moment of silence was acknowledged for those lost Lopez began, "Every single person that has ever made the trip still seems to have difficulty understanding just how huge our solar system is and how far away from Sol we are. The screen changed from images of the victims lost to a diagram of the solar system once more. The sun was taking up the whole screen. It got bright and Elton squinted. The view zoomed out to a scale of the Sun and Mercury, then it zoomed out again and more orbits were labeled. Then it zoomed out again and again and again. The last time it zoomed out it was just moving so fast that when it stopped, the sun was nowhere to be seen. Then a circle was drawn around the sun.

"That's where Sol is." As Lopez said this, another circle was made right next to it. "That is the Kuiper Belt." These two circles were at the bottom of the screen. A circle popped up at the top of the screen. "That's where we are right now." Gasps and awe were heard from everyone on board. Indeed, they had only traveled halfway to their destination. The screen zoomed out some more and another circle was drawn at the top with only one bottom circle left. That was their destination.

While they were busy studying, eating, having sex, even taking a space-shit (which was surprisingly uncomfortable, Elton thought), their skyscraper sized ship with a floorplan area of 3 American football fields, was going faster than any manmade object had gone before that didn't instantly travel to its destination. He felt his stomach knot up. The distance covered was unfathomable to him, and yet there he was. He was in a ship filled with humans who felt a sense of togetherness but felt alone and hollow at the same time. He was literally in the middle of nowhere. Yet... he hadn't left his solar system. He wasn't going to anytime soon, he realized and swallowed hard.

"Because of the warping of spacetime from our higher dimensional point of view, you can't really see the stars like you normally would. This works in our favor because this lets our passengers look outside while we are back in normal space reorienting the ship. It is an impressive new sight to all. Enjoy it for the next couple of days. I recommend leaving the wall pulled back until we start decelerating." Lopez floated to the treadmill and enjoyed her champagne as everybody else drooled over the inspiring view.

Not Elton, nor Alexa, could make out Sol in the distance. Vera pointed out where she thought the sun would be relative to the constellations. She was close but Lopez showed them where Sol is located on the monitor. After almost an hour of people talking about what they thought the Orbital was like, Lopez again chimed in.

The particle accelerator, which was the main thing that was built up there was basically a giant ring in space. At first only a minimal number of people were there, governments couldn't risk being tied to this project. Wealthy investors decided to pay for most of it. Once the wealthy elite grew disgusted by how their hometowns looked many decided to move to this wonderful station where cutting edge research was being made. Not wanting to leave without their luxuries, they demanded products and services. Waiting almost a year for their toys, clothing or food form world famous chefs was unacceptable. With their vast amount of wealth, which dwarfed even the mega rich tycoons' decades before the E was created, and with global warming causing mass migration all over the world, they funded the exodus from Earth to the RHSSO. They understood the risks and conditions from those in charge of the orbital and so they decided on taking people with nothing to lose. This alleviated pain and suffering in many impoverished parts on Earth, gave them many workers and permitted them to quench their thirst for those luxuries that were left behind. But where were they supposed to house all these people and everything needed for them?

These same people, which funded the orbital, and subsequent migration also decided to fund another far-fetched project for their own entertainment. They located asteroids, rich in metals and even found some that had ice, methane and other usable chemicals and requested that they'd be made into stations. So, that's what the team did.

The first asteroids were found and all the metals were hollowed out. Once the machines were done with their mining operations, they would jump from that asteroid to the next, making sure that the shell of these asteroids were strong enough. While the second asteroid was mined, the first asteroid would have other machines divide up the inside into sections, provide internal structural support and then everything needed would be built. Reactors were built first to supply power and some clean water. Then oxygen makers and tanks were made and installed in various parts for safety and redundancy. Once that was finished, water purifiers would be made and installed. One supercomputer was dedicated to program and order these robots around. The machines only needed a regular and dumb computer CPUs from the early 2040s. That is all it took. Programming and ordering were done by the supercomputer and its A.I. under the direct supervision of Huang and Lee. Ramirez moved on to other projects, again.

The next thing to do took the longest: growing plants. Once plants were planted, they were left to grow while the rest of the asteroid was divided up into living quarters, common areas, docking bays, and multiple airlocks that would be used to connect to other asteroids. At first it was really slow going but by the second asteroid, the first couple thousands of humans (those who weren't busy making the wealthy comfortable) started to help and maintain machines. The wealthy had an insatiable appetite for luxuries and jewelry made from space gold. New jewelry got old... really fast. More luxuries meant more people and more people meant more room and that meant more asteroids. The wealthy and everyone else felt pride as more asteroids were made habitable by their robots and their employees. This itself sparked some innovation and R and D. Some even bet on how fast they could beat their rivals' asteroid hollowing operations.

Lopez continued the story of how the Orbital came to life. Some of the mega wealthy, who didn't go bankrupt, ended up with their own, smaller, asteroids to themselves. These dwarfed even the largest castles and mansions back on Earth. Every single room that was meant to be lived in, has giant screens showing scenes from earth. It always gave the illusion to people that they were still on Earth. Some even changed images to make them seem like they were in their old homes or other important structures like cathedrals and mosques or outside of them in vast open areas.

Those who did go bankrupt ended up in a similar position, regardless. The rest of the people were so grateful for them that they were given huge sections of asteroid with the same luxuries. Not only that but they could eat and do what they wanted. After all, they paid for it. If the child of a former wealthy sponsor wanted to learn to play an instrument, people would volunteer to teach them. If they wanted new clothing, they would have it made and not be expected to pay for it. This didn't sow remorse. No. Instead it gave people purpose and taught them how to cooperate and live without money. It placed the wealthy on a pedestal. This could bring on its own sets of problems but anything could be better than Earth now.

By 2105, several dozen asteroids were already habitable. A couple of dozen other asteroids were already being worked on when the team on of the largest asteroid, which doubled as an observatory, located 5 asteroids that were just ice. Pure ice. Pure water. Well, mostly pure water. But the bits of silver, titanium and lithium were a welcome impurity to the five giant ice rocks. They were irregular shape and were roughly 65 km in diameter. The largest was 78 Km in diameter. These five rocks were promptly placed in the center of the ring, which made up the particle accelerator and the rest of the smaller asteroids were in between the larger asteroids and the actual particle accelerator. This arrangement made the orbital look like a bicycle tire.

Once the 1000th asteroid was deemed habitable people started showing up by the thousands. Every day, for the past 26 years, ships, similar to theirs docked. They were similar in ability and size but carried way more people. There was no way that all of these people could be taken off world through traditional chemical rockets and so Es were used from the ground on Earth all the way to the orbital. These ships weren't supposed to use Es on Earth, but they were launched from deserts and other isolated areas and so only a couple thousand metric tons of sand were lost. Most were launched from long ago abandoned oil fields or areas deemed uninhabitable. Since Es didn't leave a giant trail of smoke when taking off, nobody noticed.

Once they traveled for a day using their Es, their MEs would take over and instantly travel to the orbital. Not only had humans already have teleporters, but they had been used for decades now. The scientists that were being transported the, if you could call it, old fashion way seemed genuinely confused. Lopez continued, "With the hostile environment down there on Earth, we couldn't risk the possibility of radicals capturing one of our ships. After all, in their mind, we are transporting wanted men and women. This would also give you a chance to catch up on research and learn about each other. You are expected, once you reach the RHSSO, to be experts in a particular field. You were obviously not ready at the beginning of your trip but you will be. I promise."

"Is that why we also have two traditional pilots instead of a computer flying us?" Sonya asked, concerned.

"Yes. We couldn't risk our flight plan being discovered either." Lopez added. Lopez yawned and excused herself. Biometrically locked navigation plans with genetically modified docile clones were the only way to fly.

This trip was meant as a catalyst for their minds and character. While they were on earth, they were an egg and larva. While in the ship they were a pupa and once they made it to the orbital, they were expected to be fully grown butterflies with colorful wings, with their own defining characteristics and patterns. The Cheddar was their cocoon. They couldn't just pop up in the orbital and had been the truth. Some of them threw up from the shock of the news when they were just being told what was really going on, while in a ship few seriously understood how it worked. Elton, thought about M Hall. If he had been told this while there, he would have laughed in their faces and walked out. But after he experienced that traumatic episode, his mind was opened to other possibilities. He was completely overwhelmed and in total shock when he heard the SCN was down. That was never supposed to happen. It never happened in third world countries. Once it was up and running it stayed up and running. Then he saw the death of Alexa. Sure, it was fake but when it happened it was real. Then he himself was about to die. Instead, he was taken to a secret lair and told through a dream what was happening.

That's what happened when you experienced something that would never happen. It opens your mind to more of the unexpected. He had read a history book that started with the author explaining that history was just a string of impossible events. It all started with life being formed, then giant pyramids being built by people who didn't know about the wheel. Conventional wisdom was continuously proven wrong during thousands of wars where the underdog won. Penicillin was an accident and therefore impossible to discover. Radium was also discovered accidentally. Now, he was living through history on a spaceship that had also stemmed from an accident. He just hoped he'd be able to tell his grandchildren about this one day. But first, he had to make sure history continued. That made him swallow some saliva nervously. He also had to swallow his pride and his fear and become, along with everyone else on board, the person they needed to be.

CHAPTER 15:
THE ARRIVAL

Months passed and the crew continued their work. Alexa mastered a couple more languages and to practice her A.I. spoke to her in random languages. The caterpillars aboard The Cheddar were all advancing towards their goals. Their daily study times increased progressively. Maybe it was due to coffee, determination, or news from Earth about new small protests surfacing.

Everybody, including Sonya completed over 90% of their studies.

Elton couldn't help himself and one day asked Lopez what would happen if they had finished a couple of weeks before they docked. She responded with a sly smile and said that no one had ever completed 100% of the lesson plan. But if that ever happened, they had more subjects to study. He was assured of that.

Elton let go of a sigh in his room.

"Something on your mind?" Alexa asked.

"Our lives are just so different..."

Alexa nodded, "If you think about it, you accomplished your goal of working to save the world and make it a better place for all of us."

"Well, yeah... it's just... is humanity really this desperate? And what if we can't crack it?"

"We've got time. That's why they are taking so many people. It's a Massive research project. They're approaching it with the shotgun approach."

Elton sighed again and nodded and leaned into her, "I'll try. We all will."

"Alright, crew," Lopez said over the speaker system. "Today is the day. We will drop down from 3.5 in a couple of hours and cruise for a bit. We will take a medical exam while still docked and once we are cleared, we will join the others at the RHSSO." Mumbled cheers were heard. Lopez had announced this a mere 3 hours after the last one of them had fallen asleep. "So, please eat something soon, shower, shave and suit up."

An ancient song started playing on the intercom, "GET READY FOR THIS!" As they all had no choice but to get ready. They met in the kitchen area and some ate while a few of them showered. In the meantime, the ship was slowing down and getting ready to dock. Elton made his way to his console where a doctor introduced himself and told him to spit in the sink and urinate. After that, he was told to go to the recreational area with the rest of the crew. They stood there in line as the treadmill was disassembled and, in its place, sprung a circle where they could stand. They were instructed to stand there one at a time as a ring, surrounding the pad rose and scanned their bodies. This was like a CAT scan or MRI.

Once done, they gathered their belongings, and made their way to the CM. Nothing to do now, but wait for the hiss of the airlock and the final clank of the door once it was fully opened.

The door opened and they walked through a tunnel that was approximately 600 feet long. The tunnel had a floor, to not incite vertigo, but around waist height the tunnel was plastic. The entire top half was plastic and see through.

They all made their way through, being careful not to bump into each other and used the handrails. Above them was endless sky with thousands of stars. To their left was the front of the ship, which housed the pilots. They had their own quarters. It was traditional to still have a cockpit in the front even though the pilots' position inside the ship was meaningless. After all, sensors, cameras, and computers fed them information through their display, headbands and tactile input through their control gloves and control socks. The cockpit had its own tunnel to the orbital.

They saw their connections leading to what seemed like a large and smooth building. If you imagined grass to their immediate left and in between their ship and the orbital, you'd think you were entering the ancient Convention Center in San Diego, except a lot taller. To their right more stars were above a giant tunnel connecting their ship to the RHSSO. This was easily 10 times taller than their connector tube. Elton soon realized that was the cargo hold. Had he really spent the entire trip in just a small fraction of the ship? Yes. The rest were supplies.

After the long see through tunnel they made their way into a small square room. It was lined with comfortable-looking chairs on two sides. The other two walls had giant steel doors. One led back to The Cheddar and the other into the orbital. A person appeared on screens above the seats. It was a young lady. She looked like she was 16 or 18 at the oldest. She had dark skin and was without her left arm from just above the elbow. But she seemed happy enough, welcoming them to their new home. She asked them to try and sit down. It was difficult to do since they were still in 0G. But they managed and as soon as they were all somewhat seated, Layla asked them to grab on. Artificial gravity was about to be turned on. They felt it. Some even slouched. After being in almost 0G for so long they didn't know how to react. and this was only 0.2G, Layla assured them.

"Please stand."

They did. Some took longer than expected.

"You are feeling fatigue. This is normal. You were all injected with vitamins and minerals on a regular basis, but your bones still lost considerable mass. To help you grow accustomed to gravity you will be in the Welcoming Center of the RHSSO for an entire week. Don't worry. This is the briefing area. The WC is approximately the size of a stadium subjected to 20 percent of Earth's gravity. Here, you will find anything you want or need. All relevant information has been uploaded to your A.I. On your sixth day you will be briefed together to determine what you will be working on and where you will be staying. After you leave you will be expected to work diligently. Feel free to watch more historical videos on our Orbital, past, and future research. Also, spaceship launches to other systems are occurring on a regular basis. The next one is scheduled for tomorrow. You may watch it live. Also, the ships regularly go through testing and travel all around the RHSSO's vicinity for your amusement. Your screens in your room also have live feeds from the common areas of the RHSSO, and news from Earth and the rest of the Colonies in segments. Once you are in your permanent housing unit, you will also have access to sensors in your designated laboratories and workstations. Enjoy your stay in the WC."

The doors opened and they walked into a large lobby-like section of the WC. Despite them having all of the information available to them via earpiece some people opted to simply discover the area and go exploring for themselves. This is why there were screens on all walls with directories, signs, and an interactive menu.

Alexa pointed to seating areas which resembled malls down on Earth. Doors led to food dispensaries and other shops where they could get clothing and other basic needs. Even though their rooms equipped everything they needed and wanted, people still wanted something to do. And browsing like on Earth seemed to be less of a shock to their system.

Alexa grabbed Elton's arm and pulled him and he almost tripped and fell on top of her. She screamed and laughed and kissed him after he regained his footing. They had finally made it to the orbital. It seemed like any other public space on Earth except that all the 'stores' and 'restaurants' were not manned. "What do you want to do first?" She asked.

"Honestly, I want to check out our room." He responded. Their A.I. said that they could do whatever they wanted that week there. All they had to focus on was regaining their ability to walk comfortably and regain bone mass. They were welcomed to explore everywhere, except the maintenance section and go into other occupants' rooms without first being invited. They were also highly encouraged to go to the public gym space.

Alexa and Elton made their way to the nearest elevator, which took them to their suite. The RHSSO put them up in the same room unless either one of them wanted to live alone. John and Sonya also made their way with them. They had gotten close and had started an official relationship recently. They were automatically put in the same suite as well.

"This seems like a dream," Sonya mentioned, unsure of what others may say.

"Yeah, it seems like we are treated a little too nicely," Elton responded.

"Yeah. I got those same vibes... it almost feels like we don't deserve any of this," John said, biting his lower lip again.

"I guess they want us to be as comfortable as possible to work as hard as possible. Also, we just went through a traumatic experience on Earth and then went through a trip, which we were never supposed to take... or at least not any time soon," Alexa reasoned.

They all nodded slightly, "still," Elton said. "The first time I met Lopez, she was so stern. I thought she was a robot."

"Really?" John asked.

"Yeah. It was during my interview at UC San Diego. I got accepted to work for the government back on Earth." Elton confided. "I also met Smith."

"Who?" John asked, curiously, matching his whispering.

"Big Mike..."

"John, isn't that..." Sonya asked. He nodded, "Shit." John whispered.

"He was Lopez's partner..." Elton said, worriedly. They all exchanged glances.

"Just don't ever mention it to her..." He requested. They all nodded nervously in agreement.

"Alexa, what do you think?" Sonya asked, changing the mood and subject.

"Honestly, so far everything Lopez has said has sounded far out there. But we are now on a space station super far away from Earth. We are so far away we can't even tell where our sun is. So far, this part is true. Maybe they really are desperate to fix this problem. Think about it. It's like we are at war against the disintegration of our civilization. We want to prevent its undoing from within. What people think is impossible in times of peace is done within weeks during a war. Look at the Manhattan Project. Look at Project Orion from the US back in the 2070s. They started beaming solar energy from space to fuel the smart-industrialization age within two years of starting the project."

"I guess." John said, genuinely interested.

"Yeah," Alexa responded. "I don't see why we can't trust her. All the questions we've asked she has answered in a seemingly honest way."

"Yeah. If she wanted to kill us, she could have just let Earth First do it for her. Also, despite being secretive, she did spill a lot of beans on the trip over here." Sonya agreed.

"They had beans on board?" Alexa asked sarcastically.

They all let out a light laugh. The truth is, they were still too immature both on an academic level and on a social level to really grasp the gravity of the situation. 50 years to solve this problem seemed to be so far in the future they disregarded its severity. Of course, for anybody who studied history, 50 years was nothing. So many things changed in 50 years.

Within 50 years, Spain went from a dull little kingdom in Europe to basically dominating most of the Americas. In 50 years, Russia went from one of the most backward nations in the world to the first one to launch a satellite into space. In less than 50 years two European-centric total world wars were fought, which shifted the center of the world from Europe to North America. More recently, humans had gone from barely landing on Mars to sending humans to a different star system.

The rest of the quick elevator ride was made in awkward silence. Their rooms were next to each other and after a quick 'see you later', they entered their respective apartments.

It looked like any other apartment back on Earth. But instead of windows, they had screens, mimicking scenery portraying different angles as people walked by. The floor resembled wood and with the lights off, the floor lit up dimly for discrete moving around. The bed, was in the room next to the living area and was at waist level, with the area beneath it being occupied by drawers where their clothes or other personal items would be. On either side of the bed two square nightstands sat. As Alexa wondered aloud what round ones would look like, the square shape transformed to a round shape. She gave a look of approval but asked to change the color to a more natural material. It changed into a green and black pattern that resembled granite. Both desks on the other side of the room also changed colors. They made their way back to the living area and turn to their left to a small table with chairs and a small kitchenette. No way they could prepare food there. Premade meals were sitting in a refrigerator, which was next to what resembled a meal prep machine back on Earth.

CHAPTER 16: INTRO TO THE CREW

The next several days were leisurely. During their down time they explored the levels available to them. It was a very boring place to be and was the size of a large stadium back on Earth. It was organized like one as well. It had airlocks on one side and at different heights so various ships could dock. If all airlocks were occupied, which rarely happened, the passengers could be ferried on small transports to emergency landing pads. But for the most part, people just waited, as using small transports required suiting up properly like first-generation astronauts.

Each level had living spaces like theirs. The distance between habitat entries gave insight into their size and how many people it was intended to house. An open door was rare, like a hotel. All levels had their own communal area, like lobbies with sitting areas and restaurants. Elton noticed a stark contrast: screens were all over the place to show landscapes or famous hotel interiors. The image changed every 4 hours. Food establishments' screens would make the Parisian café of one day look like a Mexican food restaurant the next. It removed the monotony of the Welcoming Center

Along the corridors and doors, plants were sprinkled throughout. Some of the corridors, which were placed at the edge had thick reinforced windows, which permitted pedestrians a view of stars and some ships flying by. Every so often one could make out a new spaceship docking, bringing new scientists, engineers, and wealthy families.

On their fifth day, once accustomed to stronger gravity, they met for dinner, thinking they would not attend future social events regularly. They requested the restaurant nearest to their elevators be transformed to an Italian one. Towards the end of their meal, Elton saw Katelyn and others coming from the briefing area. They locked eyes and he waved. Alexa turned around and waved too, slightly mocking him. He turned to Alexa and she gave him a sarcastic smile.

"Hey!" She yelled at their direction. She was greeted with cheers from the entire group and raised wine glasses. Elton and Alexa got up and welcomed her. She was introduced to everyone and Alexa asked her join them. She waved some crewmates over and introduced them as well. Katelyn's cremates excused themselves because they were tired and headed to their rooms.

"Welcome aboard," Elton teased, sipping some wine.

"Thanks. Glad to see you are the first here. We didn't know. Security reasons... We launched a day after you and during the retrograde alignment, we voted to stay in normal space an extra couple of days. We had several astronomers onboard and we took advantage of our time to learn a little astronomy the old-fashion way."

Elton nodded. "We didn't think we could request our trip to be prolonged."

Katelyn tilted her head ever so slightly and grabbed a glass from the robot, along with her plate of food.

"I'm starving. I thought our boarding from The Black Hole would be faster. One of our passengers went a little nuts and had to be restrained for the last couple of weeks. He was tested a couple of times and wasn't fit to come on board. He was sedated & is now being transported to a special housing unit that specifically deals with space-mania."

"Oh, no. I hope he is alright." Alexa seemed concerned. Katelyn gave her a dismissive and pity shrug.

"The Black Hole?" Vera asked.

"Yeah. That's what we named our ship. Why? What did you name yours?"

"The Cheddar," Alexa responded as she almost choked due to food being in her mouth as Katelyn and the rest laughed.

"We noticed tons of cheese get loaded and Michael suggested the name. Vera liked it and so we kept it." John said.

Most of them were finishing up as Katelyn barely started eating. "Your name is John? What brings you here?" She grabbed some bread, barely making eye contact with him.

"John Brolin," he started. "Astrophysicist. 25. I'm from Idaho and moved to San Diego for school. Halfway done with my Masters."

Katelyn glanced over to Vera, "keep it going..."

"Vera Ivanov. Originally from Arica y Parinacota in Chile. Bachelor's in Art History. 28. My girlfriend was a physicist. We were having lunch near her laboratory. I was supposed to meet one of my clients in downtown but then the first explosion went off and the cars stopped working and..." a small catch in her throat made her stop.

Katelyn nodded and apologized for that.

"Sonya Sarali. I'm from California. No major yet. 18. I was at the wrong place at the wrong time just cutting through the biology building to get a coffee in their little shop."

"Michael J. Johnson. 58. Virologist and amateur Astronomer. Also, from California. I was on the 5th floor of the building Sonya was cutting through when it all went down."

"Michelle Thomas. 61. Experimental Physicist. I like to write in my free time. I was in San Diego, attending lectures and was touring campus. Didn't want to be cooped up all day in the hotel. From Occitanie in France."

Mahina straightened up, "Mahina Iona. Astrophysicist & astronomer. Aloha. From Hawaii. I've won the World Championship of Surfing three times. It was going to be four next year but..." Mahina looked over to the woman next to her.

"Erica Jameson. Chemist. Researcher for American SM Corp. 49. Originally from Florida. I don't surf. My kids and husband took up my time. They will join us here soon."

Elton took a sip of his beer as Henry lifted his glass and

drank.

"Henry Suzuki. Aerospace engineer. I dabble in guitars. 66. Born and raised in Washington State."

Katelyn put her utensils down and continued to chew. Elton saw Katelyn look at Elena and react the same way most men do, "You're a beautiful young woman. I'm sure more than one man on Earth will mis you."

Elena waved her off, showing she was used to that compliment, "Elena Ellis. Biochemistry major and model. 22. Originally from Nevada. I was Miss Nevada at 18 and 19 and 20."

• Elton C. John. Physics student. 29 years old. Originally from California, USA.

• Alexa B. Garcia. District attorney. 29 years old. Originally from California, USA.

"Thank you all for letting me sit here. We were so annoyed at each other on The Black Hole that we just wanted to get off the ship. I am so tired and stuffed," Katelyn said.

"Understandable. Most of us went straight to our rooms. Except Elena and Henry, which just fell asleep at this restaurant for a couple of hours after eating a heavy meal." Erica said. "I stayed with them for a little but I did make it back to my room to sleep."

"In that case, I will excuse myself. I feel a nap coming." Katelyn yawned.

"We all should. Sixth day tomorrow," Michelle mentioned, making eye contact with them.

"What level are you on?" Alexa asked.

"12"

"We are on 14. We'll make sure you get to your room, if you'd like," Alexa offered.

The tray-robot cleaned up as everybody said their good nights. Sonya and John walked to an elevator farther away to watch a small shuttle undock. Katelyn, Alexa, and Elton were the last ones standing in the elevator as everybody else had their rooms on lower levels. They accompanied her to her door and after she went inside Alexa and Elton walked and held hands.

"Are you afraid we won't get set up together after tomorrow? After all, a physicist and a linguist usually don't have their labs together," Elton mentioned casually.

"I am sure we can work something out. We can talk to Lopez about it tomorrow."

"You know... they said they are more accommodating to researchers that have been here longer and newly married couples..." he smiled at her.

"You want to get married?!" her voiced echoed in the hallway.

"Well. Sure. Don't you?"

"I do. Let's do it!"

In their room they asked their A.I. on what the procedure was like. It's simple. Both parties shall be no less than 18 years of age & have been together for no less than three years. The screen lit up with the relevant paperwork and they both signed and consummated their marriage. It was efficient.

CHAPTER 17: SILVERLAND AND ASTEROID RH580

The small classroom like setting was a nurturing and comforting one with the necessary desks already formed and Lopez at the front. This is why remote learning was only done during irregular circumstances, like students moving regularly, pandemics, and other natural disasters that prevented attendance from teachers or students.

"Good morning class. I trust all of you are responding to 20% G well." Lopez looked around the room.

"Before we begin, I would like to take a moment to congratulate Alexa and Elton for their marriage performed last night." Lopez clapped lightly to everybody's surprise. They followed suit and started demanding they kiss. They did. This was filled with lust and highly inefficient.

Once they settled down, Lopez started to explain how the orbital was intended to run.

• All asteroids and structures that could house people on even a temporary basis were connected to other asteroids nearby. Some were connected to 20. Others were only connected to 5. This depended on proximity to other asteroids and their size.

• All asteroids have artificial gravity set to 70% of Earth's. This works by stimulating HPs in our spacetime continuum without going anywhere. These HPs, in turn, bring down and align gravitons, manipulating a gravity field.

• Each asteroid had emergency shuttles and spacesuits. They would have to be trained in how to operate these. Every single person over 5 years old knew how to operate these simple ships in case many died and/or the A.I. network was down.

• All asteroids have redundant life support and service systems and limited reservoirs of everything needed in case of emergencies. Large oxygen tanks were also used as a backup power generator. In the event the power for the air went down the large tanks could be manually opened by a valve which could be opened by a smaller tank using its pressure as a power source. If everybody was unconscious every asteroid also had the inverse of that. In case of power failure some tanks would be opened automatically by the power going out.

• All asteroids have emergency spacesuit drones that would fly to as many people as they could to save them to get them to help the rest.

• Almost all asteroids have permanent housing units.

• A high percentage of asteroids have labs for every discipline

• All asteroids had a public area which resembled a park or mall.

• Only the largest 10 asteroids had stadiums in them for live sports.

• Everybody is required to be at their station working at least 34 hours a week.

• Those who fail to meet the quota will be disciplined. This can vary from rationing of non-essential foods and items to revoking access to doors, lifts and transports. In drastic circumstances even jail is possible. Jails are rarely used. One could also be sent to work in undesirable jobs in the station.

They were assigned their stations. Asteroid RH580. This asteroid originally contained titanium, iron and some aluminum and cobalt and carbon as impurities. It was one of the first ones to be hollowed out. As such, it was a little smaller than average but just as modern. The Saudi prince who funded it was disowned from his Earth family and now he just wonders around in his palace with his wife, while his children are researchers and grandchildren are learning to be chefs.

"He loves requesting scientists' and researchers' presence at his palace every weekend for dinner. We encourage you to meet with him. He's 129 years old now and has many stories of Earth and the Station like a walking encyclopedia.

"And... there is room in this asteroid?" Vera asked.

"Of course." Lopez assured. "The most densely populated asteroid is only at 65% capacity. The rest are mostly empty. We don't plan to fill any asteroid to capacity any time soon. Life support and everything else needs to be upgraded and of course we need to have escape pods for every 120% of permanent residents."

Vera raised her hand again. She, along with the rest of them, wanted to know why it was 120% capacity. Since people can freely move around to most asteroids, visitors are always gathering in different places and we need to account for that. Of course, the only asteroids that are off limits are the three huge ones in the center and some of the smallest ones, which are basically private property. In special circumstances, ships that are not needed from some asteroids can be sent to where they are needed.

Lopez continued her talk about procedures and what was expected of them. Besides working, there were a couple of rules that had to be followed. She gave the usual speech of how they should be dignified and represented the best of Earth and as such there were certain expectations they had to meet.

To complete their hours of work, their last hour or so had to be spent in classes, interacting with people of different cultures and customs. After all, there were so many different people on this orbital that they all needed to be prepared to not offend anybody. The RHSSO had replaced the USA as the melting pot for people and their culture.

John, Vera, Michelle, Henry, and Erica were teamed up together. Sonya, Michael, Mahina, Elena, and Elton were teamed up together. Alexa would be sent to her own team where her first job was to try and crack the Voynich Manuscript. Vera and Sonya would later discover they prefer to be linguists. The details of the two teams' work were very straightforward. They would need to first fully understand the ME. This would take a couple of years at least. After that, they would need to master anti-matter weapons theory and why we shouldn't use them. That would take at least another two years. They also need to branch out and prove every single particle exists and what it does. All in, they were expected to keep learning, without performing useful, new research for eight to ten years. Ordinarily, this work would take decades. But they were in a hurry and they only had 10 years out of 57 to come up to speed on a complete understanding of what humanity has discovered in the universe so far.

The next day was their last true day to rest. From then on, they all had to focus with the weight of the fate of humanity on their shoulders. They could not let up. Sure, in the WC they were rookie baseball players barely signed on to double A teams. But in a couple of years, with dedication and luck they could make it to Triple A and eventually go on to the big leagues.

Elton and Alexa, along with the rest of the original crew of the Cheddar, decided to go on a transport ride around the entire orbital on their last day there. It was an exciting sight to behold. The WC sat directly underneath the particle accelerators. There are three complete rings with a diameter of 390 km. They were about a kilometer apart from each other and beneath them they could make out a couple of Welcoming Centers. Most were too far away to be seen from their tiny transport.

They made their way 'above' the orbital several kilometers away and saw the entire wheel in front of them. In the distance they saw a tiny center that seemed to change shapes as they got closer on a wide turn. Beneath them lay countless asteroids. That seemed to be held in spokes of a bicycle wheel. All of them had lines connecting to many asteroids next to them, above and below them. Some asteroids had large domes over several sections. These are viewing domes, the transport's A.I. link said. As they flew over a certain asteroid, data sprung up on the screen filled with information about the asteroid. Most had metals that were used for construction.

They flew over a very small asteroid, compared to the rest and Mahina read its information aloud, making the A.I. stop speaking. Its robotic voice sounded condescending. Nobody protested to her reading aloud.

"Asteroid SA-S115 was discovered in 2098. It is egg-shaped and has a small diameter of 1.8 km and a large diameter of 3.9 km. Over 80% of its silver was mined, turned into jewelry, given a certificate of authenticity, and exported to Earth. This resulted in over $7 Trillion in revenue. The asteroid's thickness now is approximately 250 meters all the way around. Some of the original silver is still in several of the Salman's palaces in exhibit back on Earth. Some was given away as gifts to leaders of other nations and friends. Tons of silver are still inside of it. This makes it the brightest part of the orbital. The inside is now structurally supported by aluminum and steel beams. It has a mansion which occupies most of its inside. It has four pools and several Italian and French restaurants with personal chefs. Although it is private property, the restaurants and small stage are open to the public on the weekends. 25 thousand people can safely occupy its public space. People can visit the Saudi Prince by visitation only on the other 4 days of the week. As of late, as the prince says he is nearing death, he wishes to transform this asteroid for newcomers after he dies. These renovations will start immediately after his death. The prince is 129 years old."

They all took turns reading information on many asteroids. A lot of them had metals while some had water and methane. They made their way to the center of the ring after a couple of minutes and found out that only 10% of one of the asteroids that had ice in them had been mined. The rest was still there. The information provided revealed that this was water for emergency use but would most likely be tapped into when another Orbital was built. There was no plan to build another orbital at this time.

All this time, while on the trip, the Cheddars confided in each other their doubts about the space station being as large or as utopian-like as it claimed to be. In reality, it seemed much bigger and better. At first, Elton and Alexa thought it would look like a Death Star or one huge cube, but transporting all of those raw materials, workers, and robots from Earth seemed like, and indeed are, a Herculean task. But these robots multiplied exponentially like a virus. With cold fusion reactors providing an unprecedented amount of energy, they could create anything they wanted. Es and MEs provided the right kind of energy to manipulate gravity waves to create artificial gravity. That, along with the vastly more densely populated Oort cloud than previously thought, provided everything they needed. Most people there could just enjoy the show, sort of speak. But humans' insatiable appetite for luxuries, fresh food, the latest and greatest toys, coupled with ingenuity, propelled us to innovate, inspire and consume. This was indeed a capitalist's paradise with the French Revolution motto of Liberté, Egalité, Fraternité.

All of this started because a handful of people wanted more and more. But they wanted the right kinds of more and more. Their wants, through coincidence, was helping everyone else's needs. Because of this coincidence, humanity's next great experiment was unfolding: a moneyless society without economic classes, which resulted in the first true equal society. The only difference between the RHSSO's wealthy and elite and those on Earth is: they knew when to quit. They knew when to subside and permit others to take over. Ironically enough, it was funded by an exorbitant amount of money. Regardless, humanity's future rested on whether this experiment succeeded. It also rested on regular people ready to take on extraordinary problems.

BOOK 3: HAVING DIFFERENT PERSPECTIVES AND GETTING ONE'S HANDS DIRTY

PROLOGUE

The Observer was heard all around them and even through them: The First Test is now inevitable. It will happen within your lifetime.

All three of them responded simultaneously: Excellent. Our faith has paid off.

ONE OF THEM SPOKE: WHAT IS THE FIRST TEST?

The Observer was not heard. The station kept on rotating, ever so gently as only the humming, servos and clicks from computers and machines were heard in their small station. Their permanent location was no bigger than a large living room, but the asteroid itself was the size of a large soccer stadium.

The three of them continued to wait for a response. The next day The Observer was heard again: The test will be made known once it has been taken.

CHAPTER 18: THE WOOD SHOP

Henry Suzuki's focus on work grew the first year. He awakes at 6 AM, gets ready, and takes the moving sidewalk or a small car to his lab, waving at friendly faces as he goes. The large screens he passed showed two to three-week-old news.

The lab resembled a large lab from college, with a multitude of screens over large tables showing status of the accelerators & other sensors throughout the station. The particle accelerators run 24/7 to keep up demand for HPs and were crucial in helping create artificial gravity.

He helped his team proof theorem after theorem and time slowly ticked away. Every morning he got the coffee going for everyone. Years of dedication and hard work for private companies on Earth had instilled upon him discipline and focus, which caused his teammates to praise him.

"Morning, Mr. Suzuki," John greeted him.

"Morning, Mr. Brolin," Henry reciprocated his professionalism.

"I saw that you caught up on our work on Sunday morning." John mentioned.

"Just for a bit. I was bored and wanted to get a head start." Henry replied while John put on his tactile gloves and grabbed his pencil and started manipulating the desk as some images and words flashed on the screen.

John and Henry got off to a rocky start. Henry's greater completion rate was a way to get back at John. Henry, along with the older members, mistakenly assumed they would be in charge.

'This never would have happened in a private company back on Earth,' he thought.

A smaller screen over the center console announced that Spaceship RX1895's signal had finally reached the orbital the day before. The system has three stars. One had just gone supernova. No rocky bodies orbiting any star. This system is 31 light-years away. The search continued.

"Do you think we'll ever find anything?" John asked pointing at the screen. The screen went back to scrolling through all the main spaceships' data that had been received. Some had a lone star. Others had two. Some even had 5 stars. Many had icy and rocky bodies. Plenty of systems had gas giants. Some even had moons orbiting moons orbiting gas giants. But none were habitable. Many moons were made of different valuable metals, but none were habitable.

"Hard to say." Henry started, "I'm sure there must be one. Too bad we actually have to go visit each system independently. I wish our telescopes were strong enough to see. Too bad 21st century telescopes were poorly designed and the supposedly habitable planets found were actually desolate."

"It's very unfortunate." John said, quietly.

"Maybe a spaceship already found a good system but just didn't have any HPs and we just have to wait. But until then, we just keep sending ships out."

John nodded. "Sonya and I are trying to keep busy when not in our labs. Sometimes we think about the time we are dedicating. I wish we could do more..."

"Yeah... at least 8 more years of studying before we actually become useful..." Henry trailed off, not wanting to continue that conversation. They all felt helpless to a certain degree. Talking about it wasn't going to help anyone.

As Henry got back to his station and started running over scenarios for their last experiment, trying to figure out where they went wrong, Vera, Michelle and Erica walked in.

"Good morning, guys. Man, you guys missed out this weekend. We went to Silverland again." Vera started and paused when she got a glance from both John and Henry.

"I know. I know. No talk about non-work stuff until at least after a couple of hours. I just bring it up because the band that was playing broke up while on stage." Vera continued.

"Yeah, it was a mess," Erica hopped in. "It turns out the guitarist was sleeping with the drummer's wife and the drummer threw his sticks at him and walked off the stage. It got him right in the eye."

"Long story short," Vera continued, "The guitarist was kicked out and they need a new one. Henry?"

Henry gave her an inquisitive look. When he first boarded The Cheddar almost two years ago, he promised himself to make the most of his time that was granted to him by Lopez and her team. He wanted to make a difference. But, on the other hand, when he was first taken hostage by Earth First and had been given his first ever black eye in his life, he also promised himself that if he ever got out of that situation he would try and enjoy life more. The last year had helped him prove his dedication to the cause. He glanced over at Vera and Erica and gave a slight nod and a subtle smile.

After work, he went down to the engineering lab where he tinkered around. It wasn't technically his own but was empty 99% of the time. He had created dummy cleaner robots with single programs. His last project was taking spare parts from recovered damaged transports that were deemed DOA and making them into a completely immersive virtual reality pod. The wall and ceiling screens couldn't match an immersive pod.

Henry opened his console and browsed through services available. He wanted to design and build his own guitar. He found a couple of instrument shops and makers but decided to make his own. He knew exactly what he needed. He needed a bridge for the mouth, a titanium rod for the neck, some nickel and silver. He also needed some plastic and he needed to manufacture strings. His search guided him to woodshops.

This meant real Mahogany for the neck. Real maple. Or rosewood. There were three independent carpenter groups in RHSSO. They grew their own wood. Two specialized in furniture. One group was led by Victor Hugo, who specialized on wooden instruments.

Henry set up an appointment for the end of the week. That Friday he left the lab an hour early and took a little cart from a small communal area near his place. It was two asteroids over and at max speed the 30 km would take him around 15 minutes, if the lines to the tunnels were short. During his short trip he caught a glimpse of a couple of spaceships running tests, getting ready to travel to a system approximately 36 lightyears away.

He loaded some video messages from his children. Waiting two weeks for messages made having a conversation impossible. If he and his team succeeded, and if it was safe to do so, he could have real conversations with Earth from the RHSSO. That would come in handy, especially during this time. It is nearing his wife's death anniversary. She worked for the city of Seattle and was one of the Seattle 77 victims. Some lunatic, like so many before him, entered the county building, where his wife worked and opened fire. He made his way up five floors, killing 77 people before committing suicide.

He sent new messages to his three children and logged off. It would take around 15 to 21 days to get to Earth.

His car stopped, he got out and it went to park in its designated area. The woodshop was the size of a large warehouse store on Earth. He sneezed as some sawdust caught him off guard. He took another deep breath through his shirt and he knew he enjoyed the smell mahogany.

A small flying drone welcomed him and relayed his arrival to Victor. At the entrance, a dozen large round wooden tables were spread out. Each had monitors and each monitor showed updates of different projects at different stages of completion. It was clean for the most part, if you ignored a light layer of sawdust encompassing everything, including the floor.

Some people were gathered near a kitchenette, enjoying coffee thorough a sippy cup, and talking amongst themselves. They waved and he waved back. He passed tables and went through sliding doors that could be completely pushed to the side. They separated the design area near the entrance from the work area farther in.

Victor Hugo approached him from a doorway on his right. "You're Henry right? I'm Victor." He shook his rough hand and he could feel the skin didn't bend like it should form years of hard work.

They exchanged small-talk and Henry asked, "Hope I'm not taking you away from urgent projects..."

Victor waved a hand dismissively, "Nah. On earth I made instruments the old fashion way but here we have robots for that. We still use natural materials but for the most part I am available. I had to adapt. When the 2110 recession hit, we couldn't compete. Our quality was better but it took way too long. So now, I make instruments a little faster with the same quality."

"Have you been here since 2110?" Henry asked and added, "... I don't mean to pry..."

"It's fine," Victor waved at Henry to follow him. "I was 20. My dad ran the shop. The riots killed him. With nothing left, I heard of a ship taking refugees to Mars. I got onboard and instead came here. Never looked back."

"They let you in just like that?"

"My mom died when I was 2. No siblings. No family. Once I answered their questions and verified my info I was permitted to board."

"Glad you're here even if it was under less than ideal circumstances," Henry moved with him, passing metallic lockers with power hand tools.

Victor pointed at them, "Here we got the lockers. You can see they are spread out. Separates everybody's own working areas. Everything you need is inside them except for the larger machines. Obviously. You have, paint thinners, paints, supplies, drills, jig saws, handheld sanders, nail guns, routers, measuring tools. Anything you can carry. Just put it back when you're done."

Henry nodded.

"In between we have table saws, lathes, jointers, band saws, belt sanders. Those are shared. First come. First served. Work surfaces are considered your own so make sure no one is using one of those large tables before claiming it.

"Sounds great. When can we start?" Henry asked, feeling the table on his fingers.

"Depends."

"On?"

"Your experience."

"I've been playing since I remember. Making instruments however..."

Victor grinned and gave him a nod, "In that case you'll need to go through our basic lesson plan."

"Hmm," Henry slightly nodded, "OK. What do you recommend, professor?"

"We have a huge library on wood-working classes. It ranges from basic to advanced. Anything that can be made with wood is in our database."

"Alright." Henry agreed.

"Here. Hollo-glasses." Victor opened a drawer beneath the table. "Put them on when you are ready to start. Find something on the menu and follow the prompts. In case you make a mistake the A.I. will let you know to grab more wood. Over there." Victor pointed further back to where wood was stored. Behind it was the prep station. Large stacks of tree trunks were getting ready to be processed.

Henry nodded once more.

"In case your mistake causes injury to you or someone else, don't panic, your health stats are automatically being monitored in here. It's a moderate risk section." Victor said.

"Got it." Henry agreed. "Do I need to set my permissions?"

Victor shook his head, "It's one of those good for your safety lack of privacy things. Got it?"

"No problem."

"Any questions the A.I. can't answer come to me. If you need to lift something heavy and the bots are unavailable grab someone to help you." Victor patted Henry on the shoulder and left to his office.

The following weeks, Henry progressed. He completed a birdhouse, a small nightstand with two drawers, and even used the lathe to make bars for a crib throughout his lesson plan. He sent videos and pictures of his progress to his kids back home. Because of what had happened they did not question 15 days to 'decrypt' their messages. Sometimes his joy distracted him from Earth First, his main objective or even the guitar he wanted to build. He would show up and get his hands dirty.

Then, the day finally came. He made his way to the wood reserves and picked out his pieces for the head and body but couldn't find a nice piece of Mahogany for the neck. Victor walked over and handed him the perfect looking piece. It was long enough for 24 frets.

"Found it yesterday. Thought you might like it," Victor said.

Immediately after thanking Victor his earpiece spoke to him. News. "Spaceship RX1999's data has been received. It has been analyzed and it has shown that this binary star system has a total of 16 small icy bodies in orbit, 1 gas giants with moons and rings." None were habitable. The search continued. He let go of a slight look of disgust. 'Damn,' he thought. But he quickly pushed the news out of his mind.

He walked over to his same station, put on his hollo-glasses and started building, picturing what the guitar would sound like at the end and imagining himself tuning the strings. He smiled: he was making an electric guitar for himself at 68 years old on a space station 15 or so light-days away from Earth, to join a jazz band while focusing on making an instant interstellar phone.

CHAPTER 19:
THE WRITER

Michelle Thomas sat in the transport as it grunted its way approximately 2 km *above* the giant particle accelerators, taking diligent notes and sketches of the three particle accelerators. His dream is to be a published author and wants his book to be held in the reader's hands; to hear the crackling of the spine and smell the paper and ink.

He saw a couple of welcoming centers and many asteroids connected, far away in the distance. He could barely make out the center section. Silverland was easily spotted. The ship that docked earlier that day was still there and it resembled The Cheddar.

The bottom metallic plates folded back, making the floor see through. He laid on his belly, notebook and wooden pencil in hand and started drawing a rough sketch of the section of the RHSSO. This is his 104th trip out of the station, averaging a trip per week. He found the emptiness of space soothing and didn't even need to take the vertigo meds anymore. His minor stomach knotting subsided quickly now.

He needed the feeling of loneliness to clear his mind to focus on writing. in his room he was always interrupted or distracted. The communal area near his place has a giant dome with a beautiful view of the stars but all the regulars also became a distraction.

He continued his short story on lizard-like aliens who had stumbled upon this orbital after falling form hyperspace, after their mothership was destroyed in battle against more of their species. They were fighting for control of their system. He wanted to capture how humans would react to such a unique way of making first contact. His story ended with one of the anti-matter bombs going off and destroying the entire orbital. "Ugh!" He grunted and ripped the page from his notebook. The notebook is now considerably thinner than when it was brand new.

"Spaceship RX2048's data has been received," The transport started, displaying its information on the screen. "It has been analyzed and it has shown that this binary star system has a total of 48 small icy bodies in orbit, 7 gas giants with moons and rings and two earth-sized rocky planets." Both planets were insanely close to one of the stars. Neither had atmospheres. and both were tidally locked. None were habitable. The search continued.

"Hey, babe," Erica Jameson's voice was overheard. "Are you going to be there much longer?"

"Maybe just a couple of more minutes. What's going on?" He answered.

"Remember. We are supposed to meet with the C.A.O. today."

"Oh. OK. I'll start heading back now." He responded. He had forgotten about the Chemists' Association on the Orbital event. Today is their anniversary of their founding.

His friendship with Erica, while on The Cheddar had grown into a romance once at the station. They were even talking about possibly moving in together. The RHSSO's policy was that of always promoting and even suggesting possible mates so people could move in together with each other. This served two purposes. The first is to cut down on wasted space and energy. The second was to promote social activity on the orbital. Humans, don't do well in isolation or in dark, closed places. We need an active social framework.

He got it! 'What if the only human on the orbital with the access to these weapons died of a heart attack as soon as he/she saw the lizard-people aliens? Yes! This would prevent me from blowing everybody up in the story.' He quickly jotted this down in his binder as he smiled. He took one last glance at the orbital from above, closed the metal frame up again and ordered his descent back into the docking bay. During the last minutes of his trip, he frantically wrote bullet points he was sure would make for a good story.

* * *

Vera Ivanov moved her way up and down the row of student consoles, quickly glancing over the shoulders of the worried test takers. She heard feet and pencils tapping out of sync. 'You could at least have talked before your final and come up with a set pattern.' She thought everything needed to be collectively organized.

One by one the students finished and made their way to the back of the long classroom, letting the others finish. To prevent cheating, none of the students were connected to the system and had to remain in the room until everybody finished.

The tests were finished and the A.I. went through them, highlighting some possible errors. Vera reviewed and agreed with most of it. Despite the advancements in A.I., it was not perfect when it came to advanced Cantonese poetry and other Altaic languages. It's a win-win. She spends less time grading and the A.I. learns, slowly.

It took her 15 minutes to review all tests and most students passed. The ones that failed left, disappointed in themselves. Too bad, they couldn't learn it using headbands. Some people were prone to seizures and in rare cases brain damage was notable.

A group of eight students waited for everyone else to leave.

"OK. Grab a seat..." Vera instructed.

"Last week I promised you evidence of this new type of company working. They're in chronological order." She motioned for them to read their screens.

"Co-ops have been very popular in many industries. From

car manufacturing, to egg production, to farming to pencils to bakeries. Anything you can think of that can make a company can be made in this way." Vera saw them scanning the document.

One of them asked, "This is great stuff but how can you get it started? It says here that the average loan rate to start co-ops is considerably higher than for other companies."

Vera nodded, "That's from private banking. Unfortunately, most loans are given by governments, and they have a limit imposed by banking lobbyists on how many to provide at any given time."

"Either they go with private banks or wait..." another student said.

"Agreed," Vera started. "It's very complicated. Providing money to companies who genuinely put people first because everybody is part owner and has a word in what to do with the profits contradicts their own business model of a top-down, lack-of-input, hierarchy."

"Even with all the problems the banking system has caused?"

Vera sighed, "Yes. Banking is in too deep with the governments. Anybody wanting to disband them would need a heck of a reason to do so..."

"Like what? The end of the world?" the student laughed.

"Something like that. Maybe close to it. The banking system would need to do more than deny billions of dollars to millions... there would need to be some sort of existential threat... something so huge that they wouldn't be able to come back from, even with all their money invested in PR," Vera concluded.

"Several examples exist similar to your families' problems. There are risks. They can come together and put their mobile homes as collateral and buy the land. If they fail to make the payments, they lose the land and their homes. If they don't come together the most likely outcome is that the land will be sold and they will have to move away. With limited options they may end up losing everything regardless."

CHAPTER 20: A KICK BACK AMONG THE STARS

Michael Jacob Johnson took another sip of his beer as he continued his story about pranking his lab mate. "He was running late. I had it set up. The solution had pepper to cause sneezing and similar in color and viscosity as the new influenza type virus and solution we had just created. Very deadly. I also borrowed a tiny amount of dynamite... just enough to crack a petri dish and disburse the chemicals into the air."

Everybody at the table was staring at him. They had just finished their dinner and Lunar New Year was starting that Tuesday and everybody had that week off. It's a more popular holiday than Christmas on the RHSSO.

"I wait in the bathroom for him to show up. I hear him getting ready at his locker and wait for him to enter the cell. I come out, loudly wash my hands and we wave at each other. He's inside the sealed cell now. I tap my screen and detonate the dynamite. He sees the petri dish crack and the smoke gets right in his face. His skin turns pale. I mean, it is completely white as a ghost," his laughter paused his story. Everybody's face was mixed with shock and laughter as he continued.

"I run towards the door and press the fake sanitation button I Installed earlier that morning. Then I see his eyes become wide open and he froze. He started sneezing his brain off.

When he finally stopped, he looked over to me again with terror in his eyes. Then, a small banner with some confetti, was released reading the word, 'Gotcha!'"

He always enjoyed telling that story. He had to clean up the lab afterwards but the joke was worth it.

The laughter died down and The Orion crew started speaking amongst themselves. He turned to Ashley, smiled, and felt her bare shoulders on his fingertips. "Ready to go?" She asked, running her finger down his chest. He nodded and they excused themselves. Michael's friend and crewmate, Michelle, a minor celebrity now did not want them late the next morning for transport take-off.

It was nearing 1 AM, Orbital Standard Time, and he wanted to be well rested to keep his promise to Michelle and Erica, of joining them on their trip outside the RHSSO.

They walked down to the open elevator, and they went in, alone.

"That was fun," Ashley smiled, revealing light wrinkles around her face and even though she was a year older than him, she looked younger. People, initially, doubted her age claim of 63. She had gotten to the orbital 10 years before Michael and had gotten the nano-bots treatment then, slowing her aging way down. She could pass for a 50-year-old back on Earth.

"Indeed," he gave her a light peck on her lips. As the elevator made its way up a news story appeared on the screens in the elevator after confirming their identity and positions. "Spaceship RX2147's data has been received," The transport started. "It has been analyzed and it has shown that this binary star system has a total of 12 small icy bodies in orbit, one gas giant without moons nor rings." No HPs in this system either. No planets were habitable. The search continued.

They both shook their heads in disappointment. Had it really been four years since The Cheddar docked with the Orbital? He briefly thought about his trip to the RHSSO. It was relatively recent but seemed like a lifetime away. The crew adapted nicely, spread out, met new people, and even attended funerals of some of the first arrivals to the station. Both died near 150.

He missed his children and grandchildren on Earth, even though he enjoyed his new life on the Orbital. He focused on his research with his team and Elton and joined a lab that helped doctors in the orbital. It was grunt work, but fun. His work focused on physics and astrophysics and he missed studying viri. He loves astronomy and looking out on the telescope aboard the tiny transport vessels was the main reason he would accompany Michelle. He enjoyed viewing stars and asteroids as Michelle spoke incessantly about his new story. He found it soothing and Michelle enjoyed friendly ears.

They got off the elevator and bumped into Elena Ellis, who waved at them, "Where are you going?" She asked.

"We're turning in for the night. Michelle hates it when we're late for lift off." Ashley mentioned as she hugged Elena.

"Do me a favor and tell Michelle to hurry up with his next part. I can't wait to see what happens." She hugged and gave Michael a slight kiss on his cheek.

"He mentioned he may finish it tomorrow."

"He better," Elena replied.

"So did you make the cut?" Ashley was going to visit her the following day but decided to ask her right then and there.

"I did actually!" Elena shrieked. Ashley shrieked and clapped back. They hugged again. Elena had made the final cut to become Miss Orbital 2147. It was down to her and six other women.

Elena was a model and had won Miss Nevada at 18 and once at the station she sought out a group of models after, an older man at a bar said she reminded him of his daughter, who had won Miss Tennessee. His daughter had started the Miss Orbital Pageant upon her arrival as a hobby. That man's daughter is Ashley who is now dating Michael.

Michael and the rest of the team went out for dinner and Ashley bumped into Elena and that's when Michael and Ashley met. From that day forward, Michael would follow Elena like a creepy uncle. But he wasn't after her. Eventually, Michael got enough courage to ask to meet Ashley alone and they hit it off as well. Biochemists and Virologists always seemed to find enough in common to gravitate towards each other but enough differences to keep talking for hours on end.

That was several months after arriving. They have now been together for almost four years. Their first year, the A.I. persisted on the benefits to them and the station about living together. They made the commitment.

The next morning, they awoke and got ready for a quick breakfast. Afterwards, they made their way to a car, which took them to Michelle's and Erica's place. As the car stopped, Michelle and Erica stepped outside to greet them. Afterwards, they were well on their way to the docking bay.

"Elena wants to know what happens next in your Lizards Trilogy," Michael mentioned, casually as the car made a turn down a corridor.

"Hell, if I know." Michelle responded. "I figured there are several ways the story can evolve. Can't make the jump."

"That's why we're going up again, right?" Erica asked, supportively.

Michelle nodded and smiled.

"Did you guys hear about RX2147?" Ashley asked, trying to take his mind off it.

"Yeah," Michelle said and everybody nodded in agreement.

"Over 2000 missions and none have had good news," Ashley mentioned. "At first I was really hopeful but now... over a decade. Maybe we should re focus our efforts on Mars."

"We are," Erica jumped in. "What do you think those new ships are for?"

"Meh," Michael scoffed dismissively. "What they really need to do is fund an asteroid station around Earth, like this one. We need more rare metals."

"Yes!" Ashley agreed. She nodded. They had all heard the news of those ships lacking raw materials, being underfunded by governments.

"The problem is that an E failed with an asteroid near the moon and it almost hit it. The six major regional governments will never forget that." Erica mentioned, upset at her own conclusion.

In 2122, the CEO of the largest private launch vehicle manufacturer, Argo Aerospace, cut corners on an E design to bring asteroids closer to Earth. Unsurprisingly, the ship malfunctioned and the asteroid almost swung into the moon. After that, it was decided to use Es to bring asteroids outside the moon's orbit and slowly guide them into orbit using chemical rockets. This is so inefficient that asteroids are rarely brought into Earth's Sphere of Influence. Argo went bankrupt after being embarrassed by seeking help from the Japanese government.

As the car slowed down near the docking bay, a small group of people were standing there with screens and playful holograms of lizard-people depicted on the covers of Michelle's books.

"Fuck me..." Michelle whispered beneath his breath, smiled, and waved.

One of the guys, book in hand, approached him, "Happy Lunar New Year Missour Thomas." The kid had a surprisingly strong handshake. Camera drones buzzed around as they posed. A 15-year-old girl approached him and said she was committed to the cause but also wanted to write.

After the pleasantries they were soon off into their reserved extra-large transport. This type of transport had food, drinks, and a larger telescope.

They suited up and moved towards the giant bus looking thing. It was the size of a newer, larger shipping container. Its rectangular shaped showed its functionality and practicality. It had a large bulge in the top rear which housed its E. He saw small Stability and Control thrusters on all its corners. They made their way into the lift, and it raised them into the center of the ship. Once securely onboard, the walls of the lift retreated into the floor, reinforcing the hatch they had moments before gone through.

They sat down on the oversized, comfortable chairs and waited for the lift off check procedure to conclude. Red and orange lights came on all over their bay and soon they heard the air being sucked out of the bay. The giant bay door swung open. The inside of the bay had 2 PSI of carbon dioxide. When combined with the removal of the locks, this naturally opened the doors without wasting energy and the hydraulic equipment was only used to close the bay door. This helped expel undesired gas from the tank reserves. It was a carryover from an old emergency design.

To them, these trips were an escape from their immense responsibilities. Michelle could focus on writing. Michael could focus on observing stars that he could never see from Earth. Ashley loved socializing and the free time to focus on reviewing data from previous missions. Michael could see the hope in her eyes, wanting to discover what others missed. She was a data analyst and sought anomalies. Erica took this time to plan future events for her Chemists Association. On earth, her events were created to get funding and she missed them. On the RHSSO the events linked her to her past at Chapman University in Orange, California. People could show off and even compete a little. Lopez encouraged behavior that made people focus more on the cause.

In 52 years, if the A.I.s were right, Earth would go into such disarray that their work could be paralyzed. If it all went to shit before their new telephone was invented, their space station would be used as a lifeboat for humanity. Holding only 3% of all human population was unacceptable.

* * *

Sonya Sarali watched as her dad's index fingers were held by her daughter's tiny hands, going up and down, prepping her toddler legs for walking in the near future. Her kid smiled and screamed and drooled while her dad tried to guide her forward.

It took Sonya and John the entire third trimester to convince Lopez to let them visit her dad near Bakersfield, California. What sealed the deal was when her mom died in a mass shooting during church service. Her dad was ill with the flu and couldn't go. Now her dad was alone and when she gave her the news, besides being ecstatic for her, was saddened that he wouldn't get to be present during his first grandchild's birth.

She walked towards them, "Having fun?"

"Oh yeah. She is really going... Wish you could stay longer..." her dad replied.

"I know..."

"I put in my retirement papers last month. If you moved back, I could help with her..."

Sonya smiled, "Well, you know my work and John's work is very important."

"Yes, I know. Very hush hush. Won't ask. It's just..." He lifted the baby into his arms and walked back to the porch and Sonya followed. The sweat ran down his face without a cloud in the sky.

"You know we can't..."

"But..."

"But you can come with us. I convinced our handler, Lopez."

"Where is this exactly? I don't even know..." his smile made her smile.

"Can't say exactly. It is far away. I... we want you to come with us," she noticed John nod at them, with a precipitation-covered beer bottle."

"But, what about my home?"

"You can sell it or keep it. John knows people that can do maintenance here. It's a big decision." Sonya said, as her dad's eyes wondered over the trees and the roof and the old shipping containers used for storage.

Then, he nodded, "When do we leave?"

CHAPTER 21:
PARTY POOPER

Erica Jameson was hurriedly directing volunteers around the large ballroom as her hand gestures remotely controlled drones hanging decorations. She was recently kept busy planning Henry Suzuki's 74th birthday/ Sonya's 27th. Henry wrote a song to commemorate his birthday, which was near the date of The Cheddar's arrival eight years ago. Sonya, John and Allison, her daughter, would also show up. They got married the year before. The entire crew from The Cheddar and The Black Hole would be there, with their respective partners and friends.

Several minutes later people started showing up. She glanced at her arm to see the time and her A.I. told her it was 7 PM. Darn. 'I'm late,' she thought.

She finished the decorations as more people walked in. Server drones flew to guests and they grabbed drinks off them. Everybody from all those ships that docked right alongside hers were there. Some of the original founders also showed up. Those who were too old and frail to make the trip from their asteroids sent servants or robotic representatives in their place.

She walked around, shaking hands and exchanging friendly, short kisses. She didn't see Michael. In the sea of people, she could barely make out people she knew. Everybody was talking, laughing, greeting. The party got off to a good start. As people passed her, they made their way to tables or various bars placed around the area. Others, sat near decorative plants and others took advantage of the event to ask for clothing or other items that would commemorate the event.

The ballroom is in one of the largest asteroids able to hold over 25,000 people easily, but today, levels replaced the empty vertical space and now it could easily hold twice that. The event is also being streamed over their network to the rest of the asteroids.

A swarm of camera drones buzzed around the entrance, showing absent people the event as it unfolded. It was customary for those at home to gather with their own friends and family and have their own party with their own drones. These parties would be streamed to the monitors in the ball room and so even more people could be a part of it.

Erica intended for this party to be focused on just her two former crewmates but the council suggested that they'd invite all who had birthdays around that time, so they could all celebrate together. She eagerly accepted. This was the first time in the orbital's history that a massive birthday party was held. While some monitors showed people all over the station, others showed images and names of the birthday boys and girls. Only a fraction of people who celebrate showed up as other parties sprung up throughout the Orbital.

People continued to enjoy themselves and Michael was nowhere to be seen. As she was about to call him, she answered his call. He was stuck outside the ball room with Michelle and Ashely. The walk inside was taking longer than expected with Michelle's fans.

Her long walk with a champagne glass was made longer by a continuous stream of greetings with co-workers, friends, and new people. More people made their way slowly by her, away from the entrance. She finally saw Henry. He was setting up with his band on stage. When she asked him what he wanted for his birthday he said he would like a bunch of people to listen to him play just like any other weekend. Nothing special. She decided to indeed make it special.

"When I said a bunch of people, I didn't mean almost 50,000," Henry smiled and approached her for a hug and kiss.

"Oh, you know me... always looking for an excuse to plan a special event." She flashed a smile and she greeted everybody else on the stage.

More people were coming in, in a slow but steady pace. Their chatter was not deafening, yet. They saw each other every day but mostly spoke about work. When they were in lab, it was all business. Sometimes they would have coffee together. Henry confided that his last romantic relationship had ended recently

"So, how are things going with you?" She asked.

"Fine. Just staying busy. You?" He responded.

"Me too. I have a little present for you," she showed him a monitor showing him their lab.

"What's that?"

"On the other side of the orbital they started growing a little bit more coffee bean. Our progress convinced Lopez to relax the rules about limiting personal luxuries. I'd figure you'd enjoy making your own espresso like back home. You're always complaining about those robots never getting it right."

When he saw an espresso machine, milk steamer, and coffee bean grinder on their lab's counter he let go of a wide smile. Whenever they drank coffee, they'd have to take the car to the nearest common area. It was only 400 meters away, but he never liked how the robots made their coffee. He joked about the robots lacking elbow grease due to the lack of elbows.

"Hey! Thanks. Lopez approved this?" Henry was genuinely surprised. There was an unwritten rule that people would limit kitchen appliances in their own places.

"I told her that we were more effective when full of caffeine and wouldn't waste time traveling on the car anymore."

"But I rather enjoy our little coffee trips," he said.

"I mean, we could just make the drinks and drive around for a little while we drink it," She suggested, trying push aside the extra pressure coming from Lopez with respect to their projects. This giant party was not going to happen every day and people needed to unwind. She may raise work time from 40 to 44 hours a week, or even 48. None of the teams from her docking era eight years ago had started on original work and new research into the quantum telephone. Katelyn and her team were ahead but only because her team had no social life.

"That works. Best of both worlds. Better coffee and a free ride." Henry started tuning his guitar, and his band followed suit.

"Are you taking requests?" Erica asked, jokingly. She knew he already had his song list for the event.

"Maybe after a couple of beers," the drummer answered.

She told her A.I. to send a drone with beers. She also asked them if they wanted food. They all said yes and she ordered that as well.

She waved bye at them as she made her way down the steps. She raised her dressed a little, trying not to step on it while making her way down. At the entrance, Michael, Michelle, and Ashley had finally come in.

They claimed a table near the stage and the screens flashed birthday celebrants, partially being blocked by delivery robots filled with drink, food, and recreational drugs.

"This mining hole really looks great, doesn't it?" Erica asked.

They all nodded. "I enjoy the combination of manmade supports with the rough rocky wall, decorations, and screens. It reminds me of what humanity has accomplished." Ashley said as some men near her overheard and raised their champagne glasses.

Erica tasted the light spices on the pork chops and the slightly bitter taste of her spinach as more thanked her for setting up the party. A biochemist and astrophysicist asked her opinions on a light purplish glow on an asteroid 1AU away. There were signatures of life and they were coming up with a probe to test samples from that asteroid.

The party grew louder as the alcohol and Henry's music flowed freely. In between songs Henry or other band members would wish people they knew a happy birthday as people raised their glasses and cheered.

Around one in the morning, erica approached mic and cleared her throat, "First of all, I would like to…" The screens went black for just a second. Then, a popular reporter from Earth news in the EU, came on.

"The six councils from the 6 major regional powers voted unanimously to suppress the pockets of uprising and violence within their borders. The following areas are in full lockdown martial law/mode:

Chiapas peninsula with Central America, New York metropolitan, Atlanta Metropolitan, Yellowknife, Eastern Europe, Egypt, Nations of Central Africa, Mumbai, New Delhi, Beijing, Siberia, all of Japan, the eastern coast of Australia and Madagascar.

This is in response to the violent clashes between protestors of the Earth First Neo. These protests, though peaceful initially, have overtaken several cities and engulfed dozens of buildings in many cities in flames. Despite all of the property loss, there have not been any reports of fake trials like those that happened almost 9 years ago. Peacekeepers will enter these regions within minutes and try to maintain order and protect property.

The protestors have demands similar to before, but this time they have added that the President of the NAC, along with the three country's own leaders must all step down and at least face some sort of trial for their poor management of the ongoing crisis. This includes, famine, lack of health pods, power outages and cracking down on internet censorship. They concluded with demanding that the government work for everyone not just the wealthy elite."

The party quickly dispersed, and two hours later, Erica and Michael were getting ready for bed when she got a message, "Spaceship RX2255's data has been received. It has been analyzed. This star system has 4 stars, a total of 78 small icy bodies, 3 gas giant without moons nor rings." None of these planets are habitable. No HPs found. The search continued.

She sighed and waved to turn off the lights, kissed Michael good night and soon fell asleep.

* * *

Elena Ellis walked back from the restroom to her latest conquest's loud snoring, 'Why do they always feel compelled to sleep here afterwards?' Instead of climbing into bed she went back to the living room and pulled up the stats for her children, sleeping. Her eyelids felt heavy, but a loud snore coming from beyond the wall knocked the sleep away from her. She sighed and tapped her screen to get coffee started in her lab as she got dressed and notified her nanny of their overnight guest.

CHAPTER 22:
ORDERING MORE
ELBOW GREASE

Mahina Iona, sat in her car, on her way to Silverland, with her favorite surfboard. It was 5:00 AM on a Wednesday and hadn't surfed since before the party and the news show, two weeks back. The images he had seen in the aftermath shook her and she needed to clear her mind from all the speculation and incessant chatter.

Ahmed, the owner of Silverland had made modifications to one of his pools for her. She remembers him being flirty during their first meeting shortly after arriving, but not in a creepy way. In fact, after she mentioned she was flattered for him taking the time in speaking with her he came clean and asked her to meet one of his grandsons. She reluctantly accepted. It didn't work out, but he liked her honesty and admired her sport. He implied that she most likely looked great in a bikini. She does. He described her as a bronzed goddess with cocoa colored hair. She was one of the few people in the RHSSO who had access to Silverland freely.

The car turned into the corridor and accelerated. She had that nasty habit of waking up really early to surf. The pool can automate waves on command but she surfs at dawn religiously. The car stopped at the doors and she approached the scanner.

"The pool is not currently available. Please try again, later."

Odd. If the pool was down for maintenance, she would have gotten a message. She tried overriding the lockout with her pin. Nothing. The screen next to the scanner came on, with a pre-recorded message of Lopez, "The facility you are trying to access has been deemed not essential. Because of recent events, some rules at the Orbital have changed and resources will be allocated accordingly. There will be a meeting with team leads later today. They will fill you in on the changes. I do apologize." Lopez seemed sincere.

"What the hell am I supposed to do now?" She hit the screen and returned to her car. She cooled her heels by pacing back and forth, next to her car in the small dimly lit hallway.

Once back at her place, she grabbed her surfboard and bag, which had a towel, change of clothes and some wax, and went back to her room.

It was too early to call Elton. She went to her kitchenette and got a cup of coffee with a wrapped pastry and started watching the news. They're delayed just over two weeks and it churned her stomach thinking how bad whatever happened in the last two weeks had gotten. The major powers were cracking down hard.

'Why would this affect the orbital? We couldn't help them. Not now. We still hadn't even begun original research. Were they going to send us to another station further away? Were they going to execute Plan D or whatever it was and just start sending people into the unknown with a one-way ticket? Were they going to send us back because we weren't working out for them?'

She waited an hour before visiting Elton. The pit of her stomach knotted up, feeling similar to immediately before being taken hostage. The screen came to life. "Spaceship RX2258's data has been received," The screen displayed information. "It has been analyzed and this system has 3 stars, a total of 14 small rocky bodies in orbit, no gas giants, and three large clusters of asteroids, continuously hitting the inner planets." Uninhabitable planets, no HPs and the search continued.

She walked to Elton's apartment, deciding not to yell at him. 'Whatever is going on isn't his fault.' she reasoned. Once in front of his door, she paused her arm in mid-air, halting her knocking. 'What should I say?' She bit her lower lip, letting her brain play catch up. 'Did he even know anything?' He has constant communication with Katelyn and Lopez and the other team leads. He must know something. 'Would he even say?'

The door opened, and Elton stood with messy hair and eyes half opened.

"Do you know what time it is?" Elton, asked. He yawned as Alexa was in the back pouring herself some coffee.

"Sorry. Look..." she started.

"I know. You went to Silverland and was denied access to surf."

"How do you ..."

"As soon as you were seen outside my door, I got a summary of your locations this morning. I put two and two together..."

"Creepy..." she started but was interrupted again.

"Equally as much as being outside your lead's apartment first thing in the morning..."

"Elton, be nice." Alexa released a light laugh. "Come in, Mahina. Coffee?"

Mahina shook her head. "I already ate." She stepped in and took off her shoes and left them by the door. She made her way to their tiny table, which grew a little bit as she approached it and she saw a chair, growing out of the floor. She sat down. Having a chair on command anywhere is a nice feeling.

"Before you say anything..." Elton started speaking, putting a finger up and having a sip from his coffee. He swallowed, "These new rules and changes will start to be implemented today. All new. Long story short: there are going to be big changes around here. Why? I don't know. Who decided? I don't know. How will these changes affect us all? I still don't know." He bit his cinnamon roll, while Alexa ate some oatmeal.

"He's not lying," Alexa added. "I got a similar message from my team lead." She showed her the text. Mahina was still not satisfied.

"Why don't you take her with you?" Alexa tilted her head at her while looking at Elton.

"Might as well..." he murmured.

"Take me where?" Mahina asked, confused.

Elton took a deep breath and spoke, "Earlier today all team leads received a message from Lopez. We all have a meeting with her at 8AM. Other assigned Liaisons like Lopez are holding similar meetings with their team Leads at the same time. Lopez suggested that we appoint a second in command. Since you seem eager to find out what happens..."

Mahina's screen on her arm lit up. It was an official letter asking her to take the place of Vice Team Lead. She eagerly accepted and signed the screen.

"Great." Elton said, "Now, go back to your place get dressed and meet me at that location before 8AM." Her screen lit up again. RH-580-11505.

Later, she turned the corner, nearing the large hall and heard diminished chatter from everyone waiting for the meeting to start. She hadn't realized how many people Lopez regularly interacted with. She counted no less than 25. Elton and Alexa were there and nodded at her. It was kind of a sad yet respectful nod, like in a hospital lobby or at a church or a funeral. Alexa excused herself and made her way to her team lead. He is a short man of about 65 years old. He looked Native American. She had only really seen them in pictures and videos. Elton waved her over and as people settled, they made their way to a small table with two chairs.

Lopez walked in to the room and slowly approached the stage, not acknowledging anyone, and reached the podium with a giant screen behind her. All the screens placed on the tables came to life.

"What I am about to tell you is classified. For your ears only. In the event of a class 3 and higher emergency we implement a secret communications program. Approximately 8 light-hours away from Earth in our direction is a small uninhabited space station. It has a fully functional ME onboard. When, activated from Earth, by the appropriate authorities, a message from Earth is stored. The ME fires and is instantly placed approximately 8 light hours away from the Ramirez-Huang Super Star Orbital in Earth's direction. This enables emergency messages that need to be sent to us from Earth to reach us faster than any known E capable ship and the speed of EM waves. This is to inform and/or warn us of what is happening or what is about to happen. Exactly 16 hours 3 minutes and 12 seconds after the news segment we all remember was sent from Earth this ship appeared near us. For security reasons and concerns we could not tell you all that we already had this news available. We had to wait until the 16.3 days to stream that to you. 8 light-hours is farther away from Earth than even Pluto is. In the event that this ship is hijacked, it would appear to the pirates as a malfunctioning navigation system onboard the ship. It's a decoy messenger pigeon that has been trained to get close enough to its destination without exposing the destination to prying eyes and ears."

Mahina, and more people, gasped. She thought, 'Maybe they're afraid the more it's used the more likely it's spotted.'

Lopez continued, "The following can be shared. A summary of our conversation will be posted publicly online. We received a message from Earth. The analysis, which previously predicted a mandatory completion of our new communications device by 2198 has been updated. to 2194. Four years sounds insignificant but events on Earth are accelerating and worsening. Our guess is that 2185 sounds more reasonable. This update has enacted big changes for us."

Lopez continued her speech and after an hour of Q and As they were dismissed. All of these were to take effect within the next couple of months:

- All luxury food and items will now be made at 25% capacity. Resources freed by this action will be made into necessary items and food for future residents.

• Worktime is now 44 hours.

• Alcohol availability will be down to 36 from 72 hours.

• No more individually housed citizens. A minimum of two humans per apartment. This will be done in stages and completed before new arrivals show up. You may choose roommates or pick from our suggestions.

• If you have been studying 'catch up' for at least five years you officially graduated and will now be working on new research on The Project. Furthermore, each person will be leading and supervising new teams. The original intent was to only have the lead and vice lead with new teams, but last minute calculations by the A.I. showed everybody getting a team was marginally better for the cause.

• Your new teams will be made up younger Orbital citizens and newly arrived citizens.

• Approximately 50 million human citizens will be brought to the Orbital from Earth in the coming two years. Their trips will be much shorter at a week and so we will need extra help for our psychological teams.

• Every new inhabitant of the orbital will be closely monitored and their communications will be recorded for quality purposes. Their A.I. link will not have a privacy setting because background checks are unreliable.

• 5 million will be professionals and students.

• The rest will hold supporting roles and may be family members.

• Linguistic teams will be used as greeters and tourist guides as most of these people will come from nations that don't speak the 5 main languages.

• There is not enough golden nano-bots vaccines to go around. Only essential personnel will receive vaccines.

• There aren't enough docks in welcoming centers so many people will need to be brought to the stations via transports.

• Non-essential usage of transports and other facilities will be limited to one day a week.

• 250 new asteroids intended for usage have been located and will be relocated and added to the RHSSO. This will require satellite operators. A.I.s will assist pilots for relocation operations.

• People on board will be given the opportunity to request their families left back on Earth permission to come to the Orbital, permanently.

Mahina and Alexa exchanged glances. She had a look of despair mixed with excitement. All Mahina wanted to do was surf and continue work on dark-matter weapons and maybe start on dark-energy weapons theory in the coming months. Now, along with everybody else in the multiple rooms across the station, she was thrown into leadership roles. At 45 years old, she still felt like she was 24 and wasn't sure if she was ready to lead a team. How had Elton done it? He is seven years younger and seemed to be handling it well. and how was she expected to perform? It scared her that many more people coming to the orbital had no knowledge of anything going on. She got the sudden realization that she had just been placed on babysitting duty. They all now had just 45 years to reach their goal. 'Can I... *we* do it?' she wondered as Lopez dismissed them.

CHAPTER 23: ALEX THE GREAT

Elton Cuauhtemoc John was working in his lab when he heard a beaker smash into a thousand pieces. He rolled his eyes and let out a sigh of disapproval. 'Not again,' he murmured and stopped touching the controls next to the screen. He turned around and noticed Phil, an 18-year-old, on the floor cleaning up the mess.

"Sorry, Dr. John," Phil said, genuinely scared.

"It's ok. Clean up and you may leave early today." John said, looking at everyone in his lab, hurrying to clean up their stations.

This gave him a chance to catch up with his own work. It felt more like a class than a team, he thought.

The equations on his screen mocked him, just like they had done many others the last 10 years. He manipulated variables and he was able to derive the other equations everybody else had. After a couple of hours of running scenarios to solve specific cases of the differential equations, he decided to call it a day. As he was leaving, Katelyn was seen on the monitor in front of his lab. She walked in like anybody else on his team. Both, along with all leads had unlimited access to laboratories. But they were always being watched.

"Hey," Katelyn said, rubbing her eyes. The golden nano-bots cocktail only disguised six out of the thirteen years on her face at the orbital.

"Hi. No Biff today?" he asked. They agreed to have a quick dinner with the crews of The Cheddar and The Black Hole.

They inter-mingled a handful of times at the RHSSO. Lopez agreed to give them a semi-luxurious dinner if they promised to talk about work.

"He is busy with some of the last arrivals." Katelyn answered. The migration of 50 million was behind schedule and after several governors from African nations' states, Mexico and Japan were assassinated by EFN, the regional powers on earth added 20 million migrants. The orbital will half that. The culprits were caught and executed but this accelerated their timer and lost two more years. The new arrivals had been sent in a hurry and rumors on earth started circulating about secret ships that vanish with people who complain about how bad the situation was getting.

"Yeah. I heard." He said.

"He'll join us at dinner. What about Alexa?"

"Same. She is on her way back from RH-950 as we speak." As he spoke, he realized they are now good friends. They had not repeated their brief love affair and both were fine with that. When she brought it up a couple of years ago, they agreed to leave their brief romance in the past and on earth.

He closed his screens and they made their way out of the lab and onto a car. They passed by hallways of newly arrived people. Most of these people came from the Pacific Islands that had gotten beaten up for the last 100 years. Rising sea levels displaced many, which resulted in friction between nations. News media never really covered these undeserving victims.

They smiled uncomfortably, knowing they were on a car and these families had to walk the 10 kilometers to the next asteroid over. Elton soon realized that he is about to enjoy a pretty nice dinner while these people had to eat their blocks of compressed food bars or paste. The thought made its way from his head and sat in his heart for the rest of the ride.

Once at Silverland, they got out of the car and it went to the nearest corner and finish charging. It charged a little on the ride, thanks to wireless and radio-focused charging but that was still quite inefficient.

They were greeted with a yell and a wave like at a sushi restaurant. They made their way to the large table and greeted everybody from the other crew. The screens in the restaurant flickered and showed information to the new refugees. They showed the rules and news from Earth in several languages. The restaurant was filled with refugees who had won a raffle to eat there.

The pesky messages that indicated the system was uninhabitable popped up on his tablet. This was 'need to know' and only appeared to essential personnel on their personal devices. "Spaceship RX2466's data has been received," The screen started displaying its information. "It has been analyzed and it has shown that this star system has 4 stars, a total of 3 small rocky bodies in orbit, 2 gas giants and a neutron star." None of these planets are habitable. No HPs in this system either. The search continued.

Everybody sighed almost simultaneously. He took a moment think of the almost 2500 nearby systems had been fully explored by humanity. It became easy to visit star systems and get definitive data. The manufacturing cost and inefficiencies were a no brainer when it came to building interstellar spaceships as oppose to gigantic satellites to observe from Sol. Few ships discovered resources but no HPs. Several systems have planets made up of almost pure diamonds and gold. If they could be retrieved, they would devalue diamonds and gold so much it may cause other, violent issues.

"Here is to another failed excursion," Henry raised his champagne glass. Everybody followed suit and drank. More drinks flowed and soon the food came. Then, Alexa showed up and a chair appeared for her. She sat next to Mahina, whose birthday was approaching.

The conversation continued from Michelle's last book in his Lizard-Aliens series to Henry's band and Erica's coping with the lack of special and planned events occurring at the orbital. Eventually the conversations broke into more intimate talks between people with similar interests.

To their surprise, Alex Henderson brought their drinks. Delivery bots were busy hauling heavy luggage, food, and medical supplies to the newly arrived refugees. Even toilets were portable and self-driving, deciding where to go based on specific criteria of people in hallways and waiting rooms. Cars were scarce and the moving sidewalks only quickly added to pedestrian traffic buildup to corners.

On Alex's third drink trip he approached Katelyn and greeted her with a hug and quick kiss on her cheek.

"No. Come back here. I thought you didn't recognize us," Katelyn smiled and gave him a longer bear hug. She was surprised as everyone else. They knew he had been treated for schizophrenia and space-mania. The last they heard he was helping grow food on an asteroid on the other side of the station. He seemed to be doing a lot better. He did look older, however. The nano-bots were taken out of him. Doctors thought this would help him. They had re-administered them again when he was doing better a year ago.

"Oh yes. So many people can now help with food growing, and doctors said I am doing so much better they recommend I socialize more." Alex mentioned, slightly smiling.

"That's great," one of his former crewmembers said.

"In fact, I am doing so well, I might be able to transfer to a lab and be an assistant next year." His smile got bigger. It was a slow and grueling process but the advanced therapy available on the orbital was really helping him.

"Well, why don't you join us for a bit? After all, this is a reunion of the crews of The Black Hole and The Cheddar." Another person said.

"Yes. I saw the invite, but I wasn't sure... with work being so strict..."

"Nonsense," Katelyn motioned her hands to the floor to bring up a chair.

"What did you focus on growing?" Ashley asked.

"At first, I couldn't do much. After a year, I started

transferring soil. I got my hands dirty. Then, I washed tools for a couple of years. After that I would package fruits and vegetables. I liked that. Gave me time to think and focus on counting and the smell. It took me back to a Farmer's market on Earth. Then, I started helping Dr. Filey grow potatoes and corn. I've been here part-time six months now." He was a theoretical physicist in Riverside, but he had been dragged down a tunnel of amnesia and terror and finally made it out.

"Have all of you finished your catching up courses? That's what they are called, right?" Alex asked. He seemed very lucid to Elton.

"Everybody that was supposed to, yes." John started. "Alexa, Vera, and Sonya are all linguists now."

"Kinda," Elena added. "All of us were in the last section of courses when that stuff happened on Earth. After that, we were assigned teams and now we're all babysitters... I mean... leads." Elena shared Elton's frustration.

"So, what made you go crazy on the Black Hole?" John asked and got a look from everybody and Sonya started to tell him that was inappropriate.

"No, no, no. He's fine. It's a valid question. I was just having bad dreams and it almost felt like I was living an extra life in dreamland. Then I was hearing voices... almost like if I was being told impossible math. Katelyn and I went to Agent Grant, our handler, and he said he'd seen this before." Alex said, not showing signs of irritation.

Everyone nodded at Alex. Elton felt like Alex must have felt like an outsider. He tried to change the subject, "Do you live in Silverland?"

"I do. I stay at a guest room in the mansion. Ahmed spends most of his time in his bedroom or office now. He thinks his time is coming."

"I spoke with him last week," Mahina said, "He told me that as well. During lunch, I did notice him moving slower."

Alex's look of surprise made Mahina explain how she knew him. She did. They continued talking about current events and the extra focus they were demanding of themselves.

"You know, if you think you're ready for it, maybe you can come down to the wood shop with me. It's a very chill environment. You can be creative and focus on something else." Henry mentioned.

"The way they are pushing us, I would rather have him help us in the lab," Robert, his former crewmember and experimental physicist, said. He said it in a half-jokingly and half serious manner and took a sip of his beer. Some of them laughed a little, while others gave a look of acknowledgement.

'Couldn't hurt.' Elton thought.

"Yeah, but they'd probably make you finish the catching up courses," Elena jumped in. More heads nodded.

"I actually did glance through several of them in my free time. Lopez and my doctor said it was fine to keep my mind busy for a couple of hours max a day. What are you stuck on?" Alex asked, as he grabbed his head like if it started to hurt. He had a long sip of his beer.

John gave a mild look of derision. Sonya gently tapped his arms, indicating he was being rude, again. Elton could relate. But at this point what could they lose? They did promise Lopez they'd talk about work.

"Well, as you know the quantum entanglement equations are set. We can solve them for various scenarios." Elton started.

"Yes, they seem to work, if you don't mind breaking the laws of thermodynamics." Alex smiled.

"Exactly," Elton continued. "We're all stuck on the divergence of the differential equations. They only work with a negative temperature."

"Negative 64 Kelvin. To be exact." Michelle jumped in. Alex nodded.

"Have you guys tried solving it in higher dimensions," Alex asked.

"Michael and Erica did that a couple of months ago. On every dimension the solution diverges. It only seems to be solvable at zero." John jumped in. "The solutions slowly diverge in 3 and 4 dimensions."

"Ah, yes. Obviously, we can't go into the zeroth dimension," Alex responded.

"I mean, I guess we could try to take an E ship to the 3.5^{th} dimension and attempt to send the signal from there. But that would mean...

"... that would mean that we need to solve the equations in 3.5 dimensions..." Mahina jumped in.

"... but that won't work. Those solutions are unstable and diverge on non-integer values..." Henry added.

"... wait... doesn't the Lee Transform help solve those Huang-Ramirez equations in irrational numbers?" Erica said.

"...no. it's only for rational numbers..." Elena said. "Wait, couldn't we apply the Lee Transform on those HR equations in 3.5 dimensions?"

"Yes! But it has to be in the exact dimension: 3.4888314159..." Elton said.

"Fuck, that is insightful," Mahina yelled bringing up the equations. She punched in the values and the menu screens quickly changed to her work. After a couple of seconds of quantum computing, the answer was revealed. The infinite series did converge on the initiation but not at the reconciliation. But the values didn't make sense. They weren't matching up to the initial conditions.

"It was a nice try. But it doesn't work." John said, taking another sip.

"Of course, it doesn't work," Alex said. You are trying to converge the first set of equations from 3.5 dimensions and 3 dimensions on the other set. Both need to match. Input and output. Like a radio. When you send a signal in a frequency the listener must be on that frequency as well. Try again." he grabbed his head some more, squinting.

As she did this, everybody was dead silent. Elton was in complete awe of what had just transpired. Of course, these equations with exotic particles from higher dimensions wouldn't consolidate well in our flatter universe. How could they? But for some reason, taking their math and hardware into the 3.5^{th} dimension worked. Scientists still didn't understand exactly how it worked but it did. Only Ramirez, Huang and Lee thoroughly understood it.

He thought some more about how this could work with communications. They couldn't communicate faster than the speed of light because that was a universal constant in our universe. Of course, the temperature wouldn't make sense. There is no temperature in those higher dimensions. If there is, then it seemed the temperature could be negative. Maybe this enabled a primitive form of time travel for energy particles with miniscule amounts of mass. He realized what Alex was trying to say. Send the transmitter in the 3.5^{th}, send the message through 8th and listen to it on the other side in the 3.5^{th} again. All of their experiments had failed miserably because they were trying to make it work in 3 dimensions without the Lee Transform. This completely blew his solution back on Earth out of the water. But he got to thinking about it. If he extended that equation and solution into higher dimensions it could work. Using that, he thought, it would make sense to derive this specific solution in the 3.5^{th} dimension.

"Um... Guys..." Mahina said. "The solution is converging and stable."

The solution was beautiful. and it showed that the negative 64 degrees kelvin fit well when they were solving this in the 3.5^{th} dimension. They had just proven that the laws of thermodynamics didn't apply in the 3.5^{th} dimension and possibly higher. At least, they didn't apply in conventional methods. Furthermore, they had solved the issue they had been assigned: how to instantly communicate between two distinct points in the space above theirs. They could easily send messages back to 3 dimensions without a problem. Sure, they had to be going really slow; barely staying afloat on the water like that lizard running in super slow mo.

The problem is that they were trying to send a physical letter faster than the fastest ship could travel across the Atlantic. The only way the phone was able to connect faster was to leave the known universe behind: the normal sized universe. They had to send electrons through wire and decipher these electrons and then electronic signals and then computer signals on the other side. The same principal applied here so simply, that nobody had thought about it before. To communicate across the galaxy instantly they had to let go of the known universe. They de-bent spacetime. They already had the technology, but it took someone who wasn't bogged down by rigid/ conventional thinking to ask the right questions. It didn't matter if he grasped the concepts as readily as they did. All that mattered was to ask the right questions. Once we know which questions to ask, we can find the answers.

All their screens lit up. It was Lopez. She was in shock and demanded everyone involved in that conversation go to Elton's lab to iron out the details and prepare a plan to build a prototype and commence testing as soon as humanly possible. They all complied and Alex was the first one to walk in through the lab doors, beer in hand.

CHAPTER 24:
TESTING THE QUICK

Alexa Bane Garcia-John was manipulating controls, wearing her gloves and staring at screens in her transport. She had been physically and digitally isolated for the entire morning. There was no communication coming out or into her transport. She was preparing an encoded message that only she knew.

The day they all wished for had finally arrived and everybody involved was hard at work. It took them a little over six months to get prototypes built:

- Set up two transports with modified MEs.
- Each transport will have a crew of 1 onboard.
- Send one transport to 15 light-seconds away from the orbital.
- Send the other transport 15 light-seconds away in the other direction.
- Alexa will then start up her communications again, with the ME and E being perfectly in sync
- Alexa will send a message the old fashion way to the orbital and to Vera.
- Vera will then send the message back to the orbital and Alexa with the characters in reverse order.
- Once Alexa confirmed she got the message she would then tell Lopez and the rest at the orbital that testing had concluded the old fashion way.
- This should take approximately a couple of seconds. However, the orbital would need to wait the entire 75 seconds, since they needed to confirm the results the

old fashion way.

A silly and truthful message popped into her head and she decided to send it. She typed it in to the console. Then she revved up her ME to minimal levels, making sure it was in perfect sync to the receiver. Vera was in the other transport, ready to receive and reply and confirm as well. Alexa, let the engine settle and all the numbers on the console looked good. She wasn't moving anywhere. That was a good sign. She wasn't supposed to. She then turned on her E and made sure it was also perfectly tuned and working at the desired conditions. She looked out the window and couldn't see a change in the stars. She confirmed with her navigation system that her location and super-location had not changed. Perfect.

She flipped the old-fashion switch and the console displayed that the message had been sent. Also, a reply was already on her screen. It was her message exactly but backwards. She received another message on the screen, "Are you fucking kidding me?" She laughed and shed a small tear as she realized Vera had successfully read it. She replied with a simple 'yes'.

30s from Alexa to Vera

30s from Vera to Alexa

15s from Vera/Alexa to RHSSO

75 seconds later her screen lit up and saw everybody in the lab, cheering and jumping at their success. Elton was on the chair, chin in hand. People around him had their hands on his shoulder expressing happiness and congratulations.

"You know; you could have told me you're pregnant at a better time than this." Elton spoke. His voice was just as clear as ever. He was using their normal communications with the 15 seconds of lag. She smiled and waved at the camera.

After a couple of minutes of celebrating, Alexa was getting ready for the second test. She revved up her ME again, while turning off her E and punched in the coordinates to exactly 10 light-seconds away from Earth. In an instant she vanished, leaving the tiny reflection of the orbital behind. She reappeared in a polar orbit around Earth. The E thrusted her into a long elliptical orbit and it stabilized. Her orbit would take 250 days to complete with continuous corrections do to being outside Earth's Sphere of Influence. She could barely make out a tiny blue dot in the distance from her window. She opened up the metallic sides of the ship, exposing herself to the vast unknown. She floated there, suspended on invisible strings just like her baby was doing inside her. She touched her lower abdomen and smiled as she imagined what it felt like in there. Was she feeling the same sensation as her 5-week-old baby was? She got a bit nauseated and threw up, splashing vomit into the cabin and staining the sides of the transport. Some of it bounced and was coming back at her. Yuck!

Maybe they should work on how to get artificial gravity on smaller ships now that they had solved the quantum telephone problem. She calibrated her antenna and sensors. The ME was humming and she turned on the E as well. Location looked good again. Perfect.

She manipulated the controls, which still had a little bit of vomit on them, and started relaying normal internet and telecommunications from Earth, up to the orbital. This was the real test. The orbital now had cable at an approximately 26 second delay. John's computer was recalibrated to permit such high ping. The internet was now up and running between Earth and the Orbital. Her lonely transport hovered above earth, almost 7 times farther away than the moon. She turned on one of her screens and started watching the news from San Diego, California.

The newly elected mayor had to be taken to the hospital after EFN attempted to kidnap him and was stabbed during the ensuing fight. EFN was beginning to sound more and more like the Mexican Cartels from the previous century. She was so close to Earth, she could easily drop in, say hi to her parents and then go back in a matter of minutes. They had decided to stay on Earth. They said they were born on Earth, lived full lives on earth and will die on earth.

A message appeared from Vera on her screen. "Video

communications are still spotty. We are receiving text data OK, though. Must be a calibration or bandwidth issue. Lopez said to give them an hour to try and solve the problem on their end. After that, solved or not you are ordered to come back to the RHSSO."

They wanted to build a communications device capable of shrinking the galaxy to the size of a small town and partially succeeded. Sending video data costs extra. They have limited bandwidth. At least it was a problem that was easy to be fixed, she thought.

She didn't really understand the technical stuff like the others did. She asked them why they could send data instantly but not ships instantly back and forth. She was told, by Elton, that it was like the old landlines from the 1900s: they got power from the source of communication. The source, that which initiated the conversation, sent enough power for the receiver to send data back, even without HPs. Traveling in between spots where no HPs were present, or where only one place had HPs was still very much science fiction.

She continued chatting with Vera using the QEEIC (Quantum Entanglement Enabled Instant Communicator). They all just called it the Quick Telephone, since the abbreviation sort of sounded like the word 'Quick'.

"Want to see if I can send still images?" Alexa asked.

"Sure"

Alexa used the telescope camera and zoomed in to Earth and took a picture. From that distance she could only make out some white surrounded by blue and green. Not very impressive. She sent the picture.

"Looks fuzzy," Vera responded. A picture showed up on the screen. It was of the orbital, but it was out of focus and almost seemed faded, like a thin layer of white wax paper was covering it. That was weird.

Alexa floated to the refrigerator and grabbed a pouch of apple juice. She was getting hungry and was craving some nachos. Real nachos with beans, cheese, sour cream, guacamole, and spicy red salsa. She remembered she had eaten some a long time ago in Old Town San Diego. She missed the good old days. She stopped those thoughts as she noticed some of her drool float away.

Another message, "OK, it's time to come back. They'll try and fix the video and image issue later. For now, we have tested successfully."

As soon as she read it, she turned off the communications console and punched in the coordinates of the orbital. A second later the orbital was in her sights. More cheers and clapping were heard from the lab, via her screen and speakers. As she let the transport auto-dock a new message appeared on her console. "Spaceship RX2525's data has been received," The screen started displaying its information on the screen. "It has been analyzed and it has shown that this star system has two stars, no rocky bodies, no gas giants and no asteroids." No HPs were found in this system either. The search continued.

'But this time the search has been accelerated greatly.' Alexa thought as she walked out of the transport and rode the car back to the lab.

CHAPTER 25:
PLAYING CATCH-UP

Vera Ivanov sat in her pod, directly connected to the dozen Quick Telephones on board their own ships. The video distortion and image quality problem had been solved but was too time consuming to be implemented. Instead, the people above Lopez, whoever they are, decided to press on with missions. Now, that the Quick phone worked well enough for text messaging, they decided to build a dozen ships with Quicks and send them to well-chosen locations:

By 2156, several hundreds of ships were sent to systems that have not had enough time for their signals to reach the RHSSO. However, A Quick was not necessary in every system. Instead, they picked one ship in each section that was near other ships in nearby systems, since all the ships communicated with each other via normal light speed signals. They would go to a ship that had already received data from other, nearby ships but had not had enough time to send it back to the orbital. This cut down on time and resources. Others suggested to abandon incomplete missions. This suggestion was quickly shut down.

Vera looked over the large bent screen in her pod. She had a direct connection to the ships, Lopez and the rest of the team leads

In the 8 months since her successful first test with Alexa, ships were still being sent out as usual (without Quicks). The first Quick enabled ship was sent a couple of weeks ago to a system where an original ship without the Quick had already finished its system analysis. These antenna scouts reported no habitable planets.

Simultaneously, Quick enabled ships were also sent to new systems. Once in their system they traveled with Es and drop off drones. Their analysis took at least six months to complete, depending on the system. They were still receiving data, streamed q-bit by q-bit. 'This must have been how people felt in mission control with ships sent to Mars in the early 2000s,' she thought.

"Ivanov, ready?" Lopez was heard in her ear.

"Affirmative. All Quicks working as intended. You may start delivering when ready."

"Understood. Firing now."

A couple of seconds later her huge screen was bombarded by text, indicating the information all those ships had found. It was going way too fast for her. Luckily, the program Elena and Michelle wrote together was able to filter out the important stuff. A minute passed and the text disappeared into a corner near the bottom right of the pod. The rest was displaying the information from the systems. It is 355 systems total. and all of these were over 400 light years away. Some had just one star. Others had two. Many of them had three stars. Almost all had icy bodies or gas giants or both. None were habitable. The search continued.

The calibration and manufacturing procedure for the Quick was a time consuming one. That, coupled with the fact that none of the ships with Quicks has access to HPs, means that they need to wait for a couple of months at least and continue testing. Other data from the Quick was now being analyzed by the A.I. and Vera. She prayed they pick up signals or text from another civilization. 'I can hope, can't I?' she thought.

Ships without Quicks continued being sent. There was no point in waiting for production to catch up to demand. Now that they had open communications, exploration was going to go increase. The ones in charge wanted to focus on the systems that had already been explored. That included any system that had ships that had left approximately 3 years before the present. This bought some time for manufacturing and to let recently sent ships complete their exploration. No point in sending out a Quick if probes weren't done with their analysis.

This was going to be Vera's job for the foreseeable future; maybe even for the rest of her life. In a couple of months, once production was running smoothly, Sonya and Alexa would get involved to analyze newly received data. Then, more trained linguists will join them. They had two main jobs. One is to help facilitate migration and to review data from other systems.

But for now, it was limited to one person and one pod in a session reminding her of her first sexual experience: quick, enjoyable, and leaving her desiring more. 'Whatever happened to that guy?' She wondered. She brushed the thought away just as quickly as it popped into her head.

The pod door dematerialized and dragged the screens to the side and shrank, giving her an exit route. It was barely 3:00 PM. She had carved out the entire day for this session. She had been ordered to, was a more appropriate phrase. Now that their mission had concluded, the next mission was at hand: finding a habitable planet and start moving people on to it.

She moved over to her other desk and started looking at the theorem and solution they all had done together that one fateful night. It left her amazed and equally upset. She wanted to blow up, knowing she couldn't share their discovery with the world. At least, not yet. It could end her career.

If the tech behind the Quick was leaked, who knows what people or companies would do for it. It cuts down communication times and facilitate searching for distress calls. This could save lives.

She lost her soulmate and the chance at a normal life. Now, she had been offered an extraordinary one. If she threw it all away, what could become of her? 'I am not willing to risk my career for this. Maybe for something more compelling and momentous, but not this. After a terrifying moment, she stopped thinking about it and focused on her work of overseeing the A.I.'s analysis and data received. She double checked her work and sometimes checked it again before going to bed.

Several hours later, while going through metadata, she realized something a little off. All temperature values were reading zero. They weren't tiny values rounded off to zero. The instruments on the ships have a precision of 250 significant figures. All read zero. Odd. The more she looked at them the more she realized what the problem was. Theoretically, the temperature should be negative 64 degrees kelvin. But they didn't possess anything that could read negative temperatures. 'Can we even design something to read negative temperature? She brushed the notion aside, and refocused on the data received, trying to decipher anything useful.

Both her earpiece and monitor communicated she had a guest at her front door. It's Belmira Flores. She nodded & her lab went into civilian mode, and everything about the ships, the Quick and other planets disappeared as Belmira entered. Her screen turned off as the entire lab turned into civilian mode and Belmira entered. She was hiding something and quickly smiled and showed Vera, her hands. She had baked her a dozen Pan Amasados.

"Hey, look at that. They smell nice, too!" Vera was genuinely surprised at how good she had gotten at baking. She grabbed the basket and deeply inhaled. She uncovered them and the smell intensified and Vera was instantly transported back to Chile when she was barely 6 years old. Her grandmother had picked her up from school, which was walking distance and had given her, her daily Pan Amasado.

"Thanks, babe," Vera went in for a kiss. Belmira happily accepted and put her arm around Vera's waist. Vera felt her hand slowly getting lower and smiled, "you know we're being recorded in here, right? All labs are."

"So? Let them enjoy the show."

"Come on, let's go get dinner and I'll thank you later." Vera gently bit Belmira's lip as both smiled. She saw her light brown eyes reflect the lab lights. They made their way to the car, holding hands and drove to the neighboring asteroid for Brazilian food.

Vera's routine continued throughout her tenure at the RHSSO. She practiced her linguistic skills with refugees having trouble adapting to their new lives. She teaches the new arrivals English, Spanish, Russian, Chinese, and French. Every week she jumps into her pod and analyzes more ship data.

She loved the look of people understanding different people. It made everyone more relatable and minimized barriers. Her classes filled up quickly and soon would be focused on more advanced to train other linguists. Only people older than 59 were excused from her courses and relied on their translators more heavily.

That's how she met Belmira. Belmira only speaks Portuguese fluently. She is struggling through Spanish and English. She is originally from Brazil one of the many refugees who had gotten to the orbital around the same time they were performing their Quick test. Vera was assigned to a couple different transports and greeted them all in Portuguese. Belmira's younger brother was so scared. Her family is from a tiny town in the Amazon rainforest who were recently displaced by the river's ever widening ferocious flow. They had heard of boats and seen pictures of cars but never even imagined spaceships. Belmira made the trip with her parents, younger brother, and grandmothers. Both of her grandfathers had died.

After a couple of meetings, Belmira kept on staring at her and at first it made her a little uncomfortable but they got to talking afterwards and had decided to go get some coffee, under the pretense of providing an in-depth tour. After that, they became inseparable. Belmira's family adapted, slowly and soon she was accepted into the family. But her new family highlighted some emptiness left behind in her. Her extended family was back on earth. They exchanged messages frequently and she yearned to be with them.

Vera is one of the lucky ones. She was grandfathered in and convinced Lopez to let her keep her place all to herself. Lately, Belmira had been spending every night at her place. They basically lived together, but it was still in the early stages. Vera was enjoying her time with her and so didn't push the subject; afraid she'd make it awkward for both.

CHAPTER 26: THE PILOT, THE ASTEROIDS AND MORE REFUGEES

John Brolin grunted in disapproval, "No. No. NOOO!" His hand started to hurt as he slammed the screen. The Es were not responding to his commands and had to be recalibrated, again. Just like the week before that.

He made sure everything was as stationary as if they were all in Lagrange points. Sometimes he regretted volunteering for this mission. At first it had seemed fun: fly around in a ship, locate worthy asteroids, and take them back to the orbital. The first couple of weeks were fun. But while everybody else was trying to advance theoretical work, comfortably sitting in chairs, he was the only idiot who was outside working his butt off. The problem is that, he was stuck with older Es. These Es had not been used since the orbital was first being built. Back then, those people didn't have to worry about an extra 30 million refugees coming in a couple of years.

The governments, under tremendous pressure from its citizens were forced to push the 70 million refugees to 100 million. More homes, and everything else that came with them. Newer Es and MEs were sent to other systems with Quicks. In the meantime, John was building his own habitats from scratch.

He got into a space suit and did an EVA as soon as the transport was attached to the first E, which was hauling a 45 km rock filled with aluminum, cobalt, iridium, and some iron. He recalibrated the tiny ultra-smart relays and moved onto the next ship. This continued for many hours. Once he was back in his transport, he grabbed a snack and water and finished what he was doing: placing the half dozen asteroids into position, near a spoke.

The Ramirez-Huang Super Star Orbital had the shape of a flat disk. From his point of view it resembled a solar system minus the blazing ball of gas in the center and has a very distinguishable outer limit. He snapped a picture and continued to gently place the asteroids into position. After a decade or so, the orbital would increase in depth/ height. The asteroids he grabbed were one of the first to be built upwards and not outwards.

His work continued to take up three or four days. He easily worked his required 44 hours in 4 days. Sometimes he would get them done in three and spend those three days in his transport. Henry, Michael, and Erica, made it into a mobile space home.

After correcting everybody else's work with minor details and a couple of well-placed coefficients, he had perfected the Quick. It now transmitted superb video and audio quality. The only problem is, they needed to use a special type of procedure to make the smart materials unique enough to mold to the HPs they were using to send signals back and forth. This took time and lots of money. In fact, it took gold, silver, and other extremely rare metals.

He was asked what he would like to do, just like everybody else on the team that had cracked the secrets of instant communications. He wanted to fly in space. He had always dreamt of becoming a fighter pilot in space and bringing peace and justice to the Wild West Colonies that were outside the sphere of influence of the asteroid belt. That's all he ever wanted. There was also a quiet dignity in this work. He felt much more useful doing what he presently was doing than doing what he had done: sitting at a computer screen and solving equations. He enjoyed piloting the transport manually. He loved feeling so powerful he could literally move worlds and then provide shelter and resources for those in need. Let the linguists deal with them hands on. 'I'm happy,' he thought.

His dad was a cop, and his grandfather was a fighter pilot. His grandfather took down rebel ships before they could do more damage to satellites in the mini civil war. Every time he would meet up with his grandfather, he asked him to recount tales of space battles, limited as they may have been.

Now, there was no need for fighter pilots or war heroes. What humanity needed was scientists and actual manufacturers. For the past couple of decades all the fighting was done on Earth; fighting between those who don't have power and those who refuse to share it. Mars had seen some minor protests that didn't result in anything. It is hard to protest when all those in power had to do was click some screens to lower your oxygen supply.

So that's what he did. He moved worlds and provided homes and resources to those in need. Some people jokingly nick named him Robin Hood. He wasn't taking it from anybody else. The asteroids were just there.

As soon as all the asteroids were in their pre-determined place he would contact Robert, his partner on the ground, sort of speak. Then a large hook and thick carbon fiber rope was blasted onto the rock from three different locations. Then little robots would make their way on these lines on to the asteroid and start digging. Each asteroid first started with 6 robots and once there was enough hollowed out more would be sent in. These mined materials, along with other premade raw materials, were used to build bridges connecting the old asteroids to the new.

While this happened, the E fired pulses continuously, to keep tension on the ropes in conjunction with the robotic rope holders until all three bridges were sound. Every now and then a robot would break off and he would have to go after it and place it back to the asteroids, using the giant mechanical arms of the transport. Attaching engines and fuel to each little worker robot was inefficient. It was easier to have a single transport on the lookout. This rarely happened and one transport could easily oversee a dozen asteroids.

After a day of waiting for the bridges to complete and only having to go and retrieve one lost worker robot he packed up and docked in his home asteroid.

Before he disconnected, he got a message from Erica, asking him to confirm he would show up to their 15th year anniversary. This surprised him as, that wouldn't be for another 9 months. 'Why so soon?' He wondered. He happily accepted.

CHAPTER 27:
THE BEAUTIFUL
DOCTOR WITH
EIGHT CHILDREN

Elena Ellis was in her lab, supervising and confirming the new creation of golden nano-bots. The only difference was a modified protein that is made in half the time. Only 10% of the recently arrived refugees had received the shot. Lopez agreed with her: this is unacceptable.

Screens all around her displayed information from machines which resembled those found in a high-tech research and development laboratories from the most profitable companies back on Earth. She was in a biochemist's heaven.

After her team cracked the Quick, she began following her real passion: longevity. Elena, like others, was also asked what she wanted to do. Her answers were simple: improve the golden nano-bots, which she had studied on her free time on the RHSSO, and making being a mom a priority. But she didn't want to be just any mom. She wanted to have at least 5 children.

When she went home, she would in single mom heaven. The first three children she had were from a boyfriend, several years after she got to the orbital. Children 4-6 were with casual relationships. Men desired her, and she could have her pick. 'Being supremely intelligent and a model back on Earth does have its perks,' she always thought. It made her feel invincible. Soon she noticed that relationships with men, were not important. She liked casual relationships. She just wanted to focus on her children. It also didn't help that a couple of previous partners got into a very public and very embarrassing fight in one of Erica's many high life and rare parties. After that, she decided to just be a mom. She had no desire to be a wife. A lover? Yes.

Her last two children were conceived through IVF. When she noticed how easy that was, she had regretted conceiving the rest the old fashion way. 'IT was fun, though' a smile showed up on her face as she remembered her many conquests.

She got a message from Lopez, acknowledging her successful trials. She asked how long it would take to inoculate everyone on board. Elena indicated it would take at least a year. 'Maybe before I am forty, we can have most of the people vaccinated,' she thought. She was going to be forty in almost 9 months. Yikes! It dawned on her she had been at the orbital for nearly 18 years. That was the age of a fully grown human, she thought. She did some more thinking, and after comparing 18 years to the lifespan of many other lifeforms, she stopped.

The Council, she remembered it being called that once, decided accept another 5 million people. The population was now at 180 million and growing every day. Kids were being born every day, while some people, too few in fact, died. She briefly thought about John, again. Her good friend and former crewmate out in space all the time now, it seemed. He wasn't alone. A team of asteroid ship operators was up there all the time. It didn't seem like they were going to slow down any time soon.

She got into a car, which was already waiting for her outside of her lab and started going to the local park, which was where some of her kids were most of the time, along with their nannies. The older children were probably with some friends while the youngest ones were most likely back at home.

As the car turned and slowed down to let her out, she saw one of her nannies, a recently arrived refugee, shriek playfully as Donna, her 4-year-old daughter was coming down the slide. Immediately after landing she jumped into her nanny's arms. She threw her up in the air playfully, and Donna shrieked and laughed.

Eric, who was a year younger was playing in a sandbox with his nanny handing him small plastic tools and cleaning them as he grabbed them again.

She approached them and as soon as they noticed her, they dropped what they were doing, screamed mommy, and ran into her extended arms. 'This is the best thing in the world,' she thought. Both started running their mouths about their incredible day, which was just like any other day. But to them, it was always the best day. They ate, cleaned, washed up, did a little studying, and then watched some cartoons and then went to the park. She didn't even have to track them on her A.I. sleeve. On the rare occasion they were not at the park, the nannies would notify her.

On her way home, her oldest son and daughter of age 13 and 12, respectively, snuck up behind her and started walking with her. They, too would talk to her about their day at school. They were looking forward to a class trip to another asteroid where a lot of the food was grown.

Once home, she visited both pairs of twins. She was helping her live in helpers prepare dinner for everyone, when she got a call from Lopez and asked her to go immediately to Asteroid RH125. The newly arrived refugees were showing symptoms of the measles.

She got in to a car, went to her office where she got a dozen of the new nano-bots-filled vials and continued to the docking bay. As she made her way to the console to request a ship, she saw John standing next to it. She jogged towards him, loudly. He turned around and she made sure she was bouncing a little more than usual. His eyesight went directly to where she wanted.

"Are you going up?"

"Hi. I'm fine. Thanks for asking, Miss Ellis. How are you?" John said, sarcastically, pointing out her rudeness.

Elena rolled her eyes and asked him how he was. Before he could answer she asked him for a ride.

"Sure, I guess," he answered, a little confused. "What's the rush?"

"I'll tell you inside." She guided him, with a rushed foot and a sure hand, by the elbow. They both got in and she undid her top zipper just a bit.

"OK! No! Whoa!" John shook his head and waved his hands. He took a giant step away from her. His eyes were still fixed on her cleavage, though.

"What?"

"We can't. I can't. Not again. You're a great lay but... Sonya and I just got back together again. I don't want to mess that up. I'm not single anymore..."

She gave him an authentic look of confusion and disgust. "What?"

"We are not going to do this."

"It's hot in here," she started. "Look," she rolled her eyes, "this is serious." She took a second to zip up her top and could already feel the sweat.

John got into his seat and tapped screens and pulled a lever. They were off. She felt the acceleration, realizing John had removed the gravity softener to make room for his sleeping quarters.

"I don't think I can tell you but since we're both leads..."

"Tell me what?"

Elena thought about it for a second. "Lopez just called me. Some new arrivals have the measles."

"What? How? Hasn't that been eradicated since like 2045 worldwide?"

"Apparently not. Where are these refugees from?"

"I don't know."

"How many?"

"I don't know."

"Do you know where we're going?"

"That, I do know." She showed him her screen and he nodded.

After a minute of silence, John cleared his throat, "Sorry about before. I just thought…"

"It's ok. Don't worry about it. I wouldn't do that to Sonya."

"Good. Question though…"

"Wassup?" she gave a slight nod of approval.

"When I still thought you wanted to… you know… again… you looked like you smelled some really bad cheese. Why?" John asked, keeping his eye on the screens.

"Sorry. It just caught me off guard. For the record, it was pretty good. Really good, actually." She saw him give a sly smile and a gentle nod. She rolled her eyes again, gently shook her head and let out a smile of approval.

Immediately after her second to last pregnancy she had a bad case of post-partum depression. John, like everybody else from The Cheddar and other friends she had made along the way, tried to make her feel better. Coincidently, he and Sonya were going through a rough time, and she offered to talk with him. They were both lonely and sad. One night of regrettable love-making. Fun. Both felt cheap and weird afterwards… and relaxed.

"You know what this means, right?" John asked.

"No. What?"

"That stuff down there has been getting worse."

"Yeah. But how could it get this bad? Measles? After a couple of pandemics, the UN and CDC really helped underdeveloped nations eliminate older diseases so they could all focus on new ones."

"I'm just saying. I got a message from my sister and parents. Some regions were going into martial law… again. Smaller regions but still…"

"I heard about that. Now… we are importing extinct

diseases."

"I thought Lopez scanned everyone before they disembarked."

"She hasn't done that for several months now. It's random now. You've seen the ships and transports. They keep getting uglier, older, and smellier every year."

John gave her a quick nod.

"This will accelerate the timeframe." Elena said, undoing her top, trying to cool off. "Don't know how you guys can tolerate it so hot in these ships."

"Sorry," he said and turned down the temperature. "You get used to it."

She moved to the vent, feeling refreshed. "I've seen your ship from the domes. You fly hella hectic sometimes."

He grinned, "Makes the time go by faster."

The transport entered the docking bay and landed with a loud hiss on the pad, and made her lose her balance just a bit. She noticed he opened the ship's door for her. "Thanks, hun," she said and gave him a quick kiss on the lips. "Let me know next time you're single." She smiled and winked. He shot her a look of approval mixed with a little terror and gave a quick nod.

She walked off the transport and, sensing his eyes being fixated on her as she joyfully walked away, let go of another smile.

CHAPTER 28: STAR SYSTEM EAPR-N-103

Sonya Sarali-Brolin was sitting in her new control pod. Henry, Michael, and Elton had helped her put it together a couple of weeks before. She liked that it made Alexa and Vera a little jealous. The wooden chair had feathers for cushioning and it molded to her body. It's more comfortable than the new synthetic fibers or smart materials she had been used to. It didn't make her sweat even without having perforated seats that let cool air hit her body.

New Quick enabled ships with MEs were being sent daily now and required linguists like herself to be present during data analysis. Today, she was to analyze data from a ship sent several months ago. For the most part the computer did the work and she looked it over. Sometimes she even fell asleep in that heavenly chair and had to analyze data after it had already been logged. But, luckily, or unluckily, the messages, videos, and photos received were in essence, the same: beautiful planets and breathtaking visuals coupled with disenchanting data of uninhabitable planets.

Some planets did merit scientific study, however. Some had diamond rain, while others had lakes of gold and lithium. Others were entire planets made up of iron and nickel and other heavy metals. Her favorite planet was one with a really hectic magnetic field and every so often giant rocks on its surface would bounce and flip and sometimes even shatter and come back together like a video of an exploding grenade but on slow motion and backwards. Sometimes giant rocks would even levitate for a day or so. But that system didn't have any HPs. No useful planets, either. None did.

There was talk about just building a giant orbital similar to theirs but much smaller, orbiting Mars. Phobos and Deimos already had colonies, and they could easily be used to anchor more asteroids. But some politicians opposed that idea. If something went catastrophically wrong, then Martians would be in danger. That's why so many people were being sent up to the RHSSO. But the lies told to the refugees couldn't be held much longer and the truth would inevitably come out. The refugees were told they were orbiting Jupiter, but were always in the dark side of it to prevent harmful radiation from hitting them. It was bullshit, but for the most part, the people on board didn't care. They were just happy to have a home, work and have real medical treatment and an education. They completed their assigned tasks without questions. As far as they were concerned, they were employees and didn't have to know what the employers were doing.

It almost seemed like these people had been accustomed to being working drones back on Earth. Many of the children wanted to be scientists and the truth couldn't be held from them much longer. This was reflected in Lopez's sense of urgency. She had turned into somewhat of a bitch lately. 'We all have our days,' she said, pushing the thought out of her head.

What could she do? She couldn't magically click on the screen and have a habitable planet pop up out of nowhere. As her thoughts raced, she tapped on the screen and controls trying not to think about it. 15 Years of muscle memory took over. Her eyes scanned through the data, like they always had. They were only given fractions of a second to look at spots where keywords would or unusual numbers were likely, indicating something was found.

She was going so fast she had to stop herself. "Wait..." she said and noticed a field wasn't empty like it was supposed to be. She made her way back to the beginning of the data. Video wasn't ready. An initial scan of a planets orbiting one of the stars was ready. Star System EAPR-N-103.

'We really need to stop letting the A.I. name the systems,' she thought.

She looked at the text on her screen:

- Main star: Class F Main Sequence. Mass = 1.5469 Solar masses. Solar radius 1.3048. Surface Temp = 6900 K. Age = 3.45 billion years.
- Sister Star: Class K Yellow-Orange. Age 3.45 billion years. Mass = 0.5352 Solar masses. Solar radius = 0.6996. Surface Temp = 3741 K.

The main star has two inner rocky bodies and five gas giants. The sister star has 1 rocky body and two gas giants. The gas giants had several moons. 340 were counted so far. Only 5 gas giants had rings. The nearest rocky body to the main star was too close. It showed similar readings as Venus: toxic atmosphere, high pressure/ temperature. Yuck!

However, the second rocky body was a little farther away. It is in the habitable zone. That seems promising. She continued reading. The second rocky body is huge. 1.988 earth radius and 1.25G. Surface temperature varies from 170K to 315K.

"What?!!!!???" Sonya started having a panic attack. Her breathing suddenly quickened and shortened. "OK. Sonya. Calm the eff down. Just keep on reading through the data. Maybe there is something wrong here. I can figure this out." She calmed herself down.

Atmospheric properties include 75% nitrogen, 23% oxygen, 1% argon, 0.9% helium and 0.1% other gases, including carbon dioxide, methane, water vapor and neon. "FUCK!" She screamed, as her hands pounded on her thighs in direct competition to her heart pounding inside her chest.

* * *

Alexa passed out the last of the water bottles Elton and her were carrying to the newly arrived Australian refuges. The entire hallway was lined with people waiting to be processed with their own personal A.I. link and necessary medical check, which provided them with enough nano-bots to combat the small amounts of radiation that made it through the thick meteor walls.

They thanked her and Elton and they walked down the corridor and made a left into the linguists' labs section. They had recently been cut down to half size to double up the staff, while still providing privacy.

"Junior is still nervous about working with Lopez," Elton said.

"Lopez can be scary. I remember the first time I met her..." A scream from inside Sonya's lab. She saw surprise in Elton's eyes and she quickly pressed the pad that overrode everything, opened up the lab while setting up in civilian mode and sent an alarm to security and Lopez.

* * *

"Guys! The screen! The planet! Oxygen! 315 degrees Kelvin! Guys!" She screamed and jumped like a cheerleader and clapped her hands. For security purposes, her pod was directly linked to the Quick enabled ships. No one else on the orbital had access. She saw Elton roll his eyes and hit the pad to close the door and cancel the alarm. She leaped into Elton's arms and gave him a French kiss right in front of Alexa. They were both so startled that Elton didn't kiss her back and Alexa didn't have a chance to slap her. Then, when she was done with him, she said, "oh what the hell," and gave Alexa a longer, frenchier kiss.

She felt them staring at her demanding answers. Lots of them. Her room had gone into lockdown mode when the doors opened with a universal emergency code, and after the scanners verified her friends' status, the screens lit up again and she showed them.

Once the initial shock died down, both of her friends started looking at the data on separate screens inside the cramped room. Elton was in disbelief and excused himself to throw up in Sonya's private restroom. Alexa stood still alternating stares between her, Elton, and the screens.

This star ship, which had given humanity hope, had only been at the system for approximately 4 months. A preliminary scan of the stars, gas giants and the rocky bodies was present. As soon as the ship noticed a planet in the habitable zone with a decent atmosphere it sent multiple probes with Es to it. They hadn't made it there. They would be landing in a couple of days. But the extra data acquired looked promising. The ship didn't bother sending probes to the other planets. It was programmed to focus on the first habitable planet it found. At this point, not finding HPs wasn't a problem either. By the time Earth was back in good health, humans on the new planet could come back if they wanted to. But even then, it wasn't really planned for. After all, the settlers that went west from behind the Appalachians didn't bother coming back. What for?

"Guys..." Elton said with a frail voice. "The detector picked up HPs..." As soon as he read this, Space Ship RX-3966 was picked up on their console. The ship had returned.

BOOK 4: A NEW WORLD WITH WAR AND PEACE

PROLOGUE

*One of the two men spoke: The Observer
has been silent for over 25 years.
The other man replied: Yes. Maybe
we did something wrong.
The woman replied: Maybe the First
Test will start soon. Humans will
soon be upon Planet Beta. Maybe that
is where the First Test starts.
The first man spoke again: Perhaps
we will not be witnesses to it.
The second man spoke: At least
we have witnessed the creation of
the Quick. That should console us.
We were right. It does work.
The woman asked: Observer, will the First
Test start soon? And if so, what is it?
A couple of days of more silence passed.
Then, suddenly they heard The Observer
again: The First Test is now imminent.*

It will begin shortly. May your species act with grace and humility.

All three of them still didn't know what the First Test was. They had asked The Observer on several occasions. The Observer merely replied that knowledge of the Last Three Tests will not be known until the First Test is passed. Telling them the nature of the Three Tests would undoubtedly interfere with the outcome.

CHAPTER 29: PLANET BETA

Henry Suzuki made his way into the same ballroom they had been when they heard the news from Earth about the degrading situation. It had been divided up into parts, and no longer used as a ballroom for mega parties. Now it was partially set up as living quarters, farming, shops, restaurants, and a couple of small parks. It also had additional storage for crucial supplies and resources. It could still hold 10,000 people. All the team leads filled that up easily.

Lopez had sent out an encoded message to all relevant citizens and requested their presence. What she was about to say could not be transmitted via the network. Even with encryption, nothing was ever truly secure.

"RX-3966 returned exactly one week ago. Its data has been analyzed. We have found a habitable planet. As is protocol, if the ship detects HPs, then it is to return immediately to prove it. It did."

People gasped. Hearing the news for the second time was still shocking. This news was too big to hide. But everybody made sure that the news only traveled verbally in secure rooms. All knew what was at stake.

"After we confirmed that the ship was the same exact ship and not just a clerical error it was sent back to system EAPR-N-103. This planet is basically a super Earth. It's slightly larger, and with stronger gravity. It's also a little bit cooler than Earth. It will be a good place to colonize. 3966 has landed probes on it. It has found animals, plants, and some sort of fungus looking thing. This planet does have oceans and lakes and rivers with water. Regular water. Potable water. Our data indicates that the oceans have a slightly higher level of salt and other chemicals we humans don't like. We have only explored from the air and only one robot has successfully landed. The rest crash landed as they ran out of fuel, due to the higher gravity, to land safely. Relevant information to your field of expertise will be sent to all. Your teams will comb through the data and make sure nothing is off."

A giant screen behind her lit up. It was actual live video of Beta's surface. It looked like the Martian surface before humans showed up. In the distance the horizon was moving. Then they realized that the robot was moving forward. A couple of seconds later, green and yellow plants could be spotted. It looked like a sunflower but had more green and less yellow and black. Its center part was split up into sections with green borders. Then a small bug was seen landing on it. It looked like a pink, fatter and longer figeater beetle.

"We are planning a human mission to that planet, which is now known as Beta. We are accepting applications from volunteers." She paused as everybody stood up. "Everybody, sit back down. We are not going today. and if we were, none of you would qualify. All of us are used to being at 0.7 Gs. This planet has 1.25 Gs. If we went there tomorrow, it would be a slow and humiliating process. Trust me. I have trained at 1.2 Gs a while ago. It will kick your behind. Everybody that wishes to apply will have to immediately move to a 1 G environment. Then, we will move you to a 1.1G environment and then a 1.25G environment. This will take time."

Lopez paused and marveled at the beetle still on the flower. The lander humans sent had picked a large flat area to land on. It was running out of fuel and had to land on the desert. It's in a valley that is deeper than Death Valley, relative to its sea elevation. From what the satellites have recorded and sent back, most of the land around that desert is green and hilly. Some hills are huge and steep. Of course, this was only one continent. The much larger continent is on the other side of the planet and the other satellites had run out of fuel in geo-synchronous orbit on this side of the planet. The planet has islands sprinkled throughout its one large ocean: two archipelagos connecting both continents.

"I should tell you something else. Because this orbital was partially funded by governments and granted permission to private citizens to build, explore and basically keep anything they found, the governments back on Earth still have a claim over all habitable planets found. This means, that Beta is now the property of the 6 main regional governments on Earth. That was the deal they came to at this orbital's inception."

People looked around the giant stadium-like area at their friends, colleagues, and crew members.

"Because of this clause, any and all ships which detect a habitable planet were hard-coded to convey their data back to key Earth leaders directly at the same time it was sending the data back to us. Furthermore, with the invention and implementation of the Quick, all ships were now in constant communication with Earth and their own Quick enabled satellites."

Loud screams and roars rumbled in the giant area. "What the fuck? That is fucking bullshit!" Elton screamed at the top of his lungs. Henry could relate. But it was inevitable. That was part of the deal. IPs developed could be used however they wanted. Resources found could be claimed and were. People made hundreds of trillions of dollars off asteroids with precious metals. The governments only wanted in return was a habitable planet and access to new tech invented to use for themselves. When the government made this deal with the private corporations, the private corporations thought they'd never find a habitable planet. Joke's on them.

"Calm down, everyone. Please." Lopez made a settling gesture with her hands. "The governments back on Earth, have requested that some of their people be trained and sent as well. In fact, they have already started training in 1.25 G.

Technically we are behind them on this. But we are the ones that will be in charge of the mission. We will be piloting, analyzing, and exploring. They are just going as sightseers and to confirm our findings. Furthermore, the governments down there realize that having their people have access to MEs and Quicks on a regular basis can only spell problems for them and us. We are the ones that know how to use this technology and we are the only ones who will be using it."

Henry saw Elton relax a bit. Henry had an inkling some bullshit like this was inevitable. There is always some bullshit in contracts in fine print. Laura leaned over to him and mentioned that Lopez wasn't sure about sending non-scientists to the planet. After all, it had to be studied for a couple of years before colonizing it. Henry nodded at her, making sure he got a glimpse of her green eyes.

Laura is Katelyn's linguist. They had met that fateful night when they all met with Alex and accidentally talked their way into solving the Quick problem. Henry was now 92 years old but didn't feel a day over 66. Sure, his wrinkles got longer and his hair, whiter, but he felt like he could keep this pace up for another 20 years and then retire for the last 3 decades of his life. Those golden nano-bots worked wonders. Laura is 85 and had come aboard with Katelyn on the Black Hole. They were the only loners in both groups, feeling like outsiders as their research continued. After their meeting with Lopez that first night, they stayed up all night in his lab, sharing espressos and an intimate conversation that took them back to places they had visited as children on Earth. He let go of a small grin as he remembered and it faded as he realized these memories were lifetimes away.

Henry saw his tablet as it lit up with Lopez's instructions. Because of his age, it was recommended that he stayed at the orbital. But if he wanted to go to Beta, she would approve. Henry, along with Laura, signed up as volunteers and then were given reports, instructions, along with everybody else.

CHAPTER 30: THE NAKED WRITER

Michelle Thomas was writing in his journal, in bed, nearing lights out. The first couple of days training in 1G had kicked his ass. He looked over at Erica, sleeping next to him. She snored, but it never bothered him. His insomnia stemmed from him worrying about washing out. 'If Henry can do it then I can do it.' He wrote in his journal.

He put the leather-bound journal on his nightstand and the lights turned off automatically. His shoulders and thighs were sore. He wondered how he could keep this pace up.

Training was fierce and very competitive. It was just like boot camp. But since they were used to a lower G, it was tougher. Their first two weeks they were moved to a small asteroid where the gravity was raised to 1G. After, training, reading, and watching videos with information about Beta, the gravity was upped to 1.1G as promised. After two months of dragging ass, the gravity was increased to 1.25G. They were all exhausted and heavily relied on robots doing most of the work for them.

They all walked and ate slower, and even took longer on the toilets. Showers with too much pressure differential were like tiny knives stabbing their backs, a worthy metaphor for how their bodies in accustomed to lower gravity were betraying them. To reduce weight they walked around in their underwear. 'The guys must have loved that,' Erica told him. But for Alexa and Elena, it was not fun. Their large breasts weighed them down. They came up with stronger bras but then John, Henry, and a couple more of them built suits that would supplement their own muscles. It was a rudimentary exoskeleton that was powered by wireless energy coming from the floor, walls, and ceiling. All of their devices worked this way, but Mahina had to up the juice being sent out for other stuff. These suits needed more energy. Not just to help them lift things and walk but also because its connections go hot and needed automatic cooling smart materials that also required more energy.

During their time in 1.25G, whenever Michelle was home, he'd be naked. Erica didn't seem to mind. She would keep her bra on. When they felt tired they'd wear underwear underneath their sleek and thin mech suits.

The last couple of weeks on that asteroid, none of them was wearing the mech suit to do everyday things as they had grown accustomed to the extra weight on their bodies. A couple of the team leads that weren't part of the Cheddar or the Black Hole ended up dropping out.

Michelle awoke his last day in 1.25G and made coffee for him and Erica. She had fallen asleep before him but was exhausted from her last 5 mile jog the night before. As soon as he sat down to take a sip from his coffee Erica awoke, "morning. Have the results been posted?"

"Not yet, darling. Coffee?" Michelle replied. He was looking over new pictures of Beta. It resembled earth. But for the most part he was more interested in aiming cameras back towards Sol. He was adamant about getting to name some constellations. Lopez denied his request to control the only robot that made it down to the surface. Her hands were tied. People on earth insisted on being able to see that first. She promised him he could do all the star mapping he wanted when he landed. 'This means I have to be picked to go first.' Michelle thought. 'Viva La France.' He thought some more.

He saw a message pop up from Lopez: We regret to inform you that you have not been selected to be part of the first landing party on Beta. You will be sent shortly thereafter, however.

"Bordel de merde!" he screamed as hi sent his tablet flying to the wall. As it hit the wall, the wall softened, acted like a cushion, and the tablet fell to the ground. A drone came out of a cabinet, lifted it and carried it back to him. He slapped the drone with the tablet, causing the glass to break on the floor. Then, almost to annoy him, the floor grew a little over the pieces, like to catch them and moved them like waves of water to a corner where a different robot discarded it in a recycle bin.

He looked over at Erica, with anger and light tears in his eyes. Judging by her reaction, she knew what he had read. Her tablet lit up. He nodded at her. She let go of a light frown and shook her head. They were both not going.

CHAPTER 31: A HARSH REALITY

Michael J. Johnson was arm wrestling with his mech arm against Elton, who was also wearing his mech arm. They were both panting and making constipated facial expressions. He stared into Elton's eyes as he realized he was beginning to lose. He saw his arm slowly get closer to the table as Elton's determination grew stronger. Elton stared back at him, giving him the look of disdain mixed with superiority. Michael crossed his eyes and Elton's facial expression changed to that of confusion, followed by laughter. Michael easily made Elton's hand hit the table. He won.

"Guys, you're gonna get hurt." Mahina said, as she shook her head in disapproval as everybody else in the room traded papers, like if it was betting money.

"Nothing got hurt. Just his ego," Michael sneered at Elton.

"You cheated." Elton massaged his arm and let go of another laugh.

"This is serious." Alexa jumped in. She nodded over at the large wall, which had turned into a screen with a live feed of Ship Envoy 1, going through the final check off list.

It was going to detach in a couple of minutes and it was an event that equaled the Moon, Mars, and Europa landings.

The entire crews of the Cheddar and Black Hole were there, in silent protest, over not being selected. While some of them pouted, most were just there hanging out. What could they do? It's not like they could hi-jack a ship and go to Beta. Alexa and Ashley and Vera had suggested that but it was quickly overruled.

The countdown started and the screen went black. He felt the ground shake and heard rumbling. Then, alarms and lights turned on. Everybody looked up and around seeking answers from their confused friends. Then, Lopez appeared on screens, explaining that there had been an explosion, and that the orbital had been put into total lockdown.

After two months of being under house arrest in their apartments with little to no contact and sporadic news about the ongoing investigation, Lopez gave more news.

This time, Lopez was talking to all leaders. A shorter, vaguer explanation will be sent to the rest of the people on the RHSSO. Here are the investigation's findings:

- Earth First Neo infiltrated the group of people that was selected to go to the orbital.
- EFN heard about a secret mission to a new planet just outside the solar system.
- One of its members sabotaged the ship and when the ME was turning on for initial checks the whole thing exploded. All onboard died. Luckily, this only caused external damage to its host asteroid.
- The two-month lockdown was to screen everybody on the orbital. The goal was to weed out any EFN sympathizers.
- A total of sixty-four were found. Lopez oversaw their executions with little objections from within and without the RHSSO. Earth governments agreed this needed to be done swiftly. Minor protests about this decision spurred but were quickly subdued.
- The leaders on earth, along with the council agreed it was best to just send people they already had on board the RHSSO and who had gone through training.
- The Black Hole crew would be sent first, to set up base, followed by The Cheddar crew.
- The missions were to be made public after leaving.
- The timeframe had been changed. They had to do

everything before 2182. That was only 15 years away.

Michael, along with his original team and Alexa had agreed to meet to discuss how they could best state that they should be the ones to go to Beta first. They had met for dinner and had gotten Lopez's message as they were finishing up in Elena's place. Since they couldn't be out in public, they decided to go to her place, which was the largest they had access to for those two months.

After the video of Lopez ended, Alexa screamed, "What is wrong with these idiots? Are they retarded? Do they even know what we are doing? Do they even care?" She kicked a table leg, as everybody nodded and let her vent for a little. Some were already sitting on sofas while Elton and Elena were drinking some wine at the kitchen counter. Michael was next to Alexa and was startled when she jumped out of her seat.

"First, they take thousands hostage all over the NAC and then, just when we are this fucking close to helping everyone, they sabotage our operation. Fuck these people!" Her pacing continued for a bit longer. They had all dedicated their entire life up in the orbital to try and find a habitable planet. Sure, now they were all going as intended. But this was a drawback. One more fuck up and it was game over. Civilization was on the brink, like sanity. All it needed was a little push.

She shook her head and sat back down. Michael put his arm around her, comforting her. She leaned into his chest. Those 25 years at the orbital they had all grown closer. Michael saw his daughter in her and could relate to her frustration. Elena and Henry had a similar relationship. There was too much at stake to take this lightly. He had to get ready for the next mission. They all had to get ready.

CHAPTER 32: ANOMOP

Erica and the rest of the crew were waiting for their departure. Every so often, she heard humming, clicks, beeps and saw different things being highlighted on the screens. As the navigations officer, her job was to make sure they were exactly where they needed to be when they needed to be there. Henry, plotted the course and is the space ship engineer. Mahina was the co-pilot and John was the pilot. Elton, being the original leader, was put as the captain of the ship.

Michelle, Michael, Alexa, Vera, Elena, and Sonya and were up there purely as scientists and possible first contacts.

The crew of the Black Hole had already left the week before and had started setting up a gravity softener, to permit them to have a base where the gravity was closer to Earth's. Based on their power needs and available resources, the gravity softener could be as large as a circle with the radius of 1750 meters. This was big enough for them to have a couple of small labs and sleeping quarters and maybe even a small garden to test grow crops.

"Affirmative," John said as he grabbed on to the controls with gloved hands. He moved the steering wheel looking thing and Erica noticed the map of stars vanish, only to be instantly replaced by a new field of stars. The entire trip had taken less than a second. Erica soon realized that John simply had taken them about one light-second away from the orbital. The spacetime distortion caused by the powerful ME of their giant ship would shred their nearby inhabited asteroid.

"Mahina, how are we looking?" John asked.

"All go." She responded.

"Erica, how's navigation? Are the coordinates set?"

"Yes. All go." Erica responded.

"Henry, is the course still looking good."

"Yes. All go." He replied.

"You may take us out when ready," Elton said.

John manipulated the controls and tapped the screen and suddenly Erica felt a sensation of falling, fast. She remembered the roller coaster ride back on Earth when she was only 16 years old. But at the same time, she also felt like someone had grabbed on to her head and started squeezing it like a large egg. Furthermore, she also felt sparks coming out of her toes and fingers lips and even vaginal lips. She saw nothing for an instant and then a rainbow of colors. First, they were very opaque and then not so much. After that she felt like if somebody had gotten a hold of all her bones and squeezed while at the same time tried to get her soft tissue pulled from her bones. This uncomfortable, yet still acceptable sensation lasted the duration of the flight: 38 minutes.

Then she heard John say they were about six light-days from Beta. After an hour or so of confirming their location and checking systems John asked for an OK from everyone and soon, he made another trip. This one was much more comfortable and shorter. Then, they were in orbit around Beta with chemical thrusters pushing them into the correct path. This part lasted approximately 4 minutes as their main engines performed several mini, almost purely chemical burns to stabilize the ship's orientation and into orbit.

The Black Hole had already placed satellites in orbit around Beta. These communication satellites were analyzing, taking pictures and video and mapping the entire planet in UHD. It'll take three years. The satellites also created a primitive satellite/cellular communications network. The sat network ensures there would never be a comm blackout by placing four satellites in geo-synchronous orbit (or Beta-synchronous orbit), four in Molniya orbits, and four more in polar orbits.

Erica saw Katelyn on the screen and heard, "Hi, Erica. Everything ok? What is your status?"

"We packed extra fuel for the descent. We want a proper landing... unlike The Black Hole..." Erica smiled. The Black Hole almost ran out of fuel and nearly crashed. The ship missed its target by 12 km.

"Yeah, yeah, yeah..." Katelyn replied, seemingly amused at her jab. The Black hole, landed on an almost flat large hill covered in grass and a thin stream cutting it in half, perfectly. The base was also set up so the stream cut through it right down the middle. The gravity softener's ring was already built and powered on, providing a visible border on the ground. The diameter of their first town is 1600 yards. The gravity experienced in that area is 1.06G.

"Will be in position to initiate entry and landing procedure to Anomop Base in fourteen minutes. Be advised, we will be coming in from northeast."

"Copy. We look forward to your visit and seeds in your cargo." Katelyn said. Seasonal calculations state seeds need to be in the ground within 18 days to have a productive harvest. The initial probe with seeds crashed into the ocean, delaying their planting.

We landed on Beta as Fall season started in the southern hemisphere. The seeds are genetically modified to withstand the harshest winters on Earth.

Digging machines had started to make foundations for their living quarters and laboratories that were to be built. The Black Hole's living quarters were dropped down and are still being used by the crew. Initial testing of the air showed no deadly viri, bacteria, nor fungi. There are some flying bugs but none of them seem to want to bite them. There are small lizard-like animals in that area and living around in some bushes. These bushes do not look like any of the ones on Earth. They are similar to the Banksia integrifolia from Australia but smaller and instead of green leaves they are yellow and the yellow flower on top is blue with some pink.

Mining robots were sent out to look for anything in the ground that could be useful. This was more to calm their curiosity. The plan was to never mine anything on that planet. That's what asteroids are for.

Soil analysis showed the dirt where The Black hole landed was very similar to terra petra but with slightly less nutrients. This sure was lucky. Too lucky, some thought.

Anomop, was completely uncovered (no dome-like structure was needed) and only had thick yellowish-greenish grass. Its northern part was near an endless sea of trees and plants which looked like the Amazon Rain Forest. A wall was being erected to enclose Anomop, starting at the north side. They didn't want to take any risks with the wildlife.

A wolf like creature with giant fangs and two tails with spikes at the end was spotted further south. It is the size of a hippopotamus. Various other bugs and small birds were also discovered. Having never seen humans before, they were not particularly shy and some were captured. They were placed in cages outside one of the labs for observation. The plan is to let them go after 2 days, Beta time.

The modified Cheddar ship made its descent into Beta's atmosphere and slowly stabilized itself with parachutes and hisses and bursts from its S and C thrusters. It was shaking, but not too violently. Some alarms were heard and Erica could see that the blackness out of her window was now a deep and smooth royal blue.

As the ship landed, they all let out a grunt. Erica thought the ship could have made a better landing. After a couple of seconds Mahina told them to prepare for separation. The New Cheddar was now split up into three parts: the CM, their living quarters and a large cargo hold with machines, materials, and resources. All together, the spaceship that landed was as tall as a 14-story building with a base area of approximately 90k square feet.

The hardened outer materials of the ship opened up and

were pulled out of the way. Wheels came out and the smart materials converted part of itself into joints for the wheels, which were quickly and firmly placed on the ground. Then, the separation ejected materials on the outer ring of the connection, and then the connecting rings unlocked and rotated and pushed their portion away from the other. This whole process took almost three hours to complete.

After another couple of minutes of sitting still the computer let the crew disembark. Their belts were released at the same time as the locks. They were all assured they didn't have to wear their helmets nor use their oxygen tanks. They still took them with as they all left the ship one by one.

The air lock opened and when it was Erica's turn, she got out and stumbled her way down the steps. The sun (she kept on calling it sun even though they were in another system) was annoyingly bright but it didn't feel too hot. She squinted and before she could put her helmet on, Laura handed her some polarized safety glasses. She thanked her and hugged her and hugged everybody else.

She didn't feel the immense weight of 1.25G, thanks to the gravity softener. But it only affected Anomop to an altitude of 500 feet. Laura grabbed her by the hand guided her into a large room, where everybody else was already waiting for her and the rest of her crew.

CHAPTER 33: WE ARE NOT ALONE

Mahina Iona settled in nicely on Anomop. In the mornings she awoke and got ready and walked out into the bright day on short grass that never needed to be mowed, pass the labs with animals outside of it and make her way to the commons. Most of the time she ran simulations, trying to understand the weather patterns and took soil samples. At nights she spent time with a large telescope with Michael.

A couple of weeks later, Mahina grabbed her warm stew, leafy greens, and soft bread, and made her way to her usual seat, next to the window overlooking an arcade and could see the wall being erected in real time. She sipped at her spoon, testing the temperature. Chicken and tomato soup. It wasn't her favorite, but was better than what was on the RHSSO and the freshness was unparalleled on all of Earth.

A monitor near her showed another section of the wall being built and when she focused on it, heard the noises in the environment. She helped place those cameras and many more around Amonop.

She glanced to another monitor and saw a live feed from farming robots working on planting wheat, corn, beans, and lots of other vegetables and her audio feed automatically switched to it. The weather satellites predicted a very mild winter, resembling that of northern Baja California. She also saw a recorded clip of the cargo hold open and a couple of pigs, cows and dozens of chickens were let loose within its walls, which were moving into position to separate them from each other. The walls converted into stables and pens.

The soup smelled good and the warmth tickled her nose. The hard work burned extra calories and she enjoyed eating extra calories in the form of hot chocolate with real milk from the cows outside. As she bit into her biscuit she focused on another screen, showing a live feed from the bipedal robot making its way through the jungle. The flower colors were outstanding and it seemed like an acid trip gone bad. The last large monitor showed a rover making its way across the desert east of them.

The chatter surrounding her was lively but not overwhelming. Her teammates interrupted her thoughts every now and then It was the typical questions. How was she feeling? Was she excited? Could she believe it? What did she want to do next? How long would it take to start bringing people to Anomop and make other settlements? Can you believe I'm the first to do this and that? Everybody got asked those questions.

She spoke with them, with gusto, but there was something bugging her about this planet. It was too boring. It was a little too perfect. Of course, they had already virtually visited at least 5000 other systems and none showed promise. So, was this really a surprise? This planet is approximately 780 light years away from Sol. Maybe great coincidences do exist. She brushed the thought away and continued to enjoy her meal with Alexa by her side and everyone else. Some were drinking beer, numbing the soreness from long days of labor-intensive work. But she was not convinced. Not yet. She felt like it was a dream. She brushed the thought away once more and simply enjoyed the fruits of their collective labor.

A week later, with the wall fully built and only one event where the werewolf made it close to Anomop (werewolf was what they named that giant dog with two tails), they were reviewing data received from all their drones out in the wild. One had gotten stuck, 70 kilometers into the jungle. It was assigned as a stationary camera, as no one wanted to walk the

70 kilometers in 1.25G to dislodge a robot. The flyer drones were not strong enough to lift it. The other one had made it all the way across the desert: a total of 3255 kilometers to the ocean. Once at the beach, it saw waves crashing and giant streams of water and air go straight up like a tiny volcano. It was a whale-like creature with red eyes and fins that resembled that of a bat. It was a disgusting, nightmare inducing monster. One of them jumped like a whale sometimes does and its tail had a couple of long tentacles.

"Not surfing anytime soon," Mahina smiled at Erica, who returned a nod.

There was a small section of the rainforest that separated their area from another area which was slightly steeper. Under direct orders from Earth, they were to build another 3 gravity softeners to their west and southwest where most of the land was flatter and with considerably less plants. They protested but they knew they had to do it. In their briefing with Lopez that evening, she confided in them that now that they had been there for a couple of weeks without dying the leaders on Earth were ready to start colonizing. She thought about who she would have been willing to sacrifice to keep this planet from being bombarded by colonists. She grinned at the macabre scenario in her head.

"In fact, three of those giant ships carrying 50,000 people were already en route to you and will arrive next week." Lopez confirmed in a stale tone.

Mahina grabbed a seat with all of the other Cheddars and Black Holes. She saw Lopez look around and waited for them to settle.

"Hello. I know you are all very busy and so I will make this short." Lopez said, quickly glancing at everybody seated. "As you know, Earth leaders were immediately informed of planet Beta. As expected, this news leaked. Doesn't matter how. Long story short: to come clean about our discovery of Beta we were forced to disclose our technological advancements even before the Quick was invented."

Mahina and others gasped. She covered her mouth and was about to stand up to ask but Lopez silenced her with a look of disapproval.

"To explain how we found planet Beta we disclosed information of the RHSSO and migration patters and everything else that we have been up to. We couldn't hide over 200 million people in an amalgam of asteroids around 17 light days away. With this, the leaders and the RHSSO gained leverage over Earth and we asked every single nation to place every single EFN sympathizer on a terrorist watch list. This will reduce the amount of red tape to act on neutralizing these monsters." Lopez took a deep breath and continued with more good news.

"The leaders who announced our new tech were praised by their constituents. Our A.I. predicts most of them to win by landslides. On a personal note, my mother has gone down in history as a hero to all humans."

Mahina could see Lopez fidgeting and about to deliver news she would not like, "The debate on whether or not to start sending people so soon to Beta was quick and decisive. 90% of the initial colonists were to be made into producing water, food and shelter. Once the food supply was abundant, we will send more colonists."

Mahina and the rest spoke amongst themselves. They all hated the idea of having to start building three giant gravity softeners in a week. Their concerns were quickly squashed when most of their robots started going to the areas where the new settlements were to be built and waited for automated ships filled with materials and more robots to land. Earth had already sent supplies to start building. Mahina saw Elton's look of disapproval. Mahina shared his pain. Earth had commandeered the operation. They really were just scientists now. Either help or get out of the way. Mahina started feeling like an employee at a multinational corporation: either ease the process to deliver goods faster or get the hell out. She and the rest of them felt used. They were asked to do the impossible, succeeded and then the fruits of their labor was stolen from them. But like Lopez said, 'that was the deal.'

Later that week, while Mahina was running a simulation for a tropical storm that was going to hit near the coast the gravity softeners were finished and fully powered on. It was the night before the colony ship arrived. The murmurs from her teammates were a somber and morale was affected. She saw the robots shut down for the night and started to charge when, Laura rushed into the room with a long rock in her hands. She made her way over to Alexa while at the same time calling over Sonya and Vera. Mahina and the rest got a good look at it as well. Laura was holding in her hands a mini-sized obelisk with characters etched onto its sides she had never seen before.

"Did we just find evidence of intelligent life on another planet." Sonya said quietly. She passed out. Mahina held her breath so long her heart rate increased. Alexa, slowly took the item from Laura's hand and said, "These markings resemble those in the Voynich manuscript. But they seem bigger and stranger... fuller... if I could use that word." Laura and Vera nodded in agreement. They all stared at each other for what seemed like an hour, breathless and motionless.

CHAPTER 34:
HUMAN NATURE

News travels fast. Within a couple of minutes of Elton and the rest finding out about the tiny obelisk, the news had reached Earth. We are not alone. But who were these creatures who created this artifact? Where are they now? Did a virus or plague wipe them out? Were they killed by each other in war? Maybe, the truth would never be found out. The Olmecs disappeared without a trace. If it could happen on Earth, it could happen on Beta. All their robots and sensors had not detected anything remotely strange like settlements or other artifacts so discovering this artifact was strange... stranger somehow.

Despite Alexa's and her teammates' plead to postpone the settlers' arrival, the leaders on Earth were not budging. They were seen as saviors. They couldn't tell the suffering public to hold off just a bit longer because scientists wanted to dig for possible alien life. The news of Beta had somehow already cured humanity. Hope, is an enticing medicine and all of those left on earth had a spoonful of it every time new news streamed.

The few fringe voices, which doubted governments were quickly silenced in debates. The winning argument was, "anything can be better than this..."

When asked, Laura and Katelyn conceded that there was no other evidence of an advanced civilization or intelligent life. She tried to convince Lopez and the 6 regional presidents to no avail. Mahina saw the passion in Alexa as she argued that they had only explored approximately 1% of the surface and there was no way of knowing. Real archeological work would take years or even decades. The leaders were not having any of it. 150,000 settlers were already on their way.

Alexa, along with Robert Hemingway, the lone archeologist among them, got those in power to permit them to start digging where the obelisk was found. They were scientists and that was implied in their job description. They were to use a handful of robots to dig deep where they thought they could find more evidence of this unknown civilization.

Alexa, and the rest of the linguists were busy observing the live feeds from the robots that were digging. They stayed up all night. But nothing else was found. John offered to help by rigging up a flying drone to map that area using LIDAR and the ground bots as spotters.

Mahina, along with Michael were up all night as well. They were outside with telescopes trying to see if they could find any relatable shapes and name constellations. They mapped and named several. This planet seems to have a southern star, like Earth has a northern star. Here is a list of what they came up with:

- Werewolf – the stars seemed oddly symmetrical
- Crab – It was just the outline of its shape
- Lighthouse – two base stars and one bright one above them
- Sunflower – This one had the most stars at 18
- Squid – 13 stars
- Whale – 6 bright blue stars
- Dolphin – 6 not so bright stars
- Surfboard – 4 stars
- The Joker – 16 stars that were mostly in the shape of a jester's hat.

They uploaded a lot of their information and to their surprise, they were accepted. They kept on going and spent all night outside in the pleasant cool breeze with a smell that resembled nothing on Earth. They were intermittently interrupted by Elton. He had to oversee the operations of the gravity softeners booting up properly. That was a boring job. One gravity softener was already powered on when the three megaships with 150,000 settlers were detected in orbit around Beta as the morning sun rose.

The other two gravity softeners came online without a problem. Several hours later in that same morning all three ships started to break apart into smaller sections. These smaller sections were everything they needed: machines, food supplies, housing units, water extractors, energy reactors and fully stocked health pods. The flames they produced by entering the atmosphere were dwarfed by the giant yellow star but could still be made out. They saw those ship parts go beyond the horizon, leaving a trail of smoke and their ears ringing. Sensors and robot cameras, along with satellites all confirmed that the cargo had all landed safely where it was supposed to.

All three new settlements were outlined the same. They were a dozen concentric circles with each ring having a different purpose. At the center, the energy reactor would be placed. Immediately surrounding it would be a plaza approximately 25 meters wide. Then in the next ring buildings for those in charge would be placed, along with the control center. This housed politicians, business leaders, and solar panels as a backup energy source. Immediately surrounding that would be another narrow ring with more greenery and walkways and parks. Outside of that would be living quarters with all the necessities. Neighborhoods would also be placed in rings with parks, schools, hospitals, markets, community centers, firefighters' quarters, and police quarters. Smaller reactors, along with emergency supply reserves would be sprinkled throughout the remaining rings. On the outer most ring, there would be areas for cars, transports, and large drones. Food would also be grown on the outskirts. But citizens were also encouraged to have local farms in their neighborhoods. Most citizens, initially, will work as farmers on their own private garden. The plan is to grow specific fruits and vegetables to trade and have variety.

The mistakes from earth would not be repeated here. Industrialization would occur, but it would all be through green, renewable energy. The new cities would be planned in such a different way than they evolved naturally on earth. Neighborhoods on Beta would not be a tightly compacted mega-metropolitan area with giant roads, wasting tons and tons of resources, no parks for dozens of square miles and half the land surface area dedicated to cars and landing pads. Instead, the density would be that of a heavily populated suburban or rural area. Sure, there were buildings that housed many people but surrounding them would be parks, farms, solar panels, and plenty of space to avoid the same problems cities in the 20th and 21st centuries saw.

Mahina saw people via the screens and many were happy but impatient.

"Gravity softeners are %100 functionality," as soon as the robotic voice announced this, ship parts started being dropped into the atmosphere. She made a fist and pounded the table next to her console. Alexa and her exchanged angry stares. She could feel the anger stemming from the others. She didn't want to seem ungrateful but the speed of things gave her emotional whiplash.

Lopez assured her that Earth leaders were in a tight spot. With this news, crime dropped drastically in even the most violent of areas. Wealthy people donated money to causes and paid for thousands of people's tickets to Beta, showing the best of humanity. Even rival politicians stopped criticizing each other... for a bit. Productivity and the stock market was up.

There was even talk about transporting asteroids from our Oort cloud some people had their eyes on to Beta's SOI for known raw materials to speed up colonization. Starting a search for asteroids in Beta's system will take too long. Beta's surface was forbidden to be mined or drilled. Period.

"This is a new beginning and I think we have learned from

our mistakes on Earth," Michelle muttered, and Mahina felt his arm on her shoulder.

But as the first ships with colonists started nearing the surface, other, smaller ships were seen by their sensors. They started blowing up every transport one by one. It was a massacre. Within a couple of hours, the defenseless transports were all gone. There were no survivors.

CHAPTER 35: A HOSTILE TAKEOVER

Lopez came on the screen in front of Elton, "What is going on up there?"

"Anomalies. All of them. They're all gone. Was this EFN?" Elton remarked, confused, and terrorized. The rest of his teammates were also glued to screens in disbelief of what they were seeing. A transport camera was able to get a good look at its attacker before it was destroyed: it was definitely not human.

"It's those EFN motherfuckers!" Alexa screamed, manipulating her station, trying to get more information, frantically.

"There is no way that's EFN. Their ships don't look like that. No way!" John remarked. They all believed him but at the same time questioned in disbelief.

"Well, who is it then?" Michelle demanded.

"I'm gonna go out on a space limb here and say it's the same aliens who took out the ones who were living here?" Henry said. After a moment of silence, it seemed like they were all in agreement.

"The artifact we found is made of stone and looks old. If it was an advanced civilization capable of defending itself, we would have seen more advanced things surviving. There are no radiation levels. This means these bastards didn't just get nuked. There was no need to. Primitive weapons sufficed." Erica tried to convince them and herself.

"Well maybe they wanted to take over this planet, which is

why they didn't get nuked." Mahina asked.

"No. Nukes or antimatter weapons would have made this place uninhabitable. But they didn't colonize it so..." Elena responded, looking at her teammates trying to make sense of this.

"But their ships don't look so advanced. I mean, they only looked badass because our transports are defenseless. It's like watching a hawk take out a baby chick." Michael said as John nodded in agreement.

"Fuck me!" Sonya screamed. A giant ship, bigger than one of their settlers' spacecrafts was picked up in orbit around Beta. All of them were now stranded and at the mercy of whatever the hell that was. Elena went running outside to get a firsthand look.

As the alien fighter ships retreated, presumably into the mother ship which doubled as a carrier, a single ship, larger than the fighters was seen exit the mothership. Then a couple more broke off. They were flying in formation and making their way into the atmosphere. Mahina and Alexa followed Elena.

Several minutes later Elena came back inside, "The three ships are getting closer to us. They're headed this way." She grabbed her head and obviously looked worried. She walked over to one of the monitors and started changing images, trying to gather more information.

A paralyzing terror took hold of Elton's body. He made eye contact witch each one of his teammates, thinking they would all certainly meet the others in the afterlife.

"Um... OK. What do we do?" Vera demanded, looking at everyone. "We were trained to meet with aliens in a peaceful way. But these bastards just took out 150,000 of our companions in a matter of hours."

"Should we wait for them outside? Where is the weapons crate?" Michael asked.

"The crate with small guns and tiny rocket launchers was left isolated, far away from any building that could potentially be damaged by the weapons exploding." Michelle answered, almost robotically.

"I guess we could overload our tiny reactor. Or turn off our gravity softener. Or max it out. We can do something. But what?" Alex said, worrying and biting his nails while he paced.

They tried to communicate with Lopez for several minutes but nothing was happening. Then Mahina and Alexa came back inside and announced the ships had landed. As they said this, they were thrown into the room and knocked unconscious by an invisible force. Elton moved towards Alexa but as soon as he kneeled next to her, he saw their attackers enter the room as well. It was most definitely not EFN.

Two creatures entered and everyone else backed up against the nearest wall to them. They both had a weapon in their hand. It was large and black and narrow. They pointed it at them as they moved out of the way for the next creature.

They looked almost human, but with bright pinkish skin and no hair. They were taller and thinner than Elton and the rest. They all had blue eyes. Their clothes resembled something similar to attire from the old west. All they lacked were spurs. Elton looked them up and down, completely frozen by what had just happened. He met their gaze and if he didn't know better, he would think that they looked just as scared as they all were.

The third alien, who was obviously in charge, threw a liquid on Elton's face and stared at him. Elton let out a small shriek and wiped his face with his hands. It was just water. As he did this, the aliens observed him and saw his hands. They were all staring at his hands. Elton, on the other hand, could not see theirs. They were wearing black leather, presumably leather, gloves.

The alien said something to his companions. His voice sounded high pitched with a lot of T, L and K sounds. The other two aliens pushed all of them closer together. One of them looked at Henry and pointed at Alexa and Mahina on the floor. He made a gesture and Henry understood. He tapped Elton on his forearm and they both dragged a woman to where the others were standing.

The other alien with a weapon hit John on the arm, making him fall to his knees. As the alien approached Vera, she got the message and dropped to the floor. The rest of her companions followed suit.

"What do you think they want?" Michelle looked at Sonya.

"Why the fuck are you asking *me*?"

"Aren't you the linguist?" John added.

"That doesn't mean I can read fucking alien minds, now does it?" Sonya replied.

The weaponless alien screamed something to Sonya and she stopped talking. The alien touched his ear and muttered something. He was on a call. The alien nodded and looked at Elton. It muttered something to the ones holding the weapons and walked outside. It was definitely having a conversation with someone else outside of the tiny building they are all in, which was now officially a prison.

After several minutes, John suggested, "Maybe we can take them out."

"To where? Dinner?" Henry asked.

"No, smartass." John whispered back. There's only two of them. I am wearing my exosuit and it's still powered on. How about you, Henry?"

"Shouldn't we just wait for Katelyn and her team to come back from their scouting trip?" Michelle asked. The rest of the Black Hole crew nodded in agreement.

"For what? They'll be walking into an ambush. Elton, what do you think?" Sonya replied.

"Hold on. Let me see. Are you guys seriously asking me if I want to try and kill two armed aliens?" Elton asked.

"Well, now that you put it that way..." John replied.

"I am wearing mine. and they do look thin. Maybe you and I could take them." Henry said, quickly backtracking his previous answer.

"Guys, hold on." Elena whispered, hunched over, trying to

avoid attracting attention from the pink man duet. "There's only three of them and one is outside. Maybe there are more outside or in their ships. Didn't we see three transports detach and land?" She said, while others nodded.

"Yeah, but with weapons we have a better chance," John said.

"Don't be an idiot, John." Vera said. "We don't know how to use their weapons. What if they're biometrically locked? Also, for all we know they could have just thought they were destroying cargo and not killing people. If they wanted to kill us, they would have done so already." As she said this, she looked over at Mahina and Alexa. Both were unconscious far away in dreamland.

"OK. So. What do we do then?" Henry asked. The two pink aliens looked at them. They obviously heard them but weren't telling them to shut up this time. It's almost like if they were listening to their conversation intently.

"We need to buy time." John said.

"What if they won't give us time?" someone else asked.

"They obviously need us alive. Maybe they want to try and communicate. We should say Alexa is in charge." Michelle suggested.

"Are you crazy? Look at her," John responded, wiping his forehead.

"Exactly my point! If we can communicate with them, we need a linguist. This will buy us time until Lopez sends in reinforcements." Michelle said.

"What makes you think they'll send anyone that isn't just going to be space fighter fodder?" Erica asked.

"Think about it. If we say Alexa is in charge, then their leader would have to wait until she awakes to try and communicate. Also, communications are down. and we aren't heading back. The last thing Lopez saw was 150,000 dead civilians explode on an alien planet. This will definitely warrant the military coming in here." Michelle reasoned. Elton liked the sound of that. The rest nodded. It was the best plan so far.

"OK. Not to be a downer, but what if Alexa doesn't wake up?" Erica asked. She made eye contact with everyone around them. Some shrugged while others looked at others.

"We can say that Mahina is next in command," Michael suggested.

"This will never work. Besides I was the pilot..." John was getting anxious.

"Exactly. You are the pilot. Not the captain." Elton responded.

"This is a military situation now..." John snapped back.

"So? You're not military." Vera snapped back. "None of us are."

It was settled. Alexa was now officially in charge, followed by Mahina. Also, just to shut John up; if they both didn't wake up, he could be in charge.

The two pinkish guards still stood by the door. Several minutes later the third one came back, with another companion. This new alien was significantly shorter and darker pink. It looked at all of them and said something. Everybody looked at Sonya.

Sonya shrugged her shoulders and started making hand gestures. She pointed at all of them and then made a flat hand horizontal. Then she pointed at Mahina and with her other hand put it at a higher level. After that she pointed at Alexa and gestured her hand higher than all of them. The pink alien just looked at her. It mumbled something over her and nodded. It then mumbled something to the guards and left.

After a couple of hours, some of the captives were telling Sonya that they needed to use the restroom and getting hungry. Sonya stood up once more and stepped over the snoring Alexa. She approached the guards and started making more gestures and speaking words to accompany them. First, she pretended to eat from an imaginary plate with her bare hands and then she rubbed her belly and made a look of distress and moved her hands from her butt to the floor. The guards didn't seem to care but one of them spoke something to her and simply made the noise, which sounded like the Nahuatl word for food. At least that is what Sonya thought she said to them.

One of the guards pointed at Henry and demanded he walk over. Sonya made the eating gesture again and pointed at Henry and indicating with hand signals that he would walk over. Henry and Michelle had to use the restroom. Both were escorted out, while the other guard stayed and watched the rest. Elton heard Sonya say something to the guard, trying out a Nahuatl word on the guard. The guard seemed shocked but nodded nervously.

"What are you telling him?" Erica asked, nervously and tugging on her elbow.

"I think I just said thank you." Sonya replied.

"There is no fucking way you know their language." John scoffed.

"No. But I did study Mesoamerican languages and it sounds similar to what we already know. But I can't make out any words. I don't understand enough of it. Alexa might know more. I focused more on Navajo and Native American tribal languages." Sonya responded. She looked at Vera, as did everyone else.

"Don't look at me. I didn't learn Mesoamerican languages at all. I focused on ancient Chinese and other Asian languages." Vera responded. "I practiced ancient Zulu with Belmira but that was it."

The only person who could potentially communicate with the aliens was in dreamland. The other guys returned with the guard after several minutes, which seemed like an eternity. They had brought food and water. They explained to them that the guard was watching them from about 6 feet behind them.

"I am officially the first human to have been spied on by an alien while taking a shit," he said. The rest of them giggled and even lightly choked on their food. They only brought energy bars and water. No way, the aliens would let them start cooking.

A couple of hours later, Sonya requested to go to the restroom with other of her companions and the guards seem to accept but only let one person out at a time. They ate some more and as they were getting ready to sleep John whispered to Sonya, "Look... I gotta tell you something. In case we don't make it..."

"Is this about you and Elena?" Sonya replied. John looked shocked and looked at Elena. She seemed surprised as well. John nodded. "I already knew about it. It was obvious. We were separated. I dated other men as well."

John looked inquisitively towards her. "Wait. What?" John said. A couple of them laughed a bit. "Just go to sleep, John." Sonya said. Soon, they were all asleep.

Elton was shaken awake by the dark pinkish alien. It came back. It was the middle of the night and it yelled something at Elton while pointing at Alexa. Elton shrugged. Then, the other alien, who had come in with the guards also came in. It woke Sonya up. This, in turned woke everybody up. Mahina and Alexa were still sound asleep. They had been out for almost 18 hours now. Maybe they weren't ever going to wake up. Elton shook the thought away.

The guard pulled him and Sonya towards it and started screaming at Sonya. It pulled out what looked like a century old tablet. The words, "Who are here? Why attack we?" was shown to them. Sonya looked at Elton and shrugged. "I think they are trying to ask us who we are and why did they attack us? No. That doesn't make sense." Sonya looked perplexed. Elton responded, "Could they be asking why we invaded their lands?"

"Could be." Sonya responded. Then, the alien with the tablet, slapped Sonya across her face and as she dropped to her knees as it yelled something at her. With everybody wide awake now John ran towards the alien, above Sonya and tackled it to the floor and started cussing at it. At the same time Henry punched one of the guards in the torso and pulled the gun away from it. Vera was nearest to the other guard and swept its legs with one smooth motion from her left leg. It fell and she got on top of it, punched it and pulled the gun away. Henry, and Vera now had guns aimed at the alien who had slapped Sonya.

"Alright, Pink Man Group. You better calm down," John said, as the others moved to stations and tried to reestablish communications with Earth and observed that the other guards were on their way to them. A couple of them locked the doors and Michelle moved to the station and turned on the gravity softener all the way up. The whole area slowly floated and they could see the other guards struggle to remain on the ground. As they all hit the ceiling of their room, Elena was already talking with Lopez.

"Our three carriers were being prepped but the government leaders decided to launch without them... goddammit. The council will discuss this with them afterwards... the fighters will arrive in seconds. Ensure they get your data and ready to transmit as soon as you pick them up," Lopez said as Elena manipulated controls upside down while floating.

"Yes. Ready to transmit upon arrival," Then, the sensors picked up the carrier with a dozen space fighters detaching from it and head towards the alien mothership. The Calvary had arrived.

CHAPTER 36:
DREAMLAND

Alexa let out a sigh at a familiar location. She saw her nightstand, screens, and the large unreflecting mirror. 16 years old. She remembers that night. It was the first time she had her boyfriend over. His shoes were in the corner, next to her dresser. He was hiding underneath the bed as she heard footsteps approach the door.

Why was she here again? Despite it being a recurring dream, she had not experienced it lately. Why can I see my room? In her dream her dad was coming to the door. But in this dream, she felt a different presence. As the footsteps slowed to a halt, she realized it was more than one person.

She caressed her pink comforter and noticed a small table start shifting and transforming into a long bench. She heard the squeak of the door and slid open. She was instantly transported to the courtroom in San Diego where she had spent a lot of her last four years.

She was on the stand, apparently a witness to a crime. There was no judge. No jury. There wasn't anybody there. She looked at the seats in front of her and two tables where the opposing sides sat. Nothing. Then, suddenly, she heard the gavel to her right. She looked up. It was her dad. and then she saw Elton and Lopez sitting at the two tables.

"What's going on here? I haven't committed any crimes. Is this EFN again?" She screamed and started to sob. She noticed Elton and Lopez trade glances of derision.

"I told you this was a bad setting," Elton said. Lopez nodded.

Then, suddenly, Alexa was sitting in the Judge's chair and her dad was the witness. But then her dad disappears. He turned into her team lead back at the orbital.

"Alexa, we don't have much time." Lopez said.

"Our computers were able to hack into the Kletlop's communications as they approached Beta. The A.I. has analyzed millions of conversations in the last couple of hours." Elton said.

"What are you talking about? What am I doing here?" Alexa shrieked in between gasps of breath as her crying continued.

"Relax," Yurig said. "We are here to teach you the Kletlop's language. Klentakli. Kletlop's are the aliens that destroyed the transports."

Alexa turned to everyone frantically. She thought she felt her heart racing but when she moved her hand to her chest, she felt nothing. "What did you do to me? Am I dead?"

"No. You are dreaming. You just came from your bedroom. Remember?" Elton asked. He had a still look on his face. It only looked like Elton.

"OK. That makes sense... kinda..." Alexa muttered, halting her crying. Lopez smiled. "Good. Please stay calm. We are simply going to have a really long and fast conversation. By the end of it you will learn Klentakli."

"Wait. What is a Kletlop and how does this work exactly?" Alexa asked. Then she replied to herself, "That is the name these aliens call themselves. The headband I have worn throughout my stay at the RHSSO has rewired my brain to accept a new language faster through it." She felt a soothing motion all over her body.

"Remember that theoretical Olmec language you and I invented?" Yurig asked.

"Of course." Alexa nodded, confidently. Her eyes were still read.

"For some unknown reason, Klentakli sounds a lot like what we invented." Yurig said. "We were even able to determine that some basic words are the same as other Mesoamerican languages. Food. Death. Person. Water. But beyond this, Klentakli evolved much differently. Our A.I. was able to decipher this language. It only knows how to speak it. Reading and writing will come with time."

Alexa felt a sense of power. She had helped develop a language which now laid the foundation for inter-species communication. 'This is gonna look great on my resume,' she thought.

"This is going to go awfully fast, but we think you can handle it. Besides, you will only learn enough to communicate at a basic level. With time, you will learn more complicated phrases used in all sorts of literature," Yurig said.

Alexa nodded.

"Let's start with basic verbs," Lopez suggested. Alexa focused on all their words and one by one, they became stuck in her head as she pictured actions attached to those verbs.

CHAPTER 37: THE FIRST SPACE BATTLE

Vera Ivanov secured Mahina and Alexa to the floor with some rope and tied them gently to part of the floor, which transformed into loops. The rest of them continued to float. Others had secured, with shorter ropes, the pink aliens. She snuck a peak at one of the screens showing the alien and alien transport floating 500 feet in the air. She hoped the remaining floaters would float over the wall, and instantly fall to their deaths like the other one.

Other cameras and sensors showed Katelyn and company return. Vera established comms with them, and after an update went to check on the alien corpse. They decided to wait outside, in case more pink aliens approached. Their weapons intended to protect against the only real threat: werewolves, were believed to be effective against the invaders.

"Also, we can't go in with the gravity softener cranked up all the way," Katelyn confirmed.

The space battle was in full swing. The human motherships, which were smaller than the alien mothership had surrounded it. The human ships, which had continuous use of their Es could maneuver in ways spaceships that were slaves to orbital mechanics could never dream of. The mothership was seen burning thrusters to get a better orbit, to match the human ships. The alien fighters detached one more time and started engaging the human fighters. The alien fighters were now in prime condition to attack the human ships. But the human ships vanished. They all had Es and the larger ones had MEs.

This enabled them to move around in the 3.5th dimension and reappear behind the alien fighters, or next to them or above them. As the fighters vanished you could still make out a silhouette moving, like a ghost ship.

Then, when it was in an advantageous location it would drop down to 3 dimensions, regain its full shape and image and blast the alien fighter away. This went on for many hours. It was a slow, gruesome fight. It looked like snails fighting... if snails could be in space.

The alien fighters could only use up most of their fuel to reorient themselves, while being in the same orbit to try and counter the human ships. Vera noticed some of the human fighters struggle to stabilize themselves as well in an orbit. It was almost like these specialized pilots were relearning Sir Isaac Newton's laws of motion. The alien fighters didn't have a special force field like humans expected. In fact, they seem to just have really thick hulls.

"I bet they are extra thick to protect against asteroids and the like while traveling. No way they're wining this," John mentioned to Vera. She gave him an inquisitive look.

"Looks like they can't travel in 3.5 like we can. Which means they are more prone to asteroid collisions. That's why they have thick hulls."

Vera nodded at John and saw Elton give her a nod of approval.

The human ship cannons took a ridiculous amount of time to penetrate it. The alien ships were almost as maneuverable as the human fighters and landed several shots and destroyed some of our ships. But for the most part, humans were winning the battle. The first interstellar and interspecies space battle. Thank goodness for humanity's obsessive compulsion to annihilate itself and arm itself to their teeth multiple times over. Now, they could do serious damage to the Pink Man Group.

On the monitors, one of the larger human motherships launched a single missile to the bigger ship. But the alien's ship's defenses destroyed it before it got close. Vera didn't know whether to cheer for the 18 minutes the missile was in flight or to sit down and bite her nails to the bone. Several of the human motherships made their way towards the giant alien mothership, surrounding it in the 3.5th dimension. The alien ship couldn't do anything to stop them. It fired at the ships but the human ships would disappear, reappear, fire, and disappear again. This violent, endless, almost comedic dance went on for several more hours. It was painfully slow. It was like watching a Star Wars battle in slow motion. Finally, after humans had lost a couple of their own large ships, and the alien mothership was badly damaged, it seemed like the battle was over. Vera was in awe of the stamina portrayed by the human fighter pilots. Maybe they had an illegal amount of stimulants on board. She remembers reading a history textbook that some of the earliest space battles between humans were so agonizingly long that a lot of pilots died from space battle fatigue and overexposure to stims.

As everybody in the room watched the battle conclude, after almost 30 hours, Henry reduced the gravity softener and they all barely stayed afloat. This would make it more comfortable for them but prevented the aliens outside from coming in. The alien mothership was seen with a lot of white and pink lights all over it. It had a smooth glow and this made the human ships stop attacking. Later, they would discover that this was their version of the white flag.

Vera smiled and nodded as the battle concluded. It was a forced smile as being awake for over 30 hours with little to eat and almost no water had drained her, despite being near weightless. She noticed Elton make his way to the alien, and grabbed it by its vest, "Alright motherfucker. You lost. Now, you are my prisoner." The alien muttered something to the armless guards and they looked up from the floor. Elton punched the alien and demanded to know why they attacked. The alien, not understanding, simply stared. The bright blue eyes had tears in them and it said something incomprehensible. Elton looked at Sonya, who merely shrugged her shoulders.

"Elton, my love. Stop," Alexa said, floating angelically, feeling her head, and readjusting her headband. Her words were deeply more impactful as she floated skillfully and had a calming tone to it. She started speaking in the alien language, almost instantly. The alien seemed shocked and Elton let go of it and backed away, making his way back behind Alexa.

She stood up on the floor as Henry reset the gravity softener. Elton glanced at the monitor and Vera snuck a peak of the aliens outside fall to their deaths and Katelyn approached them.

Alexa neared the alien. She spoke to it in their tongue and Vera instantly heard Alexa's voice in plain English through her earpiece.

"Why did you attack us? We came in peace. Our ships were defenseless. You slaughtered innocent humans," Alexa was heard in her earpiece. Alexa glanced at her teammates and Vera nodded, confirming she could understand her.

Then the alien spoke, in a frail voice and the translator spoke in everybody's ear. "You came here with the intention to take over our planet. We had no choice."

"We surveyed part of this planet and only saw that small artifact. There are no signs of a civilization anywhere. This isn't your planet." Alexa said.

"It is. It is in our system. This is our agricultural and vacation planet. We use it every 12 to 15 revolutions around its star. That's when it is closest to our home planet."

"Your home planet?" Alexa demanded.

"Yes. This is our secondary planet. We come from another planet called Tlaculipoxtli."

"What do you call this planet?"

"New Tlaculipoxtli."

As Alexa nodded Lopez came on the screen. "Alexa, you, and Vera know what you need to do. I will be listening in. Prepare for the UN Peacekeepers to secure Anomop." During their conversation a heavy transport with visible guns landed just outside their building. The UN peacekeepers took the other guards' weapons and restrained them after saluting Katelyn and her followers.

Vera greeted one of the UN peacekeepers and took cable ties, a holster, and a gun. She worked on the alien's arms and legs. She motioned at Henry and John to carry it into the smart materials storage area, closer to where the barn was set up.

"That is a neat trick, Alexa," Vera winked at her, on their way from their commons to the storage unit.

"Glad you liked it. I've got the worst headache, though... I hope our new friend talks fast. Or else..."

"He'll have an even worse headache." Vera confirmed and saw Alexa nod.

"Where do you want him?" John asked.

"That large crate in the corner is fine," Vera said, as John shoved it into a seating position. It's knees still came up at an angle, sitting on the largest crate.

"Thank you. Go ahead and help Katelyn," Vera didn't break eye contact with the alien as Henry and John left.

"A.I. Isolate our conversation to us and Lopez. Standard encryption," Vera ordered, mentally wishing she had been knocked unconscious. She forced herself to stop grinding her teeth. She unholstered her gun and touched the alien's knees with it, "if I don't like your answers, you will not walk again." The A.I. took an absurdly long time translating it and she heard the speaker in the corner convey the message to their prisoner.

Alexa shook her head and Vera knew it would take too long. She nodded towards the prisoner and took a step back.

Alexa started speaking in Klentakli and Vera heard the translation.

"You will call me Alexa. What should I call you?"

Vera undid her holster, reinserted her gun and gently felt the grated portion of her sidearm. The alien looked at Vera and she saw its facial expression resemble that of a scared human.

"I am Tulip. Kletlop Space Force. I oversee the large ship in orbit and two more stationed elsewhere," Vera's A.I. spoke in her ear with an intonation of a small boy.

"Good. You said your species claims this planet. Why is there no evidence of your stay?" Alexa's voice rang twice. One in Klentakli and once more in her ear via her A.I.

"My species has traveled for over one thousand years in twelve-to-fifteen-year intervals to let this planet heal. We come, plant, harvest, and ship back food. Our home planet... it's incapable of feeding all of us."

"Why don't you just colonize this planet?"

"We did at first," the alien shifted and his face showed pain from where John and Henry hit him. "We are one people. Our leader didn't want a potential future conflict between planets. We also don't want this planet to suffer as Tlaculipoxtli did. New Tlaculipoxtli is a new beginning for my species. When we noticed your ships, we had to act..."

Vera nodded Alexa over and stepped away from the alien, "They obviously don't have MEs and seem to be more in tune with their version of mother nature."

"At least he is cooperating. He knows we are a superior fighting force..."

"He's making it a little bit too easy..." Vera doubted.

Alexa moved to Tulip again, "Why should we believe you?"

"I have no reason to lie. You took out a third of my fleet. You invaded our planet. We killed your kind. You retaliated. Let's call it even..."

Vera thought to herself, 'he is being so pragmatic, "We are even... for now." She glanced at Alexa and Alexa translated. They didn't want to wait for the A.I.

"1300 years ago, our species went through a big change. A great war took hold of every tribe. At the end only one tribe remained and took over the entire planet. To avoid more wars, our King funded a technological revolution with a simple goal: improve everybody's lives. At first it went well but then our planet got sick from the waste we created. Society began to crumble from migration, disease, and filth," Tulip coughed.

"When we finally made it into space, we discovered New Tlaculipoxtli. We took advantage of the naturally occurring cosmic river between our stars and colonized it. However, we infected this planet too and it was decided to let it heal and only use it to grow food in cycles."

"You conveniently left out the destruction of the natives here..." Alexa said.

"This planet had no intelligent life. The dominant species was giant feathered animals with large beaks that breathed fire. It produced molecule Six-Dash-One-By-Four and combined it with sparks in its throats."

'Methane,' Vera thought.

"If you did find anything it was from us. We must have forgot something.

"Our first colonists almost died out, fighting these creatures. After years no more were found."

Vera pulled Alexa back, again, "Without MEs or Es his people can't produce enough energy in space to grow food. That is why they need to come here. Maybe they don't even have Cold Fusion..."

"And what is this cosmic river he referenced?"

Vera heard Lopez in her ear, "It appears there is a cosmic jet stream like the flowing of water in our oceans. They get to near the speed of light and once they exit it at their destination, they use the returning cosmic ray as a brake and exit at the perfect time to match a good orbit around this planet. It's ingenious, actually..."

"They must be centuries more advanced than us, for their food to not go bad for years and still be fresh," vera said to Alexa and Lopez.

"How do you know they don't just freeze or can it?" Lopez asked.

"They could probably do that on their planet. The purpose of this planet is to provide fresh food. If our food stayed fresh for years or even decades, we could end Sol hunger once and for all," Alexa looked amazed.

Alexa gathered more info from Tulip:

• Their home planet orbits around its star every 1.2 Earth years. and this new planet orbits its host start every 1.3 Earth years.

• Kletlops mastered longevity and lived for over 1000 Earth years.

• After attaining a balance between their population, and their planet, they were able to backtrack some of the ill effects on modernization on their home planet. Now, their 12-year cycles are the norm.

• Ever since this harmonious balance, technology meant to travel to the stars was deemed non-essential by Kletlops.

• They didn't possess knowledge of HPs or their version of the ME and therefore had only sent probes to nearby systems. The furthest one they explored is approximately 6 light-years away. It took them 150 years to reach that one.

• Also, since they already had a second habitable planet in their own system, their need to explore was not there and soon space travel was almost completely abandoned. Instead, they focused on how to maximize food production and maximize longevity and make their lives as comfortable as they could.

• Neither side could explain how their similar ancient languages evolved separately.

CHAPTER 38:
THE TREATY

Everything screeched to a halt on Earth as the space battle concluded. Then, in the following months people, the governments and Kletlops alike sprang into action. Tulip's words rang true and both sides agreed to a ceasefire.

Upon an agreement in principle, Alexa, along with Lopez and the rest of The Cheddar's crew was sitting on an ME enabled ship on their way to a Kletlop space station orbiting Tlaculipoxtli. They were escorted by Tulip and guardsmen.

Alexa hated instant travel. It made her feel like she was falling infinitely fast with no end in sight.

She looked out the window, sitting next to Elton and the rest of them. She saw an enormous space station. It spanned the entire circumference of the planet approximately 750 kilometers above its surface. Incredible. It was thicker than the RHSSO asteroids. She swallowed some saliva, completely amazed at what the Kletlop had accomplished.

Alexa looked at The Vice President of Extraterrestrial Affairs; an old man of 115 wearing his headband and glasses that had a constant stream of information available to him. Everything he did or said on official business was recorded and observed by the President of ET affairs and the six regional presidents and their staff.

The Battle Above Beta cemented Humanity's foothold in the Kletlop System. The VP's visit was merely a formality.

Humanity, with little effort relatively speaking on their part, had bested the Kletlops in a space battle. Humanity was taking a page from former American President James Polk, and had created the Milky Way Galaxy Manifest Destiny Doctrine. This ensured that human's continuous exploration of the galaxy would end up on favorable terms. This assumed that other civilizations were at an equal or lesser technological level.

The terms of the Peace Treaty are simple: No aggression between Kletlops and Humans; Humans, having lost over 150,000 people were now the owners of the smaller continent on Beta; Beta would be referred to as Beta, even by the Kletlops. Every 12 years, the Kletlops would land on Beta and 15 Earth years or so later would leave just like they had done before. But they could only land and grow food on designated areas on the larger continent. Humans would control all space traffic between Tlaculipoxtli and Beta. All precious metals discovered by either species of strategic importance shall automatically be handed over to humans.

Humans will have a space station orbiting Tlaculipoxtli without weapons. Its purpose: to keep an eye on the Kletlops, making sure that their intentions were not of a sinister nature. As a token of goodwill, each species will have three embassies on the other's planet. This promoted cultural dissemination in the host planet. Alexa didn't like it. She could already feel the watchful eye of Big Brother over the Kletlops. The Kletlops also didn't like it and didn't have to. They only possessed more of those battle space stations that had already lost to humans.

The Kletlops reluctantly accepted. It could have been worse for them. Another, more advanced species could have wiped them out. Sure, humans could have sent nukes and anti-matter weapons of mass destruction. But that wasn't the purpose. Humans understood how rare intelligent life is. We also understood Karma and suffering on a global scale. Had we subjugated the Kletlops outright, it would sow remorse and trigger future conflicts. We explored over 5,000 systems and only two had life. The situation on Earth is so volatile, it would be nearly impossible to sell the public a war; especially one against a species without the technology to travel to Sol. The threat would have been seen as imaginary at best and fabricated at worst.

Like many previous stealthy and wise leaders, the six regional leaders agreed to stop a war before it started and understood that you didn't necessarily have to annihilate your enemy: just shake them enough to give you what you wanted and feel grateful while doing so.

The transport and its escorting space fighters made their way to a docking area of the orbital ring. As it got closer, Alexa and the rest of them could make out the odd design of the ring. It looked like inconsistently stacked Legos of all colors. Alexa saw many Kletlops behind large glass inside well-lit areas of the orbital.

The ring's colorful nature is in complete contrast to our metallic and rock-surfaced ships. Our ships with logos could not compete with the sea of colors Alexa saw curve around Tlaculipoxtli.

The transport landed with a slight jolt and hiss and soon their belts became unfastened. The space fighters did not dock. They hovered, if you could call it that, in the 3.5^{th} dimension, ensuring they wouldn't be hit by Kletlop fire and had their engines pre-charged. In case they needed to make a getaway fast, they could. Yes, humans and Kletlops are signing a peace treaty but that didn't necessarily promise peace.

The inner airlock door opened and Tulip, along with his guards led Lopez, the VP, Alexa, and Elton to the orbital ring. The rest of the human crew remained on board, to keep the Kletlops' pink hands and prying blue eyes away from our far superior engine technology.

They stepped onto the orbital and saw a half dozen Kletlops standing there. They stretched out their right hands and shook it with all of them. Their hands were stiffer than human hands and their five fingers resembled that of human hands but the smallest finger was the size of just one joint of the pinky and did not bend.

The one who was the tallest, a little older and wearing all white spoke, "We are so honored to welcome you to our orbital ring, Tlaculipoxtli Tlicalukiti Tlicalukitu." Alexa stared at Elton, indicating it was a mouth full. It translated loosely to 'The Ring of All Rings of Tlaculipoxtli.'

"We are honored and welcome your hospitality." Alexa said in their native tongue. It sounded almost like she was singing to them. As she saw Elton's eyes give the impression of confusion, all their feet were grabbed onto and she felt an odd sensation go up her calves, and thighs and up her butt and lower back. The floor beneath them transformed instantly into seats. She didn't notice it at first but the narrow chair also went up all the way to hold her head upright. Then, that same alien guard continued "My name is Tlukip. Tulip is my son. Please hold on to the seat. We will be transported to the meeting hall." As soon as Tlukip said this they started accelerating slowly. Several seconds later they reached travel speed and stopped accelerating.

Tlukip spoke in that high pitch noise and made some gestures with his hands. "Tulip tells me you would be coming here on your M E ship. He tells me it travels instantly from one spot in space to another. Is this correct?"

Alexa responded. "It is. We have had this technology on Earth for some time now. We have visited thousands of star systems. Some of which are further away from our home than yours is." She said this with a bit of condescension and a smile which meant to show humanity's technological superiority to the Kletlops.

"Perhaps, in an act of good faith you will share your discoveries with us, so we may learn more about star systems we have yet to visit." Tlukip said.

"Tell them that astronomical discoveries will be happily shared with them. But they must share some of their secrets as well. Perhaps their longevity technology." The VP said.

Alexa nodded and relayed the message in their language. Tlukip seemed a little irritated. But he smiled and simply said,

"I doubt our discoveries will be of little benefit to you humans. After all, you are the ones that visited us."

The VP smiled, not wanting to push the subject. After all, they couldn't jeopardize the peace treaty signing.

"Is it true that your home star system only has one habitable planet and one star?" Tlukip asked, changing the subject.

"Yes." Alexa responded. "We have colonized all the planets and moons that we care to. All locations are self-sufficient and flourishing." Alexa was obviously lying. They couldn't roll over and expose their bellies to the Kletlops.

Tlukip nodded. "We, too have colonized many parts of our system. Beta is the only planet we only visit occasionally. It is precious and we do not wish to treat it with the same disrespect we once did."

The car kept on moving at the same speed. They were in a mini-subway system. The top half of the cylinder is glass and they could see Kletlops going about their business through windows and some common areas and stops.

"After our ceremonial signing, I would like to meet with one of your experts in your language." Alexa said. "We have many questions. I am sure you too have many questions."

Tlukip nodded. "Our king has already asked for volunteers to be sent to your home planet. We would like to experience it. Reading about it or watching videos is never the same. I hope you understand."

The VP, nodded and spoke, "Absolutely. Our leaders back on Earth have also requested the same. In fact, I am the leader of the new organization that will oversee and direct our cultural exchange. I trust I could meet with my counterpart on your home planet."

Alexa, spoke again, but struggled to come up with their word for president. The best she could do is 'the chosen one to lead.' Tlukip didn't fully understand and asked her to elaborate. "Kings? You have more than one?" He spoke his tongue and Alexa didn't hear the translation anymore. She was fully immersed in Klentakli

"We don't have Kings anymore. Our leaders are called presidents." Alexa confirmed, saying the last word in English.

"Pre-si-dent?" Tlukip asked, confused. He said the word slowly but accurately at a higher pitch. He had gotten his own translator and he was picking up English quickly.

"Yes. Our planet has six regional presidents." Alexa said, trying to eliminate confusion. It didn't work.

"I was under the impression that you are the leader." Tlukip said, looking at the VP. Alexa clarified how six main regional leaders controlled all of earth who were elected by people living within their borders. They had elected VP Frank O'Brien to be the leader. This concept of elected rulers amazed Tlukip. He became more confused at the concept of having multiple leaders. He confided that ancient and small tribes had tried such experiments on their home planet long ago but they never ended well.

The awkward conversation continued. Tlukip is a regional/non-political leader down on his home planet. He and his wife and family control all of the export and import of crops grown between Beta and Tlaculipoxtli. Tulip, only being 150 years old was barely starting out his career in their Space Force. It turns out he was the one to have discovered the initial scouting spaceship from the RHSSO. At first, they thought it was a relic from their distant past. But when they realized the ship was not theirs they lunched their mothership/carrier to investigate, fearing the worse. Their space ship engines, not matching what humans had, took all that time until the humans started showing up to get to Beta. Once there, they saw all of these pods with humans and strange equipment. They panicked and initiated the destruction of this invasion. Tulip's reputation was ruined. He is the equivalent to Moctezuma or Atahualpa when the Europeans arrived.

Their little car slowed down and the humans were let out first into a large lobby where some familiar plants were placed. Alexa remembered seeing similar ones on Beta. The chairs disappeared into the floor as they were standing up.

There were 50 or so Kletlops waiting for them. They made eye contact with them and she was notified that the translators stopped working. It had become overwhelmed by all the incoherent chatter.

The area had no permanent seating. All their hosts were standing as they made their way in between them. They approached a large metallic table of beige color on a stage without steps. Both sides of the stage had screens with images of Kletlops gathering like they were right now. Flags were seen as well. They were very colorful and had odd looking symbols slightly resembling stars, moons, and triangles.

As Alexa and the rest approached the stage, the floor grabbed on to them and lifted itself and them to the stage level. They made their way to behind the table, which grew in length, to accommodate all of the other Kletlops who were also present.

Tlukip made his way to the front of the stage and started speaking while, the rest of them quieted down.

"Although our first meeting was unfortunate for both of our species, we would like to thank the humans for not escalating the conflict. Humans and Kletlops both understand how rare habitable planets are. In order to preserve Beta, we have both agreed to sign this accord. This is a new beginning for us and humans." He made a gesture to Alexa to come forward to speak. Frank looked annoyed at this but permitted Alexa to get up. Tlukip, as well as the rest of his species had a new found respect for Alexa. She was the first human (alien to Kletlops) to fully speak their language. Alexa and Sonya, who also learned their language were the de facto representatives of humans. Frank was under direct orders from Earth to make this as smooth as possible.

Alexa, stood up, unsure of what to say. She approached the microphone, which had also magically appeared from the floor and now was lowering itself to match her height, and began to speak in their language. "My name is Alexa. This is my husband, Elton." She waved over to him and he stood up to give a quick wave and nod. She introduced the VP and as Frank attempted to approach the microphone, Tlukip made an uncomfortable gesture and Frank simply copied Elton's actions and sat back down. Tlukip motioned to Alexa to continue.

She cleared her throat, which startled some of them. She didn't know what to say at first. She was asked to address one of the most historic moments in Kletlop history: in human history. She took a couple of extra seconds to collect her thoughts and started speaking, "Thank you Tlukip for facilitating this treaty signing. I would just like to say that on behalf of my species, we will honor our commitment to peace and prosperity with the Kletlop on Beta and in both of our systems. I ask of you to do the same. As more time passes, our initial meeting will be seen as an outlier and soon we will call each other friends, neighbors and even family." The room exploded with a cheer. It startled her and her eyes opened wide. She had just said exactly what they wanted to hear and meant it. In several years, she would see that the Kletlop took her words a little differently than what she meant them to be. Her words, which seemed so perfect and so genuine and filled with the best of intentions would be the underlying motivation for future conflicts between both species.

BOOK 5: THE FIRST OF THREE FINAL TESTS

Prologue

The King sat on his throne, cushioned from the fiercest of Clahktlaks' feathers throughout history. His prophets made a circle in front of him. They chanted the ancient song of prophets. Half sang in modern Klentakli and others in ancient dialects lost long ago to the rest of them. The chant grew louder and louder and the King tilted his head upwards, letting the smoke hit his head from the golden pressurized spouts. He inhaled deeply and raised his ceremonial staff when he heard The Messenger speak. This time they all heard him.

The Messenger – The time will come. It is inevitable. Your test will commence.

The King – Your message humbles me. Wise one, I beg you; please share more.

After some minutes, the King didn't hear anything.

The King – Thank you. I will be decisive and lead with compassion.

The chanting continued for another hour as was customary.

One of his advisors approached the King. 'Will it be dire?'

The King replied. We will triumph. It has been decided.

The advisor – What kind of triumph? The previous time there was plague, famine, and death. Lots of death.

The King – with faith we will come out of this. Let us prepare.

The Advisor – Prepare for what? All we know is that we will be

tested soon.
The King – have faith. We will know when the time is right.

CHAPTER 39 – KLETLOP SYSTEM – EAPR-N-103 AND LIFE AFTER THE BATTLE OF BETA AND DECISIONS

Spaceship RX-3966 arrived at EAPR-N-103, the Kletlop home system, a mere couple of months after the last Kletlopian ship had left Beta in 2167. The Kletlops detected this ship once it stabilized into its orbit around Beta and at first thought that it was a relic from their past as its travel in 3.5D was never noticed. Once their satellites were able to intersect some of its signals, they realized that it was an extraterrestrial craft. They didn't know how it got there and who placed it there. They sent one of their stations to that planet that was orbiting Beta's star in an outer orbit. It took the cosmic highway to get back. The Kletlops don't possess anything like the E nor the ME. Instead, they have very efficient and powerful Ion/nuclear engines that take advantage of the magnetic fields found in space, like wind and ocean currents found on earth. Sol's system doesn't have these phenomena. They didn't know it at the time, but those engines only needed the algae unique to Earth, its enzymes and an atomic layer of water to make it similar to an E.

When the cosmic rivers aligned and the planets were closest, the Kletlops trip from Tlaculipoxtli to Beta lasted just under two years. The return was the same.

After the battle and subsequent treaty singing, relations started to normalize. The Kletlops discovered that besides the ME, they also wanted something else from humans: democracy. Despite humans being violent and disrespectful of their home planet they got that right. That was the Kletlop point of view.

In between the time of first contact and the next cyclical migration (or just 'the first cycle') to Beta, the Kletlops, back on Tlaculipoxtli started experimenting with councils and acting out democracy and requesting the King's attention. For the first 10 years these were unrecognized and unorganized attempts at merely speaking with the King about specific and important topics. Their inexperience and tradition did not upset the new band of Kletlops advocating for democracy. It was only a show at the beginning. But that is how all revolutions start: as an unorganized show craving attention and recognizing that there is something amiss in the status quo.

During this time, humans back on earth were both mesmerized and repulsed by the Kletlops. Some humans wanted to learn from the Kletlops and interact and exchange ideas and culture.

Alexa and Mahina spoke about this several times.

"We should all be working with the Kletlops. Imagine what we could learn," Alexa said.

"Imagine what we could teach them, too," Mahina winked at her.

Others, didn't care for them. In the eyes of the vilest humans, the Kletlops lost their claim to Beta. This animosity materialized in the taunting, harassment and even harming of visiting Kletlops on earth. Hate crimes were rare, but did happen. These voices were in the minority, but they were loud voices. To have proper relations these loud voices were silenced.

Despite these rare and violent events, humans did crave something else from the Kletlops, besides a second planet; longevity and a sense of harmony with their planets. Humans had started their crusade into green and renewable energy long ago, but the damage to Earth had been done. Humans would like ecological stability, but craved longevity. Of course, that was our ignorance talking. Kletlops could easily live for centuries longer than humans could. With long lifespans, came long memories and long memories fueled old resentment.

The first 10 years or so slowly ticked away one after the other. Ship after ship filled with humans, usable buildings, and resources, escorted by space fighters arrived to Beta. For the first two years, migration was slow as people had to wait for the gravity softeners and essential infrastructure to be built. It seemed like every week after that, tens of thousands of humans would appear. This made the Kletlops nervous. These new settlers came from every corner of the world, especially the areas where people had been displaced. Under the threat of revolution or other wars, people from these unstable regions were rushed to Beta. It was analogous to the first pilgrims leaving England in the 1600s.

All human settlements were placed in the smaller of the two continents, which is approximately three times the size of Australia at 22,500 square kilometers. Its geography varied wildly, like most continents on Earth do. For the most part the coastal regions were fully green, which stretched deep into the continent. Around 70% of coastal regions are lined with cliffs, much like the California coastline. The green interior is mostly hilly and steep, lined with bushes and small plants that bloom after showers and turn yellow and die in the hotter months. The mid-east section of this continent is filled with a large mountain range that resembles those found in Canada and Alaska. The trees there were quickly dubbed 'everyellow' instead of evergreen. They resembled the great Sequoia trees in California but only in size. The top most branches were blue with a hint of white fuzz on them while the rest of the leaves were mostly yellow. In the colder months these snowcapped mountains were untraversable but in the summer months they replenished the rivers and smaller lakes beneath them. At the request of the Kletlops, humans agreed to not heavily modify the geography. This means no dams, no clearing of jungles or forests, no removing of mountains, no flattening of steep hills and definitely no fossil fuel burning and no heavy industrialization. This was easily agreed upon by humans, as that was the original plan.

Most of the settlements were placed near the coast or bordering the giant lake, which was named Lake Alexa, at the request of the Kletlops. In fact, different regions on Beta in the human continent were named after the crews of the Cheddar and the Black Hole. The Suzuki Mountains. The Erica desert. Vera's Jungles. Sonya's short stature was deemed desirable because it is a stark contrast to their own towering heights. Therefore, they named a small island Isla Sonya. She didn't like it at first but when she was told that island had huge reserves of gold, she felt flattered. Some of the leaders from Earth even suggested naming other areas of Beta after some of famous historical figures. The Kletlops eagerly declined.

The exact center, where Lake Alexa laid, was soon discovered by human geologists as a crater from a meteoric impact long ago. This lake fed rivers which fed smaller lakes and some even drained to the ocean. This lake, coupled with the snow from the colder months gave humans more than enough water they could ever need or want.

Lake Alexa, though massive, was still dwarfed by other, larger lakes, which resembled interior seas on the other continent. The largest continent was as varied as Africa, the North Pole, Europe, Asia, and South America. Some humans demanded we take over that larger continent and maybe even attempt to invade Tlaculipoxtli but wiser men and women understood that this would add insult to injury to the Kletlops. Like many wise generals and leaders before them they understood that victory didn't necessarily mean annihilating the enemy but merely to contain them. Besides, Tlaculipoxtli had 19.7 billion Kletlops. Humans merely numbered at 11.3 billion and that was including all of the colonies and the RHSSO.

Alexa and Elton, having completed their two impossible goals discussed their future with Lopez, were given 50 million Dollars each, their own ME transport and a room reserved at all times at all major Human colonies.

During the mass migration to Beta, Alexa was named Human Ambassador to Tlaculipoxtli. Alexa and Elton were welcomed with open arms, were given their own mansion on Tlaculipoxtli, and were always sought out to provide insight into the human psyche. They gave lectures and countless interviews before the First Cycle started. They were practically nobility. She was the first human to learn their language and he was seen as a scientist with a pure heart. They took their children to Tlaculipoxtli and all four of them completely immersed themselves in Kletlop culture.

Henry Suzuki, under normal circumstances, was supposed to retire at the age of 95, and more or less live the last 30 years of his life in quiet dignity. However, since he turned 92 right before the Battle of Beta, he was given the option of retiring. He, along with all of the Cheddars and Black Holes were given 50 million dollars as well. He returned to Earth for the time in between the Battle of Beta and the First Cycle. Now that he had the golden nano-bots he didn't know how much longer he would live and he figured he could spend some time on Earth and then some time on Tlaculipoxtli. Laura had more work to do but returning to Earth was enticing and she was able to work something out with Lopez and work from Earth.

Michelle, also close to retirement age was given the option of working anywhere. He and Erica both decided to lead cultural research teams back on Tlaculipoxtli on behalf of humans. They moved to one of the largest culturally significant cities back on Tlaculipoxtli. Sure, it had all of the modern amenities but they were there for the history. and this city was approximately 48,000 years old. The temples there resembled those of central Mexico. But there were also some other buildings that resembled the Borobudur Temple. Michelle and Erica, however, decided to only work on this part-time. They wanted to focus on their hobbies. Michelle, being a small celebrity on Earth now, was also gaining popularity on Tlaculipoxtli. Some Kletlops thought his stories were factual accounts of humans' experiences. He assured them they were not. Physical books had gone away long ago on Tlaculipoxtli and his stories resurrected it. A lot of other limited edition printed books were made on Tlaculipoxtli and some were exported to Earth. Erica, on the other hand, continued her work with her passion: setting up parties. To her surprise, the Kletlop happily did outreach during her events. Sometimes they were small and intimate dinners, while other times they went sightseeing in groups and other times, especially during popular holidays, they were large parties that ended in all of them drinking something like Ayahuasca but whose effects only lasted several minutes instead of hours.

Mahina was approximately 33 years away from retirement after the Battle of Beta. Given that she had so much time, she decided to go to, and the Kletlops complied after their similar request was granted back on Earth, the leading observatory back on Tlaculipoxtli and track the stars the old fashion way for the time being. 33 years was more than enough to track a lot of the stars and all the planets in their system. During this time, she noticed that a lot of the same techniques the ancient Kletlops used were also used on Earth. For instance, to measure the circumference of Tlaculipoxtli, the ancient Kletlops had to use a stick and measure its shadow during their summer solstice at two different locations with their known distance to each other. They also used a third location on the equator. They also used a compass, which amazed her but at the same time made sense, since both planets had similar magnetic fields. Many human and kletlop scientists agreed that a strong and stable magnetic field is needed to protect life from being fried by their host star and external sources. The similarities continued to amaze her. But there was one thing she was an expert at that Kletlops had never imagined doing: surfing. She introduced them to it and even established the first surfing academy in Tlaculipoxtli. Luckily, those half-squid half-whale monsters were not found on Tlaculipoxtli. The largest animal there was a jellyfish the size of a whale, but they mostly lived in the Polar Regions.

Vera completely mastered the Kletlop tongue in a matter of weeks with her headband immediately after the Battle of Beta. Soon thereafter, she decided to go back to Earth with Belmira and her family. They settled in California where her popularity guided her into political campaigns and she even sought a career in politics.

Belmira's family never adapted well to the space-faring life and Earth did need actual teachers to teach the Kletlop language. But this didn't mean that she stayed on Earth permanently. She did teach courses at a UC San Diego and neighboring universities but during the summer she would take a group of students to visit Beta and Tlaculipoxtli. Belmira would always accompany her. She soon realized that the golden nano-bots had changed her brain chemistry. It changed everyone's brain chemistry who took them. That, along with decades of training and mastering every single human language made her easily teach the Kletlop language to anybody who knew any language. It turns out that the headband that taught her the new alien language in a matter of weeks would not work with normal people who only knew 1-3 languages. It caused migraines and in some rare instances brain damage and seizures. In her down time, Vera decided to explore the possibility of accurately reading negative temperature in higher dimensions. She knew it was impossible but it gave her something to focus on.

It seemed like everyone except John wanted to settle down. Despite his advanced knowledge, degrees, and contributions to the Quick, John Brolin decided to be an interstellar taxi driver. Lopez was unsatisfied with his career choice. He persisted, mentioned he would only transport high ranking officials and she backed off. After all, they all achieved the goal set by Lopez and then some. Lopez made him promise that every year he would dedicate four months to developing an ME that would work in any system. He reluctantly agreed. Every so often he would also consult his former teammates on their various projects. He had become the de facto interstellar team lead of the next project. Everybody knew it was impossible to create an ME without HPs and read negative temperature in higher dimensions. But his teammates collaborated as a fun way to pass the time nonetheless.

Sonya wanted to settle down, but couldn't pass up the opportunity to have face to face meetings with powerful Kletlops. The A.I. translator wasn't perfect and figured she could translate for the most powerful and wealthy people while in the transport. She even made John do a couple of flybys around Neptune, Jupiter, Mars, and the moon just to give her more time as host on most trips. Kletlops enjoyed it. Alexa was the ambassador and Sonya was the escort and the first to hear about what had just occurred on meetings on both planets. This made Alexa a little jealous, which was a plus.

After traveling and living out of a suitcase for six years, sort of speak, Sonya grew very close to some powerful Kletlops, especially the male ones. They had explained to her on several occasions, she was seen like a tiny trophy wife. She was only 5 foot even and the Kletlop adult males were never under 7 feet short. This made John uncomfortable and after several years Sonya and John split up. He wanted to continue traveling. She wanted to settle down with their children and decided to move back to the RHSSO to help their kids finish their studies. She also joined in on some remote work with the others but for the most part spent her days interacting with other linguists and wrote books on Klentakli and how to master it and how to master human languages for the Kletlops.

The remote teamwork experience was a welcomed one to Elena. When asked, Elena chose to focus on longevity. Now, the Quick had its own network and she used it to collaborate across Sol and the Kletlop System. She improved the golden nano-bots a little and now it seemed like humans could live for 300 years in ideal conditions. This was still a far cry from the Kletlops and she was curious about successfully combining human and Kletlop DNA. Lopez wholeheartedly disapproved over ethical and treaty violations. Even if she showed it could theoretically work, the Kletlops won't ever cooperate: if Kletlops weren't getting an E or ME or the Quick, then humans weren't getting the secrets to immense longevity.

Elena agreed to not follow that path of her research, but still chose to improve longevity on Tlaculipoxtli. 'Maybe I could get a male Kletlop scientist to give me the secret.' She thought. She laughed at the notion and decided to merely ask for help from biologists on Tlaculipoxtli under the pretext of teaching Kletlops about human biology. The idea of living on an alien world excited her six younger children. The older two, however, having received a BS on the Orbital a couple of years after the Battle of Beta, decided to continue their education back on Earth. She wished them well and took her other children to Tlaculipoxtli. For those several years they would visit each other at least once a year. Usually this was around Christmas or to celebrate the discovery of Beta, which had become an Earth holiday.

Michael and Ashley chose to live on Tlaculipoxtli. Michael wanted to focus more on Astronomy and Ashley decided to focus more on longevity with Elena. They compromised and decided to live near Mahina in a town at the base of the mountain. Michael would have to take a hydrogen lift to the observatory every day, but that 65,000-foot trip only took 4 minutes and the view could not be beat. Ashley would commute to Elena's lab, only two hundred miles away. The cars took the trip in under twenty minutes. She would sometimes accompany Michael to marvel at the far stretched out lands filled with Kletlop households, business and their popular yellow-colored trees and work remotely.

To Michael's and Mahina's amazement, the constellations they first mapped out on Beta were quite similar to what the Kletlops had already mapped and named. During the early years Michael, Ashley, Elena, and Mahina grew closer. They all even started surfing with Mahina. They also learned how to snowboard, which the Kletlops were quite good at. It turned out to be one of the most popular sports in their competitions held every twenty Tlaculipoxtli years, which resembled the Olympics. Since they had just held their event couple of years before the humans arrived, they had time to try and convince the board to let them start competing in surfing.

CHAPTER 40:
THE BRIDGE

As the First Cycle neared, the Kletlops' incessant requests to travel on board ME ships kept on being met with a harsh no. Humans cited the Treaty: only official political envoys and emergencies are seen as exceptions.

After a Kletlop ship was almost lost to a meteor impact, the Kletlops became less patient and argued that they wouldn't be slaves to this cycle if humans transported them using their ships. Kletlops even tried to get some crewmembers from the Cheddar and the Black Hole to speak on their behalf but any motions to amend the Treaty was DOA. Despite Tlaculipoxtli being so close to Beta, Beta was stuck in Earth's SOI for the time being.

Besides that one heated tele-argument, the First Cycle was uneventful. They arrived, after being scanned by human vessels and permitted to land, grow their food and then leave 10-11 years later in their Return Cycle. But just as the Return Cycle concluded, humans liked having Beta all to themselves. Some politicians back on Earth revisited the idea of colonizing all of Beta. This was quickly shot down by the King, with the help of the crews of the Cheddar and the Black Hole.

As the Second Cycle was only three years away from starting, many more politicians joined in the argument to colonize all of Beta. The King and both crews worked overtime in PR and eventually got that vote defeated. Barely. As the first couple of Kletlop ships were being prepped to head to Beta, Sonya called Alexa over their Quick. Alexa and Elton had a

Quick communicator in their house on Tlaculipoxtli, which beamed its data to the station orbiting that planet and sent it to Beta's satellites or back to Earth. Quicks worked in higher dimensions and didn't need to relay messages. The satellite is only for record keeping. This was supposed to be a secret and only the King and his guards knew about it besides Alexa and a handful of humans.

"She's calling again." Alexa sighed. She was eating a fruit salad on her balcony overlooking the other houses and nearby small garden she had planted with terran fruits with the help of some of the Kletlop children. The only thing on that planet to like those earth fruits were small rodent-like animals that resembled squirrels with pink fur. They spun webs and hung out like bats from those webs. It was a nasty sight. Other than that, they were very harmless, as no virus or bacteria from Tlaculipoxtli had crossed over to humans. Yet.

"Maybe it's important." Elton responded, lifting his hat form his face, raising a brow at Alexa's direction and setting the hat back down. This day was the equivalent to a Sunday back on earth. Very little work was expected to be completed on that day. Their 'week' was 12 days and the last four days were always set aside to rest.

"I doubt it." Alexa said, "She always tries to show off who she met with the day before under the disguise of just making conversation or talking about that pointless ME or neg-thermometer." She said this in Klentakli. They rarely spoke English or any other human language even if they were alone like they were at that moment. Elton waved at her dismissively, and continued to relax in the shade of the exotic trees that cast a shadow over them.

They hear the phone ring again and Alexa decided to walk into the secret room which housed the Quick. The smart wall opened up just enough to let her through and giving the illusion of her walking through the solid wall. It was a small room, barely enough to have two sofa chairs, a desk, chair and large screen, which was connected to the Quick, which was now the size of a large gaming PC from the 2040s. It had just as many lights. Its cooling system was underneath the large house and it was the size of a small car from the 1980s.

She sat in her chair and waved her hands at the Quick. Sonya's face came up instantly. She was talking with somebody else on another screen and John, Katelyn, Alex and some other people were there with her. Sonya soon realized Alexa had come online and greeted her, "Finally you talk to us. We need to talk and you've ignored our calls the last couple of days." Sonya said, annoyed. Some Kletlops could be seen behind them. They weren't really supposed to be there but none of them would ever snitch on the Kletlops who had become close friends and allies.

"Well, we already spoke two weeks ago and haven't had time go over that data. Elton and I keep thinking that your neg-thermometer won't work." As she said this Elton walked in through the wall and sat in the chair next to her, waving at the screen as he sat. "So what's the big emergency?" He asked, with a mojito in hand.

"Long story short: the Kletlops found out that the leaders on Earth have enough votes to start a scouting trip onto Clahktlak. They even want to put up a permanent scientific base there." Katelyn responded, ditching the small talk, despite not having spoken to Elton nor Alexa in a couple of years. Clahktlak is the name of the larger continent on Beta. It is named after the giant fire-breathing chicken that inhabited that continent. It produced electric shocks like an earth eel and methane like an earth cow. It was a deadly combination and the humans were thankful for not witnessing that giant animal burn trees or other items. Some human scientists wanted to study it, and the Kletlops happily gave them all the relevant scientific data. Every now and then, the Kletlops would clone several and ship them to zoos all over Tlaculipoxtli.

Elton gave them a dirty look, "Shit. You think they'll try to get a scouting trip again? So soon?" As he said this, all of the screens had a breaking news story appear. The 6 regional earth leaders, along with their cabinets called an emergency meeting. A couple of minutes later, after they watched older clips of similar votes, the EU president announced that their intention was not to take the second continent from the Kletlops. Their goal was to study it and see what other things they could find. This was basically a trip to determine where humans could build permanent housing and infrastructure.

Protests on both sides of this new act erupted on Earth, its colonies, Tlaculipoxtli and their colonies and Beta. For the next couple of days they all went on their PR crusade once more to try and defeat the bill. A couple of weeks later, once the vote was held, they noticed that their efforts were not in vain. They defeated the vote again.

CHAPTER 41: THE ONLY CERTAIN THING IN LIFE

Henry, now being 125 years old, was in the upper limit of normal human life expectancy when the second cycle was in its early planning stages. He decided not to get the improved nano-bots and was unsure on how long he really had. The second cycle was to begin a couple of years later in 2202-2203. Of course, healthy people could expect to live up to 140 years old, but countless pandemics, a worsening climate and increasing terrorist attacks significantly lowered the life expectancy the last 100 years. Scientists calculated that without even just one of these three factors, human life expectancy could be 150+ years on average, even without the nano-bots.

He pushed the thought away and got ready for his day. He now lived with ancient looking Kletlops in a retirement home on Tlaculipoxtli, after his health deteriorated quickly. Most Kletlops were over 900 years old at that same facility and he was dubbed as 'The Baby' by the much older Kletlops. Laura technically did live there as well but kept busy with her work.

Henry walked slowly to the communal area after waking up a little later than usual. The last couple of years had been hard on him. He focused on PR against the scouting trip vote. Those damn earth politicians didn't quit and he, along with the rest of them, had their work cut out for them.

"Henry, over here," Larta spoke. He was one of the oldest Kletlops there at 1365 years old. He was much shorter than the average Kletlop. Like humans, Kletlops shrank in size as their bodies became frail and old. Henry waved and walked slowly towards the table. He refused to use a wheelchair/hoverchair or let the floor turn part of itself into a stool and pull him to his destination. The chair materialized at the table across from Larta. The game had already been set up for Henry. Instead of using an old chess set, which Henry printed out a long time ago, or using a screen or a hologram, they opted to use the smart table. It would materialize the shapes of the chess pieces on a board and would give a really nice graphic of a new chess piece consuming the opponent's when a player moved to an occupied square.

Larta moved his white piece first. "You OK, Henry? You look like... what's that word... shit?" Larta practiced his English with Henry during their matches. They all practiced their English with him. He, in turn practiced their language, which was flawless, just like a linguist's. Some even practiced small amounts of Japanese with him.

Henry let go of a snicker, "Thanks, friend." Henry moved his black pawn up to spaces. "I've just been tired is all."

Larta nodded and his thick wrinkly cheeks jiggled. His skin had lost that bright pink and red glow. Now, he looked almost human. "We all thank you for your efforts." Larta smiled at Henry. Henry nodded back, "Ay."

Their match continued with their conversation. More Kletlops showed up next to them in their own tables. They were gathering for lunch. When Henry was two moves away from declaring check-mate, Larta put his King in check-mate. Henry smiled and nodded. "Ah. You've been practicing, I see." Henry still had lots more victories than Larta had but he was improving.

"I have a good teacher." Larta smiled and gave a short bow of his head. "I will enjoy my victory. I am sure tomorrow's match will result favorably for you."

As Henry waited for his plate of food, his hands got clammy and his breathing started getting faster. Larta asked if he was OK. But before Henry could answer he got a sharp pain in his left arm and it reached his chest and he lost consciousness.

CHAPTER 42: HENRY'S VISION AND WARNING

Michelle was still wearing his black suit and tie when he got home. Erica, with puffy eyes turned on the screen and started watching the news. Another Kletlopian ship had been damaged in its voyage and a human vessel saved them. This news story was a welcomed change. Henry's death had been the headline for the last couple of weeks leading up to the funeral. Some ultra-conservative Kletlop new shows even made fun of humans for dying so young. Others, demanded that this was a sign that the humans were not fit to be a space-faring civilization. Other more liberal shows highlighted what humans could learn from Kletlops and what Kletlops could learn from humans. Sometimes the news was serious or somber. Other times it was almost treated like a fiasco.

"Maybe we should have stayed with the rest of them?" Erica suggested to Michelle. She changed the news to an Earth show. This one was blaming Kletlops for Henry's death: death through negligence. One of the guest speakers highlighted that his death could have been avoidable but the Treaty made it illegal for the Kletlop to intervene. Kletlop shows were just as sensational as human shows. Freedom of speech is a dubious gift if not used responsibly.

Michelle lightly shook his head. "What can we do?"

"I don't know." Erica replied as she sat next to him placing her hand on his shoulder. The rest of the crew of the Cheddar were left at a hotel near the cemetery where Henry was put to rest. Michelle and Erica, living so close to the cemetery decided not to stay with them. Laura and Elena were the most distraught at the burial.

"We can go back. Maybe we can convince Laura to come live with us for a little." Michelle suggested and Erica gave him a nod of approval.

They got up and started heading outside. Michelle waved the car over and the car opened its doors as it reached them at the front door. It usually charged itself nearby but away from their front door. The stairs in between the driveway and the door covered such a short distance that the car would just be in the way if they just wanted to go for a walk or greet visiting friends.

The driveway is a small roundabout with a small water fountain in the center surrounded by bushes with plants with flowers that resembled penguins. The outer leaves were black and the center had a cotton-like material and the back reached over and formed a smooth round top with a pointy end in the front. When they first showed Kletlops earth penguins they were amazed at what appeared to be walking and swimming flowers.

Their host star was setting in the distance, barely visible over some tall pink and yellow trees that outlined the street in front of their house. The sister star could be seen right above them. It was brighter than earth's moon but much smaller. At nights it would cast a good shadow and when the sister star was out one could easily be outside with minimal lighting.

As they got back in their car they both got a message from Henry. Michelle and Erica exchanged confused glances and played it on the screen. Henry was seen on the screen, alone is his former room:

"Hello Michelle and Erica. I asked my dear friend Larta to send you this in the event of my death. I hope I didn't scare you too much

with an unexpected message from me. I am sending this message to everyone. As you know the last couple of years I have not been feeling like myself and wanted to share something with you." He let go of a light cough and excused himself while he drank some water.

"First, I would like to say that I have lived a wonder filled life and that is thanks to every single one of you. Our minor differences and hiccups now and then only strengthened our friendships, I believe. Second, I know you will miss me. But please try to keep your mourning to a minimum. I am gone and you feeling bad over my death isn't going to help anyone; especially Laura." He paused and was lost in thought for a second. "The purpose of this message is simple: to say good-bye to all of you and to make a simple request.

As you know, I spent some time after we discovered Beta back on Earth. At the time, since I was enjoying retirement, I did not notice a subtle change in people. Once I moved to Tlaculipoxtli that change became apparent. In my years with the ancient Kletlops I learned to abhor that subtle change. It tore at my insides. Luckily, Larta told me that our change is very recent and can still be reversed. It is too late for the Kletlops, but he confided in me that now that humans and Kletlops know of each other that change may be able to be reversed." He drank some more water and wiped his mouth with his right sleeve.

"What change am I referring to? You all know what I'm talking about. Whether you're conscious of it or not, you can feel it, too. I know it. Larta made me realize it. The change is simple: a sudden slow and even grinding halt to innovation on the behalf of our species. Larta was explaining to me one day that once they developed extreme longevity and an engine capable of taking them to New Tlaculipoxtli and back safely, their innovation died down. Even their singularity project was abandoned long ago. The only funding from the government was in weapons. What else was there for them to accomplish? They lived for one thousand years or more. They found a second planet capable of helping their species out of a similar problem humans faced in the last couple of centuries. Even now, all of us are barely dedicating an hour a week to John's

ME project and Vera's neg-thermometer. Larta begged me to tell you this, but I never was able to get everyone together and feared I would be ignored. But think about it. Suddenly grants for STEM research on Earth have dried up. Mars terra-forming has basically been ignored. Mars is actually losing people. They're moving to Beta. Even Lopez has stopped harassing us about research. When was the last time any of you even spoke with her? The only things that seem to be advancing on Earth is how to exploit bigger and bigger asteroids." He let go of another cough and excused himself.

"Like I said before: at first, I thought it was just me. Then I thought it was just us. After all, we are all nearing retirement age and we have accomplished our remarkable mission. All of the glory bestowed upon us on Earth and its colonies and even Tlaculipoxtli are warranted. But now what do we do? Will humans only innovate when there is an immediate and looming threat? Look to our newly found friends. The Kletlops, after finding New Tlaculipoxtli stopped innovating. And what happened? They lost the first inter-species space battle to us; a much younger civilization/ species. Their cities have been continuously occupied for dozens of millennia and they are barely a couple of centuries more advanced than us in longevity and other things like food production and material science. But that's it. If we fail to innovate when not threatened, then we will not be ready when the next threat arrives. Again, look at the Kletlops. Now is the time to help each other. They can help us with longevity, and we can help them with space travel. What will we come up with together? What happens when another, more advanced species bumps into us? Just because we bumped into the Kletlops doesn't mean our next encounter will end on favorable terms for us." Henry shed a tear as he concluded his statement. "Tell Laura that I love her and the rest of my family back on earth that I love them so much."

The screen went black and they exchanged confused looks of amazement. The remainder of the trip was short and they expressed their views on the meaning of Henry's message as the car reached the hotel again. As they stepped out of the car,

Laura sent a message asking them if they had seen Henry's message. She asked them to go up to her room where everyone else had already started a heated debate about what to do with this footage.

The lift took them to the top floor and as they stepped out, they could already hear the loud conversation in the first door. That's where they were all waiting for them. The entire crew of the Cheddar was together again, minus Henry. Larta, and other Kletlops were there as well. As they entered, John stood up and pointed his hand at them, "They will tell you exactly what I think. That this was just Henry's old man syndrome talking."

"Don't talk about him like that," Sonya reminded him of his rudeness.

"I'm just saying that those are his private thoughts and we have no place in showing this to anyone." John replied, as he paced towards the rear wall.

Almost everybody was sitting down, except Mahina and Vera who were standing in the kitchen with drinks in hand. They waved at Michelle and Erica, welcoming them back. Michelle looked at Alexa, confused. She was sitting on a couch while Elton was sitting at a small chair near a table, rewatching Henry's message.

"Guys, what did you think of Henry's message?" Alexa spoke, immediately silencing everyone. She stared at them and repeated her question in English this time.

Michelle put his left hand over his mouth and lowered it to his neck and let go. "I don't know. I guess Henry's observations are correct. But what exactly are all of you discussing?" He took off his coat and two chairs materialized next to him. Erica and him sat.

"Basically, there are two points of view on this. Some of us are taking his warning very seriously and trying to figure out what we can do with our influence. Others disregard his message and merely want to move on from Henry's untimely death." Michael said, delicately as Laura started crying lightly.

Michelle shifted uncomfortably, "Henry has a point. Our investment in research slowed. Companies back on Earth aren't really innovating. What ever happened to terra forming Mars? Nano-bots improvement? Also, our own singularity project fell off a cliff. Has anyone heard anything about it? Are spaceships even being sent to other star systems anymore?"

They all looked at him. Mahina cleared her throat. "I have spoken with Lopez about the spaceships to other systems. Where before we would send one ship every week, now we are sending one every month or so. We haven't sent one out to another system in 39 days. Vera still goes over the data, but mostly we are focusing on our own hobbies."

"That's exactly what Henry was saying. Which is why we need to share this message and expand on it." Sonya said, in stark contrast to John's statement. John lightly shook his head at her.

"Look. Henry is entitled to his opinion. Does this mean we all have to agree with it? Our tech slow down," Mahina said the last part in a sarcastic way, "is inevitable. Even Alexa mentioned this to us. Remember? You told all of us that during wartime tech advancements one thought impossible were done at an amazing pace. Well, we are not at war anymore. Some slowdown is inevitable. Besides, we are still trying to fix this problem. People are still showing up to Beta. Not to mention that we have to share that planet with another species." She said this and Larta and others looked at her.

"Ah HA!" Erica finally stood up. "No wonder you didn't do as many interviews against the settlement of Clahktlak. You don't want Kletlops there just like the other morons back on Earth."

Everybody got up in favor or against that statement and everybody voiced their opinion, regardless of whether or not Erica's statement was true. "She never said that." Vera defended Mahina.

"That's true." Mahina started. "I wanted to focus on that meteor shower. You know, the one that could be seen for several months across both skies in this system and damaged several ships and satellites? Remember?"

"OK. Fine. Do you take Henry's warning seriously?" Michelle asked, firmly.

"Well..." Mahina trailed off. Another outburst from all voices in several languages started again. Michelle met Vera's stare. Vera started, "I agree with Mahina. We are still trying to figure this new system, new civilization, new planet, and settlement thing out. We don't have time to advance research." There was some truth to Vera's words. But that didn't mean that this tech slowdown would end once Beta was the way it was meant to be.

"Vera. Let me ask you this: do you honestly think that once we figure this whole thing out that we will start innovating and advancing science even without any need for ending our uncomfortableness on Earth or Beta? The grand unification theory was abandoned after the death of those physicists at the orbital. I don't see anybody else pick up the slack. Not even me, I confess." Elton spoke calmly.

"Elton, you, Alexa, and everybody else in this room has earned their time off. Remember how tough it was on the Cheddar and at the orbital? If innovation is slowing down, it isn't purely our fault." Vera responded. She wasn't wrong.

"But that's what Henry was trying to tell us. We have the power to kick start more research. If we all unite..." Michelle trailed off as others sighed. Once everybody settled down again, Alexa spoke again, making everybody silent. "We still haven't heard from Elena. She's been very quiet." Alexa and the rest of them stared at Elena. Michelle could tell she was uncomfortable. She was still drop dead gorgeous and was used to commanding the stare of everybody in the room. But this stare was different.

"Henry does have a point about us not focusing on research. Vera is also right. We have earned our time off. I'm over 81 years old now and I feel like I'm 40. We have plenty of time to work. Even if Henry's death does prove that wrong sometimes." Elena untied her hair and it fell gracefully over her shoulders. She didn't have one white hair on her head and the wrinkles around her eyes were barely becoming visible. "Will humans follow the same route as the Kletlops? Maybe. There are similarities. But there are differences. The Kletlops never encountered another civilization. The beasts on Beta were just animals. No hint of intelligence. No civilization or ruins of a civilization has been discovered there." She walked in between the crowd. Some were standing and some were sitting. All were quiet. "The way I see it: innovation has slowed and as scientists we all have a duty to push science forward, not hold it in place. Furthermore, I do believe that once this era of getting to know each other is over we could probably learn a lot from each other." She focused on Larta and his friends from the retirement home. Larta nodded. "Maybe Henry's death is an opportunity to get both species to cooperate on tech at a slower pace, if another war doesn't break out." Alexa nodded with approval. Michelle stood and nodded. Erica followed, and then everybody else stood up. "But Vera is right. Those who wish to live their remaining years in peace and without stress has earned every bit of it. I don't really take Henry's warning seriously as I do not believe it to be as dire as he made it out to be. I, for one, will still focus on my research at my own pace and privately." She muttered the last words and made Michelle uneasy.

More exchanges like this happened throughout the night. Sometimes arguments sprung up again. They all watched Henry's message multiple times and nothing was settled. In the end, coffee cups were scattered all throughout the hotel suite, with all of them sleeping on the floor, sofa, or improvised beds from the floor.

They all did agree that from their reference point, tech advancement had slowed down. John, Vera, Mahina, Ashley and Michael agreed to ignore Henry's message because in the near future others would pick up the torch and keep moving it forward. Sonya, Elton, Alexa, Michelle, Erica and Laura all understood their point of view but referenced Larta and Kletlop history. One could try and make excuses for the sudden disinterest in science and technology but ultimately, humans as a species had become complacent. The imminent threat, once eliminated, didn't push humans to proceed on to the next step. Elena agreed to ignore Henry's warning but still chose to let others decide their fate and to continue any research.

Soon, the sister star set and the main star rose. Michelle, Erica, Laura, Sonya, and Elton went back to Michelle's and Erica's place. John, Vera, Elena, Mahina, Ashley, and Michael stayed behind in the hotel, letting the others continue their crusade but refusing to actively participate in it. Michelle confided in Alexa, on the way back, that if only half of them were backing one side, the indifference to Henry's message would most likely prevail, making their fight an uphill one. Alexa nodded at him and only said, "We can only try."

CHAPTER 43: THE HENRY AMENDMENT

Michael got into the self-flying drone on his way to Mahina's observatory with Henry's funeral still fresh in his memory. The initial aftershock of Henry's message going public had died down and now he and the rest of them were moving on with their lives. The cold and dry air was held at bay by the transport's thin smart walls. That day was a rare one in the winter in that region. The sun had finally come out during the day after a snowstorm had swept the region for almost thirty days. That didn't affect him nor Mahina, as the observatory was on a mountain above most of the storm clouds that hovered over the large mesa beneath them.

He kept on being bombarded by messages from the media to comment on what his companions were up to. They were pushing for more resources to be made available for STEM research. Others wanted those resources dedicated to migrations of both humans and Kletlops. Others still, much to his surprise, flat out insisted that humans had achieved so much that those resources should be plowed into the arts and other cultural aspects. He ignored all of those requests. He didn't care much for what his former crewmembers were doing. Neither did half of them. He was happy living his life and felt that trying to push others to dedicate their time to unwanted hobbies was a sign of disrespect.

Regardless of what he thought about all of that, the politicians on earth were busy working on amending The Treaty. For the last couple of days, politicians from Earth and

Tlaculipoxtli met on neutral ground in a station orbiting Beta and argued relentlessly about what the amendments should cover. They were in a gridlock and no one expected anything fruitful.

His trip concluded with a loud thud and a hiss. The door opened and he breathed in thin and cold air. No human could be where he was for more than thirty minutes without having their oxygen level in their bloodstream drop to worrisome levels. But he enjoyed the view. The Kletlops called their main star Curicavet. The sister star was named Curicavetu. Curicavetu was seen in the distance barely above the horizon to the northeast. Curicavet was about to set in the west and he barely had enough time to get into the observatory and avoid freezing to death.

He walked in and all of the Kletlop scientists and Mahina were glued to their screens. "Good evening, all." He said in plain English. The Kletlops waved at him, almost dismissively. Mahina waved him over to her screen which was shared with Kuarta. Kuarta was one of the tallest Kletlop he'd seen. He was full of muscle, too. He towered over everyone else at almost ten feet tall. He easily weighed 450 lbs. He was also one of the smartest there. He took of his jacket and sat next to them. The screen was clear and they could almost touch the tiny people inside it.

"Wait, are they voting already?" To Michael's surprise the politicians were ready to vote. Mahina and Kuarta both nodded. Frank O'Brien was the lead at the meeting with his Kletlop counterpart, one of The King's many nephews. "All in favor of the Henry Amendment?" Frank spoke. In two minutes, the votes were in and the resolution had passed 650 to 131. None of the representatives missed the vote. The number of delegates was in honor of how many light-years the Kletlop system was from Sol. But to avoid ties, they added an extra vote.

"The Henry amendment? Wasn't that DOA?" Michael asked aloud.

"It was. Until more stuff was added to it earlier today." Kuarta noted. The Henry amendment was simple: when a human or Kletlop was in danger of dying both species' doctors were legally obligated to help if they could within reason. This benefits humans more, as we die sooner and our bodies are more frail. Kletlops demanded that, for a reasonable fee, they could get transported to and from Beta all of the time. Basically, this new act let pilots freight Kletlops as private taxis. Companies could now also transport goods for the Kletlops for a slightly higher fee than they did humans. This amendment harshly punished the sharing of technology. Humans maintained control of our ships 100%.

The voting continued on the next several amendments. When it was all over, around an hour later, a lot had changed and was to be implemented immediately. The Henry amendment essentially ended the Kletlop migration cycle to Beta. Furthermore, since the Kletlops now could travel whenever they wanted, there was really no reason to leave Beta after twelve years. This helped promote another addition to The Treaty: Kletlops would be permitted a permanent presence on Beta on the larger continent, similar to humans on the smaller continent. Humans could now freely travel to the larger continent and the Kletlops to the smaller one.

To celebrate this, both sides sent a scouting trip to the larger continent on Beta a couple of weeks after the vote. These scouts found:

- The continent being 4 times bigger than the smaller one does not really put into perspective its massive scale.
- Potable water is plentiful on this continent. In fact, natural ridges and canals give a third of this continent a high agricultural value.
- The north pole, which is on the larger continent, gets colder than Earth's. No life exists on the surface there, But with an active small volcano beneath the surface, the water is teaming with alien life.

- Most creatures in the ocean resemble jellyfish, squids, and whales. There are few species of smaller fish.
- There is a new type of bacteria in this ocean which 'breathes' lithium and expels 'lithium superoxide'. It also glows in the dark. It is the dominating one in the ocean on Beta.
- The tiny deserts on this larger continent don't get so hot.
- Besides the werewolf and other small dragon-like reptiles which seem to become invisible during the day, most of the animal life on that continent are birds and insects. Most of these birds and insects resemble and vary little from those found on Earth.
- The werewolf is the only mammal or mammal-like creature found.
- But none of the animals give birth to their young who can readily walk.
- The seasons on this continent resemble those found in Europe and North America
- There are a total of 127 large salt lakes in this continent.
- There are over 5000 fresh water lakes. In these lakes is where more small fish and other animals are found. They even found an animal which looks like a platypus but with poisonous claws and bite. It looks cute but has been known to kill Kletlops in the past. It is also deadly to humans.
- In the jungles of this continent, which only cover approximately 10% of its land, there are giant worms and spiders. The worm resembles the extinct Hallucigenia worm, which can jump from large tree to large tree. It feeds off the internal sap of a rare tree species that is short and round and bushy. The spider resembles the Hobo Spider and has been known to capture baby werewolves who get lost near the jungle.

In order to permit Kletlops and humans to use their own technologies on the others' planet, teams of both species would need to settle permanently on the other planet. On Earth, the purely academic team was to discuss longevity. On Tlaculipoxtli MEs would be stored with human-only crews. 780 Ships and crews were loaned to the Kletlops for their own use on their home planet and their colonies. This was a welcome change to the Kletlops.

Other, less crucial technologies were to be shared more openly. For instance, Kletlops had somehow been able to produce plants and vegetables that were resistant to all known pathogens and could feed lots of people and Kletlops. They also have better smart materials than humans do. Those materials moved almost like magic when compared to human smart materials. Humans, on the other hand had better computers and A.I.s. Kletlops also had the ability to regrow body parts on a living person who had suffered a tragic loss. At the end, Kletlops were liberated from orbital mechanics and slower than lightspeed travel and communications while humans now had access to centuries more of life and a higher quality of life.

Mahina gave Michael a nod of approval at what they were watching. Some Kletlops near them celebrated and even hugged each other. Both sides felt like they had won something and have come out ahead. But this was better. No war was fought. The only casualty was Henry Suzuki. She internally wept for a moment, again.

"Looks like Henry's death inadvertently resulted in better lives for all." Michael told Mahina in French.

She replied in French, "Yes. Looks like our teammates got what they wanted."

"Well, there is no clause forcing either side to cooperate or forcing any one person to cooperate."

She nodded. "I can live with this."

For the rest of the night they all made comments about how

these changes would be implemented and how Kletlops' lives would differ moving forward. Kuarta, in between drinks and documenting his work, said, "I will tell you this: Tlukip will stop making money."

"Who?" Michael asked, knowing he had heard that name before but was unsure.

"Tlukip. He's the one that owns the import and export business and has... had the largest transport contract in the cyclical migrations for the past 400 earth years. Give or take."

Michael nodded at him and looked at Mahina who reflected Michael's worried expression. Michael didn't know how this would affect everyone. But back on Earth when a man's business model is made obsolete in a matter of days, he tends to act rashly and sometimes even violently.

CHAPTER 44: TO WHAT END?

Erica Jameson laid in bed fully awake in the middle of the night and let out a sigh as Michelle snored next to her. Her insomnia had been kicked up a notch ever since she had started planning her 115th birthday celebration which would take place in a couple of weeks in the summer of 2202. Her mind alternated between her birthday party and how tired Michelle seemed lately. They all pushed themselves extra hard the last three years since Henry's funeral trying to promote Inter-Species-STEM research. That in itself didn't bother her. Michelle was nearing Henry's age when he died and she couldn't help but torture herself thinking about blaming the golden nano-bots.

Ever since Henry's death, she had secretly been helping Elena and Michael try to figure out if the nano-bots they were injected were to blame for his death. So far, their research had come up empty. It didn't help that Elena wasn't really into it. She had hit a roadblock before Henry's death and her attitude of not pushing anybody too hard was prevailing and annoying Erica. Erica had even stopped seeking Elena's input after one heated argument when Erica was pushing Elena to work extra hours on their project. They would still talk every now and then, but their relationship was not the same anymore.

Erica got out of bed and walked towards the bathroom as the floor dimly lit up beneath her feet with every footstep. Afterwards, she sat down on the couch and started watching some news segments. A couple of media outlets had picked up her party. That made her smile. Other outlets that covered her party in a different light: as the first party where all the original Cheddar crewmembers would not be present. A tear ran from her eye and it dripped as she saw her espresso machine, remembering Henry's gift. Minutes later she fell asleep and was later awaken by Michelle.

"Again?" He asked.

"Yeah. What time is it?"

"Almost time to leave to meet with Lekelop. Remember?" He asked.

"Alright." Erica got up and took the coffee mug from his hand. She drank and had a light breakfast and soon was getting ready to meet with one of the most respected historians on Tlaculipoxtli, again.

On the way to meet Lekelop they started watching more news about John's new transport company and how it was making lots of money at the expense of the Kletlops. Photos of him in his pilot's seat were put up next to photos of banking executives from Earth who were funding his endeavor and indebting the Kletlops.

"Can you believe this crap?" Michelle asked her.

"Instead of trying to prolong human life or working on the universal ME he decided to make more money." Erica shook her head at the screen. "We're the ones that made that possible. He disliked Henry and the 50 million isn't enough for him."

For the past three years Kletlops and humans were settled in practically every single colony and on all four planets permanently (Earth, Tlaculipoxtli, Beta, and Mars). Kletlops provided healthcare machines to humans on Earth and other places. This eliminated illnesses that had emerged again like measles and small pox and HIV. This caused a boom in the transport business by humans. But the increase in business also meant an increase of debt; Kletlop debt. Humans demanded that their currency and thus their banks be used. Human banks sprung up in the Kletlop system. This indebted Tlukip, who was trying to hang on to his business empire. At the same time it permitted people with no jobs to join crews on ships. A more aggressive version of The Jones Act for space was ratified, intended to protect human tech from the Kletlops.

"Have you invited them to your party?" Michelle asked.

"Of course, I did. But will they show up?" She wondered aloud.

"Sure, they will. It's not like they have something else going on. I was just thinking you don't want them there..." Michelle trailed off and started reading an article on a screen.

To get to Urukintlo, the ancient city that now is a huge collection of giant museums, they had to travel for an hour from the modern section of the city to the ancient cultural sites. The drive was 400 miles of deserted landscape that had been set aside for future archeological digs. The Kleltops always had the intention of digging that area up and finding more about their pasts but, as Henry stated, they had become complacent and a lot of the money for research was being hoarded and /or spent on getting food back from Beta.

Erica saw a lot of ruins, just like she always did, but today it was different. Being so close to a celebration without her friend made her realize that he was right all along. A lot of those sections were fenced off and the bureaucracy had simply stopped working on the permits and everything else needed to make these archeological digs possible. She had been able to get some digs going with her influence and help from Lekelop. Lekelop used her ignorance to his advantage and a lot of the sites were meant to awe and inspire humans who knew nothing about the Kletlop culture. She knew, however, that to get this whole area excavated would require more funding and more interest and more qualified people and Kletlops.

As they sped over the unmaintained road, Erica could only make out far away trees. The trees nearest to the road were a blur. She glanced at her own screen, trying to see if she missed anything from the previous tests but easily got distracted when Michelle started talking about his final book he was finishing. They had decided for him to push it off a couple of months so it won't overshadow her birthday party.

The drive continued for several more minutes and as they reached their destination, they noticed Alexa and Elton's car near the entrance of the museum. They exchanged confused glances as they were not expected until the following week.

She stepped out of her car near the entrance of the museum. It resembled an old Greek temple with columns and a triangular shaped roof. Except, this building was much taller and made completely out of glass and plastic. It was a marker for an ancient building lost long ago. During special occasions, the glass was as clear as the purest glass but most of the time it is opaque and resembles granite, marble, and other natural materials.

They took the walkway from the drop off area and made their way through the garden with tables and shops selling food and knick-knacks. She approached a table, which had some pins and looked them over. There was a new one she didn't have. It had the outline of the profile views of both a human head and a Kletlop head. In between their foreheads, there was a small pink gem and, on the outside, there were 780 tiny diamonds. Erica bought it and decided to wear it for her party to try and get the conversation about more cooperation started and guide the conversation to archeological research.

While she made her way to the museum, Michelle was surrounded by Kletlop students on a field trip. Some of them were asking for more insight into his book while others still gave him their condolences on Henry's lost. Mourning, on Tlaculipoxtli, sometimes lasted decades. Long lifespans permitted longer everythings. She left him outside, being used to this happening. She met his gaze, winked at him, and went up the stone steps towards the huge open gap into the first room, which housed the concierge. The nine-foot attendant greeted her and waved her through.

The floor was concrete with letters from their language all over them. No words were made out. Some letters are modern while others are ancient and others are from different languages the Kletlops used before. Several groups still speak those languages as a hobby, like humans did back on the RHSSO with Nahuatl or ancient Chinese or some Viking languages. The Kletlops now only had one language. Humans were moving in that direction as well. She passed walls with paintings of the ancient gods the Kletlops worshiped. These paintings are nearly 40,000 years old and perfectly preserved in a case with nitrogen gas. They reminded her of the renaissance paintings except these looked brighter and bigger and had more text around the painting.

Her walk continued down a wide hallway with benches lining either side and plants in between them. The walls had paintings of previous kings and queens and other nobles. Each painting had a monitor beneath them, showing a clip of the history of each painting. Most artists were known. Few paintings only had dates of discovery with guesses on the artist and when they were completed.

At the end of the long hallway there was a sitting area where many of the Kletlops waited for the rest of their party to conclude their tours. This area had 7 hallways leading to different exhibits and those separate areas quickly turned into a maze and many times Kletlop children were caught crying for their mom, panicking like a child in the supermarket back on earth.

She went through the third opening on her left, which had a less exotic area: literature from 1000 years ago to the present. Sometimes authors or their children/ grandchildren would come and share stories. But for the most part, holograms did the talking, whether it was recordings or a live interview. They even had statues made from sophisticated smart materials that mimicked the movements of the Kletlop talking on the other end of their phone. They still creeped the shit out of her.

This area is a long and wide hall with concrete floors, thick and tall granite pillars, covered in smart materials. Cases with ancient books and tiny screens lined the walls on both sides. The middle area has lots of circular tables with seats around them where authors would meet with patrons or where people rested and looked over notes on history about a particular exhibit.

She walked by the security guard and into the back research area where she and Michelle worked with Lekelop. Alexa and Elton were already there making small talk with Lekelop. She overheard them talking about how Lekelop's 650-year-old mom who went to Earth and tour Africa for the next couple of years, now that tourism was open to the general public.

"Well, look who it is." Elton smiled at her. She greeted him with a hug and a quick kiss. "How have you two been?"

"We're fine. Thanks. You?" he replied showing a genuine smile.

"Could be better. Insomnia. You know." As she said this, he nodded and Alexa greeted her and they hugged.

"Where's Michelle? I thought..." Alexa's question was interrupted.

Erica rolled her eyes a little and said, "Fans. He'll be right in."

"Lekelop, good morning." She greeted him as always.

"Good morning. I brought the coffee beans I promised." He glanced at the espresso machine at a table across the room. It sat on a fixed table that is too high for humans. In front of it is a stepladder. The museum didn't have the funds to upgrade the tables to smart materials in the research center. Erica thought that would have changed by now but the bureaucracy on Tlaculipoxtli is on par with Earth's.

The coffee beans were almost %100 identical to earth coffee beans but were bigger and sweeter and had lots more caffeine in them. He always brewed her a mean cup of Turkish-like coffee and regretted not ever being able to share a cup with Henry.

"Perfect timing then." Erica glanced over towards the door opening and saw Michelle walk in. She let him make small talk with their old friends while she and Lekelop approached the table and started the coffee making process. This process had been perfected over time on Tlaculipoxtli. Cold lasers and cooled grinders made sure the coffee stayed cool, preserving its entire flavor during the grinding process. Once it was in the espresso machine the temperature was kept exact throughout the entire machine, ensuring the taste flowed evenly.

Once everybody had a cup in their hands, Erica noticed Elton was fidgety and uneasy. "Told you it was packed full of caffeine," she smiled and nodded at Lekelop towards Elton's direction. He smiled. His bright red lips moved a little. She could barely make them out from her angle. Lekelop was one of the shorter Kletlops but still was well over 7 feet tall.

"It's really good." Elton replied, eating one. Erica had eaten those many times. It had a hint of pineapple and was a little bitter. It was quite popular there, resembling one of the oldest recipes the Kletlops had. The small talk continued for a bit longer. Alexa finished her cup and sighed, "Remember how several years ago Elton asked you two for copies of some old books?"

Erica nodded, having forgotten about that request made long ago. At the time, the Kletlops just handing over ancient texts to aliens was a complete shock. She soon realized that Alexa was very well respected and admired. Furthermore, what humans thought as ancient was only kind of old from a Kletlop's point of view. She took a sip of her coffee and noticed Elton guide their eyes with his open palm to one of the books.

"I see you finally brought them back." Erica saw the stack of books on a table on the other side of the room. Only half of the table was blocked off by a grated steel wall. The half that was hidden housed an automated computer that would digitize books. It had been broken for a couple of decades now and Elton jumped at the chance of doing that manually as a side project while learning about Kletlopian history.

"Well," Elton started, "the half I finished." He waved everybody over to the table and started walking. She saw him tap his glasses and a projection appeared on the wall above the open book.

"Show and tell time?" Erica asked smiling at Lekelop. He smiled back and gave her a quick fist bump. Elton rolled his eyes and started showing an old documentary of the Voynich manuscript.

"Hey, I've seen this one before," Erica said sarcastically, "this is the one where at the end of the hour you still don't know anything about that stupid book." She saw Lekelop's expression change. He was interested after a couple of minutes.

"This looks familiar," Lekelop said in English. "It almost looks like..."

Alexa interrupted, "Almost but not quite." She shook her head.

"So, you came here to tell us nothing?" Erica asked and smiled, teasing them.

"Let me start at the beginning," Elton said. Erica nodded and Lekelop seemed worried but nodded just the same.

"We all know the history of the Voynich Manuscript. Right?" Elton started, but was quickly interrupted by Erica, "I don't think Lekelop does."

"I don't." Lekelop said.

"Ok. Back in Earth year 1912, a book dealer named Voynich purchased this book. Carbon dating states that it was most likely written in the early 1400s with some hints of it being written in the 1200s by more recent testing."

Lekelop nodded, "Interesting. Please continue."

As Elton spoke, images from many documentaries were displayed on the wall for all to see. "Thank you. This book is named after this book dealer because there is no author information and no one really knows who or when it was written. It is written using really weird symbols which resemble nothing on Earth. It also has drawings of women and plants, which also don't resemble anything on earth." He took another sip from his coffee and the rest of them nodded. Erica didn't seem to care and gave him a fake yawn. She, like most scientists, had already gone through her phase of meta-science and fringe science. However, she didn't interrupt with anything else.

"Some people speculate that Voynich himself wrote it as a prank or a hoax. Or he hired someone to write it. Others say that it was a book of knowledge that was encoded to elude spies or other unwanted eyes. Others go to another extreme and state that it could be from a person who was transported to our dimension from another, that evolved this language."

"The Mandela Effect?" Lekelop asked.

"Very good," Elton seemed genuinely surprised.

"Thank you. I researched it after humans arrived. We were thinking that maybe you came from another dimension. It was a fun and interesting theory. Obviously false but back then we thought anything was possible."

"Wait a minute. The Mandella Effect only covers false memories. It doesn't account for dimension jumping." Erica said, doubting him.

"Right." Elton replied, "you see, there is also a theory that says that the Mandella Effect is known or materializes when a person or group of people are transported from one universe to a parallel universe. They bring their real memories across dimensions but in the new universe some memories never took place. Maybe someone from another dimension wrote the book and jumped to our dimension or wrote it after jumping."

"Okay..." Erica said, "you are telling me this because you guys found a way to travel through parallel universes?"

"What?" Elton asked incredulously, "No. I'm just saying that maybe whoever wrote this book came from a parallel universe where this language existed but never developed in our timeline for any number of reasons. That's just another theory about this book"

"... you're thinking that this is true? Do you ... you know... have evidence?" Erica asked, looking at Alexa.

"Honey, you're getting side tracked with this explanation." Alexa touched Elton's shoulder and he let out a sigh of relief.

"Right. Forget about the Mandella Effect and other theories." Elton quickly spurted out.

"You were the one that..." Erica was interrupted by Alexa's

shaking head.

"Anyway. We got our own theory." Elton continued, "The simplest solution is usually the correct one. Forget about spies, forget about parallel universes, and forget about a hoax with no real justification. The more obvious solution now that we know of the Kletlops would be that one of them wrote it." He took a long breath and another sip.

"I thought you guys said this didn't look like one of their languages?" Erica looked at Lekelop. He shrugged his shoulders and they both turned to Elton.

"Right. We looked back to Kletlopian history and even though the symbols do resemble those found in this book, nothing panned out. That's why I looked at those ancient texts. We didn't find anything. But we found out why we didn't find anything." He smiled at Lekelop and Erica.

Erica smiled back, and nodded, wanting to hear more.

"Lekelop, does the name Lekelop Xintquintlaxtli mean anything to you?" Elton asked him.

"Nope. The last name is somewhat familiar but no, not really." He towered over the rest of them and crossed his arms in front of his chest. Then, Erica noticed Lekelop's face light up.

"Wait..." Lekelop started, "it does sound a little familiar. Isn't that the name of a star explorer from one thousand years ago?"

"Exactly!" Elton and Alexa screamed at the same time. Michelle looked at Erica again and lightly shrugged his shoulders. "OK. So why is he important?" Michelle finally asked. The images on the wall quickly changed to a photo of the former astronaut and a narrator started speaking, "despite his mental health issues and his seizure inducing schizophrenia, he was still permitted to go on the last mission of discovery during Tlaculipoxtli's age of political correctness."

"Oh. Yeah. I remember him now." Lekelop interrupted the narrator. "He had a lot of mental problems and couldn't even write his own name to save his life, but his advocates pushed for him to be sent as a token of good will and inspiration to those with similar problems. That was before genetic engineering snuffed those problems out and a year before we discovered Beta. He was tragically lost in a mission. His ship was never found and was deemed a Kletlopian hero. Right after his disappearance, Beta was discovered, and we vowed to never sacrifice more Kletlops to the finding of other habitable planets. He was loved by all, and it united us and our efforts to visit Beta 50 years after that or so"

Erica nodded, "that is a touching story, but it still doesn't explain why we are talking about him." Erica was genuinely inspired by this Kletlop but still confused.

Elton nodded and looked at the screen where the narrator continued to tell his story. He brought up a page of the Voynich Manuscript next to the video being paused at an identical page. "It turns out that Lekelop the explorer could physically write but his brain mushed it all together and he wrote gibberish. It looked like a real language but it wasn't. It was literally portions of letters scrambled together to make fake words. Basically, it would be the same as you writing random parts of letters placed in random groupings to form fake words. "

"What?" Erica asked.

"Remember those ancient school texts for small children that only had like a circle or a vertical or horizontal line and they would have to fill in the rest of the letter?"

"Sure, I guess," Michelle said.

"That was basically Lekelop's writing system. He never wrote words. He never wrote code. He never wrote sentences. He never even wrote letters. His brain would only let his hand write parts of letters. And the same exact page that was found in this history book that was never digitized was also found on a sheet of the Voynich Manuscript."

Lekelop grabbed a chair and fell onto it, as if he had just run a marathon or ten, and shed a tear. He composed himself and several seconds later said, "are you saying that the man I was named after made it to Earth 1000 years ago and have found the evidence of this?"

Elton and Alexa nodded.

"Holy shit!" Erica screamed.

"Do you know what this means?" Michelle was really into this now. They all nodded and smiled. This means that the Kletlops, not humans had visited the other system first. Moreover, it wasn't even close. It was a difference of 1000 years, give or take a decade.

"One can only imagine how Lekelop survived on Earth and what he did for a living and how long he lived. No evidence of his ship landing or crashing into Earth was ever found, or maybe there was but ignored because humans didn't know what to make of it so long ago and then made into jewelry or toys or weapons." Michelle added.

"Wait. Isn't the Voynich Manuscript believed to be originally from Italy or that region? What if Lekelop's advanced knowledge somehow helped spark the renaissance?" Erica asked. "Or worse, what if he took the Black Death or other diseases."

"Maybe." Lekelop shrugged his shoulders again. "Then again, since he had mental health problems maybe he couldn't help much, especially without any source of energy for any tools if he had any left. Then there's the lack of medication…"

"Who else have you told about this?" Erica asked.

"No one. We just found out yesterday and rushed over. We also wanted to ask what you two think." Elton said with his eyes showing hope but the rest of his face showing worry.

"Well, why would you tell anyone? To what end?" Michelle asked aloud. "It's like confirming China discovered America before Columbus. So? I mean, yeah, it's a nice factoid and makes for an interesting conversation, but it won't change history and it won't change technological advancements from anyone."

"Such a downer," Alexa said.

"Well, wait a minute. He brings up a good point. What is the point of telling this? It is shocking to learn this information but it seems to me that human history doesn't cover this well at all and we don't really care on our side." Lekelop said, raising his hand to his jaw lost in thought.

"Look. Elton and I talked about it and we concluded that it will have two major impacts." Alexa said, throwing her long hair back. Erica was a little jealous of her. She had gotten the nano-bot treatment at a much younger age and she barely had a handful of white hairs and few wrinkles around her eyes. She, on the other hand, could look like she was a traditional 65-year-old.

"The first thing it would do would be to inspire the Kletlops similar to a battle cry. 'Hey, we got there first. We have technological advancements as well.' The second thing – make the Kletlop research more into STEM and their past. It would help with your funding; Kletlops may dig more sites to uncover more history. It'll help them become independent. If they managed to discover this technology before discovering Beta, maybe they could perfect it now like Ramirez and Huang did."

"Ok. Assuming it actually works out this way, humans would also invest more in STEM and create competition." Erica pondered aloud.

"Exactly. If the Kletlops know they can achieve this they will try, not wanting to fall behind and depend on humans." Alexa confirmed.

"But then humans will try to outdo them as well most likely. This can start an interstellar arms race." Erica said, worried. Lekelop nodded at her and responded, "Agreed. I don't think this will end well. Arms races never do."

"No! With all our scientists now being closer than ever it could spark an era of cooperation; an era of inter-species cooperation." Elton said.

Erica thought about it. She loved his enthusiasm but hated his ignorance and naïveté. No matter how brilliant he was, she still disagreed, "what in human history will make you think that? Our own human brothers blew up the first manned ship destined for this system. Or did you already forget about that?"

"Erica, that was only because they were in the dark. If we communicate properly with humans and Kletlops alike, it can be different. This is a clean slate." Alexa said with a firm tone and a stare that bugged Erica.

Erica thought some more, paced, and avoided their gazes. She grabbed another pastry and started eating it. "It's a gamble. I love that you two think the best of humanity, especially since what we have all gone through. But..."

"Erica, come on. We need you. We need the half that believe in Henry's message... I know you do. You too, Michelle. I know you want to do this. Maybe we can even convince the rest of them to help out, too. Maybe except John. He's all business now. But the rest, I'm sure, can be moved." Elton matched her pace as Alexa nodded and Erica could feel her eyes on her.

"Lekelop, what do you think?" Erica asked and smiled when he nodded. "We'll have to tread lightly," Erica said as she met Elton's gaze. She glanced over at Michelle. He gave her a look of support, waiting for her to make the final decision. "I'm in." She finally responded.

"We're in." Michelle confirmed as Lekelop nodded at Erica.

CHAPTER 45: FORBIDDEN LOVE

Mahina Iona started her cleaning routine after everybody left her cabin. She loved having her cabin next to a lake with automated waves. It's perfect for accommodating different experience levels at her school. The ocean was only a couple of miles away, but this lake gave her full control over the waves. Surfing Season had just ended the week before in a tournament were Pantl Miltplitl took first place. The party last night had carried over to this morning and into early afternoon, culminating in brunch. With her astronomical research being abandoned, she could focus on what really mattered to her.

She manually guided the vacuuming drones all around the lobby. She made them clean the chairs, tables, desks, and screens. The walls were also cleaned, along with the windows, floors, and fans. She never had imagined that she could enjoy cleaning so much. In her younger days, she thought it was a waste of time, but on the orbital, she quickly grew to like it. She remembered drink containers littered across John's and Elton's private offices. She never understood how Sonya nor Alexa put up with it. Sure, automated machines would clean every day but that made them lazy. When she noticed she was getting into those bad habits she started to clean.

During her busiest days at the orbital when she couldn't surf at the pool, she would take out her frustrations and excess energy on cleaning. Elena told her she needed to get laid. Sure, that worked too. But it required lots of energy and it demanded investing time into a relationship. Casual sex never really appealed to her. She could never find a man she liked well enough. Even the one who fathered her only son was just another story to tell. After her son started school on Mars, she went full throttle in to the hands-off parenting approach and only communicated with him every couple of months or so.

Her hands continued to guide the drones and after a while of buzzing and spraying, she called in other drones to clean the sofas that were just sofas. No smart materials. No screens. No massaging hardware. Just good old fashion sofas.

When the last of the robots were scurrying off, her screen turned on to show more news about the Voynich Manuscript and how her former teammates were calling for the cooperation of scientists on all four planets. She was getting sick and tired of this coverage. It had been on nonstop for the last 10 months. She didn't care which species visited the other first. However, she did notice that the Kletlops were walking with a prouder stance and didn't shy away from humans as much as before. It could also be that after 38 years of knowing of each other's existence they were finally getting used to humans and putting the initial battle behind them like Alexa and everybody else wished.

The voice in her ear reminded her that she had several messages from her former teammates. She gave a smile of indifference and headed for her refrigerator, seeing an ice coffee being brewed for her and her visitor that would walk in at any moment. When she had her second small sip of coffee, she heard her A.I. tell her that she had a visitor but could not make out who it was. She had disabled all her alarms, facial recognition and analyzing tools from her cabin. The sensors could only tell her whether there was something outside or not. It couldn't even tell the difference between a person and a chicken in this state. Mahina had programmed the house to bring up their sensors to max settings when she waved her right hand left to right with her thumb, index and ring fingers extended. This was in case her equipment got hacked or the authorities asked to see her records.

Soon, her sensors told her that there was something at her front door. She smiled and felt her hand tremble and some sweat under her armpits. Her heart raced a bit as well as she saw the doorknob turn slowly. A tall, hooded figure walked in and revealed himself. Pantl Miltplitl, the champion entered her cabin and she quickly gave the signal to lock her doors, and blind her windows. Her sensors also went on full alert. Now, they could tell her exactly what and who was outside her house.

She smiled and waved him over. He approached her and she gave him a hug and a passionate kiss that turned into a short makeout session. "I missed you!" She finally said when she came up for air.

"I was just here 6 hours ago," he smiled at her and let her climb down her step stool that always followed her around when he was nearby. Many times, she would ride it all throughout the house just so she could make eye contact with her lover more frequently.

"You know what I mean," she slightly tapped his chest, and they made their way to her kitchen.

"Mm... this smells good." Pantl reached for his cup and drank half of it in one sip. She leaned onto him and put her arm around him. He did the same. Even though they were always near each other in the presence of others, they rarely made eye contact, smiled at each other, or touched. It was all business. She trained with him in surfing and that was it. She even had to endure female kletlops, called kletlas, buzzing near him. She couldn't ever give the hint of jealousy.

"How was dinner with your folks?" She, interlocked her fingers with his.

"Very good. We had pork from Earth." He said, making a disgusted face.

She giggled, "Trust me; it's a very well received meat on earth. Mostly."

"If you say so..." he said as he guided her towards the couch. They sat and cuddled with dim lights and robots brought them their drinks.

They started watching an old Kletlopian comedy that was considered a classic. She understood it and for the most part comedy with both species was common enough. After they had watched several movies from other genres from both species, they decided to only watch comedy together. The other movies left the other side confused.

Two hours into the movie, Mahina paused it. "Let me get some more drinks." She said as she got up. She needed to take a break. Kletlop movies lasted much longer than human movies. When one had centuries to spare they could afford to watch the rough director's cut of every single movie. He stopped her and asked, "Why don't we finish watching it tomorrow?"

She smiled, nodded and led him back to her bedroom. As they walked, they were both getting naked and she asked for a report on her house sensors. Some drones had built a perimeter of 200 meters and many of them were observing Kletlops and humans in the surrounding common areas and yards that Kletlop houses shared. The sensors were already programmed to make sure that anybody with the intention of going to her house would not go unnoticed.

"Are you checking, again?" Pantl asked.

"I always do."

"Are we safe?"

"As safe as we can be." She already had her ritual down to a science. Two, semi-high-profile individuals as themselves had to be extra careful with their relationship. She had an army of drones as lookouts for both of them, even when they were not together. It was an incredible invasion of their own privacy, but they agreed to it nonetheless. It was worth it, after all. They had been seeing each other for almost two years now but they didn't dare come out. She thought about all those other inter-species couples that had been caught. At the very least they'd be shunned from their own species. At worse, they were killed by the either species out of spite or jealousy or both. In addition, the murderers were rarely prosecuted accordingly.

Things were changing on all four planets, and they knew of other inter-species couples that they confided in. But it was a tight knit group. It was similar to being gay in the early 1900s back on Earth. They met in secret, seldom spoke about it and none were open about it. Things were changing indeed, but not fast enough. 'It may never be ok,' she thought in her moments of self-doubt.

Once in her bedroom, everything proceeded as normal; or as normal as it could be. Our parts are compatible and the mechanics are the same. After, they laid in bed and simply enjoyed the moment. He played with her hair and she stared into his eyes, surrounded by bright red bald skin.

"The first time I saw someone from your species I was completely terrified. Now..." She trailed off.

"Now here we are..."

She nodded and held his jaw in her hand. Their heads were surprisingly similar in size to human heads. They were a little bit bigger but she could barely notice it. Kletlops are bald and human hair seemed to make their heads bigger. She pressed her body against his. His skin felt exactly the same as a man's and she thought about all of her previous partners. Maybe she couldn't find the right man because the right man didn't exist for her.

Soon her eyes were closing, and she fell asleep. She awoke to the smell of coffee being brewed and a message in her ear. Alexa, John, Sonya, Michelle and Erica, all had called her separately. She spent a couple of minutes listening to the messages. More of the same: they wanted her to help them get STEM research cooperation and wanted her to do outreach. Now that she was in the off-season, she had time but didn't want to waste it doing that.

She put on some underwear and made her way to the kitchen. Her sensors had picked up many small animals running around the outside. That was normal. She saw Pantl warming up breakfast in his underwear. She smiled and approached him.

"Morning," her stool made her way next to her and she got on it and kissed him. He picked her up and she let out a small shriek of surprise. He lifted her like a man would lift his young daughter. "What's for breakfast?"

"Pork for you and tofu for me."

"Fair enough." She said as she helped him with the plates and utensils.

The kitchen is large with two islands. One is for cooking and food prep while the other one acts as a bar station for her guests. Beyond that laid a table capable of sitting 12 people and beyond that was an open area of around 100 square meters where a larger table or tables could be set for special occasions and parties. Sometimes comfortable couches would be put there or be used as a play area for children. Beyond that was the welcoming area with a large triangular shaped desk with monitors. Near that was the huge double doors with traditional, non-smart doorknobs. The area felt empty but it was a welcoming sight. During surfing season and the tournament, it was always full. It filled up with families of surfers, fans, and just anybody that was interested in the sport.

They sat down at the second island, letting the robots clean while they ate. "One of my friends asked me if we wanted to go with him and his girlfriend on a trip to one of the outer planets. There's not much to do there but it is similar to what you have back on earth called cruises." Pantl spoke as he covered his mouth and chewed. He didn't make eye contact with her. She wished she could treat this like a normal relationship.

"I don't know..." She hesitated. Maybe if there were plenty in their party, she could say yes but that would mean more people would know about them two.

"Look. It's a semi private ship. We would have a large suite. Three couples and us. Trust me, I've known them for a long time now. We could even stay in our room most of the time." He tried to convince her.

"Four couples total. That seems like a lot of people and your type to know about this." She took a sip from her coffee.

"It's perfect. Two human males. Two human females. Two Kletlopian males. Two Kletlopian females. You would team up with a man and I would team up with a kletla and pretend to be with them while in public. But once we get back to our suite it'll be as safe as we are now." He chewed some more, "If we don't go then nobody can go. We could say that it's a trip to learn about our culture for humans and to visit outer world colonies. If that helps." She could see the smile fade from his face. She hadn't had a vacation in almost a decade. Whenever she felt like relaxing, she would simply stop what she was doing. She could even close her surfing school for a couple of weeks without a problem. This is common practice with Kletlops. Since they lived for so long, closing a store for a couple of weeks or even months didn't bother them one bit.

"Well, I guess we could go for a little bit. How long would this last?" Mahina replied and saw his eyes light up.

"Really? Yes! Well. I don't know. A typical Kletlopian cruise lasts over two years. I know that the company that runs these trips has employed humans and their ships so I guess it could be less." His smile returned.

"Two years seems like a lot. I was just thinking a couple of weeks or months." She replied. He looked confused, "No. If you go on a trip with Kletlops it's short duration will be suspect. I guess since humans will be going as well and in human ships, it could potentially just be one year or maybe less."

She smiled and reached for his large red hand. "OK. Let's go. But we have to be back in time for next surfing season." She said. That started in exactly 14 months.

"I'm sure we can find something that will accommodate that." He replied and continued eating.

For the next couple of days, they enjoyed their time off, completely isolated. It was just the two of them against the world. She loved it. Pantl made the necessary arrangements for their trip whenever he could find the time, which is hard for newish lovers. Her friends' calls went unanswered until

Pantl noticed she had messages pending on one of her desks' screens.

"You can speak with them. I can go to the bedroom if you'd like and you can call me back when you're done." Pantl suggested. He got up from the large couch in the secondary, smaller living room and started making his way towards the door.

"I don't want to talk to them." She said, annoyed.

"Why what's wrong? Are they still bugging you about…"

"Yes. I don't want to do it."

"Why don't you just talk to them about themselves and what you have been up to? Just catch up a bit." He suggested, sitting back down.

"I guess since we're going on a trip, I could use that as an excuse…" She paused as he snickered.

"What if…" he trailed off, lost in thought.

"What?"

"Nothing…"

"No. Come on. Tell me. You wanted to say something."

"What if you do help them out?"

"What? Why? You know my stance. Let people do what they want." She said, raising her voice a bit.

"Yes. I know…"

"Hey, if I never started this surfing school – something I wanted to do – I would have never met you. I'd probably be off in a dark museum or office or some unknown orbital millions of miles from here." She said as he sighed. She saw a look of disappointment on his face. She continued, "So what? Are you saying that you think it would have been better we never…"

"Oh, come on Mahina. Don't be so dramatic," he interrupted her. "You know I love you and you know that I would never trade anything in the world for you. It's just…"

"What?" Mahina said, more calmly now. She got closer to him and touched his shoulder with one hand and thigh with the other` `.

He cleared his throat, "They want more inter-species

cooperation, right?" He asked as she nodded. "I know you think it's silly or invasive or whatever. But what if you promoting inter-species STEM research made our situation less... less... shocking?"

"That's absurd. How is my asking scientists to cooperate going to help everybody else be OK with what we have?" Mahina raised her voice a bit but she genuinely didn't understand Pantl's point of view.

"It won't. But it'll make our relationship and relationships like ours ok sooner. Your species records have tons of examples of people in the outskirts of society showing their true colors after achieving something great. They helped normalize what was first deemed unnatural."

"OK. True but you know how things have been going lately? Remember that couple where that kletla was murdered and the man was tortured raped in prison?"

"I do. It was gruesome to even hear the news..." he looked down to her hand, which was still on his knee.

"Let's say, I start advocating for this stupid STEM thing..." She started. "I'd be even under more scrutiny and I would have less time for us; for you."

Now she was lost in thought. She didn't know what to do. All she knew is what she wanted and didn't want. If she became a pioneer in this whole ordeal, she could lose her independence, privacy and Pantl. There was no way she could justify having a wealthy surfer as an employee, or business partner or acquaintance. The end didn't justify the means to her and she didn't want to potentially lose him or have any possible harm come to either of them.

"If you do this, I swear to you that I will take any and all steps possible to help you with it and be extra careful. I promise we won't lose each other. We'll figure out a way." He smiled at her and kissed her forehead. "... besides, we'll have at least a year to figure something out. We're still going on our trip right?" He asked, smiling.

She hated him for having such a hold on her. This must

be how Elton and Michelle must feel with their wives. She thought about it for a bit. "If we're careful enough and if I only make well calculated public appearances it could work." She said aloud, as his smile grew a bit.

"Fine. I'll do it."

"Yes!" He gave her a hug.

"But..." she started as he pushed her away gently, making eye contact. "I will only advocate for the STEM thing on a part time basis. I won't ever hint of trying to justify or normalize our types of relationships. That could definitely ruin us."

"That's fine. All we can ask for is more inter-mingling. Surely, it will fuel these conversations later and normalize what we have down the road." He said and then kissed her. "Let's go celebrate." He said, pulling her upwards off the couch.

They made their way down the hallway, passing offices and went through a door, which led into her personal living area. It was basically an apartment inside the large house. Her inner apartment had her own kitchen but she rarely cooked or ate there. She only had that in case she got hungry during extra long private meetings on her Quick. As she passed the kitchen, she told her A.I. to send a message to her former group of friends. "We will talk tomorrow. I promise."

Her conversation with her old friends went from her being semi-harassed to small-talk to her finally saying that she was willing to help the cause but that she would only do it on a semi-regular basis. All she wanted to do was lend her name and face to the cause but still have a hands-off approach to the whole making others do her bidding thing. To her surprise, her former friends agreed to it and respected her space and her decision to go on a one-year vacation. She promised to record some messages on her trip and willing to have a meeting with them once or twice a month about what they could do to help the situation.

After the initial awkwardness and business talk, she loosened up and lied to them about her new boyfriend. She referred to her pretend boyfriend for her trip. After an hour of getting an update to their progress she ended the call while everybody was still in good spirits.

For the next couple of days Mahina and Pantl enjoyed each other's company some more. They ate, were intimate frequently and smiled at each other all day like fools in love. She couldn't remember the last time she had this much fun just eating, having sex and chatting.

The night before their friends showed up for their trip she sat at the couch after their comedy ended. It lasted a total of 8 hours and they saw it in 4 parts. Pantl found her lost in thought, doubting her own decision.

"Are you alright?"

"Huh?"

"What's wrong? Nervous about our trip?"

"What? Oh. That. No. I was just thinking about my decision to help Alexa and the others..."

"It's the right choice. Trust me. I'll be with you every step of the way. I promise."

"It's just that..." before she could finish her thought a news segment came on. It covered a group of dedicated 'humanists'. These 'humanists' were against inter-mingling, whether it be romantic or even friendship or a professional relationship between both species. The anchor showed videos filmed by the group harassing Kletlops and humans alike. The term 'redder' was used in a demeaning way. Some videos seemed harmless enough. They showed them throwing crumpled up sheets of paper or verbally confronting them in public. Another video showed them hitting a couple of humans with Kletlops with softballs. Another video showed them shooting kletlas with paint guns. They were promptly tackled by onlookers and subsequently arrested but the damage was done and the video was captured.

She let out a scream and saw the disappointed look in Pantl's face. His bright red skin expressed anger and worrisome just like a man's face. 'Motherfuckers,' she whispered as she ran her fingers through her hair. That cemented her decision. There was no looking back now.

The next day, their friends showed up. So many visitors didn't prompt attention but her guardbots and A.I. didn't stop guarding. After a couple of days of planning everything with everyone else they headed out on their vacation. They took a car from her cabin to the coast and a boat out to a platform far away from the mainland where the rocket platform was housed. She saw the rocket, similar to the one she had gotten on back on Earth at the beginning of her journey. She ignored the flashbacks of her kidnapping so long ago. It was in another lifetime now. Even the explosion on the Orbital seemed like a distant story told to her by a stranger in passing. Pretty much anything before her arrival on Beta was a blur. Now, all she wanted to do was live in the present with Pantl and enjoy herself and help her colleagues.

She got into the rocket with her fake human boyfriend. He was good looking enough but awfully short at 5' 8". She held his hand and smiled during lift off at the notion that she was no longer alone in her journey. She had pushed away her former friends to make new ones. Now, her soulmate was bringing her back to her friends. She caught Pantl staring back at her, which helped her push the scary thoughts out of her head. She winked at him and realized she was already having a blast.

CHAPTER 46:
BETA STAR AND
THE EXPLOSIVE
AFTERMATH

It had been almost seventy years since Elton and Alexa left Earth as the news continued to cover sporadic assaults by the 'humanists'. At least the attacks were confined to pockets on Mars and Earth. Everywhere else, with a healthy mix of both species, was spared from such horrible and ignorant attacks. Elton continuously grew more disillusioned with humans but Alexa was completely starting to despise them.

During his first decade on Tlaculipoxtli, only a handful of Kletlops asked him some minor technical details about the E, ME and the Quick. He was always under the mindful eye of humans higher up in the food chain and only recited his approved answers. After that, less and less Kletlops probed him about the ME. To his amazement, the last couple of decades of his life were relatively peaceful. After the discovery of the Voynich Manuscript, which was renamed as 'The Lekelop-Voynich Manuscript', the Kletlops stopped asking him even minor details about the human technology that brought them to their system. It was a welcome change and partly due to everyday mingling between both species. He had given countless lectures and interviews and wrote a couple of books describing his experiences on Earth, the RHSSO and Beta and is looking forward to younger scientists on both sides doing research. He loved the feeling of helping cooperation between both species.

The few humans who knew the technical details surrounding the Quick and the ME were monitored. Those who didn't know, were also monitored but less intensely. Kletlops had very little help from their own government and with virtually no funding, it was going to take them a long time before they could build a functioning ME. Despite these technologies being off limits, several inter-species and modest institutions sprung up. Hope.

He waited for Mahina's call. Her new organization with her business partner, Pantl, was aggressively securing funding for the first inter-species University campus. Pantl's family wealth got the ball rolling by putting up the first billion, hoping to entice others.

The screen lit up and Mahina's silhouette sprang to life in the middle of the room. "Hey, Elton. How's it going?" She started the usual small-talk and finally told him that John decided to give them two billion dollars with the promise to not use his name. He wanted to avoid paying so much in taxes. Mahina and the rest of them ended up with a healthy foundation for the ground-breaking ceremony of the new building on Tlaculipoxtli. Then, they caught up about common friends. However, this time they focused more on Elena. Neither of them had spoken to her lately and their call ended with both agreeing to do more outreach to her, Ashley, Michael, and Vera.

Elton started his Quick again and attempted to dial his son, Alex. Despite giving him a different name, he still called him Junior. They only spoke around twice a year lately. Alex managed most of parts of the orbital. Lopez had taken him under her wing and with Lopez semi-retired now, Alex was taking on more responsibility. Junior didn't have the same pressure as Elton did but handling 50 million residents and thousands of Kletlops, kept him busy. Elton made him promise to visit soon and the call ended.

Elton started writing a personalized letter to John, thanking him for his contribution. Afterwards, he wrote more letters to wealthy bankers and investors he met at the RHSSO. He had already secured some of them donating to smaller causes and got them to promote their message but this was different. He was asking for significantly more money this time around.

For the next couple of hours, he and Alexa brainstormed possible locations for their new university. Earth was ruled out as Kletlop patrons would be turned off by that idea. The same went for Mars as well. Furthermore, Beta and Tlaculipoxtli were also out of the question as each spot they thought of was clearly in the 'other's' territory.

Elton shook his head. A news story appeared on the screen while he let their conversation seep. Maybe the school could be split up into two asteroids in the outskirts of both solar systems with ships going back and forth at will like a shuttle back on Earth going from building to building, dropping students off. Before he could explain that to his wife, the alert came back and interrupted their conversation.

A news segment started playing where the anchor was talking about 'humanists' again. Some of them had been arrested for allegedly killing a newborn baby. According to this radical group, it was an inter-species' mix baby. Elton's eyes became wide, and Alexa gave him a frightened look.

They wanted to get as much information with their immersive news pod and made their way down the hall, passing their offices in the top floor, along with a couple of guest rooms and a couple of restrooms. He let the floor lock on to him and materialize a chair that brought him down to the first floor, skipping the second, which was just a large hall with a huge kitchen.

They moved into one of the small living rooms where they greeted acquaintances and ate breakfast most days that had the INP. She waved her hands and a large image appeared on the wall near their entrance. The story continued as the anchor asked for a clip of himself quickly interviewing the humanist who was under arrest and pushed by the cop. "I didn't kill the baby. I swear. It was a stillborn! I just wanted to beat up the mom who fucked a Kletlop..." his sentence was cut short as more reporters asked follow-up questions. He couldn't answer as more cops got in the way and he was pulled up the steps into the police station. The segment continued with coverage of protests. Some were supporting the Humanists. Others weren't. Most seemed to indicate that inter-breeding could not continue. Even some of the more liberal personalities indicated that this shouldn't happen because no baby could survive and therefore it was just creating death. But they stated that violence from either side directed to anybody was not going to end well.

"Jesus..." Alexa muttered.

"Yeah. Doesn't this make baby number nine now?" He asked as he rested his chin on his left hand and his left elbow on his right hand.

"Yeah. Five women and four kletlas have all gotten pregnant from the other species and all pregnancies have ended similarly." Alexa was lost in thought. "At least the ones that have been turned in. What if there is an actual mixed baby out there?" She seemed worried, trying to ignore previous stories.

"We've heard the reports. DNA dissimilarities are too many. Even with a team of geneticists working full-time it would take decades to crack it."

"We've had decades. We made contact in 2167. It's almost 2213..."

Elton let go of a disgusting look on his face. The thought of him being with a kletla reached his head. He became nauseated and sat down. He looked over at his wife of almost 70 years, and it completely put him in a different mood. He smiled at the fact that both of their faces had barely started wrinkling and the first of many gray hairs were being grown from their head. They're both nearing 100 years old but they could easily pass for a 50-year-old or even younger. Maybe they could live to be

300 or even longer.

"God, I hope not..." his mind shifted back to his previous thought, but stopped when he had a little throw up in his throat. He turned off the news segment and directed his A.I. to not show any more news for the rest of the day. He got himself together shortly thereafter as Alexa went back outside to their garden. She continued showing some of the neighbors how humans grew food in small gardens back on Earth. It was similar to what the Kletlops had, but it was all Earth fruit and vegetables with some flowers as decoration. Most of the fruit was still disliked by many Kletlops, except the youngest ones who were growing up with them. Their favorite is pineapple, because it had roughly the same shape as their cold fusion reactor buildings.

He caught up with her later that day and expressed his ideas about the university inhabiting both systems at the same time. It could even double as a tourist stop/check in on leisure flights. She immediately loved the idea, and they started designing it. Both parts would contain the same layout. The outer part would be representative of the system it is in. The inner part would represent architecture from the other system, with a small building in the middle of it would be a copy of an official government building from the other side to show the inner connections of both species and how each species was always in the others' heart.

For the next couple of days before their grandson showed up, they were busy with interviews that covered everything from their new school to the terrorist groups that were springing up on both sides. They focused on their design and writing letters to potential sponsors. Their physical letters with their own personal seals would take at least a week to reach its intended recipient. They knew these personalized handwritten letters would remind the oldest of the recipients of stories from their parents or grandparents about how communication took place without the Quick or holograms.

The day before their grandson was supposed to arrive,

they were getting ready for bed and made their way to their bedroom, passing small rooms in the hallway that led to one of their bedrooms they slept in when they just didn't feel like going to the third floor. As they neared the room's door one of Alexa's alarms went off, indicating there was a trespasser in the front garden. An image appeared in both of their lenses. It showed five hooded figures. Somehow, they were jamming their sensors and didn't display any data. Then they disappeared. Elton saw this terrified look on Alexa's face. Whoever was sabotaging their electronics knew what they were doing. Only higher ups in either government had the power to do that. Computers and A.I.s all came with a quanta-Hexadecimal encryption keys based on a 256 q-bits lock that no one could break. The only other people capable of doing that, in limited capacities, were the leaders at the orbital. They could only do it to people lower in the food chain, presumably because they had weaker quantum supercomputers.

Elton started getting flashbacks from when he was walking back to his apartment before he was taken hostage and subsequently thought he saw Alexa die. He started to have trouble breathing and all he could say was, "Alexa, if we die today, know that I have always loved you..."

"No! Don't talk like that. You're scaring me. Maybe we can escape through the Quick room, if we hurry."

"Let's go," Elton nodded, catching his breath. They made their way to the area where the floor usually lifts them up but nothing happened. As they made their way to the stairs, their front door opened.

"Stop!" A woman's voice said in plain English. He recognized the voice but couldn't place it. He told Alexa to run upstairs and he stood there waiting to die or be arrested and let go of his wife of almost 70 years. The leading hooded person revealed herself. It was Sonya Sarali, their old colleague.

Elton started sighing and breathing heavily, as he tried to stop his panic attack. He put his hands on his knees and slightly hunched over while Alexa placed a hand on his back and the other on his shoulder unable to call the drone with meds.

"Jesus fucking Christ, Sonya! What the fuck is wrong with you?" Alexa said as she motioned the floor to become a chair for Elton. This time it worked. She instinctively demanded answers in English once she got confirmation from the drone it was on its way.

"Alexa, I'm sorry. Elton, are you OK?" Sonya looked at them with a terrified look on her face and a face with more wrinkles than it should have. Elton looked at her as she made her way towards them, slowly. She looked like she was carrying something. He felt a short stab in his left thigh and cold liquid go in and saw Sonya glance over at her four companions and nodded at them in the direction of the hallway. Three of them walked towards the back wall to their left and chairs materialized and they sat down. The last figure stood behind Sonya and took her cover from her.

"What's that in your..." Alexa asked as Sonya walked slowly towards them.

"Is that a baby?" Elton asked.

Sonya nodded, in a frail voice with a despair look in her wrinkled eyes, "I'm sorry guys. Do you want the short version or the long version?" As she neared them, Elton got a glance at the baby. It seemed normal enough, but it had very little hair for its size and the skin looked sunburnt. Elton soon realized what he was looking at: an inter-species baby. He felt dizzy and threw up his orange juice on the floor, provoking the floor to clean itself. It looked like the floor was made of liquid and someone dropped a pebble in it. It morphed with tiny waves going outwards and soon the floor was clean and the area smelled like fresh linens.

"We can't talk about it here," Alexa noted. Sonya nodded, and Elton focused his eyes upstairs in the direction of the Quick room. The three of them and the baby made their way to the most private room in the entire house. All of the original leaders from their time at the orbital, wherever they decided to live had their own Quick for communications and it even came with an ME and an escape pod. Only Lopez, the King and the King's guard, which only numbered in the thousands, knew about it. The King's Guard were sworn to secrecy and genetically engineered to be incredibly loyal and obedient. Even regular human citizens didn't know about this and didn't know about their existence in Kletlop territory. All they knew that in the event of an emergency they should all go to an embassy or high-ranking human citizen's home like Alexa and Elton.

They made their way into their office and it went into lockdown mode. The Kletlop guards waited outside. They made their way into the Quick room, seeming like they could walk through solid walls as they opened for them. Once inside the room, some coffee brewed and Sonya gave the baby to Alexa as she prepped food for it as it started to cry. Elton looked at the baby and almost threw up again. "Excuse me," he made his way to the private restroom as the walls started showing feeds with text from Earth, local news, and the security camera system they installed. Their drones went into stealth mode and made a 400-meter perimeter. When Elton returned to the couch, the baby was drinking its milk and looked like it was going to fall asleep.

"OK, so let me get this straight," Alexa started. "You made an inter-species baby and brought it here?" Alexa wanted an explanation and fast.

"Her name is Beta Star." Sonya corrected, meeting her gaze.

"And this is your baby?" Elton asked.

"What? No!" Sonya reacted in a surprising way. She seemed upset. "I would never do something this stupid. and besides, I haven't been able to bare children for 25 years now."

"TMI," Elton said.

"Let's get the long version, then." Alexa pleaded.

Sonya started. Almost immediately after making contact Elena Ellis made a deal with the King. In exchange for longevity, she would let the King's closest science advisors try and backward engineer her E, ME and Quick. Elton's eyes showed terror and he felt sweat coming down his brow and in his armpits. The hairs on the back of his neck stood up. That was treason, plain and simple. It was also incredibly stupid. To minimize the number of people and Kletlops from knowing about this no human engineer or scientist was ever told about this and there was no way Elena or the King would have asked for help. She knew what she was getting into. Similarly, no Kletlop scientist, doctor or engineer would be told about Elena's research. Both parties had to start both of their projects from scratch. The King got Elena's private transport and she got to test on Kletlop prisoners in vegetated states. Elena had lost part of her soul; part of her humanity in the process. This is why she continuously and progressively isolated herself from the rest of her former colleagues. She didn't want to risk their safety. Michael and Ashley didn't know anything about this. Publicly, Elena always confirmed that she would never research without the consent of both governments. A lie.

"That dumb, arrogant bitch did it. Fuck..." Elton whispered. His eyes sealed shut, almost as it tried to prevent the thought from entering his brain. It was in vain and he quickly snuck a peek at the baby again.

Sonya continued. After hitting several roadblocks on her research, Elena decided to try and combine the DNA from inter-species couples. This was even stupider than before. She shared this information with Vera Ivanov after learning that an inter-species couple on Earth was trying to have a baby and Vera didn't seem completely opposed to it. Vera sent the first couple to Elena as guinea pigs. However, they modified their brain chip implant to erase their memories of Vera, Elena and even their trip. This guaranteed their anonymity, let her research continue. If successful, their pregnancy would have appeared natural to them. All nine babies that were allegedly reported on the news were Elena's creation. But there were lots more. The actual number was closer to 300.

300 dead inter-species babies.

One day one of Elena's youngest granddaughters walked in on Elena's work. She had snuck in to her lab as a surprise the night before and wanted to be the first one to tell her happy 90th birthday. The lab was as big as a large apartment from the 2040s and so hiding in it was easy with a preoccupied inhabitant as Elena. After the initial shock, it was revealed that Sophie, Elena's granddaughter, was in love with a Kletlop and they wanted to isolate themselves in their own private asteroid-ship. Maybe they would entice others alike and form their own colony. Elena liked the idea. Their plan was to scout for an asteroid to mine and make it habitable. However, before that got off the ground, Sophie had convinced Elena to test out the latest procedure on her and her Kletlop husband. Elena reluctantly agreed and eleven months later Beta Star was born. This was barely 45 days ago. A jealous couple that wanted to be the first, outed them and soon a squad of human police and Kletlop police showed up to her lab on one of the moons of the larger gas giants. They sacked the place and in their ensuing battle, Elena and her granddaughter were arrested. Her lab was burnt down, and they are now prisoners. Sophie's Kletlop husband was killed.

Elton had a look of amazement and awe. He thought about it for a second and only asked, "wait. The news didn't talk about this at all. Are you making this up? How did you end up with the baby?"

"I wish I was," Sonya sighed. "Elena sent me an encrypted message, along with Vera and John. However, I was the only one who happened to be in her own transport at the time. I acted quickly and instantly showed up in her lab. John and I perfected the sensors and calibration procedure for our ships' MEs and now..."

"Now, you can basically transport yourself between both systems no matter the coordinates..." Elton finished her sentence for her.

"As long as there are HPs present." Sonya noted. They all knew John mastered piloting and it was reasonable to assume that he had taught his wife when they were still together.

"Motherfuckers... you can basically teleport yourself now, can't you?" Elton whispered.

"Honey, weren't you working on that?" Alexa said.

"Yeah, and I got it to work. John must have perfected it and made it more efficient. That's his specialty. He makes everything better... everything except our situation..." Elton buried his face in his hands with elbows resting on his knees. "All he needed to do was figure out a way to minimize the bubble of disturbance when jumping..."

"Yeah, he did as you suggested... he used two other, smaller MEs to triangulate the ship's location and focus the computers in 3.5 Ds, which keeps the disturbance bubble at bay. Last time I checked we got it down to 2.3 mm outwards of the ship." As Sonya said this Elton shook his head.

"Anyway, so how come Elena and the rest of them aren't with you?" Alexa asked.

"As soon as I got there, I opened up the ship and Elena screamed that they had already gotten there. She was talking about the police. She gave me the baby and was going to jump in but they shot her and she fell to the floor outside my ship. She was arrested and I got the hell out of there. The door closed automatically, and I zapped my way over to Neptune, Saturn, and even close to this host star before I came over here. I tried to throw them off my trail. Hopefully their wake sensors can't find..."

"Wait, you tried? How do you know Elena is still alive?" Elton asked, without looking up at her.

"I am still reading her vitals on my lens." Sonya answered simply. "If they were on to me, they would have already been here by now."

"Wait. There is one thing that still doesn't make sense..." Elton said quietly. Sonya and Alexa stared at him. "If Elena really made a deal with the King then why did he send troops there as well?"

Sonya sighed, "One, it wasn't his call. He purposely set

up this independent task force during the last agreement. As you know this so called independent task force is mostly managed by humans. That's why he didn't want to create it; until he was permitted to increase his King's guard and have his own guards be powerful enough to stop that task force in the event of a coup de etat. Two, even if he could stop it, he wouldn't. Elena knew the risks going in. Nobody in either government could be seen interfering. It would seem like they had something to do with it, from the beginning."

"Dumb bitch..." Elton whispered, again.

Alexa took a sip from her coffee, and cleared her throat. "So why did you decide to drop in like this? The situation is very delicate. You know what the King is going to do. To keep peace, keep the protests at bay and keep having access to MEs, he will have to kill the baby." Alexa shook her head. "I bet other people have discovered mixed babies and decided to kill them and claimed they were stillborns. No way they would show pictures of a murdered baby to the public. This way they stop the inter-breeding and it seems like they are right all along..." Alexa sighed again, "this is completely fucked."

Sonya started crying lightly, ignoring Alexa's conclusions, "I know... but I just thought since Alexa is OK with this... I've thought about how you'd react since I first learned about this over a month ago."

"Whoa! What? What makes YOU think I would be OK with this? Are you fucking retarded like those EFN turds back on Earth or the so-called humanists?" Alexa's screams got a light cry from the baby but it soon fell asleep again as she stood up a little and distanced herself a couple of steps from Sonya's words.

Sonya, on the other hand, started crying more heavily. Elton gave a look of confusion with disgust to Alexa and shook his head. "OK. Sonya... what has Alexa done or said, in your mind, that would make you think she'd be OK with this?" He asked firmly but calmly. His irritated tone still broke through. He tried to recall an instance over the last several years where she would be interviewed by both species and she never indicated this would be ok. She always strived for normal relations between planets and spoke about peace and lively debates. But never this. She, like any other human, would always speak in a pro-democracy way but never actually criticized the King or their monarchy. That was seen as a violation of the treaty. Live and let live. Some of the more powerful CEOs and politicians back on Earth craved full dominance over people and they liked everybody falling in line like that, including Alexa and the rest of them.

"Alexa!" Sonya screamed. The baby gave a light shake with a yelp. "Don't you remember the very first speech you gave after the first battle?"

The screen quickly reminded her of her little speech. At the end she did say she wanted to call the Kletlops family.

"That was metaphorical. Not literal." Elton corrected with a nod of approval from Alexa.

"Well... obviously some humans and Kletlops took it literally," Sonya said. "Or at least... it became literal lately." She looked like she was in her late 50s. The younger the person was when they got the nano-bots the longer they lived and the younger they stayed looking. But the stress of knowing this immense secret took its toll; even if it was just for 45 days. The only limitation to the treatment was that the person had at least hit puberty completely. This means the person had to be at least 21 years old to get it. Despite extending a young quality of life, most women still hit menopause by their late 50s, ensuring this was not Sonya's baby. Elton thought about this and tried to piece it together. He didn't want to miss anything that could have happened.

They sat there in silence for a couple of seconds when one of the guards came on the screen and informed them that the house was completely surrounded and they had two hours to surrender. They glanced over at the screens and sensors' feedback and suddenly saw a swarm of cops surrounding them. They had hacked their system like Sonya had an hour before. The ME was dead.

CHAPTER 47: THE FIRST PRESIDENT

Alexa watched Sonya pacing back and forth, holding the baby. To her surprise it wasn't an arrest, trial, and execution. They were merely detained while the powers that be try and work something out. Elton was sleeping on his cot when Alexa took a sip of the mediocre coffee and pastries that were supplied as breakfast.

The King approached the jail cell with his guards. The noise shook Elton to life. His golden glasses and green hat glowed and reflected the lights. His bright pink skin also glowed from sweat due to the heat and the stress he was under. He looked significantly older than the last time they had met with him.

The king whispered to Sonya, "My child, what a beautiful and hated creation you have made." The King gently touched the baby's head through the jail door. "What ropes you have used to bind my hands with..." He shed a tear as they all realized what was going to happen. He motioned at the guards, and they approached the jail cell and the door slid open. Sonya backed away from them, behind Alexa and Elton.

"You can't. You won't. How can you?" was all she could say with a catch in her throat.

"I'm sorry." The king said, next to the guard who was taking the baby from her hands.

"I can't believe you would do this do a defenseless child." Alexa muttered with hatred in her eyes.

"It was Elena who sealed the fate of this baby the moment she considered helping conceive it." He answered.

It had already been a couple of days since their arrest back in their home. This was enough time for the word to get out. Massive protests on all four planets erupted. Some were in favor of keeping the baby alive while others called to study it. Others wanted to kill the baby and others still, wanted to kill the baby and the rest of the original crew of the Cheddar. All protests were intense. Plenty of them became violent to the point neither side wanted to back down nor escalate.

The protests outside were getting louder and Alexa knew Elton was having another flashback to when the mob made him run for his life into his apartment building, again. She also remembered when her building's lockdown gates were opened. Her left knee trembled. Most of the local protestors supported interbreeding with humans. But the King's hands were tied. He needed access to human technology and without it they would surely lose Beta to humans forever. He had to comply with human law, over Kletlop law. He couldn't help it, even if he was the supreme leader.

Lucky for him, his team of one scientist and one engineer were not caught and Elena nor anybody else that knew about their arrangement said anything. That was the deal. If either side was caught, they would take the complete blame. Admitting to the deceit would surely start a war. But conflict seemed inevitable now.

One of the King's guards cleared his throat and approached his leader with caution, stepping closer to the jail cell. He showed them all a hologram of a nearby street. Counter protesters were now seen marching down the streets of the capital city. Alexa got the feeling humans had started this protest one way or another.

With a single motion the guard took the baby from Sonya and slapped her as she wouldn't let go. Elton moved forward but Alexa stopped him. There was nothing they could do. She had a flashback to when the mob stormed her building after the terrifying acceptance that they had opened the locked down federal building. More guards entered the jail cell and made a wall between them and the other guard with the baby. As they made their way out of the jail cell with the baby, a loud explosion shook the building and blasted a hole in the wall down the hallway and closer to the offices.

Tlukip entered through the giant smoking hole in the wall with guards. From the looks of it, they were wearing a more traditional set of clothing. He had a shiny weapon that resembled a gun with a pointy end and aimed it at the King. The revolution had started.

"King Abkatlacat Tlaculipoxtli Abkatlacut, you are hereby under arrest." Tlukip said with a firm voice and mean eyes. "Hand that baby over and we will spare your life."

"Have you gone mad? I am the state!" The King said, standing firm and without fear in his eyes. His guards pointed their weapons at Tlukip and they suddenly were disintegrated, leaving only the King with the other guard and baby.

"Not anymore and don't make me ask again." Tlukip said, firmly raising his weapon and meeting the King's gaze.

"Under whose authority?" the king demanded, irritated.

"The Kletlop's authority invested in me as sole protector and First President of Tlaculipoxtli." He answered. As he said the last four words he looked at Alexa and smiled and let go of a belly laugh. He had said the words 'First President' in plain English.

The King, Alexa, Sonya, and Elton were all handcuffed. Once the guard holding the baby was relieved of the baby, he was shot in the head with a pulse gun and pink and grayish Kletlopian brain splattered onto Elton's face. Elton threw up once more.

They were escorted to a traditional looking vehicle. As they passed through other empty cells, they noticed that Tlukip's guards were in several parts of the police station. None of the original police force remained there. They made their way through the garden and onto the street to the car. It resembled a chariot with two neutered werewolves pulling it. The seats were lined with traditional colors of Kletlop: pink, white, and green. The seats were comfortable enough, but humans looked like babies in a large car seat. The seats automatically shrunk to their size while the rest stayed the same.

Tlukip, along with two of his guards sat across from the humans and the King. In between them was a console with several screens, showing images of Tlukips guards entering the King's palaces all over the planet and slaughtering the royal guard easily.

The beautiful granite flooring of his palaces that were lined with different metals and other expensive jewels were soaked in bright orange Kletlopian blood. In the distance they heard explosions which were timed perfectly to what one of the screens showed. They had hit the fort next to the pier and had started sacking it.

As the trip came to a close, near the front plaza with Alexa's garden, they started seeing smoke in the distance in several locations. The screaming had died down and the royal naval vessels were seen on fire in another screen and were sinking.

In another screen, they saw a Kletlop revolutionary soldier inside a huge electrical room, which controlled communications, power, and satellites inside a ship.

"Why are you doing this?" The King asked, firmly and without fear. Elton saw his giant arms tense up. The King was easily 10 feet tall, and he wondered how they could get so big and strong with stronger gravity. Maybe their bones adapted. He and Alexa had adapted to it well, but still tired easily. It was a combination of their age and stronger gravity. The Kletlop home planet's gravity is 1.15G.

"You have ruled as a weak King for most of your reign. You lost the battle to these creatures," Tlukip looked at Elton and the two women in disgust. "Now, you have capitulated and were about to kill a defenseless child. She will be a symbol of the revolution. She will be proof that humans and Kletlop can live together in harmony. and if the humans won't accept this new worlds order then we will just have to make them." As Tlukip said this he tapped one of the screens and now all of them displayed the same image.

It showed the control center of a human ship that has an ME and a Quick. Elton recognized as one of the recent models that were bigger and meant to transport up to 300 Kletlops. There are only 4 humans on board. It showed several of the Kletlops, being led by a human, forcing their way into the control center and slaughtering the other three human crewmembers.

"You monster," Alexa muttered. "But you won't ever get away with this. One ship is not enough." As she said this Tlukip tapped the console again and showed several other ships going through the same thing. It was a coordinated attack on approximately 32 ships. 32 ships could do some damage.

"My scientists assure me they will backwards engineer this technology in a short period of time. The rest of them will be used to wreak havoc in your solar system and on the continent you infested on New Tlaculipoxtli."

Tlukip had been planning his revolution since even before humans showed up. Like a weak Bond villain, he told them the story leading up to that day.

"I suppose I should thank these humans... after all, I wanted to become King but President sounds so much nicer. I will make my people see that Democracy had propelled humans into a true space-faring civilization and it will do the same for us, with my guidance."

Alexa could sense the fear stemming from Elton. It's exactly like she felt on Earth when they were taken hostage. 'At least this time, we may die together,' Alexa thought.

"I have the means and the will power to lead this change. You humans," Tlukip looked down his nose to Alexa. "Show up, and then all of the sudden my business is worth nothing. My business is a beggar in front of the building belonging to the richest company."

"So, you want money? Is that it?" Elton scoffed.

"Money is only the means to an end. I want you off New Tlaculipoxtli and out of my home system... by force, if necessary." Tlukip's face showed a hint of nervousness.

"What about Beta Star?" Sonya asked.

"On her... well... it may be hard to believe, but we are aligned. No harm will come to Beta Star," Tlukip agreeing with Sonya made her face visibly irritated. They had unwittingly made a deal with the devil.

Several seconds later Elton approached Tlukip, "it's reverse engineering, dumbass. Also, that's not how Presidents obtain power." Elton corrected his English. One of the guards hit him in the face with his gun and Alexa screamed as she saw him pass out.

The King, along with his human cell mates were all placed under house arrest. Committing regicide was not an option on Tlaculipoxtli. Much in the same way Louis the 16 was treated by the French revolutionaries early in the revolution, the King would also be kept alive and forced to sign over power to Tlukip and a small representative party elected by the wealthy and oldest of Kletlops.

Every day for the first 30 days of being held captive, a pair of guards from the revolutionary army would barge into their home, make the King sign on a tablet, slap, punch or kick the King and storm out. On their way out they would usually break a piece of decoration or furniture. A couple of times they would urinate and throw salt on the garden where Earth fruit grew.

For the most part, all of the prisoners were free to move around the house. The Quick room's entrance was hidden behind a wall of a special type of smart material which made the guards' scanners scan a normal wall with a small utility closet on the other side. The guards didn't bother to investigate further and merely waited outside for instructions. Occupying Alexa's home is also not a popular option. Despite her being a human, she has still been accepted as one of the Kletlops' own. Everyone from The Cheddar and The Black Hole were seen as a Kletlop and had certain privileges other humans lacked.

During the next several months, under house arrest the King and humans shared stories about when they were younger. The guards' daily ritual eventually turned into a weekly one.

In days after the public treaty signing Lopez, her bosses, and the King had a closed-door meeting. Fearing unrest was inevitable, humans gave the King a Quick for himself and one to place elsewhere for his own use. More Quicks were sprinkled throughout the Kletlop system. Humans insisted on having Quicks wherever high-profile humans were stationed. This included the Cheddar and Black Hole's crews.

Alexa, Elton, Sonya, and the King would take turns in the Quick to communicate with Earth and if they chose, anybody else who had a quick. They merely had to setup the quantum computers to send the signals properly. The first iteration of the Quick was a large appliance the size of a small car. As time passed, the engineers on the station found a way to merely send the data through the higher dimensions, which greatly reduced its size. Now, it was the size of a large gaming PC from the 2050s. It even had lights and fans.

For the most part, they only received messages. The news coverage of their situation proved they were OK and didn't want to possibly endanger themselves by revealing more information than necessary. The Kletlops had access to this technology and may have learned how to pin point the locations of all the other Quicks. They intentionally limited themselves to yes or no messages. Sometimes they would send several words at once. This was rare and only to give peace of mind to the human generals about their situation and about the situation immediately surrounding them.

Humans were dragged into space conflicts for the next couple of years. And Tlukip kept his promise: they would be kept prisoners until the war ended.

Kletlop pilots only bombed stations in the outer parts of Sol. Those stations were not defended as well as others inside the asteroid belt were. Humans replied in kind and easily destroyed dozens and dozens of space stations in the Kletlop system. They had not yet duplicated the ME and were merely using the ones they had stolen from humans.

Earth's space force was able to sniff out and destroy half of the MEs in the first year of conflicts. Neither side was stupid enough to try a full frontal assault on each other's home planet. This would invite retaliation from the other side. In effect, this war played out much like the cold war. Spies and small groups of soldiers on both sides sabotaged and destroyed far away installations from Earth and Tlaculipoxtli. All the while Alexa and her husband could only sit and watch with the others.

CHAPTER 48: AN INCONVENIENT TRUTH

John Brolin's time during the first 4.5 years of the civil war ticked by. Sometimes it was peaceful, other times, it was intense and other times he feared for his life. The Epoch Eagle (his smuggling ship) was getting ready to transport the last batch of Kletlop refugees out of central California. Riots in the streets were getting worse for the visiting species. Humans back on Tlaculipoxtli and Beta's larger continent were also having a rough time lately. The conflicts were at the cusp of all-out war.

He looked over at his sidekick, one of Mahina's surfing students who won third place in several tournaments. He looked more nervous than usual. But he knew what he had volunteered for: helping his species and making money.

John never asked any of his employees to risk their lives, property, or freedom. He decided early on that he would be the one doing all the smuggling... for a fee. He looked at his clock and noticed that the sun would be coming over the eastern hills in the Mojave Desert fairly soon. He had to leave before the sunrise or else risk being spotted.

His sensors indicated that the drones both on the floor and in the sky were being prepped to go out on scouting trips, just as the other set of drones were heading back to base for maintenance.

"They are still coming in. Maybe we should wait another 12 hours..." his assistant, Tricvu suggested in English.

"No. We have to go now. The longer we stay in one spot the more of a chance they will spot us..." John whispered, looking back at some monitors indicating Kletlops were not hurrying at all. "Fuck it. Close the doors!"

Tricvu, nodded and started the procedure. The loudspeaker announced the shutting of the doors and the last of the Kletlops ran inside.

The doors closed and John took off, instantly disappearing to a Lagrange point in between the Earth and the Moon. He stayed there, as was his custom, for exactly 350 minutes. Enough time to let his engine's signature fade into oblivion.

During the dissipation period he always walked around and tried to comfort the Kletlops. It was hard to do when they were all easily 3 feet taller. He sometimes gave them anti-space sickness medicine. Sometimes he took some himself. The instant teleporting from one spot to another never sat well with him, especially when it was 4 times in rapid succession.

The news started playing in different sections of the cargo bay. They were used to these types of reports. They showed Alexa and the rest inside her home through windows. Sometimes they would wave and other times they even opened the door and let everybody see that they were ok. Other reports focused on his former crewmates and some even went back to Henry and tried to blame him for this. He shook his head at the unfair treatment of his dead colleague. They never got along as friends but he still respected the man as a scientist.

The timer went off in his ear. Since no other ship appeared near his he was cleared. He let go a sigh of relief and made his way back to the command area where Tricvu waved him over.

"John, looks like we got stowaways. Only fifty-six Kletlops paid the full fare. and there are sixty-two on board, not including us."

John sighed at the lack of payment, and it was becoming a bigger problem now. The rate of non-payment had increased from 2% when the conflict started to now nearing 10%. Kletlops and humans were both getting desperate. He turned back to his own private quarters and put on his exoskeleton, making him 6 times stronger.

He approached his cargo bay door controls and spoke and let his ship project his voice into the cargo bay, "It appears we have six Kletlops who have not paid the fee. You know what happens to those who don't pay or those who try to support them." He paused for a minute. Usually that was enough to shake the coins out of their pockets. The smuggling fee was set firm at $250K per Kletlop adult and $100K for Kletlops under 40 years old. He saw his bank account grow by only $1.2M. Some were holding back, he thought. "I know none of you are under 40 years old. Come on. Don't make me get the airlock." His account ticked up a little higher to $1.45M. He was only short $50K but he had to make an example of that person that was trying to short change him. "In ten seconds, if all of my money is not given to me, I will pick one of you at random and throw them out the airlock, unless that person... er... Kletlop comes forward."

Eight seconds passed and he got a call from Tlukip as he rolled his eyes. He made his way back to his room.

The money was electronically transferred to one of his shell companies via different routes and different companies. It had to swap hands several times to make the income seem legit, making it smaller with every exchange. Digital money laundering. For the most part, nobody really paid attention to the questionable jobs he took on because of his status as one of the original crewmembers of The Cheddar. However, John was all about minimizing risk and preferred not to take unnecessary chances.

"How much do you need this time?" He answered at Tlukip.

"Not much, I just need $150M to hire human engineers to help with..."

"How many times have I told you? You can promise human engineers all the money in the world but they won't help you.

Even if they could..."

"You know how it is... It's all business. These guys are different. No loyalty..."

"Dude, it doesn't matter. Shit, even I don't really understand how the ME actually works. I just know how to troubleshoot it and tweak it here and there. Even today, there's only a handful of engineers and scientists that can build an ME from scratch. Trust me, after you pulled that dumbass stunt on Callisto last year they brought back all of the valuable people. I know because they tasked me with bringing them back." John rolled his eyes again. Tlukip owed him a total of $6.7 Billion. Every now and then Tlukip would scam one of his own kind and pay John back, but he was still in serious debt.

"Come on, man. I need this. We're close. I can feel it." Tlukip was heard in his ear.

"Tell you what... I will loan you $50 million and that's it. I need to start seeing regular payments. After a couple of months you need to start showing results. My banks are also casting doubt on your ability to make anything happen. If we ever suspect that you try to pull anything even close to what you did on Callisto, we pull our funding and go after you." John sneered.

Tlukip, after successfully extorting smaller Earth governments, was running out of money. He initially had some success raiding outposts and claiming booty like a pirate but that didn't pay well enough to cover his loans from John and his banks. John purposely put in the contract that he would only accept human money, which now was contraband for all Kletlops. Tlukip could easily use one of the remaining 7 MEs he stole from humans to seek out and find an asteroid full of rich resources. But they all had a tracker and a unique signature in its exhaust, magnetic field, and comms devices. So, he could only use them in short bursts. Humans quickly sniffed out most of the MEs within six months of his initial takeover, which hindered his progress and limited his options in using them. The only way he could undo that was to make one from scratch, which was expensive and time consuming. It was further complicated by Tlukip and his followers being chased down everywhere they went. Human spies were everywhere and almost a third of the Kletlop population didn't approve of him having the King as a prisoner along with Beta Star and Alexa. The humanists wanted all the mixed babies dead. Lamentably, Earth governments had to agree but for the time being they didn't want to risk the lives of three of the Cheddars. Killing a mixed baby was one thing. Killing the baby and three Cheddars was political suicide. To top it off, eliminating the King would highlight a void with the Kletlops and for the time being the only one trying to fill this void was an unacceptable choice.

He shook his head and transferred the money over to him. He saw the rest of the refugee money come in and went back to the intercom. "See? Was that so hard?" He observed some of the Kletlops crying in a corner. "Hey! No crying in my ship!" He giggled and went back to meet with Tricvu in the command center.

"Are we ready to go?" he sat down.

"Yes. We can go to Neptune or halfway in between here and the RHSSO." Tricvu answered.

"Neptune. I don't trust this particular batch one bit." Traffic increased 20-fold between Earth and the RHSSO since contact was made.

"It's weird... they know the price... and they know the consequences..."

John shrugged his shoulders, "I always think that Kletlop spies are in my ship. It seems like they were just stalling to see if they could track where we are... or send a signal..."

"Don't worry, I made sure to patch up the blocking software in the ship before we landed in the Mojave."

"The new patch you said you needed more time to get ready?"

"Yes. I connected to the supercomputer back home to run the q-bits analysis..."

"Did you..."

"Encrypted with 1024 Q-bits instead of 512..."

"Excellent," John let go of an authentic smile and patted Tricvu on his bright pink shoulder.

John put his gloved hands onto the control sphere and they made the jump and instantly appeared over the north pole of Neptune. He glanced over at Tricvu who was looking at his screens and had his own hands on his own sphere. Tricvu nodded and launched chemical rockets to stabilize. This would take another several minutes.

John stretched his arms and looked at his screen, showing Neptune in all its glory. He saw lighting strike in the clouds and shivered. He never got used to seeing that giant blue planet surrounded by black and barely visible rings. "I'm gonna go check up on the ex. Go ahead and jump us when the countdown is over. This place gives me the creeps." Tricvu nodded and manipulated his screen a bit.

John walked into his room again and fired up his Quick. Every now and then he liked to check up on Sonya and the rest. The King answered this time.

"How is it going?"

"Just another day in paradise," the King responded.

John nodded, "How are..."

"We're all fine. Bored. But fine. You know... we're actually considering accepting your help."

"I can be there within five hours," John eagerly responded. In order to get a return on investment he needed Tlukip to be successful. His human side, however, naturally wanted him to fail. Relations with the King were on thin ice but relations with Tlukip would be over boiling water. If Tlukip was somehow successful he could turn against him and get him in trouble with his own species. He'd be branded a traitor and a coward. He already had a backup plan if that happened but preferred not to live in isolation far away from both home worlds.

The King waved him off and shook his head. "We were thinking about it is all. All hell can break lose if we escape.

What if we get caught?" The King obviously didn't know John was behind the refugee transportation business.

"If anything changes you…"

The King nodded and waved him off again, "Don't worry. I'll tell her you said hi."

"Thank you." John said and saw his Quick turn off. The King's image disappeared. This always made him feel better. He took a nap and when he awoke, he felt the jump take place and lost his balance a bit. He looked outside and saw they were on one of Tlaculipoxtli's moons.

For the last couple of years John would smuggle Kletlops off Earth and onto a random and uninhabited station controlled by their own species. It was a simple routine. First, he would set up three routes from where he does his pickup to where we would do his drop off. Lately, however, he would need to have two separate drop-off locations ready just in case one was compromised or unexpected maintenance was needed. He disabled the tracking beacons easy enough on his own personal ships, but deep space scans were always on the lookout. Then he would send a pair of his smaller, automated ships to three points in each route. This enabled him to observe news and other chatter on the comms channels to see if anybody was on his tail. As of late, Earth governments had learned a way to detect ship wake signatures. This tech was in its primitive stage, unreliable required finely tuned expensive instrumentation looking for specific signals. For now, those sensors were easily fooled. The third point was always near its drop off location for easy and quick surveillance. If the site was compromised, he would backtrack a couple of shots and deviate to the other route.

Drop off was simple enough: intercept/block/alter comms channels coming to and from the station just long enough to get everybody off the ship, ensure they are able to get into the station using the universal emergency protocols and leave. It was just like dropping off a newborn baby at a fire station back on earth. Except in this case the baby could knock on the door and go in on their own.

Everything went off like clockwork and soon his passengers disembarked and he left with his sidekick and reappeared near a small asteroid cluster in the outer reaches of the Kletlop system. He started feeling a bit nauseated and took this opportunity to get some water and take some motion-sickness medication. The needle penetrated him and a couple of seconds later he felt better. He quickly planned his next pickup location near Machu Pichu.

He sat on his bed and made a gesture, which prompted his ship to turn his room's ceiling into a glass-like material, permitting him to see the endless landscape of stars. He laid down to get a better view and made out one of his three ships which helped him get to that precise location. He smiled and observed the stars and briefly remembered his time back on The Cheddar during their Christmas break and how nervous and excited they all were. The same feelings rushed into him but for entirely different reasons. He also felt a hint of disappointment and regret as he realized he was all alone both literally and figuratively. 'At least I am making lots of money...' he smiled. '... and helping Kletlops.' He tried to convince himself that he was doing the right thing. 'If I didn't do it, someone else would,' he thought. Others did provide smuggling. Half-assed.

He hadn't heard of any humans smuggling in a while. The last idiot to be arrested did so almost eight months back. There are still tons of Kletlops back on Earth, Mars and at the RHSSO. To get out the legal and right way took a long time. Even for those who could live for over a thousand years. With every passing day back amongst so many humans, their life expectancy dwindled. Some were killed while others chose suicide. It was a nasty sight whenever the news reported it. He shook the image out of his head.

He got up and walked around his ship to inspect it. He never fully trusted automated sensors and robots. He preferred to manually control what he could. This stemmed from his days coordinating and fixing ships during the great migration from Earth to the RHSSO. Immediately outside of his bedroom was the control room. It was a large room with two stations with chairs, displays and control balls along with the special gloves and special socks required to make fine-tuned movements quickly.

Mind control never really took off as humans had too many thoughts racing and it confused the A.I. Now, most pilots preferred tactile controls from their feet and hands. On the other side of the control room, Tricvu's much smaller quarters were present. He had his own room and bathroom in there. The other two walls of the control room lead to short corridors. One leads deeper into the ship with the engine room, and maintenance room. The other corridor leads to several rooms meant for storage that had been converted to lobby-like areas to transport Kletlops. The corridor continued to a large storage area, which was also adapted for John's current needs. Beneath that large area the engines and fuel tanks laid. This portion of the ship was not protected as well as his private quarters, which housed a lone escape pod with a fully functioning Quick and ME. If this was ever jettisoned the rest of the ship would self-destruct 0.5 seconds after he jumped.

The entire walk lasted almost half an hour. He walked slow and steady but the ship was quite large. He knew other smugglers packed the Kletlops like sardines similar to what narcos did in the 20th century to unsuspecting undocumented Mexican immigrants. It was not uncommon to have some of those smuggled die in transit. That area was large and clean-looking. The walls had smart materials, which made benches, chairs and tables when prompted. The vertices were solid now. When the ship sensed many people or Kletlops they would open at strategic areas to circulate air. Permanent vents were long gone, replaced by smart materials that morphed to the specific needs of the ship and its inhabitants. Wires were also a thing of the past. Either things communicated wirelessly and were powered wirelessly or the smart materials inside the walls, hull, ceilings, and floor morphed and changed properties to provide a pathway for current/ signals and small magnetic fields and even sound waves. This happened in the background and rarely required human intervention. When ships were docked, most would be replenished with fresh smart materials. On average, one could expect a ship to go through its original cache of smart walls and floors every 20 years or so. If ships were required or expected to be away from docks or stations for an extended period of time then they would be equipped with reinforced walls with pipes, fiber optics and smart relays with tiny plutonium rods and even old school copper wire.

He made his way back through the corridor, which resembled the same aesthetic as the large transport area. It looked clean, smooth, and white. The floor had simple tanned squares as a pattern where the material was softer when it only detected feet. When it detected wheels, it would harden. The walls were plain and the doors to other rooms were in a small indentation, clearly being marked. But the doors weren't really doors, they just looked like it to know where people should walk through. The materials would simply dematerialize to let people through. This was useful as somebody on the other side of the wall would know not to create blockages in that area. It was a carryover from ancient predetermined emergency exit routes. However, it was useful as humans easily panicked and continuously changing exit routes created problems early on and so were quickly abandoned in ship design.

He saw the empty storage area and as he made his way to pick up some trash left behind by some of his customers he was alerted to a call on his Quick. He notified the ship that he would walk back immediately and to tell the caller not to hang up. On his way back to his private quarters, Tricvu made eye contact and he replied with a gesture indicating to give him a minute more.

Vera Ivanov could be seen on his screen. She had not aged

much. Some white hairs could be seen but they were few and far between. She was wearing one of those new suits that was trendy for modern Earth politicians. Shiny, gray, 4 super thin ties.

"Hi, Vera. Haven't heard from you in a long time." John said, sarcastically. After his split with Sonya, they became closer and he decided to bank the last couple of campaigns, since her views aligned with his – Ignore Henry's warning and keep people happy by letting them do what they wanted.

"Hey, John." She smiled.

"How's Belmira?

"Oh, she is fine. She is still getting over her grandfather's death. But she's working through it."

"Glad to hear that. Did she get the book I recommended?"

"She did. That's what's been helping since I've been so busy lately..."

"Sometimes you gotta leave people alone in their sorrow. I am sure she understands..." He gave her a gentle smile and rubbed his chin. He felt his stubble and it tickled his fingers.

"How you doing?" She asked. He knew exactly what she meant. She knew about his endeavors and worried about him. He never explicitly told her but she wasn't stupid. She put two and two together and got four.

"Business as usual." He stared straight into her eyes.

"We're trying to get all the Kletlops home but it's tough. The other five regional governments are not cooperating. They're really starting to piss me off..."

"I know. I know. Last I heard most humans didn't want Kletlops on Earth."

"Yeah. I believe we have enough support from high-ranking officials and roughly half of the people to unite under one government, but no one seems to want to step forward. I spoke with my advisors, and they are thinking that I have the best shot but this requires money. Lots of it." Her eyes showed concern.

"How much?"

"Twice as last time. I hate to ask…"

"It's alright. Either I donate it to your cause or risk your opponents taxing me up my ass…"

"Thank you. Have you heard anything from Elena or Sonya?" She asked, trying to change the subject.

"Not first hand. Just what I hear on the news." As he said this he typed an encrypted message to her, providing the funds and telling her he had recently spoken with The King. He asked if she was going to do anything about it. She texted back: What can I do? Thank you, by the way.

"I sure hope you win… this luke-warm cold war between us and the Kletlops is getting old; fast."

"I know. I know." She shook her head and looked down to the floor.

"Any luck with Tlukip?" He asked, trying to make eye contact with her.

"John, you know I can't discuss any of this with you." She didn't look up as she was typing. He received another text message on his screen: We are close. He only has 3 MEs left. We believe we can get him within two months: right before election. If I am able to capture him, we can finally end this informal, mildly annoying war and we can move forward. We have informants. A lot of those inside Tlukip's inner circle are getting fidgety and restless. They keep getting funding… we don't know from where."

Thanks to Vera's experimental A.I., her text's encryption was decades ahead of anyone's; including Lopez.

As he read this he smiled internally. 'It was all business after all.' and for the most part, Sonya, and the rest of them were pretty safe. They were all merely trophy prisoners. Victims of circumstance.

"Well, either way… I believe in my favorite politician." He winked at her and smiled.

"You ever going to come back and visit us here on Earth?"

"Nah. No need to go back. Too busy mining asteroids and running my taxi service for the Kletlops and their food. I just hope you guys don't decide to make that illegal."

"No. The Beta and Tlaculipoxtli merchant routes will keep on going. As long as we only help transfer food and medical supplies, we are good. Besides, because we..." Vera paused as he gave her an inquisitive look. "... sorry... because you control the routes, we are bleeding Tlukip's operations dry. It is just a matter of time."

He nodded and their conversation shifted to how his children were doing. Vera had given them internships a while back and were learning the ropes of the political world. One was on Mars, the other, was on Earth.

They exchanged some more small talk and soon hung up. He relaxed and started organizing his finances and swapping money in and out of shell companies. Some transfers were legal. He sent messages to his children, grandchildren, and even sent one to Alexa's Quick. No response. But the unencrypted message was delivered. No sense in wasting compute units on messages going to a Quick no one knows exists. He scanned the networks for news regarding his ex-wife. Nothing. No news is good news.

After a while he ran some diagnostics on his Quick, ME and all of his subsystems. Everything checked out. He verified his next route. He hacked into all three networks: Earth, RHSSO, and SOL. The Earth Quick Space network handled the Earth, its orbiting stations the moon and its orbiting stations. The SOL network controlled everything else in the system from Mercury to Pluto. The RHSSO controlled everything outside of that, MEs in other systems that were now forever stuck there and the human vessels in the Kletlop system.

As he was finalizing his next route and ships, he heard a bang. It shook the ship and startled him. The alarms went off and he heard Tricvu's voice in plain English, "I think we've been made!"

He dusted himself off and stood up quick, and went to his closet and started to put on his exoskeleton/spacesuit. It took him just over two minutes to do so. 'Fuck! Why did I take it off in the first place?' He asked himself. Before he could finish, he heard his A.I. in his ear, "Recommend to abandon ship. Hull has been breached. External boarding party detected."

"Fuck me!" he whispered to himself. The screens sprang to life, showing him a much smaller ship. He didn't recognize it at first. It looked like one of his ships. It attached itself to his ship, crippling his external engines and deactivated the magnetic fields. This caused his ship to lose the main engine's HPs. He wondered how HIS personal ME was doing. His A.I. detected this thought and promptly replied, "All systems nominal."

"Tricvu!"

"Yes, captain. Is a Boarding..." He heard him say in a panicky voice. He hated being called that, but this was no time to correct him.

"Come to my quarters. NOW!"

"Move it!" He screamed over the alarms and he heard his voice echo from the external speakers in the other areas. He noticed Tricvu was performing his usual walkthrough in between their missions when this all started and he was soon hauling his large pink ass back down the long corridor with orange and red lights flashing throughout. In another screen, he saw the external boarding party walk through the large storage area. At least no refugees were present. He noticed this party was made up of humans and Kletlops. The height differences were undeniable. He quickly sprung to action, having his full suit on now. He manipulated his screen, which was a backup control panel. He deactivated the E, which disabled the gravity softener. He saw the boarding party start to float upwards but soon their magnetic boots turned on and they quickly landed on their feet again. He overrode the controls and opened the airlocks behind them. The swoosh of air being evacuated took out anything and everything that was not bolted down. Everything, except the raiding party. He observed one of them manipulate his pad on this arm and the doors closed. They overrode his command. He tried to slow them down with the smart materials locking onto their feet but soon, he saw the smart floor recede. These were obviously well prepared experts. His only chance was to abandon ship.

Tricvu finally made it to their control room. But he did so as the boarding party entered it from the other door. They shot him without warning. Tricvu fell to the ground. Dead. Tricvu's blood soon pooled around his corpse, staining his jump suit. He saw as the smart floor was soon cleaning this up, instinctively.

He quickly sprang into action, manipulating controls. A couple of seconds later, as the first two of the five in the raiding party approached his private quarters, he was jettisoned. He instantly fell that inevitable and unsoothing sensation that accompanies every jump. He tightened his grip, which comforted him. He couldn't do much else and he just rode the wave. He had his eyes clenched tight but then came to the realization that he was safe and alone, near Neptune, again. His eyes opened and confirmed his position. It was off by approximately three AUs. What could be expected when both of his other triangulating ships were compromised?

'Good enough, I guess' he whispered to himself.

He had to wait several minutes for his ME to energize again and so he decided to ramp up his E as much as he could. If his ship's wake was compromised, at least he could be several hundred-thousand kilometers away, making it harder for them to find him.

He accelerated his ship; or what was left of it and he felt the comforting 0.4G. He oriented his ship so the floor would be at the tail end. Soon he let the ship take over and he started analyzing his private quarters/escape pod for any damage. It was minimal. He turned off his Quick and completely disabled his ME, not wanting any residue particles or EM waves to be present if anybody caught up near his location. For the time being he was safe in his brand new and smaller ship, emulating a ship from the 2080s.

He knew that even the most advanced trackers and detectors only had a short time table to when they were usable. Last time he checked, which was the year before, it was 98 minutes for ME wakes and 134 minutes for Quick particles. Damn. He realized that with a safety factor of 1.5, he would need to be in this state for almost three and a half hours. 'Fuck,' he murmured. He started thinking about his other triangulating ships and if they, too, were compromised. He would have to scrub his network. But with Tricvu gone, this would take him much longer. He could probably reach out to Michael and Ashley. Maybe even Mahina would help him. Sure, they were all slowly backing the other half of his old colleagues, but they would help him, right? This meant he would have to come clean. If he strategically only mentioned the Kletlop refugee part of his work, they may even welcome him in. Maybe in exchange for helping them out on their outreach campaign. Rats! That was definitely out of the question.

He figured he was getting ahead of himself. First, he had to stay vigilant and safely end up at one of his bases/ safe houses. He went to his station and determined which asteroid of his was closest that had an extra ship and a docking station. Then, he calculated his location and trajectory. At this speed, his nearest asteroid was four months away. Unacceptable. He steered his ship in that direction, for the meantime. In four hours, he could jump there. No problem.

After an hour or so, his ship detected another, smaller ship nearby. It was the size of a large satellite. It was getting closer by the minute. He couldn't tell what it was. Then, a second one appeared. As far as he and his ship could tell they were the same type of ship. Both were approximately five kilometers away from his ship and getting closer. A couple of seconds later a third one showed up. They made a triangle around him and now all were getting closer. He decided to break his own rule and quickly activate his ME. It was already preprogrammed to go into a small asteroid field where his station was. The ME was heard come alive and the console booted up instantly. The countdown started. As it reached zero, he felt that same sensation, but except this time, it was quite short. This time it was short lived. Too short. His heart sank as hi saw his console with the barely moved star map. He had only moved five thousand kilometers.

Then, a ship appeared. After his ship scanned it, he realized it was the same one that had attacked him less than an hour ago. He tried to run diagnostics again and try to see if he could escape. Everything seemed to be working fine. He tapped the screen and keyboard, not wanting to use the tactile gloves this time. Countdown ended. Nothing happened. The boarding party's ship got closer and closer until he heard three distinct clanks and six thuds. They were getting ready to board again. He sensed his hull being penetrated by the other ship. The sensors and cameras showed the invading ship a couple of meters away from his hull with a tunnel connecting both.

A minute or so later he saw and heard footsteps approaching his inner room from the outer layer of his escape pod. His escape pod was roughly the size of a tiny transport vessel, which measured around 25 by 15 by 10 meters in size. His private quarters was only the size of a large bedroom and the rest of the ship was basically a propulsion, communications and fuel system. He had three small cannons but everything happened so fast he never realized they were disabled. His intention was never to fight. Usually, when he was close to getting caught, teleporting was all that was needed.

The roof to his room was slowly opening. Grinding and hissing echoed throughout his room and the sparks made him squint and the smoke made him cover his mouth instinctively and cough. Small debris fell. At least his gravity softener/ artificial gravity was still working. Then he saw a Kletlop jump down. His height was undeniable. Then another. Then two humans dropped down. He was near a small storage compartment, taking cover. He reached for a gun but soon everything went dark. Everything except small lights on the helmets and other parts of the invading force's suits. He tried to fire but his weapon was malfunctioning. It had been hacked. His realization came too late as the two smaller bodies walked towards him, with their own weapons.

"You're under arrest," the woman said and took off her helmet. Lopez. She gave him a weird smile.

"What the fu…" he started to say. The other person took off his helmet. It was a man. He didn't recognize him.

"You know how big of a pain in my ass you've been?" Lopez demanded. He couldn't tell if she was joking or genuine.

"What?" Was all he could muster.

"For the last three years I have been arresting your employees doing your dirty work. None of them spoke though. You've got loyal ones. I'll give you that."

"What are you talking about?" John was genuinely confused. He thought about it for a minute. Then, it came to him. She must think all the other coyotes worked for him.

"Wanna play it the hard way, eh?" the man asked, lifting his gun. Lopez signaled him to put it back down.

"You two. Hack in. Tell me everything he knows." Lopez signaled at the two Kletlops to start work. They picked up a couple of suitcases that dropped down from their ship, with computers and communications devices and started setting up.

"… and turn on the lights." The man next to Lopez ordered. A couple of seconds later the lights turned on and it made John squint again. Lopez took the gun away from John and signaled him to sit down at the chairs by the table at the foot of the bed, with his back to the rear wall.

"You've been busy, John." Lopez said.

"I don't know what you're talking about," John tried to stick to his story but this time he didn't sound too convincing. He sat and saw Lopez sit across from him. Lopez's enforcer stood next to him, ready to subdue him if it came to that.

"Look, John…" Lopez started. John stared, nervously. Even if they did figure out that he was behind some of the Kletlop trafficking, there was no way they would pin it all on him.

There was absolutely no proof of that. At best, she had circumstantial evidence.

"I know you and the rest of the original Cheddars and Black Holes think you are untouchable..."

"I never..." John started but halted as Lopez raised her hand, closed her eyes and pressed her lips a bit, indicating he should keep quiet. She continued.

"I would have hoped that seeing how Alexa, Elton, and Sonya, and even The King have been treated the last couple of years would have gotten your creative little brain of yours to think about what you can do and what you can't do." She took a sip from her water and placed it on the table as his enforcer walked over to the two Kletlop techs. She tilted her head a little towards her team's direction and then she brought it back to face John. He saw the wrinkles on her neck. He never found out how old she was. The current year is 2221, he started thinking as she was interrupted by a phone call. They were taken hostage 80 years ago and he still felt like he was 45. Obviously, she was alive since the mid-2090s when her mom disappeared. At the very least she was 130 years old. Yikes. He saw her nod, say 'yes' and conclude her conversation.

"Look. It's a different world now. We are at war with the Kletlops. No matter how little this affects most humans or most Kletlops we are in a de facto war. It's not all out war but we still have some basic rules to follow. You and your empire haven't been falling in line." She took another sip as her enforcer came back with a screen, which showed her what they found.

"You've been busy. It looks like you traffic Kletlops 4-6 times a week. Good job moving around your money," she said, without looking at him. She continued to read. "Hmm..."

He let out a small snicker, which she missed. The enforcer caught it, though. He was near the techs again but stared back at John, always within earshot. He let her continue.

"It looks like you have done a very good job of isolating yourself from the others we have arrested. Doesn't matter.

This is enough circumstantial evidence to arrest you on Kletlop trafficking, aiding the enemy, illegal jumping in no jumping zones and once we get some Kletlop witnesses; I'm sure some murder charges wouldn't be farfetched." She looked at him, silently and without an expression on her face.

He let out a sigh in return. "Why are you even after me? I'm doing what you jackasses can't." He adjusted his posture by crossing his left leg over his right and leaned back a bit in his chair. His right hand tapped the table. His left hugged his foot upon his thigh.

"I know. But... we still have a problem..." Lopez drank some more water and continued. "On the one hand you are correct: you are doing what we can't. On the other hand, you are still breaking the law. On the third hand, you have lots of money and a lot of the people in charge don't want to damage such a high-profile person's reputation. But, on the fourth hand, plenty of the younger politicians don't want to make exceptions and even feel we should make an example of anybody. You can understand my conundrum."

He looked her dead in the eye while another snicker escaped his face. He glanced over at the two Kletlop techs packing up and the enforcer was now standing next to him. Still. "You could just say you never found me. That's always an option."

Lopez gave a sincere, yet condescending laugh, "You really think that is going to fly? You really think it's that simple. I got so many lenses on my ass, I should be charging for it."

He shrugged.

Lopez sighed and raised her voice, "especially after that stupid stunt Elena pulled? And Sonya with the rest of them."

"Sonya, maybe I can't defend but Elton and Alexa are victims of circumstance."

"Their point of view of not killing that mixed baby falls in line with Tlukip's, which is not irrelevant... and... after the bullshit Mahina has been doing for the last several years..."

John was genuinely startled, "What about Mahina? Last, I remember she sometimes speaks up about more collaboration but that is pretty much it…"

"You might as well here it from me. She married one of her surfing students. The one that won the championship several times. I keep forgetting his name.

"That is not even legal…" he started. "Why would she even… how would she even…?"

"Technically. Nevertheless, they've been fucking and living together for so long, they're basically a married couple.

John didn't know what to say or do. He shook his head in disapproval. "So, what do we do here?"

"I have a dispersed group of people who helped humanity achieve its goal in our darkest hour. They, and you are part of them, helped us get here. Humanity will forever be in their… in your… debt. However, you all seem to think the rules don't apply to you. My task is to find, arrest and bring you back to Earth to stand trial."

"What if I refuse to cooperate?"

"Then I'd have to kill you. Let's call that Plan B." Lopez directed her head towards him as she looked at her enforcer.

'Fuck,' John thought. "How old are you anyway?"

"One hundred ninety something. I keep losing track. I've spent a lot of time in the paralyzer to preserve myself. My mom was sent at an elderly stage because we didn't completely understand how radiation would affect people. Cancer. Old age. You know." She stood up and gestured at her enforcer. John thought for a bit. Those paralyzers are supposed to extend human life by decades if not centuries. She must have the best and the brightest to keep her going. She may witness his execution, if it came to that. Seems like she's destined to flirt with immortality.

The enforcer hacked in to John's exoskeleton and uploaded a slave program. It was a simple procedure. All he physically did was make some gestures with his hands. No wires. It started leading John, to the spot beneath the invading force's hull breach. He struggled to let the exoskeleton control him but it was no use. He either went limp or got sweaty and tired and would still end up on Lopez's ship.

The two Kletlops were already in their own ship and were observing as tentacle-looking things went down and reached for John. He looked up but could not make them out. As the tentacles reached his shoulders, he felt a jolt. The jolts weren't on his body. It was felt throughout both ships and he looked at Lopez with a surprised and irritated look on her face.

"What do you mean we detected ships?" Lopez asked, really annoyed now. She touched her earlobe, most likely to get a better signal on her coms.

The screens in John's ship lit up and showed three small ships orbiting each of the three ships that halted him in his tracks. 9 ships total. Lopez started barking orders to get John back on their ship and prepare for their jump. Her enforcer nodded and replied, "Ship is prepped. We just need to get on our ship and close the boarding tunnel."

Lopez signaled for John to be lifted. It was a slow process and with the pair of ships being a little unstable, he felt his exoskeleton hit the walls of the tunnel that connected both ships. He saw lights flashing on Lopez's ship, like what he had just gone through. The two Kletlops were at their stations. Both were operating guns now, waiting to shoot. He made it all the way through and was moved to the side so Lopez and the other could get back.

Her ship looked eerily similar to his but it was bigger and it seemed cleaner and better taken care of.

His suit directed him to a wall nearby where it latched on to the wall. He was trapped and could do nothing but watch. If he could somehow reach his left and right thigh, insert his finger into the top layer of the exoskeleton's leg he could start the emergency jettison procedure. But he really, couldn't move much.

As Lopez and the last of her crew boarded their own ship, she yelled at the two Kletlops at the guns. "Why aren't you two shooting?!" She paused for a second and then answered her own question, "Are they in 3.5?"

"Yes, ma'am" both said in unison. When we boarded John's ship his drive was deactivated and so we had to drop to normal space." One of them said in plain English, not willing to make eye contact.

"For fuck's sake…" she started.

John let out a slight giggle but soon stopped himself when Lopez shot him a stare.

Portions of the wall towards the ceiling turned into screens and started displaying a ship that seemed to be doing the exact same thing as Lopez's ship did to his a little while back. Then, another ship showed up but was approximately 2 km away from Lopez's ship. No doubt, it was providing a perimeter. That ship was different. It was a cargo ship with 12 bays that each housed two small fighting ships. They were all controlled by A.I. and were only deployed if the chances of risk were high. This was one of those times and it deployed half of its ships. The other half were set to reserve no doubt.

John was getting tired of standing for several minutes and attempted to reach for the emergency release on his suit to no avail.

More screens popped up along the perimeter of the walls. He couldn't see the ones next to him, but he was sure they all had sensors on each drone.

Once again, a boarding tunnel was attached to the hull near him and once again, a boarding party was present.

"Prepare for boarding!" the enforcer barked.

A section of their roof was seen opening. It started as a small circle and got bigger and bigger until it reached three meters in diameter. However, nothing dropped down. Instead, an alarm for depressurization was heard. The typical warning was heard in several languages, including Klentakli.

Approximately two minutes later, without a single shot being fired, John lost consciousness. He was now in dreamland. He was instantly transported to his old backyard back on Earth. He saw his Siberian husky run towards him. He relived that joy and petted him. It wasn't just a memory. He looked at his dog. It was so real. It had is tongue sticking out, panting and howled at him. It jumped onto him, paws on the shoulder and let out a shriek. As it did this, it hit him on his forehead with its large, wet and black nose.

He laughed with joy and then the dog got down, looked around him and made eye contact with something behind him. The dog calmed down instantly. John heard footsteps approach him on the concrete pathway that came from the backdoor of his old childhood house. He tried to grab his dog but it ran away and disappeared into some bushes on the rear of his backyard, in front of the 8-foot-high wooden fence. He turned around slowly, and made out every single detail he remembered. He even saw some things that he had forgotten were there. He saw the small fire pit and then saw a small barn looking shed, which housed all the rusted tools his father never used. Then, he saw his dog's house, beneath the kitchen's window. He continued to rotate and the blue house came to life for him. The white window frames were freshly painted. But he couldn't see into the house. He remembers he could always make out at least a chair or some posters or smart panels. Not this time.

His wondering was quickly interrupted by Sonya. She approached him and looked just like he remembered her from a couple of years after they got to the RHSSO. He was a little surprised to see what was happening but it quickly donned on him. He hadn't had a Multi-Conscious Evenly Entangled Teachings (MEET for short) in a long while. The process was to evenly entangle neural interactions. This means that the interaction was permanently recorded into all of its participants. However, whoever initiated the MEET could end it when they wanted to and was also expected to guide the others.

"What are you..." he started.

"Hey, John. We need to talk."

"How did you escape?" John was so confused now.

"Oh. This? Thought it'd grab your attention." Sonya said,

slowly turning into Mahina.

"What the fu..."

"Just listen, John."

He looked at her and soon they were both transported to his old office when he took on his own team back at the RHSSO. It was large and filled with a musty smell. He walked over from the entrance to the left, where a table sat with three chairs. They sat down and he could still look over the counter into the small kitchenette. To the right was a small waiting area with screens, comfortable chairs and a couple of smaller tables. Directly across the front door was a glass door that led him to his actual working area.

"Do you remember where you were when you were awake?" she asked, calmly.

"No. Not really. My old house?"

"No. Hold on. Let me adjust some settings." Mahina looked up and nodded at the sky. "Give it a sec."

John felt a jolt of energy hit his spinal cord and his head felt like it was pricked from the inside. His forehead felt heavy and he reached up to it but felt nothing but his head and ear.

It all became clear. His ship. Lopez. Two boarding parties.

"Am I dead? Did you fuckers cause brain damage?"

"What? No." Mahina responded, shaking her whole body as to say, 'why would I do that?'

"Wait. Where is Lopez and her crew? Did you kill THEM?"

"Goddammit John. Shut up. Let me explain." She shook her head and looked up again.

She took a sip from a glass of water, which miraculously appeared. Either that or he never noticed it from the beginning.

"Look. There is a civil war brewing on Earth. We didn't want it to happen. But it will. The way our A.I. sees it is quite simple. Either we will have another bloody civil war on Earth or a peaceful transition. Humans are good at wars. If that happens, the Kletlops, being led by that psychopath will invade Sol. Or, we could consolidate power in one central government on Earth, like the Kletlops have. But on Earth it will be a democracy, not a monarchy. Looking back at human, and even Kletlop history, we have noticed a pattern. Whenever a new social form tries to take hold, a big fight breaks out. Sometimes it's peaceful but most often than not it ends in a bloody war. Either way, we are living through that painful transition right now. Either humans damage each other enough to have Kletlops invade in a decade or two or we become a unified species once and for all. If the latter happens, we will be able to do what some of us want and what we all need: find another habitable planet away from the Kletlops. Live and let live."

He shot her a WTF look. "You expect me to believe this shit?" He didn't know what to believe. Over 90% of MEETs were positive. The rest were mostly illegal and performed by criminals. Real criminals. Not the type that have a meaningful and monogamous relationship with a member of another bipedal species. Maybe it wasn't so farfetched. If his experience had taught him anything; it was that you can always be surprised by anyone.

Mahina waved at him and he was forced to sit down, "there is a growing movement behind the Cheddars and Black Holes to discover a third habitable planet. It started with the Kletlop Civil War. As you know, this luke-warm cold war between Kletlops and humans was primed for escalation."

John squinted at her, not wanting to believe her, "This is bullshit. The A.I. predicted our demise iff we did not create a Quick. It predicted that once we had this tech, hope would be regained. Then, we found Beta."

Mahina shook her head, "I know that was supposed to happen, but the A.I. did not take into account Kletlops. Once the Kletlops were discovered, the A.I. had more info to go by and as time went by and events unfolded it created better, more accurate models."

"So, we are back to square one?" John said, and Mahina gave him a nod off approval.

"That is what we thought at first. The A.I. is now predicting all-out war between our species. When/if the Kletlopian civil war gets out of hand humanity will have to pick a side. We think this will take place in under a decade. Whichever side we pick, it will lead to the collapse of civilization. It's 65% certain."

"This doesn't make sense. I watched Vera on the news indicating she is closing in on Tlukip." John was confused and tried to hide his involvement.

"The problem is that there is still a 35% chance Tlukip will crack the ME and cause unspeakable damage to both sides. He's gone over the edge..."

"So, to avoid dancing with the devil the outcast angels need to be buddy-buddy again?" John scoffed.

"Something like that," Mahina nodded. "Long story short, all of us, except Elena and you have been working together. The other problem is that Lopez lost faith in us... in the Cheddars and the Black Holes. She doesn't believe we can work together anymore. Can you blame her? Elena is in prison. Sonya, Alexa, and Elton are out of commission and you are going off on your own space smuggling adventures."

"So, Vera is doing what... exactly?"

"She is quietly garnishing support in the shadows for a possible peaceful transition of power. If we can prevent civil war on our end, whatever Tlukip did may be contained but we will still need to find another planet."

John thought for a little. What did they need from him, exactly?

"We have two objectives. Stop Tlukip and unify humans on Earth, peacefully. Then, we will have another two decades or so of stability to find another planet."

"So why did Lopez come for me then?"

"Apart from the obvious illegal stuff... which honestly none of us give two shits about... she wants to publicly tarnish your reputation. With that, she could say the rest of us are guilty by association and stop our plan."

John was thinking about what they needed form him again, when Mahina started talking.

"Frankly, we need your money and your import/ export empires. But, our A.I. states you won't help willingly. As a last resort, we could stick you in isolation and claim you were lost in space..." Mahina's face showed she didn't want to do that.

He was out of options.

When he awoke, he noticed he was alone in a room, like his own ship's quarters. Smaller. One tiny restroom. No kitchen. No control panels. It didn't even have displays. It did have a small fridge feeding into the meal prep machine. As he got up from the small bed and started walking around, he noticed the indentations on the walls where one would expect doors to open, were sealed shut. He was a prisoner. 'Guess it's a deal I can't refuse,' he snickered to himself.

He sat down on a comfortable sofa chair. No smart materials. 'Comfy,' he thought. He could make out the engine noise. The new TX-3000 series. 'Nice,' he thought. But every so often he heard a click. Maybe they needed calibration. Or maybe they were modified for stealth. Either way, he couldn't really make the sound out. It got a little louder. It was not the engine. They were footsteps. From the sound of it, they were three pairs of shoes. Then he heard talking. Klentakli. His was rusty but he could definitely make out the bad words. They were yelling. The intonation of the language made it difficult to tell who was talking. When speaking it, humans had to stress their throats and so their original tamber was altered.

With more words he confirmed it was one man and one woman talking. Then, another woman was heard and another man. He couldn't make out what they were saying but as they got closer the conversation became distinguishable.

"How can you defend him?"

"I'm not. I'm just saying we don't have enough information to jump to conclusions."

"Come on. Don't let your forgotten friendship blind you. He's not the same man."

"I understand your frustration..."

"No, you fucking don't!"

There was a pause and some more murmuring that he couldn't make out. It sounded like four or five distinct people talking. The roar of their arguing erupted and it became unclear chatter to him. Then: silence. It lasted only for several seconds but it seemed like an eternity to him. His heart raced.

"He's awake. I'll just beat the confession out of him..."

The door to the outer area beyond his room began to open. A small display appeared from the wall near the edge of the two walls. Near it was the indentation for the door. It finally opened all the way and he saw a really tall Kletlop walk in. He backed up, unsure of what else to do. Mahina rushed behind him and grabbed his long and thick right arm. There was no way she could overpower him but he decided not to punch him after she pleaded.

"Let's think about this for a second..." Mahina gave John a worrisome smile.

"Enough think. We need answers..." the Kletlop said. No doubt it was her husband.

Immediately behind Mahina he saw more of his former crewmates standing. Erica, Michelle, and Michael were all there. He had forgotten when the last time so many of the Cheddars were so close together. Behind them were more people, he was sure. Kletlops were in the mix, too.

"Pantl, please... don't do this..." Mahina pleaded some more.

Pantl pulled his arm away from her, but only to prove a point. He started pacing and after a minute he relaxed and conceded. He waved over the rest of the Cheddars, indicating he wanted them to talk.

"Hey, guys... what's up?" John asked, nonchalantly. He saw Pantl give him the evil bright blue eye and then kept on giving it to him throughout the conversation. It was very awkward and terrifying for John.

"From our MEET while I was under it seems you have been busy..." John started.

"We're not the only ones that have been busy." Michelle replied. He easily looked like he was 65. He must be using the paralyzer as well. He walked slowly but with a purpose and stood next to Pantl. John nodded nervously at him and saw Michael come in. His other nod was directed at Michelle and he could see that Michelle, too, was hesitant to give him a warm greeting, regardless of how much time had passed. Erica waved at him from near the doorway, blocking his path. He could see others behind her. It was a good mix of Kletlops and Humans.

"Hi, Erica," he took a step in her direction and everybody inside his room gave him a move and a look of disapproval. He stepped back. "Where is Ashley?"

"Keeping lookout," Pantl barked.

Mahina motioned to him with her head to move towards the table. He moved towards it and sat down. She sat across from him, making sure is back was to the rear most corner of the room. Deja vu.

"John, I am going to level with you. There is enough circumstantial evidence to prove that you are the mastermind behind Kletlop smuggling." She stared and paced at him. It made him uncomfortable.

"That in itself is not so bad in the grand scheme of things. However, some of the ones who were smuggled claim that you killed some of their family members for non-payment. *That*, is really bad." Mahina took a deep breath. "... if that was not enough, you are laundering money. Sure, they are paying you but things are heating up, and all of those you smuggled used human currency which is illegal for them to use. That is the worst part. You are now aiding the enemy."

He shrugged his shoulders a bit and gave her an 'I don't care' look.

"Once our A.I. goes over all of your data, we will know everything your ship has done, and what you have done. Our A.I. is better than yours. So, why don't you just tell us all that you have been up to? It's only a matter of time."

He said nothing, having his confidence in his encryption unflinching.

Mahina stood up and they all exited his room. Several minutes later, the smell of the food prep machine got his attention. He grabbed his food and started eating. Once done, he took his dishes to the automated washing machine. He sat down on his bed and started thinking about his options. He didn't get very far as he heard, "I'm going to kill him! Lopez was right!"

The doorway dematerialized and he quickly saw Pantl towering above him. He showed Pantl his palms, "whoa!" But it was too late. Pantl grabbed him by his shoulders and he felt the sensation of weightlessness as he was flung in the air like a little a sack of cement. Except he hit the ceiling and as he started falling Pantl grabbed him again, flipped him, face up and body slammed him onto the floor. His earpiece notified him that there were now 6 hairline fractures in his rear ribs. He let out a loud grunt. He braced himself for the beating of his life. But it never came. Instead, he opened his eyes and saw another Kletlop and another man he had never seen before hold Pantl back. The human was sporting his exoskeleton.

"You piece of shit!" Pantl was heard as he was forced to calm down. Out of the corner of his eye, John saw Erica grab her head with both hands and heard her say, "this is completely fucked." She started pacing and then Michelle shook his head and said, "FUBAR."

Michael helped John get to the bed to sit down. "John, old friend. You completely fucked up. Hard." John let out another grunt and sighed as he fixed his posture on the bed. "What are you all talking about?" He gave himself a slight hug. "You need to control your husband, Mahina."

A terrified look came over Mahina's face. Michelle, Erica and Michael all stared at her in disbelief. Mahina collected herself. "How the fuck... do you know that?" She apologized to the other Cheddars with her look. John was surprised they didn't know. He smirked a bit, incorrectly thinking he had just leveled the playing field.

"We'll deal with this later, Mahina," Michelle confirmed.

"Let's deal with him, first." John could feel Michelle stare at him.

Mahina took a couple of breaths and steps and cleared her throat. "You fucked up, John. Completely." He opened his mouth to talk but her look told him to shut up. He did.

"We just scrubbed your data networks and your metadata. Motherfucker," she whispered. "You've been helping Tlukip all along?" She wiped her face with both hands.

"What are you talking about?" John said, in a frightened voice. He saw Pantl give him a 'you'll pay' look and take one step towards him. The others stopped him.

"Lopez was right." Erica said, holding back a tear. "We're all collectively fucked now."

John thought about telling them to just let him go, but their looks convinced him otherwise.

"No need to hide it anymore, John" Michelle said. "You disappoint me, old friend." Michelle closed his eyes and leaned his head back onto the wall. "But why did you do it?"

'Fuck,' John thought. He was made. He didn't know what to say.

"Did you also let Tlukip take one of your ships to build his own ME?" Michelle continued.

"What? No! I would never!" John spat back. It hurt to speak. It hurt to breathe.

"I even told him I couldn't help him with that. I just loaned him money..." He saw everybody staring at him. A crowd had gathered outside the opened doorway. Everybody on the ship now knew.

"So you wanted him to win?" Mahina muttered, "you sick fuck..."

"Well..." John started. He was unsure of how to continue. He saw Erica shake her head slightly. "It was just business."

"What?!" Michael yelled. "Killing Kletlops? Was that 'just business', too?"

"At least I helped some of them. I rescued many. Got them out! What were you all doing?" John grunted some more. He was feeling tired now. "You were on vacation, writing books, planning parties, digging up old fossils. I am the only one who helped them. I am the one who really helped them. I was the only one brave enough to get his hands dirty" John made eye contact when he spoke with the appropriate person and paused for a bit. "Yes! I made money. I helped Kletlops. Some of them had to die. It was all business. The banks back on Earth also thought it was all business. I don't see you going after them!"

"You and your stupid banks fueled this fire storm! You, and your money! You are the reason we couldn't find Tlukip!" Pantl broke himself free from the other two. Either that or they let him go. "You and your money. If it wasn't for you and your banks this war wouldn't be going on for so long. So many lives lost. On both sides! So much suffering. Our King was doing fine. But now, you and Tlukip have almost ensured all-out war will break out."

"We can't let you continue doing that." Mahina muttered. "You and the banks have been playing both sides. Jesus fucking Christ, John. Jesus fucking Christ." She crossed her arms and jumped up and down and screamed. He didn't know what else to say.

"Fuck this!" Pantl screamed and walked towards him. Pantl started punching him in the face and head. At first it hurt and then he put up his arms. As he did this, he heard others scream at Pantl to stop. Then his hands and arms hurt. and then they went numb and flopped to his sides. He felt some more punching on his head and his chest. He felt his own blood running down several spots on his head and face. and then his whole body went numb. He stopped feeling and stopped seeing. "Stop! Pantl! You're going to kill him!" Erica's voice was the last thing he heard.

CHAPTER 49: BETA STAR IS EXTINGUISHED

Sonya Sarali stood and watched over Beta Star. She had developed a fever, internal bleeding, and malignant tumors. She never learned to walk properly either and was color blind. The health pod in Alexa's and Elton's home couldn't save her. Nothing could. Her DNA was much too damaged and fragile, unique, and new. This was inevitable. She glanced over at Beta star as she struggled to breathe. She looked at the screen and saw another story about her MIA ex-husband. She wept for him, too, unsure of which one of them had a larger percentage of her suffering. Maybe it was equal.

John had been MIA for 12 days and news started reporting he was dead. Some concluded that he vanished, trying to escape, after dropping off Kletlop refugees. The media threw hero paint over his name. Some of it made sense. But she knew him well. Some of it didn't sit right with her.

For several minutes after that report ended, she was lost in thought about her ex-husband. She missed him. Money had taken over him and he changed. Sure, everybody changed. But his change was a common one. Money. Power. Corruption. Other, lesser known, news sources jumped to the idea that John maybe even helped Tlukip.

'Not entirely out of the question,' she thought. But for the most part the media covered him in a positive light. When her reminisce-induced trance was over, she looked down at Beta Star. She had stopped breathing while she was lost in thought. She gave her a sad smile and shed a tear. Nothing could be done. Nothing could be undone. The only thing now, was to move on. She caressed her cheek. It felt cold and stiff and saw one of her own tears fall onto the mattress next to Beta Star's body.

"She is gone. I will come out in a minute," she said, knowing Elton and Alexa heard her. She wanted to spend the last minutes with her. Alone. She let out a deep breath and started to cry. Gently first, and then heavier. After some time, she motioned at her A.I. to take care of Beta Star's body and walked out of the room, thinking of both eulogies.

CHAPTER 50: DOING WHAT MUST BE DONE

Michelle Thomas boarded his ship immediately after Erica. They had landed on a secluded station that replenished their supplies. They needed more time. The entire crew was still asleep. Erica needed more time. But he had to return to Earth. Vera needed him close to her. He could only tell Vera, what had transpired, in person. As he sat down, he heard his A.I. notify him that ten new ships had finished scanning their respective systems. None of them had anything to offer to humans nor Kletlops alike. The search continued. Again.

Soon after they were settled, she fell asleep, and he signed on to his Quick for an interview. Most questions were about John and Sonya. That overshadowed his books. He recited the same garbage they all agreed to. He had written it. Once he was done, he got up and rejoined Erica in their bedroom. She was still sound asleep and would be for several more days. She needed more time.

CHAPTER 51:
INCEPTION

Erica Jameson shook hands with the crowd of people and Kletlops. She thanked them for their service in bringing John Brolin to justice. Some of them smile, unwittingly. Others stare at her in a confused manner. She had never been with so many people inside a MEET before. But she had to do it. Before, she loved organizing parties. Real parties. With real guests. Now... now she despised what she had started to do. The luke-warm cold war had broken her. It broke all of them in some way. She had lost part of her humanity. They all had. Some literally. Some figuratively. She hoped it all paid off in the end. She had to do her part. Part of her thought the new A.I. was full of shit. The other part made her remember the previous iteration, before discovering Beta. It didn't matter. Either she made the new A.I. happy to have it spit out favorable information or she proved it right by letting humans destroy themselves, for the last time.

This was a different type of party. Too many of them knew the truth about John. This was the only sure-fire way to have them believe in what was favorable for humans and Kletlops alike. A new type of brainwashing and mind control. There were no chemicals. There was no physical torture. You simply walked into their minds, with a key, and shook the core of their essence until what you wanted to be dropped, fell out and what remained was what had to remain.

She kept on walking around them and kept on whispering the same crap that Michelle was spewing out in the real world.

She recited it so many times she had started to believe it, herself. Every time she finished reciting the details to each inhabitant of the MEET, she asked questions to observe their response. It was not enough for them to recite the desired answers properly. They had to do it in a believable manner. There was no 'fuck up' room, this time. In order to get the correct response, both verbal and physical, the background had to change to accommodate the correct subject. Some of them preferred a small kitchen back on earth, while others wanted a nice beach or to be inside a museum. Kletlops also had a varied menu. Some were at parks, or inside their own homes or inside their own vehicles being pulled through their hometowns by werewolves. With every change, she had to change with it. Some of the words varied in her brainwashing soliloquy, but the message stayed constant. It only varied when absolutely necessary.

Some were easy enough to convince. It only took a couple of tries. Others, however, were less subservient. She recited her story over a couple thousand times. Once she was sure they were all ready, she signaled her A.I. to wake her up.

CHAPTER 52: THE NEW BANKING WORLD ORDER

Six months after John Brolin went MIA, Vera Ivanov was able to secure enough of a following to get the six regional governments to unite behind a Central Earth Government, granting her new powers. It helped that Tlukip's ever diminishing following only had one ME left. Several scouting and raiding parties were dispatched during that time. Tlukip was kept on the run. For everybody else, John was MIA. But she knew better. She had met with Michelle and Erica. The war's end was within measurable distance. But before her followers committed to anything, they had to make sure Tlukip was under arrest or dead. Preferably dead.

Every time she thought about her taking money from John, it made her sick. If this was uncovered, it would ruin her. She had to put an end to these types of practices. But banks wouldn't relinquish their power and government-controlled banking was out of the question. There was only one, risky alternative. It proved to work on a smaller scale but now was the time, she thought, for the true test.

Vera thought about it for a second, sitting in her chair, motionless. She looked up and admired the portraits of the six regional leaders on her wall, seeking guidance or inspiration or both. They were painted on canvas. No smart materials there. Her office was huge and was adorned with flags from all of the countries she ruled over. 26 total. She got up and went around her desk and imagined people in her sofas. She always imagined people being around. This kept her unconscious ticks in check.

She paced nervously back and forth in her office. She had told all of her staffers to leave her alone for a little, unless they had something to report on Tlukip. She used this time to hear herself and meditate. But there was no time for that not now. As she imagined how she could steer the conversation to a new banking system, her thoughts were interrupted. She heard a voice in her ear. The boarding party was ready. They had found Tlukip's ship and had disabled it.

Her glasses showed her feed from two cameras in the raiding party. One was from the leader. The other was from a drone. She saw them falling into the ship through the boarding tunnel. The first couple of them were shot dead. Then they dropped in an anti-matter flash bang. The camera feed went bright white. All she could do was listen in. She heard her team yell orders to surrender and drop the weapons. Then a shot was fired. Then another. Then a barrage of bullets was heard. After a second the ship started its warning about depressurization. Then there was silence. After the longest seven seconds of her life, the feed slowly returned and she heard her squad cheer. The camera feed showed Tlukip. Dead. Ha had bled out from multiple bullet holes. The camera turned to face a couple of his crewmates. Some were dead. Others were dying. Only a couple were on the floor, surrendering and being handcuffed.

The ones arrested were immobilized and the carrier drone lifted them into their ship. The one in charge ran an RNA test on Tlukip's corpse. It was confirmed. Tlukip had died. She let out a sigh of relief and a couple of generals congratulated her in her ear piece. She took a deep breath, lit a cigarette, and held an emergency meeting with her shadow government members all over the planet. The time had come.

Several months went by. The Earth Constitution

Ratification, touring of the damaged sites and small reconstruction ceremonies took place. On October 22, 2222 she held a conference and invited many leaders of Earth banks. She walked in to her meeting. It was in her government mansion, in the outskirts of Barstow, CA. Long ago, that had been decided as the seat of the NAC. Now, it was one of the main offices to the newly formed office: Chief Chancellor of Earth.

The news of Tlukip's death traveled faster than the speed of light from Sol to its colonies to Beta and Tlaculipoxtli and its colonies. This united Kletlops and humans alike. But now, the real work began. Different representatives from Kletlop provinces and local areas which once served the King were unsure of how to proceed. Would they go with Democracy? Would they go back to a Monarchy? A constitutional monarchy? Just the debates themselves in the media were enough to trigger a civil war again. Endless war. It seemed humans were good at exporting that.

It was finally decided to leave around %10 of Tlaculipoxtli territories under The King and the rest under a Democracy. The King would have limitless power like always in his territory and only symbolic power in the rest. He would be available for council but the rest of his species could decide how to run the rest of their world and their colonies.

The King was liberated along with Alexa, Elton, and Sonya. But the humans were soon arrested for having played a role in kick starting the revolution. They were sentenced to live in exile in one of the darkest colonies back in Sol. After the fiasco with Beta Star, they were deemed 'Unforgivable.' Sure, at the beginning of the war they were seen as victims. When time passed and more lives were lost, on both sides, and they didn't kill Beta Star, they were seen as complacent or even as enablers. The media and the masses slowly but surely turned against them.

Vera was too busy to do anything and aligning herself with her former crewmates could have spelled disaster for her master plan. She had bigger fish to fry.

Vera had to come up with a way to control the banks on Earth but was advised to limit her newly found powers. The war was officially over and her emergency war powers had yet to be rescinded by the council of 25,000 humans, which were representing the rest of humanity.

Once the Kletlops had a clear path forward, Vera decided to have a meeting with her bankers. Everybody crowded around the long oval table. It sat 150 people. Most of the bankers' board of directors were telecommuting.

The first part of the meeting was private. The second part would be a public Q and A. As she made her way from the door, everybody stood and stared at her. Many gave her a cold and unwelcoming look. They seemed frightened. Why wouldn't they be? Many of them had openly bankrolled Tlukip. All of them knew about it. No one spoke.

"You may sit down." She said as she reached her chair at the head of the table. Her voice echoed throughout the chamber and she could have sworn to have seen the lights flicker a bit. Maybe it was just her imagination. She reached her chair, made a gesture to the rest of them to sit down. They did. The camera showed the rest also sit at their own meeting rooms. In total a couple dozen screens showed several feeds from all over the world.

Mahina and Pantl were heard in her ear, "We are ready. It's not too late to back out... just give us the order." She knew they had said that a minute or so before. Quad encryption non-Quick coms took a while to decrypt. She was using 2080s tech now. It was so low tech that no one would have suspected it. and it was stable. She prayed that her government A.I. would be wrong. But she knew better. That's why Mahina and Pantl were in position.

She sat down and felt her armpits sweat. The A.I. had told her this was the only choice. She had her doubts but at the end the A.I. was right. It was always right. It worked too often to be a mere coincidence. She thought about what this would entail and at previous examples of what she had in mind. Some worked. Most notable – the RHSSO showed a moneyless society function well. Of course, initially, billionaires had sacrificed themselves willingly. This was different. She wasn't getting that same 'good for everybody is good for us, too' vibe.

"Welcome. As you know, we have brought you here today to discuss the matter at hand. But before we begin, let me remind you that all of this is being recorded but not transmitted. Not yet. You are all under oath. We all are."

She cleared her throat, "The Kletlop civil war has come to a close and now they have started to rebuild, with our guidance. Our rebuild era has also begun. No direct funding is permitted from humans to Kletlops. Any human or corporation, non-profit or local government is free to assist the Kletlops for free and without promises of being paid back nor promises of anything. Furthermore, those expenses accrued will not be tax-exempt." She could see the disgust on some of their faces. Her A.I. went crazy analyzing everybody's statistics. Many had risen blood pressure, temperature, perspiration and gave off the stench of stress hormones. The A.I. deemed those as hatred. Ironically, she wasn't scared of them. They showed they were going through the motions and willing to comply. The calm ones worried her. Some were too calm. This proved that they did not care and were going to do what they wanted to regardless. The courts deemed this pre-emptive accusation illegal, but it could still be recorded and provide usable feedback nonetheless. It was a good way to predict actions, even if they were not admissible in court.

Her emergency powers were still active and she acted as a prosecutor, judge and even a jailer. She continued, "with that out of the way... we need to discuss how we will fix what has already transpired: what all of you have already done. That is to say; how will we seek justice for traitors such as yourselves? You provided money to the enemy during the time of war..." she looked around the room and saw some people shift uncomfortably. "Or... you provided money to my former crewmate who then in turn provided it to the enemy with your knowledge." The A.I. and database analysis did not show John gave her money. They cleaned it well. But it was only a matter of time before they made the connection. She had to act fast. Get them before they got her. One way or another, she would be the first and shortest serving Chief Chancellor of Earth. "Don't give me that bullshit that you didn't know." She saw a couple more people shift. Except one. One of them was looking quite indifferent. Her A.I. didn't spot him as one of the ones who would disobey. This was a different type of calm. The A.I. analyzed him. He had a thick piece of paper near his chest.

"What is your proposal?" one of the men spoke to her, fixing his ties and collar layers.

"Are you suggesting we take the loss from your former crewmate?" Another spoke

"Do you want us to forget what he did and how much money he cost us?" The speaker was heard.

"Do we not have a say? We lost money. Lots of money." Several more started speaking.

"Do you really expect us to not try to recoup our loss?"

"My board will never go for that?"

"My local government promised us the ability to make money from the Kletlops. They rebuild. It's a win-win."

"What about funding for ME transports for the Kletlops?"

"Are you going to give away that tech?"

Many more questions were heard. They deafened her.

The man with the envelope stood up and fixed his collars and ties. He cleared his throat. He was wearing three narrow ties in layers and three collars in layers as was the fashion one hundred years ago when he was younger. The suit was gray and blue with hints of red on the tips of pockets and edges. He made a gesture to calm everybody down. They all listened. Those who got up sat back down. Some smiled while others gave snickers with giddy.

"My colleagues and I have our own proposal. He reached into his breast pocket and her defense drones and secret service drew their weapons.

"Whoa..." the man said, raising his hands, exposing his palms. "Let me just get something from my pocket."

"Slowly," one of her agents said, firmly. The man with the envelope smiled and pulled out the thick pieces of paper. It was several sheets. "Here I have an agreement, in writing, which includes all of our banks." He waved it at her and one of the agents that was closest to him grabbed it and brought it to her. The drones read the first page and looked through the pages and deciphered what was written on the 8 pages in less than a second. The text displayed on the screens.

In effect the bankers agreed to the following:

- The smallest 10% of banks loaned all of its money to the next 10% tier up and so on
- The money was then used to buy the banks in the tier beneath them and so on
- The last bank standing would use that money to build a small asteroid-nation in the outskirts of the solar system, making their own, independent nation where they could loan money for any purpose.
- They were already in deals about to close the purchase of all private property that housed government buildings and were going to evict them
- Some money would be used to run for office in the remaining seats they did not control in the local governments and start undoing their progress.
- The senators that were in the NAC and the rest of the local governments and those of who made it into the Earth Central Government would be a very loud and voiced opposition.
- Interest rates on loans to humans were going to be at a very reasonable %45. While loans for Kletlops were going to have an interest rate of %67, enslaving them forever.
- The media companies they all owned and loaned money to would go on a propaganda campaign hard

set on making her life miserable, citing her close relationship with John.

• All of this was going to start in 72 hours if she persisted in her agenda of preventing them their right of exploiting humans and Kletlops alike.

• Corporate Alliance of Earth Constitution was already drafted and ready to be submitted by their pawns throughout the governments.

"I promise you," the man said, handing her the papers to her, "don't fuck with us on this. You will regret it."

"Mr. Deredith, are you threatening me?" She met his gaze.

"No. I am simply telling you what can happen. Of course. Maybe you won't see any of this happen. I hear the SCN has had some troubles lately; especially in this area."

"Oh. You should not have said that."

"Is it illegal to worry about our newly appointed Chief Chancellor? Or are you just paranoid?" He smiled so much the crews feet around his eyes grew. "Should Madame CC Vera Ivanov be paranoid?"

She paused for a bit. She let his voice be heard and the signal transmitted to Mahina and Pantl. A couple of seconds later she heard Pantl's voice, "That was exactly what our A.I. said he would say." She could hear the fear and shock in his voice.

Vera's new A.I. grew from the one Lopez had. It learned on an accelerated rate. Mohr's law dictated snails while Huang's Law dictated authentic A.I. growth. Real A.I. Not that poser shit tech companies tried to shove down people's throats during the 2020s to 2040s. Espionage was mostly useless now. No need to find out what your enemies were planning and going to do in a couple of days or weeks when everybody and everything was connected. The A.I. observed everything and analyzed anything, and gave most likely outcomes based on past events, environmental factors, probability, and more inputs from others. It could predict when a new tech would be invented, who would discover it and how to plan ahead.

It could predict large acquisitions of companies and even when a company would become defunct. If a person was well connected to the grid for the most recent half of their life, the A.I. could even predict its death. At first it would pick a decade. After more time it could tell you a year. After more time and more data it could even tell you the hour it would happen.

Now, it had predicted this corporate-capitalistic coup-de-etat. It analyzed the war, the battles, the laws that were passed and human nature and how a functioning institution would function and react to a new world order. Not only that, but it had actually spat out seven possible phrases Mr. Deredith would speak. The most recent thing Mr. Deredith had spoken was number 4 on the list. Once that phrase was spoken, the A.I., had more info to predict more. This time, it predicted Vera's death: it would happen after this meeting, whether she agreed to his terms or not. The wheels were in motion. But with this knowledge came power: power to plan ahead.

The future was never and would never be set in stone. But predicting likely outcomes is possible. She understood this. She had already planned over 500 scenarios. Each one ready to execute, depending on what Mr. Deredith would say to her. Her confidence gave her a level of deserved smugness. The A.I. had predicted that if she acted in a certain way, even after phrase 4 was spoken she would not die. But maybe her fate she accepted would be worse.

She smiled at him, "Oh, how I wish you would have chosen option 7. Option 7 could have let us be friends…"

He looked at her, perplexed. He looked side to side and saw her nod her guard over. He looked back to his second in command and nodded at him. She knew what this meant. Her A.I. had prepared her for this. He had his own private army outside his boards of directors' rooms all over the planet. But she had planned for that, too. Her intelligence officers dispatched all throughout only counted a handful of armies and a couple dozen drone squadrons. But they knew that if they took control of him and key areas, they would all fall in line.

The shortest civil war started and concluded within twenty minutes. Mahina led her team and stormed the largest gathering outside of Vera's meeting. Her drones were faster, stealthier, bigger and better coordinated. Also, she had more than the bankers. Mahina's team went in similar to the rest. Drones went in, disabled everything with micro-EMPs. After the suicide drones went in, the other drones went in and did recon. Once some of those were destroyed, other drones with non-lethal weaponry went in and took out the first wave of the private army. They were few of them. But they were well hidden, using the smart walls as cover. Then, the actual soldiers came in. Some enemies were stuck in smart walls after they were disabled. Others were locked in separate rooms due to the smart materials being disabled. Other still, had unusable guns from the suicide drones. A few were dead. Those left alive were clearly overpowered and outnumbered. A few, with exoskeletons were frozen stiff. The nano-bots-filled-clouds dispatched by the suicide drones did a fine job.

While that was happening, Vera spoke, "By the power invested in me by the people of Earth, as CC, I hereby place you under arrest for colluding to help an enemy at the expense of your own species, planning to dispose of the Chief Chancellor, murder, conspiring to defraud billions of people. We will now control your banks and your money. As you will be charged with treason, your personal accounts will be frozen and anything related to your former banks will be confiscated. I will turn your corporate possessions over to the people. All of yours." She made eye contact with each and every one of the ones near her as they were being arrested. Some were lost in disbelief. Others screamed and accused her of treason. Others noted that government takeover of banks never ends well, and she will be seen as a traitor, a dictator and will be blamed for everything that goes bad from that day forward. More guards came in, ready to escort them to squad cars that were showing up.

"I'm done."

"Me, too." Mahina and Pantl reported back. Then more reported back. It took longer to report back than it took to actually subdue the enemy. Vera had lost only three humans and two Kletlops. It was a joint effort. The bankers had lost over 35,000 of their army sprinkled throughout earth. 550,000 were taken as prisoners. Every single board member was in handcuffs. All 3,544 of them. Not that many left. Banks had been consolidated after every economic downturn and now only few remained. It made their power and wealth more concentrated. They had more power but were an easier target to hit. They were a much more manageable size. After centuries of them controlling, consolidating, and buying out other companies, so few remained. The very essence of competition and consolidation of resources, power and money were their demise. Had companies decided to stay smaller and less unequal maybe this would not have worked. But they didn't and so it did. They all thought they were gaining power, but instead they had less and less support on their side.

Vera's knees felt weak and she smiled at all of them and followed Mr. Deredith, "Don't worry. I have a plan. With the lessons learned from the Kletlops about living more in harmony and the lessons you and your financial ancestors taught us in the last 600 years or so, and what the Cheddars learned from the RHSSO, we know what to do. We know there is something better than your way. Call it corporatism or capitalism. Call it boards of directors. Call it whatever you want. Call your employees, workers or associates, or partners, or call them what they truly are to you: slaves or resources. You are, were, the master and they, we, were the slaves. All of us. But now, that is going to change. You have proven time and time again that such a small number of people can not control the financial lives of the rest of us. Now, we turn to democracy. We have had political democracy for centuries but now; now, we will have financial democracy." She paused for a bit. Her heart sank. The transformation was a politically suicidal move. But if her A.I. proved to be right once more, she could cement this change. She nodded at her agents to take them all away. They did.

CHAPTER 53: THE DEATH OF BEAUTY

Elena Ellis laid in her bed and watched as the last of the bankers were sentenced to death or life imprisonment. 'The balls on Vera. Good for her... and I thought I was brave and crazy.' She thought. The robot brought her more medication. The cold liquid made her way up her arm and it cooled her shoulder. She let out a small shiver. She laid back and saw the lonely light bulb start to swing again, due to the air coming out of the vents. The robot returned to its corner. It sat there, next to the door, like a trashcan. The other robot on the other side of the door would soon activate. It was almost dinner time. Her bed squeaked as she sat up. The brick's cold easily went through her tank top. Her standard issue gray pants were ripped and her thigh had goosebumps.

She let go of a cough and made her way to her metallic toilet. She cleaned herself and saw black liquid, in the bowl again. Her internal bleeding had been kicked up a notch. Like Beta Star, there was nothing others could, or would want to do, to save her. She was sentenced to life in prison, but without an adequate geneticist's laboratory her sentence was death; and fast approaching.

Every time she went to the restroom her insides hurt and she got dizzy from getting up too fast. She would slowly make her way back to her cot and try to relax. Sometimes she was dizzy but always in pain. The last time she was not dizzy was so long ago she had forgotten what it was like to not stumble when she walked the eight steps to the toilet/shower and back to her bed.

She had gotten blood taken out the day before and her analysis confirmed that she only had a couple of days left. She laid back down and continued to pay attention to the news. Vera, after having arrested every single banker on earth, was seen as a dictator and took every single bank that was now defunct and transformed it into a decentralized entity. She, under the disguise of keeping the economy going, declared that every single account holder was now an equal parts owner, along with every single employee and the towns where that specific bank had a considerable presence in.

She giggled at the thought, 'democracy and equality in banks.' Wish I had thought of that. She thought some more of her days back on the RHSSO. A moneyless society worked there. But only after trillions and trillions of dollars were spent. Now, after the number of people controlling banks shrank and shrank, they suddenly exploded and now people truly had democracy. The irony made her laugh. Democracy given by the one person who had the most power on Earth, ever.

Democracy was not just for people. Shortly after, people took control, they voted to fund the campaign to undo laws that prevented them from making deals with the Kletlops. After all, they reasoned, it was the previous wealthy bankers who had betrayed them. It was a clean slate.

Despite having the love of most of the people on Earth, Vera was seen as a threat and after passing her one and only constitutional amendment, resigned. But what an amendment it was. It guaranteed that no one person had more say in the decision making in banks than anybody else had. It laid the foundation for converting traditional corporate businesses to worker co-ops. Sure, they could still earn more than others could, but that was up to them to decide. Everybody had a say. Wages were no longer going to be set by the person at the top. It did not stop there. Some bank owners were smart and decided to invite Kletlops to be part of it. After all, how can Kletlops not have any say in a banking system that would make decisions that would surely affect them? Then, in turn, the Kletlops passed similar laws. Now, humans and Kletlops could intermingle, financially speaking. Mahina's and Pantl's relationship was still seen by many as unnatural. Maybe in another one hundred years that would be ok, too.

As she thought this last thought, she smiled. She brought on a horrific civil war, that cost some of her crewmates their freedoms and one of them their life... but in the end she was at peace. Content. It was not what she wanted. The treatment failed. Her great-granddaughter died and now she was nearing the same fate. She didn't even regret injecting herself with experimental chemicals and nano-bots that were attempting to bond her DNA with Kletlop DNA. It didn't matter now. She laid in bed for just another couple of minutes.

CHAPTER 54: MICHAEL'S CALLING AND THE NEW CHOSEN ONES

Michael J. Johnson awoke in the middle of night, startled and sweaty. It was the same dream that had woken him up since the beginning of the war. He was never in danger. He never felt threatened. But it scared him and shook his core. It was a new type of dream. It felt so real and every dream grew on previous dreams. It was like he was living a double life.

Consciously, he could not really recall his exact dreams. But they guided and changed him. He convinced Vera to let him see the rest of the Cheddars. There was a new instinct within him. He needed to see them. They were transferred to the dark side of the moon. That was one of the last things Vera did while in office. That was almost a month ago. She had to resign. 'Poor thing,' he thought.

He felt bad for her. After delivering all of the wealth back to the people, she was seen as a dictator that could not continue to rule. It did not matter. If the people controlled the money, they would also control the government. The ones put in charge would never again be pawns to the very few super wealthy. Now, they would be pawns to the masses, as a true democracy intended.

He rubbed his eyes, as he stood from his bed. He heard

something in his head. But it was not coming from outside. It wasn't his earpiece and it wasn't a speaker. The voice spoke through him. Was he going mad? He was only 134 years old. Without the treatments he would most likely be dead but he felt fine. There was no history of mental illness in his family. But then again, everybody in his family died by the time they were 119.

He called his psychologist and sleep expert. Everybody over 133 was assigned one. After all, being over 130 was new territory. Sure, many before him have made it that far but now, with the treatment and the expectation of living over 150, the side effects needed to be clearly examined. Now, there was a big enough sample size.

He had a quick conversation. None of the other patients were having that specific issue. Sure, some had insomnia, normal health problems and some of them even developed schizophrenia. But his psychologist was not ready to diagnose that. At least, not yet.

His ship was traveling with the normal E to the moon, from Mars. He was only an hour away now and he could, for the first time, recall his dream. It was blurry at first but he was able to recall it. He was sleeping in a bed next to two others. He remembered. There were two... no... three more beds next to him. He was at the edge. The area didn't seem like a normal bedroom though. He couldn't make it out. But it was definitely not a normal bedroom.

He shook away the thought and started to eat something. Afterwards, he walked over the dishes to the robot, wanting to stretch his legs. That is when his dream fully materialized. He laid there, next to Elton, Alexa, and Sonya. He was able to make out the walls. Cabinets, a kitchen, restroom and a sink and more storage. But the bathroom and sink weren't for them. No. He was sure. But who else would use them? Who else was there?

Then his mind went blank and he remembered Ashley. She stayed back on Mars. She wanted to come with him.

But something told him to tell her to stay back. It wasn't dangerous, or terrifying for her. He just knew she did not belong and when she asked him when he would return, he honestly could not answer. But a small part of him knew. Oh, he did know. He was never to see her again. But he wasn't going to die. Of that, he was sure.

After a while the ship started the landing procedure and he settled down again. A peaceful environment came over him. As the ship docked, he got up, out of his quarters, down the long hall and through the storage section and out of the bay door.

He was greeted by the tiny flying drone and got his retina scanned. The rest of the stationary sensors confirmed his identity and a small path made of light made its way from his ship into a door several meters away. The bay was cold and dark. The only lights present were the stars in the sky that could be seen through the transparent ceiling and a couple of bulbs sprinkled throughout the area. Towards the front he saw an army of drones ready to repair, dismantle or stock a ship.

The lit path showed him the way in a steady glow in the direction he needed to walk. He made his way into the hallway and sat on one of the small carts. It resembled those on the RHSSO but were smaller and there was no one around. He passed windows and several more bays on one side. On the other was all the machinery and supplies that kept that giant base going. The ride only lasted a couple of minutes and it stopped in front of an area that resembled a lobby like the rest the RHSSO but, again, was smaller.

He got out and waited and saw the car leave. He made his way past some displays and turned and headed towards a table in the center. There was a small area on the other side that had food in it. Restrooms were in the back. The ceiling was see through, letting all of the lights from stars shine through. It reminded him of Christmas time in The Cheddar. He let go of a worrisome smile and started to point out some constellations to himself.

He only waited for a minute and then he saw the three of

them walk through a door and stood. He approached them with a huge smile. They all gave him a much smaller smile but he could tell they were genuinely happy to see him. He also got a hint of confusion from them. He got near them and went in to hug Sonya.

"Hello, beautiful. It's been much too long. I am sorry about John and Beta Star. How are you doing?"

"Hey, Michael. Thank you. Working my way through it." She replied and gave him a light peck on his cheek. Her words were slow and soft and he saw her eyes avoid his.

He squeezed her upper arms and moved on to Alexa.

"There she is. The first Ambassador to the Kletlops. You look amazing, as well. How have you been? Have they been treating you well?"

She nodded and gave him a huge smile and a close hug. He kissed her cheek and she did the same to him. They embraced and he could feel her warmth. It soothed him.

"Elton. Have you been taking good care of these ladies?"

"The best I can. How you doin'?" he answered and shot him a smile.

"Come here, old friend! Hope your arm isn't sore anymore." Michael went in for a hug and then pulled back after several seconds. He felt Elton squeeze him and thought about everything he wanted to tell him.

They sat down and exchanged awkward pleasantries. Then, after a while they regained their confidence in one another and exchanged stories of their time apart. They told him about life with The King and he spoke about his cooperation with Vera, Mahina and Pantl. They all had many more stories to share and after a couple of hours of conversation, some robots brought them food and wine. Wine in a prison. It was more of a private habitat where they could not escape and barely communicate with the outside world.

They relived their time on the RHSSO and aboard the Cheddar. Once their bellies were full and their eyes were tired, they decided to go to their quarters. He was promised a week with them and they could talk some more throughout. They all fell asleep, and for the first time in a long time he did not wake. He had the best rest in a long time. He even overslept. But he didn't just oversleep a little bit. He woke up 14 hours later. It was odd, but he didn't feel groggy. He felt renewed but felt an urge to fall asleep again. Was this death knocking on his door?

The next day went on like the first. They spoke so much they were losing their voices and ended up having to use their headbands to let the A.I. do the talking for them. They ate more and it was like a mini kick back party that lasted six days. They spoke so much, that it almost seemed like they were never apart in the first place. The last day before his departure, he became a little sad. He decided not to ruin the mood and kept silent.

The last night, when he was getting ready to go to sleep the voice came back, "Are you ready for the next step?"

"What?"

"Are you ready?"

"What are you talking about? Who are you?"

"I am the Observer. You have been chosen."

"What? Who? Chosen for what?" He lifted his arms and slowly rotated in his room. He looked up, and around, wondering if this was a cruel and an ongoing prank.

"You have been chosen along with your friends nearby."

"Wait. What?"

"What do you think brought you here?"

Just like that it all made sense. Everything. He walked out of his room, took the little cart, and made his way to the common area where they were all waiting for him. Something came over them and they were all in agreement. They had to go to the exact opposite spot as the RHSSO. Huang, Ramirez, and Lee were there. Waiting for them. Waiting to be relieved of their posts, sort-of speak.

A message appeared on screens and in their ears. It was Vera. A recording.

"Hello, old friends. I was able to secure a pardon for you

three. But something told me to make it effective today. The working of this deal on the back end is what really killed my political career. You are now free to go. Michael, take good care of them, please. I will be out of the public eye, spending time with Belmira. I promise to visit when the time is right." The recording stopped.

"We better get going." Alexa said. The rest of them said, "Yes," in unison.

They made their way to Michael's ship. They boarded, undocked and soon the E was soon powered on and then the ME kicked on and they were sucked into a small asteroid field. The ship slowed into an orbit around an asteroid. Their destination.

"Guys, before we dock, I want to share something with you," Michael started.

"Michelle and Mahina, along with Pantl and some others, helped me develop a neg-thermometer. There is an extra layer to our reality. An Anti-Universe." They all stared at him in disbelief but didn't say anything.

"As you know, the limit of our MEs is approximately 7,000 LY displacement. Anything further than that and we risk having our accuracy drop down by several orders of magnitude. The risk is too high. Without a source of HPs, we will forever be stuck in this bubble; albeit a 7000 LY bubble. But with the neg-thermometer, we discovered a new universe. This new layer will propel us into the outskirts of our Milky Way Galaxy. The neg-thermometer shifted our understanding of this new layer and it led to the creation of a new ME. We call it the xME. This new xME along with devices that were created for the neg-thermometer is now able to recall, if you can call it that, HPs 5 times from anywhere in our Milky Way galaxy. It has a range of approximately 50,000 LY. This means we now have the ability to jump anywhere in our local area of our galaxy without HPs being present in those systems. Not only that, but if we leave smaller, tracking ships in these systems we can extend our reach further, much further. Using

John's triangulation technique our range can be extended by orders of magnitude. This technique, along with the new xME will send us to locations we never even could dream of possibly existing."

They all saw him explain this and did not seem shocked.

"You know what? This makes sense. It all does. Something told us this before. But we didn't really have it in our conscious selves. But we somehow knew about it."

He nodded at them. "This new xME engine is now built and ready to go. It passed the tests with flying colors. There is a ship in the outskirts of the Kletlop system with this new engine. It is being manned by 385 humans and 385 Kletlops. Their mission is to jump to a system we have confirmed to have HPs but no habitable planet approximately at the very edge the Milky Way Galaxy. From there, they will launch crewless ships to the Andromeda Galaxy. Now, we won't have to wait the 2.2 to 2.3 million years to hear back."

They all nodded and smiled. After a second Elton shifted himself.

"What's down there, Michael?" Elton asked. Only Michael knew the answer to that. He answered it and added, "Now we will have to wait for The Observer to communicate with us. The Observer chose us to carry on for the second test. With the xME and the new treaty with the Kletlops and the unification of Earth, we have passed the first test."

"What was the first test?" Sonya asked, in a neutral tone.

"I was told the first test was just that – to unify the entire species behind a single and noble cause. Furthermore, it was to see if we ended up surviving our first encounter with an alien species that was more or less at our same technological/ sociological level as us. The Kletlops had already unified their entire species. They were just waiting for us. The Observer has not shared knowledge of a similar test for the Kletlops. We believe he or others like him, or it, also are testing other species. But telling us would compromise the integrity of tests." Michael said, mimicking Sonya's neutral tone and blank stare.

"Now *we* have to wait for the second test." Michael saw all of them and felt them. Their connection was undeniable now. Two men. Two women.

"The second test will be to see if we survive and encounter with a much more advanced civilization: orders of magnitude more advanced than us." They all said, in unison.

Their ship docked. They walked to the four paralyzer pods. Everything was ready for them. The corpses of Ramirez, Huang, and Lee were cremated and stored next to the corpses of humans that came before them. All of the chosen ones' remains before them were sent there by Lopez and her team. This was not only a communication station for The Observer but also a Mausoleum for the previous chosen ones. Lopez and those similar to her had decided that all of the ones chosen by The Observer had to be together. With every new death, the future chosen ones had a stronger bond with The Observer.

They all got naked and walked towards their own pod. They entered it while flying drones recorded them and while the A.I., controlled other robots and control panels for the pods. They glanced at everybody else and got in.

They were soon asleep, if you could call it that. And they weren't sure for how long they would need to be there. But they were ready for their next task. To wait. To listen. To encourage others.

It is said that the best of us would plant trees, knowing full well they would never sit in their shadow nor enjoy their fruits. That was true legacy. That was dedication to its fullest. It didn't require a genius, nor the strongest nor the wealthiest. It only required dedication and an understanding that they had to do their part. And that, they did.

Epilogue

The Observer reached out to Lopez for the first time – *Your species has passed the first test. They will always have passed it. They have always have passed it. It is locked in to your universe like Plank's Constant or the Fine Structure Constant.*

Lopez – *I guess I was wrong. They ended up being special and important after all.* Lopez gave a small snort of derision.

The Observer – *No. They were always special. Everybody is. But the importance of a single human is irrelevant. The task, which does have importance is the one that guides them. It is their response that warrants praise. Even if they had failed, their response is what shows character and that is what matters.*

Lopez – *Will you tell me Humanity's Second Test?*

The Observer – *Yes.*

The Observer told her.

Lopez – *What about the third test? Is there even a third test?*

The Observer – *The Third Test is the hardest. So few civilizations pass it.*

Lopez – *Will you tell me The Third Test?*

The Observer – *Your civilization, once advanced enough, must stay neutral and get out of the way of emerging civilizations. Few pass that test. The temptation and forgetfulness of their ancient struggles clouds their judgement.*

Lopez – *So you chose my team correctly all those years go.*

The Observer – *No. I chose them after you all passed. It is illogical to bestow that honor at birth and irresponsible to expect greatness before proving they are capable.*

Lopez didn't hear the Observer for several hours after that. She got out of her chair and approached the center of her command room in her ship. She laid down her Q-Transport Bar on the floor. It was heavy and only 4 feet long with a diameter of 3 inches. Its little legs dug into the smart floor and turned on. The top of the bar expelled a powerful light while some smart material from the floor grew to form a rectangular perimeter with the Bar as its base. A doorway. She walked through it and was instantly back In Antarctica surrounded by the ancient stone ring in front of her new base of operations. She walked the 40 meters to the building and took the first elevator down 500 feet. She got out and approached vertical *cylinders housing more clones of her old sidekick, Mr. Smith. 'I just hope you don't fuck me over this time,' she thought. Her A.I. responded, "The calibration procedure mislabeled a protein as it had shifted since the last iteration." Lopez nodded and made her way into a room further inside and saw more clones of her. Dozens of them. Dozens of her. She made it to her pod where a tech stood by.*

"Ready for mind-transplant?"

"Yes. I need to find out more about Michelle's new ship. My council demands to know."

"Will you go visit them?"

"When the time is right. For now, we need to replace this body. That bitch Vera reprogrammed my nano-bots."

Before the procedure started, the screen came to life. It was a former council member. A dark figure spoke, "Agent. The mission has been completed. Humanity has survived. There is no room for pettiness."

"I lead them. They imprisoned me and left me to die in space." She snarled.

"It does not matter. The council has decided to let that go."

"Go ahead. Let this go. I have seen they can't be trusted. I will live to see and lead us through the second test. My A.I. has calculated a %78.9 chance of failure." Lopez nodded at Elton Jr. and he initiated the procedure.

ABOUT THE AUTHOR

Ignacio Ramirez Bautista was born in Mexico City and his family moved to California when he was only four years old. He attended school in Orange County and attended Cal Poly Pomona, where he got his B.S. in Aerospace Engineering. He now lives in San Diego, CA with his wife. He is a full-time engineer.

www.ingramcontent.com/pod-product-compliance
Lightning Source LLC
Chambersburg PA
CBHW060149260626
47160CB00001B/186